THE LOVE SONG OF NUMO AND HAMMERFIST

THE LOVE SONG OF NUMO AND HAMMERFIST

Maddox Hahn

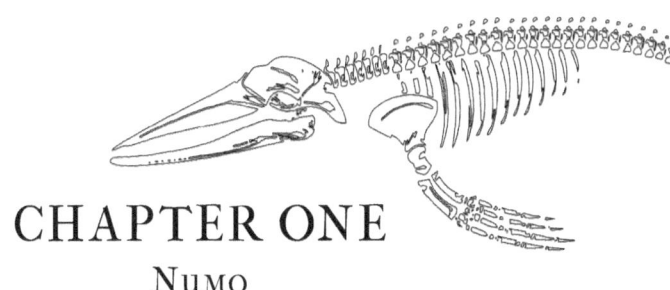

CHAPTER ONE
Numo

Numo WAS BORN of a mandrake. This was not a problem in itself—over half the homunculi in the holy city of Moaki were created this way, since it was the least expensive-and-still-legal means of making a servant. Numo had never seen the process himself, but he imagined it involved an alchemist plunking the pendulous root into a consecrated pile of goat dung and ululating majestically, or somelike.

But a homunculus born of a mandrake was small. His limbs were uneven. His movements were awkward. And as a runner, he was an utter disappointment.

It was not his place to wonder why his master had him delivering a message, though wonderment kept knocking at his mind like a wandering mime at the door. Numo banished it and pumped his legs harder down the winding streets of the enormous terraces carved into the mountain. He had to deliver the missive. Safely, quickly, or they wouldn't let him out into the city again.

Numo did love his warming-ovens in the hypocaust, make no mistake—a stoker he was, bred and buttered, all the days of his life—and his excursions into the woodier foothills for kindling and fallen branches were pleasant enough. But in the strange wide labyrinth of buildings and terraces, the sights and scents of the rock-hewn city were so intoxicating he thought he might throw up from excitement.

Throwing up, he understood, was something that exciting people did.

Numo bumbled down the steps of one of the steeper alleyways and broke into the main square on the biggest terrace of the city. He paused for his besooted lungs to heave inside him, rebelling against the mixture of altitude and calisthenics. The arena was just across the square. He'd made it.

He staggered up to the guard at the public entrance—a great swooping circular doorway made of white dragon-birch, like the grand entrances at his master's house, but flanked by stone instead of wood. Numo didn't know much of anything about stones, except that they had a general lack of flammability.

"I have—I have a—" A sad wheeze came out of his throat and his lower lip stuck to one of his little tusks. "I have a message, for master Tungsamran. I need to deliver it personally, per my master's instructions."

The guard looked down, prodded his nostrils in disdain, and went "pffaaah." It was an uncultured noise and one Numo was not accustomed to hearing in his master's household.

"Er, do you need to see it, sir?" Numo took the scroll from his leather bag and held it out. It was half as tall as he was.

"Tch. What kind of master sends a drake for such a thing? Eh?" The guard poked him in the belly with the end of his watershot torch. The human guards at his master's home had those, but he'd only ever seen them discharged on public holidays—shots of brilliant blue alchemical fire fueled by a

2

stream of water, spurting off into the sky like fountainous fireballs. Numo had never seen one used for poking.

He didn't care for the experience.

"No master who ain't a fool sends a drake with a message, unless it needs to get delivered slow and stupid. Why don't you just wait outside, mm?"

Numo inhaled sharply. It was true he was slow, and not terribly intelligent, but the fustilarian had just insulted his master. He was uncertain of the appropriate response. His master's honor ought to be defended at all costs, but the guard was a human, after all, and thus Numo was not permitted to show him any modicum of disrespect, however proper he might think it to visit fisticuffs upon the man. Or the man's kneecaps, rather, since that was about as high as Numo could reach.

But these were evil and sordid thoughts—ones he could not have, lest his servile gland exact retaliation on his physical being—so he dislodged them quickly. He took a deep breath. "It is not my place to question my master's intent, sir. Only to deliver the message." Again, he held out the scroll.

The guard sniffed wetly, then bent down and took the scroll in his knobby fingers, turning it over until he reached the seal. "An alchemist's mark," he muttered. "Sooth and balls, I should think an alchemist of all people would have slaves more suited to messenging! Or else, ain't much of an alchemist..."

Numo bristled. "My master is the second seat on the council, sir. Inventor of the process of drake creation." So he'd overheard, anyway. Most of the things Numo heard were of the overheard variety. "Do you need to see the marks on my collar-plate, sir? Is the seal not more than sufficient?"

"I got a bad back, drake; not going to lean all the way

down there to read your neck. The seal is good enough." The guard gave back the note. "The drake's entrance is just there. Follow the servants' corridors, no wandering about."

Numo set off at a jog down the narrow and ill-lit halls. The air inside the arena's bowels was moist, which was an odd sort of air for him to breathe, his lungs more accustomed to smoky dryness. The damp intermixed with the sweat gathering underneath his collar and made an uncomfortable lather around his neck. Every so often another drake would pass, nod, and continue on, but there weren't many. The arena, after all, was a place for an entirely different sort of homunculus.

He turned the eighth corner and ran into a shaft of light. The corridor had a long horizontal slit carved into it. A window, of sorts, open to the outside. Numo peered out. Above him was the squalling clamor of a crowd of humans. In front of him were the fighting infandi.

He'd seen infandi before, of course—messengers, carriers, rickshaw-pullers, guards, laborers, loggers—but these were a different sort. Prizefighters. Warriors. Numo pressed his face against the slit and stared.

Two homunculi strained against each other with iron rods in a whirling blur. They were not like drakes at all, and only a little like the wiry infandus laborers and loggers. Those types of infandus were of more humanish shape than a drake, though still smaller and more lopsided than most humans he'd encountered.

But *these*—these were like none he'd ever seen.

They were enormous. Muscular, dripping, scarred and plated with prosthetics and imbedded armor; they were as tall as men if not taller, with jaws bigger and jaggeder than a full-grown megalobat's.

One of them threw her rod to the ground. Her talons and fingers were massive, like the claws of a mole ten times magnified. She curled them into spiked fists and slammed them into the other infandus with an echoing crack. Her opponent fell. When the great-beclawed infandus stopped moving to place a dirt-crusted foot upon the fallen one, she stopped being blurry.

And she was the most resplendent creature Numo had ever seen.

Her eyes were as red as bellowed embers. Her blood-spattered mane stood up a foot or more from her head and neck, cresting between her shoulders like a glorious wave of shimmering heat. Her slobbering mouth was an orangey oven of the purest fire, a font of wondrousness gaping open down to the little iron plate stamped above her pendulous bosoms. Her blood was a magnifice—

Oh no.

She was bleeding. She was hurt. Numo curled his fingers around the edge of the slit. The humans were cheering, but underneath the noise, the infandus was quietly whimpering. Under the growling and slavering, of course, but...she was crying.

Sort of.

Why were the humans so happy about it? Numo's master would never suffer him to bleed all over the floorboards.

The dust under the infandus reddened. Numo's heart-chambers pounded so hard they seemed to choke the breath out of him. His lungs went *squee* inside him and he gasped. Was he dying? Was this what death was? He wasn't quite sure.

He'd never seen it.

Flowers rained down in blues and yellows and purples. Humans tossed them in the air like they tossed their hats on the festival of Ong-Nklak the Millipede Lord. Numo clutched his chest in relief, as if squeezing his anteventricles would slow them. Plants had healing properties, he'd heard. So humans were tossing plants at her for medicament. Thank goodness. Should he throw a flower? He should find a flower. Where would he get a flower?

"What are you doing?" a voice said. Numo turned. Another drake, his face scarred in the pattern of a waffle, shoved him in the shoulder. "Get a move on. Drakes aren't to watch the matches. Not here for pleasure, are you?"

"No, I—"

The drake didn't wait for an answer. He snorted up a surfeit of mucus and trudged away.

But he was right. Numo was here for a reason, and this wasn't it. He'd forgotten his orders. He was a terrible messenger and the masters wouldn't let him out again. He needed to move.

So why wasn't he moving?

Numo turned back to the slit in the wall. The infandus was being led away in shackles. Already. He hadn't thrown her a flower. He needed a flower.

Before he could grasp exactly what he was doing or why, his feet were racing back the way he'd come, bounding off the corners, faster than he'd ever run before. He erupted into the light, panting and wheezing.

"'S amatter? You see a monster?" The guard laughed. Numo ignored him, which wasn't proper, but he had no time. He looked up, down, to the left—there. Growing just along the stone of the arena walls was a yellow flower. He pointed. "Sir, what is that flower?"

The guard furrowed his brows and looked. "Dandelion. Hardly a flower."

"It has healing properties?"

"Do I look like a doctor?"

Numo ripped the dandelion from the ground and sprinted back down the hall until he came to the slitted window. More infandi were hurling stones and boulders at each other, whole teams of them, running between chalked lines smeared across the dust. But she wasn't there.

He careened down the hall, knocking over the occasional drake, which was also not proper. This was the first time in his life he didn't care about proper. Numo was on a mission. He didn't quite understand what it was, which was unsettling, but exciting. He was one of the exciting people.

A sign pointed downward, and Numo ran down a dirt ramp before slowing to a plod. Things were going sparkly and he couldn't seem to suck down enough air.

He emerged into a huge open space that smelled like festering flesh and flowers and musk and urine. There were sounds of desperate breathing. Growling. Dripping. Numo slunk around another corner and peered out.

The stables. Numo had seen stables for goats, but this place was different. More metal, more chains, more restraints and locks. And the stalls, if they could be called such, were full of infandi.

He padded forward, clutching the dandelion to his chest. Numo heard the whimpers before he saw her. He followed the sound, even though it pummeled at his innards. What if he was too late? What if his flower was not enough? What if she was angry that it had taken him this long to provide her with a suitable gift?

He saw her. She saw him. Her two sets of eyelids blinked and he stared into the limpid pools of beauteous inflamed lava that were her eyes. Her snowy white mane terminated in a crest of black, bedecked in entrancing spatters of brown and red. Her formidable maw hung open to her armored bosom and her fangs glinted in the dim beam of sunlight lancing through her stall like crystals in the dark. On the gate was a gold plate with an inscription. It said

HAMMERFIST

Numo's organs flipped and seemed to eject themselves right into his throat. Hammerfist! The name was a song, a hymn, the dulcet tone of a gentle waterfall pounding the rocks below it into submission.

He stepped forward. She was still bleeding. He wasn't too late. But where did her other flowers go? Perhaps they hadn't been the correct ones. Maybe no one else thought to give her a dandelion, and a dandelion was exactly what she needed, and his flower would be the best one.

"I saw you," he said.

Hammerfist leaned down. She cocked her head. She sniffed. It was a sound like a gust of wind through a cave.

"I saw you...um." All thought seemed to have fallen out of his head. "I saw you fight, and I didn't have a flower at the time. But I have one now." He stared at her. He realized he was still clutching the dandelion, and thrust it out in front of her single gaping nose-hole.

She sniffed again. An odd rumbly noise came out of her.

"I...I hope it helps. With the bleeding, and such."

She said something. It sounded like a mongoose with its vocal bits ripped to shreds and put through a meat-saw. It was their language—the infandus language. Numo didn't understand. And she didn't take the flower.

He swallowed. His hand shook. He laid it down on the ground in front of her nostril. "I do apologize if it is not meet. I just was so very sorry to see you hurt." He wrung his hands. "And I think you're beautiful."

Hammerfist recoiled and made a tiny high-pitched "hrouh" noise. Numo had no idea if she was happy or sad. Then she leaned down, under the lowest wooden bar, and nuzzled the dandelion. She pulled it into her stall with the tip of a claw and curled her massive hands around it, pulling it close to her breast.

Numo thought he might void his bladder.

The infandus crouched again, stuck out her muzzle, and gave Numo a gentle shove to the chest. Feeling her breath against his skin was like nothing he'd ever felt. It was a flush of heat in winter, a hard smack to the elbow, a cartwheeling pair of scissors in midair aimed at his face. One of her tongues unrolled, and for a second he thought she might eat him, but when it fully unfurled, it revealed a note. Numo opened it carefully, so as not to tear the spit-saturated paper. It was only a few lines, written in infandus and in the drake shorthand usually reserved for banalities of inventory and general notes pertaining to household tasks. None of the human tongue, which was strange. And possibly illegal.

For too long the alchemists have made slaves of their unnatural children. For too long have the malicious wights of humankind beaten down the innocent. The revolution comes. If you are of a willing heart to aid your brethren and end their suffering, please come to Rawang's veterinary practice on 17 Middlemonth at six in the evening.

Hammerfist reached out with a claw, straining to get her enormous scimitar of a finger past the small gap in the wood, and poked two holes in the paper. They pierced through the words "please come."

"Okay," said Numo. He scarcely knew what he was agreeing to, and didn't understand the word "revolution" except as it referred to revolving, and had no idea where the veterinary practice was, or what his master would need him to be doing at six, but he nodded vigorously, like it was the surest thing he'd ever been sure about.

With this, Hammerfist withdrew. She sat back in the shadows, her eyes smoldering at him from underneath the crescent-shaped metal browguards implanted into her face. Numo was hypnotized by them, those volcanic eyes, and his fists uncurled. The scroll he was supposed to have already delivered fell to the floor.

"Oh no! Oh no. I'm sorry, I must go." He picked up the message and bolted. He had orders. He had a job. And he was afraid that, if he didn't run, he wouldn't be able to leave her.

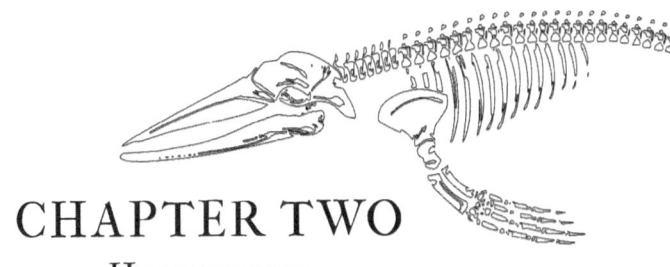

CHAPTER TWO
HAMMERFIST

HAMMERFIST CHOKED ON the swelling in her throat, trying to hold back the butting desires to weep into her claws and smash her face against the wall until something snapped. It was such a small gesture, but it was huge and fathomless at the same time, a screw of cognitive dissonance boring into her chest and forcing out the wetness in her eyes. Anger swung through her like a crazed gibbon, whooping and drowning out whatever feelings should have been there. Anger was the default coping mechanism, and she had no idea how to cope with people caring about her.

A scattering of flowers thrown for her victory meant nothing. A flower given to her with wishes of well-being meant something that was utterly foreign to her in this life.

Of course this had to happen on a day when she was extremely lucid. Extremely *human*. Everything was much more painful when she was lucid. Her brain hurt. Her body hurt. By the hells, if it didn't sound so vomitously trite, she'd say her *soul* hurt, like a weeping sore being squeezed into her nerve endings.

She wished she could say it was the strangest encounter in recent memory. Or memory at all, for that matter.

But that had been a few weeks ago, when she met her husband. Or the man who said he was her husband. She almost-sort-of remembered him, but the brief flashes of remembrance were laced with a sickening sensation of falling.

Hammerfist leaned against the wall of her cell, the wounds on her back burning against the brown-flecked slats of wood. She folded herself tighter into the shadows. She wished her mind would follow. It was easier when she didn't remember and had no real thoughts. Or was it? She didn't know anymore. There was a great blank void inside her, full of white noise and itching, only now starting to sprout little infections of knowing.

The sprouting had also happened a few weeks ago. Before that, there was glorious nothing, the stupefied existence of an infandus. Wake up, breakfast, light jog, pulverizing the bones of those she was commanded to maim in the arena, lunch, flea treatments, second and third rounds of casual murder, bath, application of salves, dinner, and, if she was successful in battle, nights with the knockwood—a uniquely-shaped and well-smoothed edifice of solid timber on iron, designed to withstand any intensity of carnal release.

It was a blessedly simple life.

Then, in the middle of a match, for no apparent reason, she'd blinked and the world had shifted and the exploding poison of *I was a human* spattered all over her brain.

Her opponent had dashed her against a wooden stake and she lost. For the first time ever. And she kept losing, until her master sent her to the veterinarian. Her husband. Used-To-Be-Her-Husband. Doctor Rawang, he called himself, though the "doctor" part sounded very strange to her.

Little jolts of the past had come. She'd been human. She'd

been a she. She'd had a life and a family and a family god she was supposed to honor. And she'd been a blacksmith. She'd done something bad, very bad, and been sent to prison and sentenced to transmogrification and did even more bad things and now—

She spread out her claws and marveled at them as she'd done hundreds of times. A fan of blades. Gods forbid she should ever have to touch something that didn't need to be shredded to ribbons. But there, in the middle of them, was the dandelion. Unribboned. Inside it was some other creature's hope that she would be all right.

Not just any creature. A drake.

It was possible, then. A drake could care about an infandus, about someone other than his masters, no matter what Rawang said. He had been wearing a collar, and thus his owners still claimed him—and the little creature hadn't seemed to be dementia-stricken to her...

Whether he was demented or not, he had his masters. Access to their homes, access to their trust. Like so many others Rawang told her they'd never reach. "Their masters euthanize them at the first sign of dementia, they can't hide it, they don't care about anything but servitude, they've got nothing but their masters, forget it"—

But this one cared.

The hope of freeing them all hadn't been just a delusion of her diseased upside-down brain. Rawang had been wrong, she was sure of it, and this dandelion was proof.

CHAPTER THREE
Numo

THE GUARD AT the stables, after another drakes-aren't-messengers-sod-off type of exchange, eventually pointed Numo to one of the master's rooms flanking the main hall. It seemed Tungsamran did not have a servant with him, so Numo would be dealing with the infandus master directly, which made his feet sweat.

He knocked at the door. A minute passed. He knocked again. Numo wondered if knocking intermittently was pointless in this instance and contemplated battering on the door like a goatskin drum, and was in the midst of weighing how impolite this might be when the door finally opened.

The smell of the master struck him first, and the sight was equally odoriferous. Tungsamran was the sort of man who looked like he slept in a barrel of brine and kept company with rogues, scoundrels, and *fefnicutes*. Numo did not know what a *fefnicute* was, but he often heard the word in association with things like knaves and stinkards, and he imagined it was some sort of dirty rodent-type of animal that carried diseases and squirted people with milk from its poisonous teats.

"Wotchew want?" said the master.

Numo held out the missive. "Message, sir, from Master Shanyang."

Tungsamran squinted. "Writing? A writing-message?"

Numo stood there in front of the large man in the doorway, blinking, feeling very awkward indeed. What other kind of message was there? Had he done this all wrong? Numo knew he couldn't be a messenger. He'd ruined his own honor. He'd have to crawl back home and tell his master he failed and get shut back into the hypocaust beneath the manor like a naughty cat. He should have stayed with his wood piles and ovens and—

"Dumbass drake." Tungsamran leaned down, kicking up a tsunami of stench that washed over Numo with an impressive sting, and snatched away the paper. He tore open the seal. "Dumbass alchemist. I knew it. Writing." He sniffed, and flicked the message back at Numo. Numo grabbed it before it could hit the floor and get dirty. "I don't suppose you can read, dumbass?"

Numo stared. *What's a dumbass?* "Me, sir?"

"I don't see no other dumbasses."

Numo supposed he was a dumbass, then. "I read a little, sir."

"'Course you do. Why wouldn't a fuckin' homunculus get a better education than a real-bred man. Makes perfect goddamn sense. Why are you standing there? Read it to me or get the hell out."

Numo unfolded the letter. It was sideways. He turned it. It was upside down. It fell out of his hands and fluttered to his feet. This was not going well. Numo snatched it back up and flicked it open. Finally, he found the starting place and began to read.

"*Master Tungsamran,*
It has come to our attention that your prizefighter Hammerfist—"

15

Numo choked on his own breath.

"Is that it?" Tungsamran snorted. "Come on, slave. Either you can read or you can't."

"It has come to our attention that your prizefighter Hammerfist seems to be cured of infandi's fall, and that she has regained her title as champion in Moaki. It would seem our alchemical treatments have proven effective. At this time, as per our bargain, we would like to request the full payment for our services. Please—"

"Bullshit. Absolute bullshit." Tungsamran slammed the door. Numo blinked. Was he meant to leave? Surely he was supposed to get some word of response. Perhaps "bullshit" was the response. Perhaps it was human vernacular for "very well then, thank you."

Numo peered down at the message. A lot of words. He could read them, but what he could understand was limited, and it all swirled around "Hammerfist" in a jumbly mush. And "champion." She was a champion. Pride burbled up in his chest.

The door swung open.

"Ah, good, you're still here. I realized I forgot to give you a response. Awfully rude of me." Tungsamran hiked up his pants. "Tell your master his alchemical treatments aren't worth a pile of sheep shit. All they did was give 'er diarrhea. The man what cured her was the new vet. A surgeon. Cut her, tinkered with her brains and fixed 'er right. So you can tell your alchemist to screw 'imself with a Tragan swordfish. I trust I don't need to get that written down? Plain words is fine?"

Numo had no idea.

16

"Good." Tungsamran shut the door on him again. Numo waited in case he wanted to come back, but after several awkward minutes of staring at the untidy sog-willow paneling, it seemed like the briny old man was staying inside.

Numo ran over the words in his head, processing, memorizing. He glanced at the note. He folded it up, over and over, until his nerves seemed to calm down a bit, and took a deep breath before jogging home.

Somehow he sensed that he should leave out the part about the swordfish.

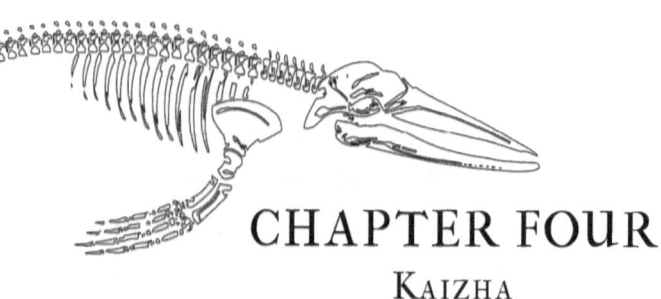

CHAPTER FOUR
KAIZHA

KAIZHA SPREAD HER skirts over the seat with a majestic flourish, and the men around her riveted their attentions on her bottom.

Such was life in the modern state. The wife of an alchemist, no longer allowed to alchemize herself, made to entertain the council members at their meetings like an ape in a party dress.

Her grandmother would have rather eaten cyanide.

She pulled up the crank-trosan to her body and set about cranking the wheel against the two strings. A low drone poured out of the instrument, and Kaizha slid her fingers up and down over the neck, making the trosan cry out in keening misery. She'd invented the instrument herself. It was the most "innovating" she could do without being scolded for breaching the bounds of her womanly station. Or possibly being arrested.

"How skilled Kaizha is! You do have a good one, Mozeh!" As if he'd accomplished somehing fantastic in getting her to marry him.

The end of the song finally came, and with it Kaizha's obligation to provide the requisite entertainment for that day's council meeting. The important business always had to be delayed with a pretty waste of time or two, at least according to the men. With the last note slid out, Kaizha set the trosan on the floor and gestured for the men to withdraw to the hearth-room.

"Gentlemen, if you please." She held out her palm and waved it a little, since no one seemed to be taking notice.

Mozeh blinked vapidly and swished around his tea. "Yes, yes, please," he said at length, and the council members shuffled out of her music room with the unharried pace of innately boring people.

The adjoining hearth-room was the greatest room in the house, with a fire pit in the center. A fine antique table encircled the pit, with somewhat less fine chairs fringing the perimeter. The men and wives took their seats with the swiftness of drunk flies in the cold. The slaves served bear steaks and honeyed wine, which perhaps did not go together at all, but if Mozeh didn't like it he could go piss in a wheelfan.

Kaizha took her seat next to her husband. She was nominally still part of the oligarchy, like her mother and Grand-Mum-Ma before her, but it was well-known that she was a ridiculous person not to be trusted with anything serious. The "failures" in alchemy she'd wrought in her younger years had not only brought down her own reputation, but had been part of the impetus for the social reformation that barred women from the practice entirely. Since the men didn't seem to understand that chaos and failure were at least half the balance of the universe, she'd become more of a mascot than a member.

So she watched the buffoons play at it and did what she had to in order not to lose her mind.

"Gentlemen and ladies," Mozeh began, "thank you for coming. I've called this meeting to address some concerns that

19

have been swirling about, and in particular one troubling trend in Moaki.

"To get to the point, fellows, I'm not sure about you, but I've noticed an increase in surgeries. Doctordom. Apothecaries who claim alternative treatments that alchemy cannot provide. And the veterinarians! Quite necessary for the woolly rhinoceroses or the goats, but now they claim to treat homunculi? The very creatures that alchemy creates? It is most nonsensical, and quite troubling for the alchemical community, that so many of the ordinary populace are being taken in by these charlatans."

"Indeed," said Goh. The High Councilman stroked his infinite beard as if he were contributing something intelligent. His little beard-holding slave Reddles petted the end of the dyed whiskers for him. A creepy smile was ever creeping across that drake's face, as though he had some sort of romantic affinity for the beard. The bandolier he wore over his chest was weighted down with an unimaginable number of instruments and unguents for beard care, though Kaizha couldn't see a need for anything more complicated than a knife. Or, in Goh's case, a hacksaw.

"We've allowed them permits to practice, for they provide valuable services to the poor who cannot afford the perfection of alchemical tactics," continued Mozeh. "And indeed, it's not as if we should go about sinking to common dentistry. But I have heard tell of a wider, more insidious spread of these practices. To the merchant class, even, and digging into the realm of alchemy where it is not welcome."

The council members huffed and snorted.

"I propose we stop issuing permits for medical practice for the time being. There are enough operating now to serve the poor. What say the council?"

The men banged sleepily on the table with their eating-tongs. Kaizha wondered if she'd put something in the tea. She could be surprisingly absent-minded about such things, although in truth she did it so often she barely thought about it anymore. It was the only way she knew to stop herself beating them all to death with a soup ladle.

"Agreed," said Goh. "And we ought to start an informative campaign. Can't have people going around thinking that medicinal sciences are more effective than our alchemy."

"Just a myth spread from the poorer castes," a younger woman trilled. Xiongnyao Haishing, wife of the fifth seat in the council. Her husband was a slow-witted infandus-maker and "anatomical expert" by the name of Turian. "I dare say that any higher order persons would know better!"

"I'm not so sure," said Goh. "For a myth, it has promulgated quite far. If masters are sending their slaves to veterinarians instead of alchemists, it could be the start of anarchy, the degradation of the holy countenance of alchemy, of Moa himself. And how would Moaki keep her proper supremacy over the city-states without her ideological authority? It's a bigger problem than it seems—more dangerous. Wouldn't you all say?" His eyes glinted with clarity. He hadn't touched his tea. Come to think of it, Kaizha hadn't seen him eat or drink anything served in their household in a few months. Clever beardface.

At this moment, the doors creaked open. A drake's head poked out between the crack. Numo, the youngest, and Kaizha's favorite, possibly because he was the last. It had taken several years of clandestine chemical tinkering, but she'd finally rendered her husband's testicles incapable of production. No more semen meant no more drakes. Not from him, anyway. And none of anything else that testicles could spit out, thank the gods. Mozeh had never liked the seahorse arrangement—one of the many innovations of her grandmother, who insisted that men should and *would* serve as incubators for offpsring rather than women—and Kaizha had refused to carry children herself, so he'd hemmed and hawed until she had time to chemically castrate him.

The very definition of good fortune.

Kaizha hurried over to Numo, bending down to his eye-level. "Yes, Numo, what is it?"

Numo spoke quietly, but the entire room had hushed.

"Master Tungsamran, er, sends his regards, mistress, but he says that the alchemical treatment was not effective, and that the new veterinarian's surgery was what, em, proved effective. I—I believe this means he refuses payment? Respectfully, mistress." Numo stammered and trembled, as though he might soon shake himself into nothing but a puddle of porridge on the carpet.

Kaizha cooed and petted him a bit. Mozeh hated that. "Dear Numo, do you mean that Tungsamran claims a veterinarian has cured infandi's fall?"

Numo nodded. "Yes, mistress, it seems so."

Kaizha smiled. "Thank you, Numo."

The council members were frozen, grimness pasting itself over their faces. It was delightful to watch.

It was too soon to know the full implications. But Kaizha would be ready to bend them in her favor, as soon as she sniffed them out.

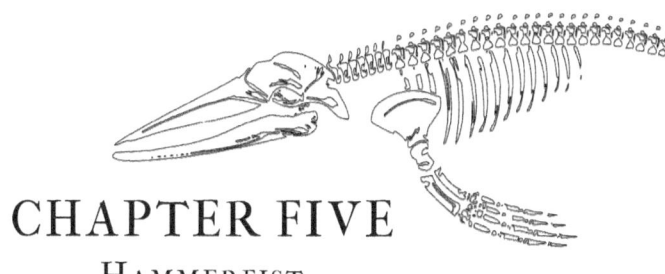

CHAPTER FIVE
Hammerfist

Her MASTER'S GUARDS dragged her through the
streets in a ram-drawn cage. The wood around it was painted
in bright oranges and blues and yellows, with a giant

TUNGSAMRAN'S CHAMPYUN PRIZE-FYTERS

written in a flourish across the whole thing. She had never
noticed it before the fall afflicted her. Before then, it was just
a box that moved.

She was only half-lucid today, somewhere in between
infandus and human. Today she remembered she was a mongrel
and a monster, and that she used to be a human, and that her
life was much *bigger* than it seemed, but she couldn't remember
any of the particulars.

In times like this, the whole thing seemed so surreal
and distant, as though she were watching a moving tapestry.
People with oddly small faces staring in awe, as though she
were awesome. She wondered if her face had been that small
when she was human. Some people cheered and nodded at her
knowingly, as if she were involved in some merry conspiracy.

Hammerfist wondered to herself why they would cheer, and a little voice in her head went *they probably bet a lot of money on the matches.*

The cage bumped over a dip in the rock-carved road. Hammerfist's thoughts tumbled out of her ears and her mind went blank. When it returned, she was licking herself, scratching at the skin beneath her breasts with her rough tongues.

It was itchy there.

The guards drove the rams through the gates of the veterinary practice. It was rather a larger affair than one might expect for a man of modest means, but she supposed a veterinarian would need the space to treat the goats and sheep. And creatures like herself.

The cage rolled into the courtyard and the guards removed her from it. A thin little infandus in flamboyant pants frolicked out to meet them. It was a very odd frolic—joyless and dull. Maybe that was just how he moved. After all, Hammerfist didn't see many other infandi that lumbered around on their knuckles like she did.

The infandus raised a piece of paper with a list of names written on it. The guards pointed.

"Hammerfist. Owner Tungsamran."

The infandus made a mark with an inky claw and handed them a slip of paper. He took Hammerfist's leash and led her through the courtyard, down a corridor, and into a large room with a beaten wooden table and a single skylight. He bowed and left her there without uttering a word.

Like the last time, if she remembered correctly. But then, she rarely did.

Hammerfist rocked herself on her knuckles, waiting. She

24

pushed herself off her legs and balanced on her claws. She tried walking around on them and crashed into the floor.

Her mind went blank again.

Then that man was walking in—the doctor. Used-To-Be-Her-Husband. Asking her if she was all right. Taking her foot out of her mouth.

"Are you that hungry?"

She didn't know. She'd ceased to register hunger; she was fed when she was fed and there was nothing to be done about it. So she was chewing on her foot. What of it? Maybe it itched. The infandus part of herself seemed very concerned about itchiness. And the knockwood. She hadn't had a go at the knockwood lately. She hoped the master would let her have a turn with it when she got back.

The veterinarian handed her a melon. "I brought you this. These used to be your favorite."

A swell of heat ripped through her again and a ball formed in her throat. He was looking at her strangely, with that obnoxious caring and worry. She snatched the melon from him. It crushed and shattered in her claws. Juice and pulp messed her hands. *Dammit.* She began the laborious process of licking it off. It was different from what she usually ate—it wasn't rotting, at least, which felt odd to her tongue. The veterinarian seemed pained, as though he'd been beaten, but he adopted a wavery half-smile.

"You've a dandelion in your hair. I didn't know Tungsamran was so concerned with aesthetics."

Hammerfist fingered the dandelion. That drake had been so kind, so heart-rupturingly kind. It hadn't made sense. Rawang was a different sort of kind, one she was used to. The sort that was like curdled milk—the only variety of milk she was allowed to drink, because it was too nasty for the Deserving People, but at least it was for her.

"I see you have some fresh wounds. Let me take care of those…" Rawang fiddled with some instruments in drawers under the table.

"I always have wounds. Doesn't matter." Her own words sounded half-foreign to her. Senseless grunts with punctuation marked by spittle. She knew what she was saying, what the human words sounded like, but all she could make of them was a loud mangle, a growling hurt that was the infandus language.

He smiled a little. Half his face was too injured to smile, scarred with the old marks of burning. It pained her to look at it. She didn't know why. She'd seen wounds and scars before. Burn wounds, puncture wounds, crushing wounds. Caused them and received them. They were nothing. But his face made her chest heavy and unsettled.

"I'm so sorry; I don't understand yet. I know I promised I would learn more of your language. I've been working on it, but I learn slow," he said. He looked thoughtful, dripping some foul-smelling fluid on a cloth. "Did you say that your skin is cold?"

"No."

"Hang on." The man leaned out in the hallway. "Bollix!"

"Yes sir! Right away sir!" tittered a small voice. A drake scurried into the room. Hammerfist vaguely remembered her from last time—all bounce and vigor. Bollix had immediately liked her. She knew because Bollix had told her so.

"Bollix, my infandus tongue is still rather lacking. I was wondering if you might translate."

26

"Absolutely, sir!" Bollix bowed in Hammerfist's direction. "Anything for the liberators!"

Liberators…a scintillating memory swirled into view. It woke up Hammerfist's synapses and seemed to light up an entire sleeping section of her brain. *The revolution.*

And just like that, her brain made the final leap from creature to human.

It was excruciating.

Hammerfist sat down heavily as the gravity of full consciousness bashed her brains into a pulp. *Murderer. Criminal. Monster.*

"Now, my dear, what were you saying?" Rawang said. That was his name. She remembered it from some clanging bell inside her head, warning her of a memory that she couldn't quite see. He pressed the cloth against a laceration on her side, wiping and rinsing and wiping and rinsing, then unlatched her collar and moved to her neck, repeating the process.

"Nothing. I don't remember." The grunts and glottal stops in her voice made her wince. She nearly remembered what she sounded like now, before all this.

Bollix translated. Rawang frowned. She scratched at the other side of her neck. Hammerfist didn't like it when her collar was off. It felt like a lie.

After she was thoroughly wiped and rinsed, Rawang pulled out a needle and something that looked like thread. "What is your mental state right now? Last time you said that you go in and out of—of awareness. Memory, and the like."

"It's just kicked in. Awareness, that is. Memory comes and goes."

He raised an eyebrow. "It happened when you saw me?"

"No. Bollix—the revolution." The revolution—the only reason she had to believe that her life was worth something. Bollix had mentioned it, sort of, on her first visit. Something she'd been imagining. A haven. A utopia. "If only we could all escape the pains of our slavery!" or something, with honest-to-sooth-and-balls twinkles in her eyes.

Hammerfist didn't believe in havens and utopias. She was pretty sure anything like a heaven was a prairie in the skies exclusively for the puppies and goats and white rhinos of Moa to retire in, and everyone else on earth was metaphysically screwed. But if she could help others avoid this, and maybe rid the world of some of the worst humans she knew in the process, then she might redeem her own existence as a monster that killed others for sport before she died.

In order to do that, though—since she had no resources, and a thoroughly unreliable brain—she had to use the doctor.

His face tightened. "Do you still not remember me?"

"I remember your name. And your face is familiar."

Rawang dropped something into a bowl and swished it around. He chose another wound on her body to clean. "That's about as much as you remembered last time." He almost sounded accusatory, or disappointed, as though she'd failed him somehow.

The guard-hairs at the sides of her mane stood on end. She tried to smooth them down with a claw, as though it would tamp down the frustration. "What do you want from me?"

He stopped wiping. "I'm sorry, Sramai. I don't mean it like that. I just wish you remembered."

"I told you last time not to call me that." Her chest felt inflamed and swollen. The anger was ratcheting to a crescendo.

Hammerfist had to keep calm. She must keep calm, or else she might lose it; the infandus in her might drown the human and take over her body. And she couldn't let herself kill him. Rawang was the one who could make the revolution happen. She was kept isolated in a stall and had nothing, but he could access the human world and the drakes and all manner of homunculi besides; he could buy weapons and explosives and hide them; he could provide a safe place…

And his brain was more or less functional.

She shut her eyes and pretended to squeeze out the anger and impatience through her eyelids like tears. Her mother had taught her that as a child.

I had a mother?

That thought was as bad as hearing her name. Or the name of some creature she was supposed to be, before she'd ruined herself.

She didn't know what she'd done exactly before she was a homunculus, but people who were innocent did not end up like this. And the things she'd done since…how many people-in-monsters'-bodies had she murdered?

Rawang's voice snapped her back to the present. "Hello? Did you hear me?"

"No. Sorry."

"I was just apologizing. I don't mean to do things that cause you pain. It was only an old habit. All right?"

Hammerfist tried to catch the tail end of a thought before it vanished. All she could manage was, "All right."

Rawang finished his wiping and scooted back in his chair. "I think I'm moving a little too fast here. For me, well, I've spent a long time thinking about you—all these years, retraining myself to be a veterinarian, becoming respectable, opening my own practice, hoping that one day you'd be delivered to me, all the waiting and experimenting—it's been a very long time for me. But for you, this is new. I keep forgetting that. After all, you only barely remember who you are. And I know last time we didn't have a chance to talk much about it; you were so badly wounded and so very insistent on this revolution business."

"Yes." Yes, she was insistent. She had to be insistent. "How are the plans coming?"

"They're coming along fine," Rawang mumbled. "More fallen infandi have been sent to me. I have spread the word accordingly. Got in a new shipment of conflagrates. Taken out a few of the more functional servile glands, so there's nothing holding them back from inflicting violence on my fellow man."

"Good." She paused, wondering how to say what she wanted to say in her own barely-functional language, if there was even a word for euthanasia. "About the drakes. Can you try? Say you can cure their brains. Or—say you can kill them nicely." She winced at the awkwardness of the words. "Get them sent to you—"

He interrupted Bollix's translation while Hammerfist was still struggling to form the words. "I told you, there's no point in it. Drakes who are demented enough for their owners to notice are too far gone to be of any use to us."

"But I met one. He seemed different. Please?"

Rawang waved his hand at her, as though he could erase her words midair. "Fine, fine, whatever. We can talk about this later. I wanted to talk about your *memory*, Sra—Hammerfist. Can't we talk about our past? Aren't you curious? Isn't there anything you want to know?"

No, no, keep your mind on the present...

But there was one question eating at her. Something that wouldn't leave her alone, as much as she tried to glue her brain to the subject of miraculously upending the entire system of slavery in order to feel better about punching people's bones through their skin.

She shouldn't ask it.

"Go on. Anything," Rawang prodded.

Fine then. "What did I do, that they turned me into this?"

Rawang shifted uncomfortably and cast his eyes at various inanimate objects. "That's unimportant. Something happened, but now it's over and done with."

She hesitated. She didn't know the word for 'transmogrification.' Perhaps there wasn't one in the infandus tongue. Ironic. "It is the most severe punishment."

"It is."

"For things like murder."

"And other things," Rawang snapped. "Look, the woman who committed a crime—that wasn't you. You aren't that person. They didn't have all the facts. They didn't understand. It wasn't your fault." His voice was getting all high-pitched and warbly.

"Fine. Never mind. Can we talk about the drakes more—"

Rawang grabbed her wrist. An instinctive growl erupted from Hammerfist's chest and she hurled her forehead into his skull, flattening him to the floor. Bollix stopped in the middle of translating and flinched backward.

"Oh no. No no no." Hammerfist bent down on her knuckles. She tried to pick Rawang back up and set him right, but her claws kept piercing his squishy hide. Hammerfist looked pleadingly at Bollix.

"I can't do anything…" Her breath came faster and she labored harder to win it. Maybe she really should kill herself and get it over with before she hurt anyone else. If Rawang died, the whole revolution was lost, anyway. Where would she find another human who gave a damn? "I can't. Help me. Please."

Bollix nodded slowly. Then she seemed to snap back into the real world and nodded faster and bouncier. "He'll be fine." She scurried over to his side. His eyes fluttered open and he pushed himself upright. "You see? He's fine!"

"Yes," Rawang grumbled. He pressed a hand to his head. "Fine. What happened?"

"She accidentally hit you, sir."

Hammerfist backed herself into a corner, as far as she could get from him. She could still smell approaching death. That smell had become very familiar over the years. "He's not fine."

"Of course he is!"

"There's bleeding inside his head. I can smell it."

The drake translated, and Rawang shot Bollix a hard look. "Get Pantaloons to take her to a waiting-room. Write a receipt for surgical follow-up and wound cleaning." Bollix hurried out and went yelling down the hall for this Pantaloons person. Rawang took a step towards Hammerfist. She pressed herself into the wall.

"Don't come near me. I've hurt you."

"I'll be fine. I'm a doctor, aren't I?"

"For sheep…"

Rawang's chin tightened, the little balls of muscle in his jaws ballooning out. "Sram—Hammerfist. Please." He reached for a tip of her claw. "I know you're hanging all your hopes on this revolution. I know you need meaning in your life. I do too. But I hope that someday, when your memory returns, you might—you might be able to hang your hopes on *me*." He gazed into her eyes as his pupils dilated unevenly. "I want you back, sweetheart. I will find a way to fix you. And we can be a family again."

The joyless frolicking infandus gamboled forlornly into the room. He latched Hammerfist's collar back on and attached the leash. Hammerfist stared at Rawang, hoping that the desperate look in his face would prompt her to say something, but nothing came. She couldn't respond—she couldn't process such a thing.

"Go on then, Pantaloons," Rawang said. The infandus led her out the door. Hammerfist stole a glance backwards as Rawang laid himself on the table and Bollix pulled something out of a drawer that looked like a crank-drill.

"I liked your drake idea," Bollix whispered to her. "Don't worry. I'll motivate him, so!" She turned away, wheeling away on the drill.

Pantaloons pulled Hammerfist down the hall and left her in another room with a single skylight. Hammerfist watched the bits of dust floating around in the beam of yellowy white, afraid to move, afraid to hurt them. Still trying to understand. But in her mind, there was only one way to comprehend it.

She had almost killed him. She was too dangerous; she couldn't be trusted.

She was a monster. She was nobody's wife.

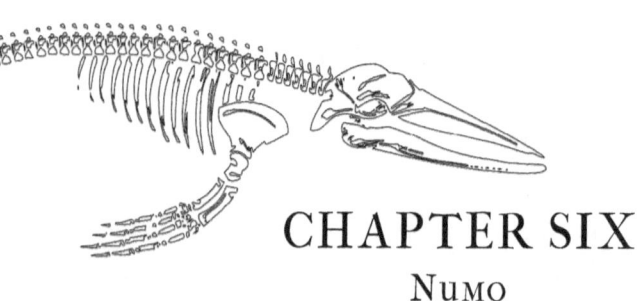

CHAPTER SIX
NUMO

NUMO ARRIVED AT the hunkerwood entryway of the practice, his body slick with sweat and his knees gelatinized to a fine mush. The veterinary practice was down on one of the lower terraces of the mountain city, in a rather dirtier neighborhood than Numo imagined could exist in Moaki. But Hammerfist would be there. And he had a flower for her. Even if its stem was now broken—he'd clutched it too tightly—and one of the petals had been lost—he'd dropped it—and it smelled vaguely of his armpit—for obvious reasons.

He'd procured the day and night off from the mistress, who didn't seem to care much about the loss of his service. But it was summer, and too warm for Numo's fires, and there weren't any logging trips going out that week that he could attach himself to for the gathering of combustibles. This season made Numo feel near-to-useless, usually, but for once, he was glad to have nothing to do. Because for once, he really did have something to do.

Today he would see Hammerfist again.

That morning, he'd flipped through the book his mistress had once given him as a gift—*The Book of All Moaki, Abridgement for Children*—and found listings of healing flowers, then climbed the long way down the terraces to the foothills and scoured the forests for a good one. An apothecary's marigold, it was called, indicated for sores and wounds and all manner of potential infections. And beautiful besides.

He wished he hadn't gone all the way back up to the upper terraces afterwards. But, even so, it was all worth the while.

Numo paced the wall, looking for a servant's entrance. It seemed to go on for a mile before he found it. He knocked. A drake opened up the peephole in the door and peered out, squinting warily.

"Your business?"

"I'm here for the, er…" He'd forgotten, his nerves making a brambly mess of his thoughts. At length, unable to sweep up any crumbs of the right words, he reached into his pocket and held up Hammerfist's invitation.

The drake's eyes widened in surprise. The peephole shut. Locks turned. The door unlatched. The drake pulled it open, full of manic energy. Numo flinched away and drew the flower tight into his chest.

The drake pounced. "Brother! My brother!" Numo was locked in a perfumed embrace from which he was too weak to escape. He froze, suspended in confusion like a mutton shank dangling in a butcher's window, clutching his flower and hoping that it would not be too badly crushed.

The drake withdrew. Numo checked his marigold. It looked a little rumpled, but it was all right.

"I am so pleased you could join us," the drake said, and slapped Numo on the back. "My name is Bollix. Yours?"

"Numo," wheezed Numo. Was the drake—she was. Female.

Well, I'll be fettered and flagellated. He had never seen a female drake before. But then, he supposed he was not very worldly. Perhaps his masters simply didn't employ any.

"My brother," she said again. How odd. "Come in, come in. You're just in time." She ushered Numo inside. The servant's entrance opened into a dark hall. Numo followed Bollix through a few turns before another door was opened and he was standing in an enormous courtyard. There was a crowd, but it was like no crowd Numo had ever seen.

There were infandi everywhere. Laborers, footmen, fighters. No other drakes besides him and Bollix, and not a human in sight.

"I can ask one of our taller brethren to allow you a view of the stage from up close," Bollix said. Before Numo could respond, Bollix was gone. An infandus emerged from the crowd and grunted.

"Hello," said Numo.

The infandus picked him up off the ground, sat Numo on his shoulders, and shuffled back into the throng. Numo scoured the place for Hammerfist. He couldn't see her. Then he realized how high off the ground he was and his anxiety over Hammerfist turned into anxiety about dying, falling, throwing up, or death by falling whilst throwing up.

Someone walked out onto a platform. The crowd went quiet, but for the scraping breaths that came from malformed lungs and throats. Numo squinted. The someone was a human.

He had a very short beard, well-trimmed at the edges, and he wore nice clothes—not as nice as an alchemist wore, and mended in several places, but nice all the same. Half of the skin on his face was puckered and rippled as though he had been burned. Was this Rawang? It must be, being his practice and whatnot.

"My friends," said Rawang, which was a very strange thing to say. No human called a homunculus "my friend."

"My *patients*," he continued, smiling a cheeky smile. A series of grunts and small chuckles wafted over the crowd. Numo again had the feeling that "patients" was the wrong word. Odd city-people.

"You have been created to be trodden in the mud, kept from freedom, kept from life itself."

Grunts and nods. Noise of an agreeing nature. Numo wasn't sure he understood.

"You toil, unquestioningly, for years. But all things degenerate over time. Your bodies, your brains—in particular, the lobe that needs to serve and love mankind. And when that lobe fails, and the masters' own creations start to realize the horrors of their servitude, they call that 'illness.' Infandi's fall, or drake's dementia, they are the same, although they'd have you believe otherwise.

"I've told them I can cure you. If you have come here tonight for 'treatment'—welcome. This is your treatment."

More snorting. Was anyone else having trouble understanding? It was odd really; Numo understood the individual words, but when they were put together, they formed a thick cloud too dense for him to comprehend.

"So tonight, after the speeches are over, you will be returned to your masters, and you must act as though you no longer hate that you are a slave. You must behave as you did before, bowing and begging and putting the worth of your very life on the line every day for them. You must lie until our numbers are large enough. Then, we will strike, and the revolution will free you."

The crowd loosed a drippy roar. Numo plugged one of his ears but, afraid to drop his marigold, the other one took the full brunt of the aural assault.

Then Hammerfist strode out on the platform, knuckle-walking on her enormous claws. Numo grinned and he didn't know why. His juices seemed to vibrate and simmer inside him like fat in a pan, and his muscles felt like they were full of bees. The line of her mighty jaw thrilled him, and the curvature of her tusks delighted him, and the delicate trail of slobber that leaked from her lips and slid behind her like a silvery thread made him weak, and her majestic ape-like gait stamped his heart with a respectful awe. But there was so much more than that. She seemed to project an aura of wondrousness that blossomed from her core and flared out to swallow him whole.

She had a dandelion in her hair.

Numo swallowed his breath.

Hammerfist reached the center of the stage and sat down on her haunches. She swung her head left and right, scanning the crowd. She stopped when she saw Numo.

"*Hruh glaaarga,*" she said. And then she glanced away, looking at the crowd, but Numo knew that "*hruh glaaarga*" was for him. He would memorize it and cherish it and recite it in his head. Maybe find out what it meant, if his masters would allow him to learn.

But oh—what an improper thought that was! Learning the infandus language—it wasn't meet, for a drake.

"*Bleah frshah! Haorurh bwar glarlrll gru roo arrgrghlblaaarrguh!*" said Hammerfist, and the infandi in the crowd yapped like amused dogs. She went on, giving what

Numo was sure was a grand speech, pacing across the stage on her fists, her saliva running more freely now, her eyes blazing. He had no idea what she was saying but she lit his heart on fire. Whatever it was she was urging the others to do, he would do it. He believed in it.

When she finished her speech, Numo realized he'd been forgetting to breathe. He gasped as the crowd erupted in noise once more. He'd never felt so wonderful and so sick at the same time. She sat down on the stage next to Rawang. Bollix then strode out to the center.

"Dear brothers," she began. Was everybody a brother to this drake? Maybe her alchemist had ululated incorrectly when she was being made. Or maybe she had the dementia. Brain problems, and somelike. Yes—she had no collar, come to think; she must have been ejected into the streets by her masters, the poor thing. "And sisters. There are so many of our infandus family here, and so few drakes. Not without reason, I understand. The infandus brain does not carry the weight of servitude as long, nor as passionately. And what can a drake do, anyway? We are small. We are weak.

"But we are not helpless," said Bollix, aiming her gaze at Numo. "There are many of us, allowed free range of the masters' homes. We can go where no one else can. And this is why, my brothers and sisters, we must convince those of us still residing in their masters' houses that our cause is just. For we will be the catalysts. We will be the watershot-torches that go off inside their homes. We will be the shackles that drag them from their beds in the night and give them to the claws of the infandi. We are the lynchpins of the revolution."

Yes. Poor Bollix definitely had brain problems. Torches and

lynchpins indeed. Numo supposed he shouldn't be surprised, as she seemed rather elderly with her wrinkles and creases, but he didn't like the hardness in her face.

"Today is a special occasion. One of our drake brothers has finally found his way to us." Numo felt a little shock go through him. Bollix's finger sprang out and leveled at him. "It proves that I am not an anomaly; that others of us are tired of the choking of our collars; that we can truly have sympathy for the cause! And where there is one, there will be more. Come, come brother, up here to the stage."

"No thank you," said Numo, but the infandus underneath him was already moving, bearing him towards certain humiliation. He was deposited on the stage, and Bollix again wrapped him in her arms. Numo held the flower out in the safety of the open air.

"Tell us, Numo," said Bollix, pulling away, "tell us what brought you here today, so that we may spread this message of change to our drake brothers."

Numo looked out. The eyes of dozens were on him. Pairs of reds or yellows or purples or flaming white. Numo shifted his feet and sweated. He wrung his hands around the stem of the marigold. The waxy feel of it made him remember why he was here.

He turned and walked across the stage towards Hammerfist, slowly, begging his knees to carry him. His legs seemed as fragile as rotten boughs in a pond. Hammerfist got to her knuckles and her feet, crouching low.

"I came because you asked me to. And I brought this." Numo held it out. Now that he saw it in front of her, against the backdrop of her soulful face and waves of mane, it looked sad and beaten and crumpled. Its battered petals fluttered in the breeze of her breath. Shame burned through him like indigestion. "It is good for wounds. And...and it was very pretty, before...before it got ruined."

He looked out at the silent crowd and felt very small and very silly. "I did not mean to draw attention to myself or cause a scene. I'm very sorry." Bollix seemed crestfallen. Maybe the flower was daft. Maybe this whole thing was daft. Numo swallowed, his throat growing a lump. His eyes burned. But his master had taught him not to let the fluid leak out of his eyes. It was not meet.

Hammerfist made that odd rumbly noise again. She took the flower between her claws and wove it into her hair, next to the dandelion.

"Hruh barlshffrf flurghablugh," she said.

"She says thank you," said Bollix. "She says you have a wonderful heart, and the flower will help."

"Oh."

There was an awkward pause. Numo considered leaping off the stage and running away. But the stage was high off the ground. He might break his legs. Which would impede the running away.

Hammerfist cupped her hands and pushed the platform of claws underneath Numo's feet. She lifted him. He was paralyzed. He'd never been so afraid in his whole life. She brought him up to her face, and then she brought their foreheads together.

The connection shoveled aside all rational thought and filled his brains with a sort of wild happiness he'd never experienced before. Then she stuck out one of her tongues and licked his face. Numo couldn't help himself. He reached out

41

and embraced her muzzle, wrapping his arms around the one giant nose-hole, letting the electricity of the moment course through him like crackly fire on a lonesome night.

A hoarse human laugh jarred him. Hammerfist lowered him to the platform. Rawang was standing there, casting his shadow over Numo, grinning in a way that was probably supposed to be genial. But Numo was not used to humans baring their teeth at him like that.

"Do you know what that was, friend?"

Numo couldn't speak. He couldn't think. It was the best thing he'd ever known and better than anything he'd ever imagined, was what it was, and at the same time it was shattering and frightening and he barely knew who he was.

"From an infandus," Rawang said, "that was the closest thing you can get to a kiss."

"Oh." Numo's ears went dark with shame. The way Rawang had said it, it was like it was a joke, something shameful he'd done, as though…the whole thing had just been an act of pity.

Was that what it was?

Rawang chuckled, his face tight and bitter. It was not a chuckling matter. Numo's whole life was in that—that kiss. It had scooped out his brain and put it back in upside-down. "I have to go," he said. He swiveled his head frantically, looking for stairs—there, in the corner, behind the laughing Rawang. Numo dodged the man's legs and sprinted down the planks, tripping on the last one and falling on his face. He hoped she didn't see. He hoped Rawang didn't see, for some reason. The man already thought him ridiculous; why should it matter that Numo prove him correct?

"Calm yourself, brother." Bollix pulled him up. "Come

here." The drake pulled Numo away from the crowd, over to the narrow hall where they'd come in. It was quiet, and the lump in Numo's throat grew even more as he replayed the incident in his head. The silence was horrible. The crowd thought him pathetic or sad or insane. And he was, wasn't he? To come here, where he didn't belong, to see an infandus who was above him—

"It's all right," said Bollix. "This is a little much for you. I apologize. I shouldn't have made you go up there. Put you on the spot like that. You're a shy sort, aren't you?"

Numo nodded. He tried to shuffle away, but Bollix sidestepped in front of him. "Easy. You know, she likes you." She peered at him curiously, as if measuring the geometry of his forehead to ascertain the location and size of the lumpy defective bits in his mind.

"We're having another meeting in four weeks. She'll be here," Bollix prodded, sidling forward. "You're welcome to come. I promise not to call you out on stage this time. Nothing you're uncomfortable with."

"I can't. I can't." Numo shook his head and said *I can't* a few more times, until it occurred to him that he was being repetitive.

Bollix bit her lip, and then smiled. "How about this. You promise to come to the next meeting, and I'll give you my notes on the infandus language. Speaking it's a little complicated, because it sort of needs an infandus tongue and throat, but you can learn to write it, even understand it. You'd like that, right?"

Numo clasped his hands. Such a thing was forbidden. His chest felt tight. He imagined his ribcage chewing up his lungs like a bear gnawing on the leg of a deer. Or of a person. Any leg, really. "It's not allowed."

43

"Well, your master doesn't have to know." She paused. "There's a decision that needs to be made. Either you choose your master, or you choose us. Her. And us. The rest of us. Sisters and brothers, Numo." Bollix cocked her head. She was breathing all heavy and strange, as though she'd been running, or the thing she'd just said was the most important phrase ever uttered. "What'll it be?"

Numo had never directly disobeyed before. There'd been mistakes, yes, and little slips into loopholes, perhaps, but this would be—blatant disregard. Unlawful activity. Wrong. He closed his eyes and rubbed his forehead. Why was he even considering it? Hammerfist would not want to listen to him, or to talk to him, not after seeing how gormless and absurd he was.

But he wanted to see her again. And he wanted to talk with her, not just at her. He wanted to know what she was thinking. Her eyes had sucked him in and the kiss had made him deranged. Numo couldn't believe what he was about to say, but he said it all the same.

"I'd like to learn, please."

CHAPTER SEVEN
Numo

ONCE SAFELY BACK in his hypocaust, Numo sat down by the sandalwood pile and opened Bollix's little notebook. It was the first time he'd ever felt unsafe in his own home. The cavernous space underneath his master's house felt, despite its actual size, close-quartered and sheltered, an effect created by row upon row of ovens connected to venting channels that led up to the main house. It was warm, and scented with all the woods Numo could ever hope to smell, the air draped with the merry ghosts of his fires.

It was safe. It should be safe. But here, now, with an illicit text of some language he was not supposed to know, Numo held doom in his hands.

I'm being awfully dramatic.

That's what the mistress would say, anyway, that he was dramatic. *Poor fretting Numo!* she'd say, and pat him on the head, and give him a bit of fig. But he had a feeling the mistress wouldn't have such pity for him if she knew what he was doing now.

He stared at the book. His fingers longed to open it. *Bad, bad servant, ungrateful wretch.* His masters did not ask much of him. Was it so hard to obey? It had never been hard before. He'd never even considered…whatever the opposite of obeying was.

His hand shook over the cover. An image flitted into his mind. Hammerfist was there, in a forest full of sandalwood, braiding dandelions into her mane. Her eyes looked raw, and her face was drawn and miserable. And she said something to him, something important. But he didn't understand, and it was like a knife in his spleen. He didn't know what to do and he gave her another dandelion, and she cried silently, and then quietly braided it into her hair.

Numo gasped, trying not to let his own ocular fluid run over his eyelids. It was improper. Whimpering noises flolloped out of him as he struggled not to react to the imaginary pike he'd run through his own heart.

He flung open the book.

The lingua infandi was developed as a result of need: most infandi are, in the process of their creation, mutilated in face, mouth, tongue, and otherlike, and can't speak a human language. As a result, they speak in standardized grunts, moans, growls, guttural expectorations, body language, and so on. The writing system is a simple character script based on slashes and dots, designed for infandi who, for whatever reason, find it physically painful or impossible to write the human script with normal implements. Indeed, it only seems to be publically acceptable to use in those particular cases.

Numo thought of Hammerfist, and imagined her trying to hold a pencil. Like a blade of grass in a crush of knives, he supposed. He wondered if she minded not being able to hold a pencil. If someday she might like to.

His mouth was drying up at the idea of asking her. Maybe he shouldn't. Maybe he should forego any mention of pencils.

After all, claws dipped in ink were much nicer, he thought. To all the hells with pencils.

Numo was, perhaps, somewhat nervous.

He flipped a few pages further.

Certain emotions are most simply indicated with head tilts. A left tilt might indicate confusion or curiosity. A right tilt usually indicates a smile.

Expressions of anger are usually self-evident.

Numo kept reading for hours, well past his normal hour of sleep. The handwriting was bad and much of the words were scribbled on the sides. He didn't understand the rules for pronunciation. A stabbing pain effervesced behind his eyeballs and crackled through his meager brain-case. But there was writing, and he could understand the writing. There was a small dictionary at the back. Numo flipped through the pages of the lexicon, searching.

Eventually he cobbled a sentence together. He didn't have the use of pencils, either, but he did have charcoal and a scrap of paper, and with these he scratched out

MY HEART IS WONDERFUL
BECAUSE YOU ARE IN IT

Did that make sense? It made perfect sense to Numo, but it was not as smart as something Hammerfist would say, he was sure. It didn't seem to say everything, though. There was more in him, more to say. He stuck the charcoal in his mouth, grinding it in his lopsided teeth, thinking, pondering. Then he added

I WANT TO HELP.

He didn't know how, exactly, but he knew she needed it. And, Numo decided, he would be the one to give it.

Four weeks of study ruined Numo. He knew the stories about what happened to a homunculus who disobeyed his masters—or, for that matter, obeyed a master who commanded him to engage in certain immoral acts. The poison of guilt would secrete from his servile gland and corrode him from the inside out. But he'd hoped the pain would develop rather slowly, and that somehow, if he really tried harder to please in other ways, he'd avoid the worst of it.

But no. Numo secreted more guilt than most, apparently. He was covered in odd wounds that wouldn't heal, his head hurt all the time, his eyes felt infected and light lanced into his pupils like a log-hook in his face.

The masters didn't call for him. Numo tried to convince himself that it was a good thing, so they wouldn't see him, but if they didn't call for him, it meant they didn't need him. That he was useless. Or that they suspected. They hated him. They thought he was buffoonish and incompetent and stroppy, and soon they'd send him to the euthanizer or kick him out on the streets to become prey for the market-mongers or the gamblers or the con artists or the muggers or the organ-sellers or the megalobats or the flesh-eating water deer.

He'd never see Hammerfist again.

The day before the next meeting, he quivered in his hammock with his body curled around the book, feeling very sorry for himself. He was learning, but not enough, and now he looked like he'd been run over by a goat cart trundling moist beast carcasses on the festival of Ong-Nklak the Millipede Lord. Hammerfist would think him even sillier than before. And uglier. Was he ugly before? Numo hadn't thought much of it. Now it seemed important, that his ugliness not sully Hammerfist and her magnificent aura.

Just when the thoughts threatened to shove him to the precipice of the deepest melancholy, a familiar prickling tickled his neck.

His skin shivered. His body jolted upright. Was he imagining…

The collar tightened. He was lightly strangled for a moment. Then the fibrous strands of whatever alchemical invention was woven into his collar with the wiry metal relaxed once more.

Good gods! By Pyri the hearth-gremlin! By the forge of Pig-Iron Nonnysteed! A summoning! They were calling him after all! Numo jumped out of the hammock and the infected cracks of his feet slapped on the floor with fiery disapproval. He wrapped up his book in the pillow-sack, concealed it in the straw bedding on the hammock, and raced towards the stairs to the main house.

It was not until the mistress looked at him with a very odd expression that he remembered his unfortunate appearance.

"Numo," she said. She rose up from the summoning bench, where rows upon rows of little woven rings were hung on the wall under tinily-printed names of each servant. "Dear Numo. What has happened to you?"

He bowed his head, exposing his neck. He would show her he was submissive, prove it to her. Keep his neck open. "I…I am…so sorry, mistress."

The Mistress Shanyang spread her voluminous pantaloons and knelt on the floor, to become nearly eye-level with him. He didn't often see her face from this angle. It looked even kinder than it did from below. But her eye contact shriveled his insides. He stared at the floor, trying to arch his stout little neck like the rams did when they pranced in the parades.

"Numo. Are you feeling guilty about something?"

Numo didn't say anything.

"You can tell me. I know how guilt hurts you. And I know how sensitive you are. My poor fretting Numo."

"Mistress. I…" His thoughts swirled. Not just about the book, not just about Hammerfist, but about how unkind to his masters he was. He did a bad job of everything, and they constantly petted him and tried to convince him that he was good—at least the mistress did, but—

"Come, Numo."

"I'm an awful servant," he blurted. "You and the master were kind enough to give me a chance at delivering messages and I ruined it. I spat upon your kindness. I ran too slowly and you and the master are right to hate me for it and not call on me for anything else these past few weeks and I will understand if you would send me away to the eutha—"

"Numo, Numo! Calm down." The mistress patted him on the head with two slender fingers. "Calm down. Heavens, is that all that's bothering you?"

Numo couldn't talk. The lump in his throat was the only thing holding back his eye-leakage and words might pierce through it. His lips quivered, locking his mouth into place.

"It's okay, it really is. You were a fine messenger. We simply haven't had many jobs to do recently. That's all."

"I was?" Numo said, the words tiny and afraid.

"Yes, yes, good gracious, yes. In fact, I have a very important job for you to do tomorrow evening."

Numo blinked. "You do?"

"Yes. I chose you because I know I can trust you." She smiled. Numo felt like she'd plunged an iron poker into his stomach. "I need you to go to Rawang's veterinary practice. He is doing a number of follow-up treatments on some of his patients there, where he treats infandi's fall. Have you heard of infandi's fall?"

"I...yes, but I'm not quite sure what it is."

"That's okay, Numo. All you need to know is that it is a horrible brain disease that the infandi get. Rawang thinks he has devised a cure. I was wondering if you might like to go in and find out what that cure is for me." She pursed her lips. "Actually, your present condition might provide a better excuse for entrance than the one I came up with."

She pulled a piece of parchment out of her pocket and crumpled it. Then she stood and crossed the room to the writing-desk, whipping out another parchment and scribbling. "You will go there and ask about treatment for an overactive servile gland. I'll vouch for you here—that it is indeed overactive. My signature should be enough to bypass the permit laws and all that nonsense." She shot him a playful grin. "Just pay attention to what's going on inside. Listen carefully; try to notice small details. And let me know what you see." The mistress strode back over to Numo, rolled up the note, and handed it to him.

Numo took the little scroll and stared up at her. He felt that he should say something, but his mind was empty. There was only that lump in his throat. "Yes, mistress." He scurried back towards the hole in the wall that led back down to the hypocaust.

"Oh, Numo—you remember how we have special things between us that we don't tell my husband about? You do remember, don't you?"

Numo stopped. "Like the little house in the woods?"

"Yes, exactly like that. This is one of those things. Don't mention the veterinarian to my husband at all."

Numo almost asked her why. Instead he said, "Yes, mistress," and bowed, before disappearing down the stairs.

CHAPTER EIGHT
KAIZHA

KAIZHA SNUFFED OUT the candle on the summoning bench and hung Numo's ring back on its hook. She wondered, briefly, if she ought to stop summoning him this way until he recovered—the flesh of his neck seemed to be sloughing off just a tad—but the strictureweed had only a mild response to the fire, after all. She doubted it had much to do with his ailment.

Besides, Numo would, most likely, be ensconced within the veterinarian's practice for the next several days. Kaizha wasn't sure yet what this sheep-doctor meant to her, but she would soon find out.

Until then, she still had things to do. Plans that were already in motion. And she was close to creating something that would bring the oligarchy to its knees.

She drew back the white megalobat-skin rug on the floor of her quarters. Thankfully Mozeh had learned not to come in unless expressly invited, although it did take some months of booby-trapping the door and whipping him with bamboo.

Kaizha felt along the wooden slat for the catch and stuck her fingernail in the notch. The slat gave way and she pulled up the trapdoor. Grabbing a fire-lamp, she slid herself into the hole and climbed down the crooked stairs she'd had one of the slaves carve into the bedrock.

She emptied some water into the top of the fire-lamp and it ignited the packet of chemicals at the bottom of the glass. Alchemical fire—grand thing. Grand-Mum-Ma had invented it. Kaizha's mother had invented the method for shooting it out in a column of flame and water, and also the watershot-torches that were now standard weaponry.

Not that anyone cared about weaponry or setting things on fire or any of the proper arts in this age. Fifty-something years of life and this was what her city had come to—using slaves to do their work for them, selling them to keep a grip on the economy between the city-states instead of exacting tribute, winning money from gamblers by making the creatures fight imaginary battles in the arenas. Yes, Moaki still held the most tenuous of grips on a few tributary states—Trago, Dailin, Raeng; those that had tried to take up their own alchemical pursuits and needed to be legally barred from going further, once upon a time—but there was talk of releasing even those from their subservience. There was still an "empire," yes, but what a sad and shriveled one it was.

The use of slaves made humans into weaker beings. A bunch of limp rags with arms and legs who couldn't do their own work or fight their own wars or suffer their own sufferings or lick their own floors clean—er, sweep, she supposed; Kaizha was even forgetting how house maintenance worked before specialized homunculus tongues existed. The male brain apparently found this preferable, and she hadn't been able to fathom it in any of the thirty years since the social reformation.

Kaizha hated having them herself, but this was how the world worked now—she couldn't get human servants anymore, and quite a lot of financial transactions had to involve the exchange of homunculi as a matter of course.

She was stuck, until something gave, until the universe presented itself ready, like a crane doing a mating dance. As Grand-Mum-Ma said, "a great invention is never born without a shift in the tides."

The tunnel inside was getting dank and spider-infested again. She rather liked spiders, but walking into their webs was unpleasant. The strands of web on her face reminded her of Mozeh's silk merkin brushing against her cheek on their wedding night. It was a memory she wished she could erase.

The tunnel was long and not very well-ventilated, and Kaizha had damaged lungs from her early experiments. When she came out the other end, she was pasted with a dirt-sodden sweat and gasping for decent air.

Kaizha pushed herself out of the hole and onto the floor of the little shack. It was quite a mad wreck, that shack, full of bottles and liquids and body parts and strictureweed and animal blood and metals and glass and bones and more than a few bloodstains from some of the accidents. Experiments came with a lot of accidents. There were the idols, too—fine wooden statues of Moa the god of alchemy in his form of a woolly rhinoceros, as well as Kuru the Bloodeater, Kaizha's family god. The only remaining inheritances from her grandmother, since Mozeh had given away most of the valuables in his silly philanthropical pursuits. Grand-Mum-Ma and her legacy might have faded beyond everyone else's memory, but Kaizha could at least keep Kuru's honor there. Somebody had to. The gods of chaos—even the greatest of them—hardly had any working temples anymore.

Hacking and wheezing, she fumbled on the desk for the nebulizer vials. They were buried underneath a pile of half-eaten porcupine breasts. She raised one to her mouth, popped off the cork, and inhaled as the pressurized air shot out a fine mist. The combination of compressed oxygen and makhat-juice was a brilliant concoction that she had to credit her husband with—oxygen brought her back to earth; makhat acted as a bronchodilator. And, fabulously, a powerful stimulant. She'd be ingesting it all the time and euphoric to distraction if it didn't cause her to make horrific life choices. Like marrying someone.

The distilled alcohol and compression was her own addition. If the ingredients were placed in a container and sealed but for access to a basic squeeze-pump, she could compress the air inside, and the alcohol would cause the contents to vaporize on release. Much faster. Much more satisfying.

Speaking of alcohol—perhaps that was what she'd slipped into the councilmen's tea? Kaizha shuffled through the jumble on her desk to find her notes.

Distilled alcohol, n. 21, ex 1: Self. Quantity: a sip. Results: tastes like fire and acid. Should probably mix with water or something. [...]

Distilled alcohol, n. 353, ex 43: Self. Quantity: 1 2 3 4 glasses. Results: who cares I want to fuck the mooooooooonn

Afterthought: Going to die. Might die. I hate everyone. Death comes. Throwupdeath. Fuck. Too much alchol in 353. Fucktup.

Distilled alcohol, n. 354, ex 44: Husband. Quantity: six vials in two cups of tea spread over a thirty-minute period. Results: took pants off, urinated in washbasin. Became desperate and obnoxious. Fell asleep.

Distilled alcohol, n. 354, ex 45: Council. Quantity: two vials in a cup of tea each. Results:

Kaizha picked up the pen and scribbled "several fell asleep or became debilitatingly somnolent. Xiongnyao showed great interest in Goh's beardservant. Seems especially susceptible. Most others became belligerent and poorer of judgment than usual."

She slumped into her chair and thought about the remainder of batch 353. She could drink it all right now...

Life would be easier if she were witless or drunk.

Grand-Mum-Ma would rip out my fingernails with her teeth.

Kaizha flipped her logbook to the last and fattest section. The distillation experiments were important, but as lucrative as a more potent alcohol could be, it was nothing compared to the business of warfare and extracting tribute—a market Moaki had barely touched in years, and the holiest of pursuits. Man pulling worth straight out of man, instead of all this bartering-in-slaves nonsense. The strongest and most innovative survived, instead of the best liars.

A holy pursuit, was killing other people for money. Good and honest.

She found the page of her latest experiment. *Weaponized quasi-homunculus, batch 509.*

She'd made mistakes with homunculi before. Kaizha had invented drakes—sort of. Her drake had been fertilized with an ovum, not semen. It had not ended well. It still galled her that she'd let Mozeh take credit for the drakes, but if the public knew all the details of what had happened with the first and only female drake, there might have been executions. And to be fair, he did come up with the "idea" of masturbating into the incubation chamber.

But using human seed was too unstable—well, created certain problems, at least for her current needs. There was too much will, too many nerve disorders…too much psychological flotsam in general involved. Sadly, though, she'd been harvesting ova and sperm of various animals since that mishap and hadn't found one yet that bonded well with the mandrake. The latest was squid, one of the squishier animals she'd yet attempted. But anything was worth a shot.

Today was the day she'd open up the incubator—a steaming-hot box of electrified synthetic fluid—and find out if the new batch was any good. The previous batch had almost fully-formed parts, and some were even alive briefly before they disintegrated into shrieking puddles.

Kaizha tried to press the tension out of her hands with her fingers. Five hundred failed attempts were beginning to wear on her.

She slid open the hasp of the incubator. The metal was hot as Kuru's hundred penises. She used her prodding-stick to open the lid.

Nothing was visible but simmering syntho-amniotic fluid. Kaizha peered at it. There should have been something in it—floating corpses or threads of half-formed eye stalks. Something. Anything.

Kaizha decided to try one of the most ancient alchemical methods. She poked it with a stick.

It screamed. Then it exploded.

Scalding liquid spattered across Kaizha's face and simmered into her skin. She yelped and flung her hands over her face.

58

"Damn it," she growled, sucking air through her teeth. The burning sensation was beginning to fade when something hammered into her arm and coated it in liquid fire.

By all the demon rectums in all the hells—

Kaizha's arm was covered in something that seemed to be made of electric membrane. Clear, with sparks shooting all over it. Tentacles. Teeth. Luminescent blue eyes—she thought they were eyes, maybe—dotted around its girth in a circle. She tried to move her fingers.

It was a mistake.

A stringy tube shot out of thing's mouth and punctured her palm. She felt the tube working through her hands and her wrists and up her arm like a half-melted sword being rammed through her body. Kaizha screamed and bit into her stick to keep from doing something she'd regret. She clawed at the chair. Brought down the desk. Tore at her own face and shoulders and chest. Anything that would not hurt the experiment.

But what if she died? What if it was killing her? Still, she couldn't kill it, not now, not after all this—

Something inside her arm cracked. She looked down. Purpley redness spread across her elbow. The thing had tapped into a blood vessel.

A glowing red trail lit up from her elbow down to her hand. The creature's clear membrane flushed with red and orange and yellow. It spread its membrane up to her elbow and form-fitted to her limb, with the mouth and tentacles at her hand. Sparks jumped between their flared ends, assaulting her nerve endings with crackles of agony.

Kaizha held still, clasping her arm with a death grip. Maybe if she didn't move, the creature would stop torturing her. She held her breath. The pain settled and the electric shocks abated.

Then she inhaled.

The tentacles shot out and a misshapen wad of projectile electricity flew into the chair. It burst into a white-hot conflagration, the flames eating through the center of her shack.

Bollocks.

Kaizha tore one of the curtains off the windows with her non-electrocuting hand and threw it over the fire. The creature on her arm protested, digging harder into her flesh. She stamped on the fire until it died and fell to the floor, exhausted, in agony, and without anywhere to sit.

With the adrenaline dwindling, the pain in her arm shoveled into her consciousness, trying to bury it deep underground. Every part of her settled into a heavy ache like a small cat sinking in the snow.

But it had worked. By the gods and their sex toys, it had worked.

Sort of.

Well, it was probably killing her slowly, but that was a small detail...

Kaizha peered down at the thing on her arm, panting. It seemed to be quite firmly attached. And since it was inside her bloodstream, there was probably significant danger in removing it.

That was going to be most inconvenient.

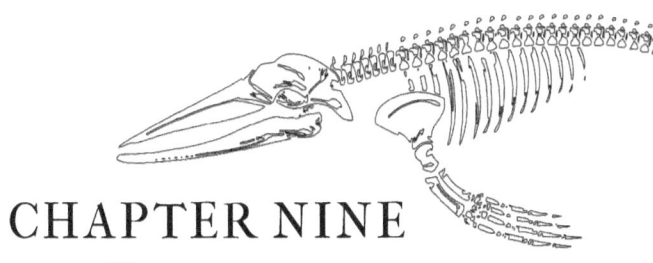

CHAPTER NINE
HAMMERFIST

HAMMERFIST WAS LOSING the match. Her brain wasn't working—she was having one of those days, when her mind was constantly dancing in and out between human and infandus, leaving black gaps of nothing in between. The arena made her dizzy and the people shouting in the stands were like little puppets spitting acid from their nostrils.

Her opponent was huge, with half a rhino's skull implanted in his face. He charged again and again. She blacked out too many times and took too many gorings. Her mind went spinny, saying *you're human you're human you have to stop this stop it stop it.* Hammerfist screamed at her brain to stay in one place, for the love of any god it remembered, but it kept on dilating and constricting like the black insides of Rawang's eyeball after she'd hit him in the head.

She had to get a grip. She couldn't lose. Tungsamran would find out—he'd find out that she wasn't really cured. He'd bring out the whip, put her in the strongbox for weeks—he'd—

He'll take away the revolution.

Hammerfist counted the beats of the charging infandus's steps. When he was close and he lowered his head to spear her

again, she shot out with one fist, grabbed a horn, flung him
aside into the ground—

I want the knockwood.
He'll take away the revolution.
He'll take away the innocents, the Numos, the chances...
I'm hungry.
I deserve to die; I want to die, let me die—
Make it shut up make it stop—

Her awareness receded into a tiny dot. She scrabbled to
hang on to that tiny dot and expand it again, but the infandus
in her was enjoying itself too much. The crowd flailed their
puppety arms and flapped their mouths in excitement. Her fists
were slamming into the other homunculus all alone, without
her mind telling them to. It was very accommodating of them,
she thought. Bones splintered. Her opponent's spine crumbled
like a snowball into little flakes.

The puppet-people wiggled their arms about merrily. She'd
won.

Hammerfist sighed in relief. Tungsamran would give her
the knockwood. For a night, at least. But she was bleeding, and
there were little pieces of her flesh sitting around in the dust,
and that meant she had to go to the doctor, which he would
not like at all.

She didn't get the knockwood after all.

The day was an utter disappointment.

Hammerfist's injuries were worse than she thought, so she went straight to the doctor in the cart, and he sewed her parts and asked her things like "What do you remember today?" and "Do you know who I am?" and "Does it hurt when I do this?" and she said "disappointment" and "yes" and "yes" and hoped he would shut up after that. She was very tired, after all. The doctor sighed and shivered and a bead of snot rolled into his whiskers before he snuffled it up and straightened. "You don't remember me at all?"

"I remember you are a doctor," Hammerfist said.

"Yes. I am. You've been here before, right?"

"Yes."

"And what do you remember about being here before?"

She blinked. "My head was itchy. There was bleeding."

"Anything else?"

She thought very hard. "I killed a melon."

The doctor threw something inside a cupboard with a bang. He flung himself down on his little stool and it scuffed angrily against the floor. Hammerfist curled her hands to her chest and tried to make herself small.

"I'm sorry. I didn't mean to—"

"No, no, sweetheart. It's not that. I just..." He smiled grimly. "After all this time, I still don't understand this thing well enough. Your illness, I mean. It seems to be all over the place, and I still don't know how to control it. I've tried, Samaak knows I have; I've lost so much sleep trying to study your language and your brain and your physiology but...I just wish I was a smarter man." He paused and breathed out.

She almost had a thought like *why does he invoke my family's god like we're still married* or something but it popped into nothing like a spit-bubble under her tongue.

"At least I've learned enough to understand most of what you say now. I suppose I can thank my tiny intellect for that." Rawang's muscles sagged, as though exhaling made them evaporate. "You don't feel it yet, but the wounds are severe enough that you'll need to stay here a few days for observation. At least—I would prefer it." He scribbled something on a paper and waved it in the air to dry the ink. "Bollix will take you to a room."

He called for the drake, and she came gamboling into the room and tried to gambol out of it, but Hammerfist's limping knucklewalk couldn't keep up. Bollix slowed herself, shouting empty enthusiasms with exclamation points at the ends all the way down the hall. The hall tilted ever so slightly inside Hammerfist's head and she lumbered into a wall.

"Dear sister! Is the dizziness getting to you? We can stop for a rest! Yes, don't you worry about a thing!" yelped Bollix, patting her claws. "By the by, I've gone ahead and convinced the doctor about your idea for drakes, and we've even gotten a few who remember where they are most of the time, it's absolutely working!"

Hammerfist had no idea what she was talking about but decided not to admit it. She scanned the hallway, searching for a point that didn't spin or list or cant, and found an open doorway. It smelled like impending death. Blood, also, but that seemed rather superfluous.

"What is that?"

"That—!" Bollix looked. "Well, that's nothing to concern yourself with. Boring veterinarian things. Spay hooks and uteruses and discarded tumors and blech. Did you have any more ideas about recruiting drakes? I do think it's of utmost importance…"

The drake kept babbling but Hammerfist couldn't hear. Her ears filled up with the smell. She drifted towards it, stumbling this way and that, but surely coming ever closer to the delicious scent.

"No, sister, no, that is not something you want to see! We must get you to the—"

Hammerfist knocked Bollix aside. Unintentionally, but conveniently all the same. She came to the doorway and grasped the jamb.

In the room was a table, and on the table was a dying infandus, shackled down and gagged with a stifling-ball. The impending death smell came off him in thick skull-drilling spirals. His bones jutted out against his skin and his fingers and toes fluttered to and fro in a mess of discoordination. Brown fluid dripped out of his mouth at a steady leak.

He was trying desperately to wrap one of the chains around his neck. Over and over, he pulled and tugged, but the chain didn't reach far enough to make it all the way around. But over and over he went, making the same rehearsed motions.

It looked familiar, somehow. Almost as if she'd done it before. Her pinprick of a brain filled up like a cyst. Something twisted into her chest. Then, a burst of realization.

That infandus was her. Sooner, or maybe later. But this was what the fall did, and this was what would she would become.

The doctor emerged from another doorway in the side of the room and Hammerfist shrank back, peeking out from behind the corner so that he couldn't see. Pantaloons frolicked glumly out beside him. The doctor looked at a scroll. He felt the infandus's pulses and poked instruments in his orifices. The homunculus didn't seem to notice, grumbling something in a voice too low for her to hear.

The doctor picked up something sharp from a tray and jammed it into the slave's neck. His body went limp. Pantaloons handed the doctor a knife and—

The doctor cut into his brain.

Hammerfist could tell it was brain because the doctor pulled some out. Pink and red with a bit of gray and black, dripping, gently going *squish squish ptpthh* in his fingers as he laid it down on a table.

That was, someday, her brain.

Then he sewed the infandus's head again. She didn't know why. The infandus was dead.

That was, someday, her.

Did the doctor not know he was dead?

"He's dead," she snarled.

The doctor looked up. "Sr—Hammerfist? Are you all right? Where's Bollix?"

"He's dead—why are you sewing him?" Her fists twitched. They wanted to punch the doctor. To rip him apart for what he'd done. But what had he done? Why was she getting so angry?

"He's not dead yet," Rawang said quietly. "I'm sewing him to find a cure. For you."

For her? The pube-face would cut open a brain and say it was for her? "Two minutes," she huffed. "He will die in two minutes. Stop sewing him. And don't cut any more brains for me."

He kept sewing. Hammerfist's brain went small and black and red. "Stop sewing," she said again, and he said things like "Where's Bollix" and "you need to get to recovery" and ignored her.

"*Stop sewing!*" she roared. Her body launched itself into the room and her fists flew out at the table. It cracked in half. Her claws went around the infandus's skull and squeezed and blood came out of the places the doctor was trying to sew and the sticking-out bits on the side of his cheeks went *snap snap* under her fingers.

"Sramai! Hammerfist! Stop it—stop—what are you doing!" said the doctor, but she batted him away and his body whammed against the cabinet. He blinked up at her, gasping.

"He's dead. Stop trying to fix him. He's *dead*," she roared over and over again, and crushed the poor dead slave's skull so that the doctor could see how dead he was and the slave could be lucky enough to die two minutes before fate made him, luckier than her—unless she stole his idea.

She grabbed one of the chains and wrapped it around her neck and she didn't know what she was doing or why. Her brain kept shifting now, quicker than before, growing and shrinking and going black and red and back to regular colors, and she pulled and pulled until it cut into her neck but she wouldn't stop breathing, damn her damnable throat, why wouldn't it stop breathing—

Something sharp went into her neck. "Sorry, Miss, I'm so sorry!" said Bollix's voice, exclamation-pointing all the way down. Hammerfist's fingers went limp and her face hit the floor.

Her brain wouldn't be fixed and she would die. The doctor wouldn't cut any more brains. She wanted to tell him. She wanted to tell him, she had to tell him before she forgot everything again, but her words and her thoughts were washing out into a blank whiteness, and she had so few words left…

The doctor wobbled in view, drifting to and fro—whether

he swayed, or her vision did, she didn't know. His image hovered over her like a child sneering at a tipped-over beetle, his eyes staring her down into sleep.

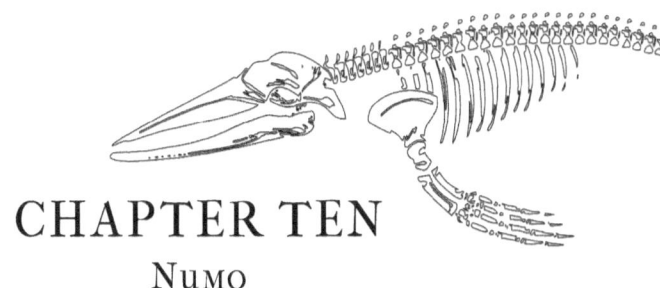

CHAPTER TEN
Numo

NUMO SPENT A long time scrubbing himself with soft cedar shavings and a bit of water. The cedar smelled nice, although he was never sure how much of its scent rubbed off on him, and the water got off most of the dried effluvium from his wounds and sores.

He scraped some brownish stain off of his little tusks and scooped out his ears before strapping on his carrying bag. The mistress had sent him some orduras to take to Rawang as payment, and there was the note and Bollix's book, but he still felt he was missing something.

A flower. Should he bring a flower? His palms broke out in abject clamminess and he tugged nervously on the strap. There was no time to find a flower, or at least no guarantee he would happen upon one on the way, and no money to buy one. He should've thought of it before. *Gnat-witted dungard!*

Perhaps he'd bring her some other gift. Numo gazed up at his log pile, the stack of kindling, the set of fire-stoking instruments, the bellows…he did think some of his woods were special, but what would Hammerfist do with a log?

His gaze fell on his little collection of resins and saps.

About thirty of them in all, from a variety of trees. It only seemed respectable to collect the saps and resins when they bled, in order to soak up their auras or somelike. He wasn't sure how it worked. He only knew that his little collection comforted him, as if the trees were all around him in spirit. Maybe a jar of tree blood would make Hammerfist feel less lonely, too.

Numo selected one of his favorites—a jar of shiverwater pine sap—and secured it in his bag. It was time to go.

This time he was slower. The aches in him throbbed harder when he ran, so he stopped running. He coughed up something black. That couldn't be good.

By the time he got to Rawang's practice, he felt perfectly wretched. The sores and wounds had re-opened and his sweat had washed away the scent of cedar. Numo knocked at the door marked "patients." The door opened and an infandus stood there, dressed up in trousers, which struck Numo as very odd. An infandus really didn't have use for trousers, as far as he knew. Numo had thought of wishing for trousers before, but his belt and carrying-bag were sufficient for toting things, and truly it might be hard to find trousers that were as lopsided as he was, and in any case, he didn't want to seem so presumptuous or haughty beyond his meager flea-witted station as to feel he was deserving of things like trousers.

"I'm here to see the doctor," said Numo, and handed the infandus his mistress's note. The infandus scanned it and ushered Numo in, leading him down a large passageway with a vaulted ceiling. The whole of it was made of deep dark hunkerwood that ate up the pale leakage of light from the skylights. He was left in a small side room containing a stained table and various frightening-looking instruments gilding the shelves.

70

The infandus locked the door as he left, trapping Numo inside.

Numo stood there for some time, clutching his bag. This was different than last time. The air was close and the ancient oil lamps only provided a faint glow to combat the dark. He couldn't hear anything. The meeting, with its crowds and grunts of understanding and whoops of excitement, must be far away, in a courtyard somewhere.

He paced. He was missing everything and he'd promised to come back. What if Bollix found out he wasn't there? What if he didn't see Hammerfist again? What if this was his last chance to speak with her, and truly know the mind that lay beneath that mystifyingly effulgent—

Rawang opened the door and hit Numo hard in the face.

"Oh, bloody cockbeans," muttered the vet. "Sorry about that, quite sorry." The doctor bent down and clasped Numo in his hands, enveloping him in a cloud of a yeasty burning sweat-sheened scent that reminded him of the Master Tungsamran. Rawang placed him on the big table in the center of the room and peered at Numo's bleeding gums. "You all right? No cracked teeth, nothing?"

Numo felt his tusks. Still intact. "Okay, sir."

Rawang smiled a crooked smile. The half of his face that sported the wriggly scarring didn't seem to move. "Good. Last thing I need is to send a homunculus home with more injuries than he came with, no?"

There was something peculiar about this man. Vacancy poured out of his eyes. His mind always seemed to be trying to look at something in another room while his pupils struggled to focus on what was actually present.

"Well, you do look like hell. I can probably guess what

71

I'm needed for, but let's see the master's note."

Numo handed it over. Rawang's eyes tracked back and forth over the lines, and one corner of his mouth turned up again.

"Numo?" he said, as if asking for confirmation.

"Yes?"

"Hm. This is interesting. I'd have thought she'd tell me to euthanize you or drag some truth out of you with surgical knives. Overactive servile gland, though…that's a new one. And from an alchemist. Imagine that, an alchemist sending their homunculus to a vet instead of—"

"My mistress wouldn't dissemble, sir."

"No, of course not." Rawang sighed. "Is this all? Just the note?"

"Well, yes, sir, what else would there be?"

"There's no paperwork here. It's illegal to remove the servile gland without approval from the Regulatory Commission. Supposed to keep you little buggers in order, you know."

"Oh." He thought. "It's possible that she does not need permission. She's a member of the oligarchy. My master is the second seat on the council." Numo didn't know anything about paperwork, but he couldn't imagine that personages as great as his masters were beholden to the rules of some lowly Regulatory Commission.

Rawang's nostrils flared. "I see." His pupils became as distant as his focus. "I see," he said again, clearly not seeing anything that Numo was seeing. "You may be right about that. Last question, then: is it truly overactive, or are you simply better than most at hiding whatever it is you're betraying your masters for? Because the surgery to fix such a thing will not be painless."

72

Numo swallowed. All his thoughts went up in belching smoke. His honor was being questioned, and rightly so. Numo pulled out Bollix's book. "Sir, when I came here last month, one of the drakes gave me this. I've been reading it. I've been... *studying* it," he spat. "My masters don't know."

Rawang fingered the pages. He looked up at Numo. "You were at the last meeting?"

"Yes. I was meant to be at this one, but I—I—well. I'm here in this room instead." Numo looked down at his feet.

"Oh...oh yes. I think I remember you now." Rawang stroked his mustache. "Sramai took quite a shine to you, as I recall."

Numo blinked. "Sramai, sir?"

Rawang waved a hand. "Er, Hammerfist, whatever the hell thing her bastard owner calls her."

Numo wasn't sure how to respond to that.

"Never mind. Let's talk about you, shall we?" Rawang pulled out some metal stick with a lens and peered into Numo's orifices. "Is the study of that book the only thing that is troubling you, Numo? After all, you were drawn to the cause of the revolution, were you not? I'd think that would cause a much bigger problem."

"To be honest, sir? I don't really understand it. This revolution business."

Rawang's mouth tightened. "I see." He daubed a nostril-scalding liquid on the wounds and Numo tried not to flinch. "That does make more sense. Why did you come, then? And why are you studying that book?"

"I came because...because of Hammerfist," he mumbled.

"What?"

"Hammerfist. I saw her at the arena and she gave me an invitation and I thought it would be rude not to come and I got a flower for her that was better than the one I got before and I wanted to give it to her so as to be properly gracious and help her with her injuries with the correct herbal remedies," Numo blurted, babbling until he had no breath left.

Rawang sat back in his chair and crossed his arms. His eyebrow went up, and his smile twitched, and he looked very amused. Numo had no idea why. "So you came out of propriety, did you?"

"Yes, sir, propriety, sir. Most important to be proprietous."

"Indeed it is. May I ask you, then, whether you told your master or mistress anything about the meeting?"

"No sir. It's only my silly desires, sir, and I'm only a common stoker, and I didn't think any of it would interest the likes of them, sir, and I'd be too confused to tell them much, anyway. Sir."

"I see. You'd do best to keep it that way, Numo." Rawang seemed to be quite enamored of saying things like "indeed" and "I see." Numo so wished the doctor would say something useful. Maybe he could *make* him say something useful.

"Dr. Rawang," Numo began, already regretting it, "may I ask something?"

Rawang grunted, fiddling with the instruments on his tray and dabbing bandages in the scalding liquid.

"Er…" Numo pulled a bit of his lip from out behind his tusk. It was always getting stuck under there. "I wanted to ask about Hammerfist and infandi's fall? I did hear she became afflicted, and I was worried—though I admit I don't rightly know what it is—but I did also hear you cured her. I wonder

74

if she might catch it again, or if she is well rid of it now? And if she's safe from harm, by this cure you have put on her?"

"Mmm." Rawang rubbed his hands with some of the liquid. Then, as quick as a mouse darting back into a hole, he took a sip from the vial it came from and swished it around in his mouth before swallowing. "Well. That's a complicated thing, that." He hesitated and squinted at Numo in the way his master sometimes did after a very long party. "Do you know how an infandus is born, Numo?"

He didn't.

"Both types of homunculus are formed with the process of alchemy from two primary materials. The standard formula for a drake is mandrake, with the addition of semen. The standard formula for an infandus, on the other hand," said Rawang, "is human, with the addition of torture."

Numo found himself sitting down without wanting to. He knitted his fingers together. "Human?"

"Yes. An alchemist can transform a human into a homunculus, but it does take quite a lot of torture to strip them of their humanity. And bloody alchemy, I suppose, to warp their bodies and minds even further. It is against the laws of the gods to enslave a human, so they need to make monsters.

"There is some element of the alchemy used for both drakes and infandi that alters their brain structure—gives them the slave lobe—and renders them subservient to mankind in essential nature. And something else that installs the servile gland, so that a homunculus can't hurt a human without being poisoned to death. I'm not an alchemist, so I'm not sure what all that is—but those are the only two things all homunculi have in common, the lobe and the gland. Are you with me so far?"

Numo wasn't sure. He stared. Words bounced off his brain, struggling to get in. Rawang continued anyway.

"Infandi's fall—and drake's dementia, for that matter—is when this part of the alchemy wears off. The slave-lobe and the gland both start to fail. A drake has nothing but their servitude, nothing else to know life by, and will try to hide the dementia until it becomes so obvious that their masters catch on and euthanize them. But an infandus may start to remember the torture, and their old life. Often, they try to kill themselves or their masters.

"The 'cure' is the revolution. The revolution will stop the humans from hurting people and homunculi. The revolution will stop slavery. And the revolution gives infandi like—like Hammerfist—enough hope to survive. I give them a little stitch on the head and tell their owners I've done brain surgery, but all I've really done is give them hope."

"But—em—will she die from it?" Numo sucked in after he said it, as though it would slurp up the words, but he'd already spilled them everywhere.

The upturned half of Rawang's mouth drooped to match the other and he stared at his shiny instruments. "The fall rots the brain. The slave-lobe happens to be first. The disease is progressive…" He stopped abruptly and banged something down on a metal tray as though it had offended him. "But the revolution will give me time to find a way to stop it. It will keep her from injuring herself or worse. It will give me time…"

Rawang shut his eyes and inhaled sharply. He took a long time to exhale again. "Does that answer your question? Do you understand now?"

No. Yes. Well.

Numo still did not understand what a revolution was or how this doctor planned to stop the fall. But if the revolution stopped Hammerfist from being in pain, and it made her happy, and it would help this Doctor person fix her, no matter his smell or rough character, it was exactly what Numo wanted.

"Yes. Yes, I think I understand."

"And you're on board with us, Numo?"

"Yes, sir."

Rawang half-smiled, but even the smiling part of his mouth looked uncertain about it. "I see. But do you still feel loyalty to your masters?"

What kind of question was that? "Can I be on board and still feel loyalty?"

"No, Numo. You cannot."

"Oh." Numo tried to comprehend this, but it was like trying to chop wood with a dead eel.

"Yes, I thought so," Rawang said curtly, and tossed the lens-on-a-stick into a tray. "Sramai was so sure that drakes could—well. Never mind. Think it over. You let me know, if you decide to prove her right."

Numo very much wanted to change the subject. "One thing—"

"Yes?"

"Is it too late to see Hammerfist? It's just that I brought her something…"

Rawang looked at him curiously. "Propriety, still?"

"Of course, sir. I promised."

"Ah. Well. Happenstances being what they are, she sustained some nasty injuries in her fights yesterday and is staying here a few days to recover. She likes you, so I suppose

77

it would do her some good. As long as she's feeling herself. But first, let's see if we can't disable this gland of yours, hm?"

"Disabling" the gland turned out to be a serious degree of painful. Numo had never had his flesh cut like that and he felt a little ashamed for some reason. He wasn't sure anymore if he should go and see Hammerfist. His armpit ached, he looked a mess, and she wouldn't want anything to do with him anyway.

Except she'd kissed him.

"She'll be happy to see you, I'm sure," said Bollix, winking like she knew something Numo didn't. "As long as she's in a good mood."

Rawang had summoned the drake to lead Numo to the recovery rooms. With every step, Bollix seemed to become springier, and Numo became more sure he didn't belong here.

They stopped in front of an average door, looking like all the other doors. Bollix pointed. "She's in there. I'd knock first. Sometimes she gets upset. And confused—her brain is not exactly tip-top. She has good days and bad days, like any with the fall; sometimes she remembers and sometimes she doesn't and sometimes it's in between. But she'll be happy to see you, I'm sure," she repeated. Her smile wavered. "But sometimes she's not in a good mood. Knock first. But she'll be happy to—"

"See me."

Bollix nodded.

"If she's not too upset."

Bollix folded her hands. "Right. If she is—run. Run fast."

Numo didn't know what that meant. His lungs seemed to

be turning over inside him, bouncing around and ricocheting off of bits that they weren't supposed to touch. He lifted a fist to knock, dreading it, hating the feeling of his fingers passing through the thickening air. He stopped. He didn't want Bollix here. What if he made a grand dolt of himself again? And Bollix was still here because Numo had her property. Of course. Numo only had to return it.

Numo took the book out of his bag and held it out. "I meant to give this back at the meeting."

Bollix's brow-skin went up. "You've finished your study already? It took me years!"

"No...but..."

Bollix shoved it back in his chest. "You hang onto that until you've finished. It's the reason I made it, after all, so that the manfolk couldn't trample us with their plod-boots of ignorance."

A thunderous crack sent Numo flinching halfway across the hall. The door slammed against its hinges and bits of wood splintered off. A gut-hollowing howl erupted from within.

"*HGRHAARR FLSH!*"

Bollix gave Numo a wide-eyed glance. "That means 'shut up or die'."

"Oh."

"Maybe now isn't a good time after all," Bollix sighed.

"She's hurting?" Numo gazed up at the door. He imagined he could see through it, and that Hammerfist was curled around a bedpost inside, weeping, alone...

"Usually. But that's not the point—"

Bollix continued babbling, but his attention left the general area of her voice and plastered itself to the door. Numo sucked in his breath. He was a dolt, maybe, but what did his shame

79

matter? She needed something. Or someone. And he would find out what that something was and deliver it to her like Someone should.

He knocked on the door.

"Brother!" hissed Bollix. "Are you mad? I mean, seriously, are you batpoop loopy nuts mad? She'll—"

The door exploded off its hinges. Numo was knocked to the floor and saw only a confetti of wood splinters flying above him. He struggled to get to his feet, but a claw came down on him, the gargantuan blades trapping him inside like a spider in a cup. Hammerfist scooped him up in a platform of palms and fingers and scythey claws and brought him to her face. It was familiar. She'd done this before. Last time she'd kissed him, and love and kindness and wonder and perfection radiated from her like stink off an unwashed goat. This time, there was only hate, and Numo was certain she would eat him.

Her mouth opened wider—it was always slightly open, but now it was a snake's preparing to swallow. Tongues shot out, tangling themselves around his body. Numo jammed his arm into his bag before they could constrict and waggled his hand free. He held out the jar of sap.

"This is for you," he said. And then he dug up the note and waved it. "And this."

She paused, her breaths heaving in ragged gusts. Numo closed his eyes and inhaled it. If he would die now, he could die happy, sharing her breath, letting the glorious ejecta of her volcanic lungs whirl about his own and infuse him with her particles.

The tongues slackened. Her hands diddered. Breaths shuddered in and out of her nose. Her livid eyes went to the jar of sap, and for a moment it seemed as if it might be working its calming magic.

Then her claws curled around Numo and pelted him into the wall.

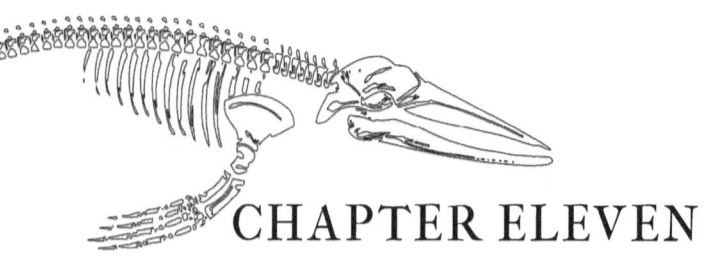

CHAPTER ELEVEN
HAMMERFIST

HAMMERFIST SLAMMED THE door behind her. This was a different room than before, she knew, because the door was in one piece, and it didn't smell like her, like a faint miniature of death in the distance riding an oozing blob of clotting blood.

She breathed in, unsure of what had just happened. Her wounds throbbed, her torn leg muscle ached, and the infection burned somewhere the doctor said it would after she woke up yesterday.

She wasn't sure if she was more infandus or human just now. That drake—she had almost remembered him, and then she hadn't, and he was just some creature who hadn't started dying yet trying to fix her, like the doctor with his brain-cutting and his killing of innocently doomed slaves, which she might not be so outraged about if it wasn't in her name.

The light from the sky-window floated in like a leaf falling. Hammerfist stepped away from it. The light was her family god—Samaak?—or was that the family dog—casting his gaze on her, and she didn't want him to see this. But of course he'd see.

If he could stand to look anymore.

She had to fix this. Make sure this didn't happen to anyone else; that it ended here with her. It was only something as huge as freeing the slaves that would make it okay. Then she'd die in the revolution, a clean death, and that would finish it off neatly, tie up the ends in a beautiful bow.

Someone knocked at the door. "Miss? It's Bollix, miss."

"Leave."

"Yes, miss, I won't trouble you long, I just wanted to let you know that Numo is being treated and the doctor says he will be all right, miss. He'll be just fine. Fit as a woolly rhino! Fit as—"

"Who is Numo?"

"Er. The drake who gave you a flower at the first meeting, miss? You seemed fond of him…you'll remember in time, I'm sure. I just wanted you to know! I'll just leave his gifts to you outside the door then. Ta!"

Numo. A flower? What meeting? What gifts? The revolution, there was a meeting, something foggy happened. The name was familiar.

The memory speared into her stomach. *Numo.*

Had she just…?

She had.

He'd been bleeding, hadn't he? Had she used all her force? Had she twisted her wrist to make sure the neck broke? Oh god, what if he—

But Bollix said he was fine. Bollix said Rawang was helping him. So his neck wasn't broken. Unless Bollix was lying.

Hammerfist should go to him. She should make sure. Make sure he was okay, that he wasn't dead, that she hadn't really hurt him, not really, because if she really hurt such an innocent creature, maybe she didn't even deserve a clean death or anything else …

She flung open the door. The handle ripped off and a hinge popped away. Outside was a broken jar with some sort of goop inside of it and a note. Hammerfist tried to pick it up and open it, but her claws shredded it at the edges.

Ribbons; everything I touch turns to ribbons.

She couldn't go see him. She couldn't trust herself, not now; she was too unstable. Too destructive.

Hammerfist slid the broken jar inside with the piece of paper impaled on a claw. She shut the door again. The metal handle clattered to the floor.

Hammerfist unrolled a tongue and licked at the edges of the scrolled paper until it opened. There, in unsteady and barely correct infandus script, were the words

MY HEART IS WONDERFUL
BECAUSE YOU ARE IN IT
I WANT TO HELP.

Her eyes burned and steam rose up from the corners. Did he really mean it? Did he know what he was writing? Or was she just twisting his words in her brain?

No. He must know he couldn't care for her. She'd snap him in half.

She breathed out. It was impossible, in any case. No one could care for her, not as she was. He must have meant helping with the revolution. He wanted to be free.

But still he had said he cared. He had given her a jar full

of sap. And she had nothing to give him.

Nothing but his freedom.

Hammerfist breathed in and out and in and out, willing herself to become stable, as if by magic or alchemy, to somehow become peaceful and non-destructive. But the more she wished it, the more an impossibility it seemed, and the faster her breaths came. Anger still pelted her like fat hailstones in an ice storm. She ripped the bedpost away from the frame and embedded it mercilessly into the dirt floor. She needed something to dissipate the buzzing swarm of anger-flies inside her body, something to disintegrate her thoughts, something to waste her violence on.

It wasn't the knockwood, but it would have to do.

CHAPTER TWELVE
Numo

NUMO AWOKE IN a room that was much too large and much too wide. The ceiling was leagues above him. It made him feel exposed. He rolled over to get up, but a feeling like a ram's hoof crushing into his face battered down on him from nowhere, and after that he didn't dare move.

Lying still was a horrible thing, but not as horrible as not lying still. Numo tried turning over his most recent memories to get a bearing on what was going on, but it was like turning a die with three blank sides. He vomited. Finally, he was one of the exciting people.

At length, a door opened. From the sound of it, it was a small door—a drake's door. His vision was fuzzy and gray.

"Mfrugh?" said Numo, which wasn't what he meant to say at all.

"You're awake!" A dish clattered, and Numo's ears seemed most irate that they had to drink in such a sound. "I'm so glad! You're going to be fine. I told her you would be fine!"

Bollix's overenthusiastic snub-nosed face leapt up into Numo's visual field, too loud and too close. There was too much of everything everywhere. "She was worried, you know.

Not right then, of course, but a bit later, when she'd come out of it—she was steaming at herself. But I told her you were fine, indeed! Well, I might have lied a little and said you were fit as a rhino, but here you are! I'll go get the doctor for you. Meantime, I brought you water...well. I spilled it. I'll bring you more water! You don't move a titch, dear brother, we'll get you back on your feet to spoil the human crop of oppression in no time!"

Later?

How long had he been here? And who was "she"?

His heart went nauseatingly aflutter, and Numo knew, even though he couldn't quite remember her name just now.

But why would she be steaming at herself? The lump formed in his throat and, before he could remember not to let his eyes leak, they were spilling over. Numo wasn't really sure why. Maybe it was because his head felt like it was full of swords and iron bricks. Maybe because there was some other lump of a thing sitting in his chest that seemed to be expanding the more he thought of *her* and the vague ghostly idea that something very bad had happened.

But she—Hammerfist, that was her name, her beautiful mellifluous name—she was worried about him. Numo wished he could feel happy about that. Maybe he did, underneath all the pain and doltishness. Maybe later.

Rawang strode in, dizzyingly tall.

"Well. How are you doing, Numo?"

"Dunno," said Numo. Properly he might have said "I don't rightly know how to answer that, sir" but he didn't trust his mouth to make words.

"You took a bad blow to the head. You're lucky a drake's

87

skull is so thick, and the brain so thoroughly encapsulated in fat." Rawang smiled, maybe. Numo's vision was clearer, but he wasn't sure exactly which way was up.

"How long..." Numo said, but it sounded like "halaaa" and he gave up before finishing the sentence.

"How long have you been out? Well, you got up after the initial incident and wandered down the hall to find me. After which you asked me the same three questions over and over, throughout the fifteen-minute examination I gave you: 'What happened?' 'You won't tell the mistress, will you?' and 'Does she hate me?' You also told me, repeatedly, to 'shut up, Weirdbeard,' which I found quite amusing the first six times or so."

Numo was mortified. He wasn't sure how he had the strength and wherewithal to be mortified, but he accomplished it all the same.

"It's all right," said Rawang, waving a hand. "It got funny again around the fortieth time. Then you hopped off the table before I could stop you and you passed out.

"So you've been here for a night and a day. It's night again, by the way. I sent a message to your mistress explaining that you did not respond well to surgery and needed more recovery time."

"Oh...oh."

"I'll give you something mild for the pain, but it won't do much. And maybe an anti-emetic." Rawang frowned and wiped at the little puddle of vomit with the edge of a bedsheet. "Luckily, a drake's brain is much less complicated and delicate than a man's, and it shouldn't take as long to recover, but I suspect you'll need to stay here at least a day or two more. After that, though, you'll still need rest. No physical strain. For a week or two, perhaps. Would your mistress be amenable to that, or shall I tell her that you've suffered a severe infection and need to stay on the premises for the duration?"

Numo blinked. In slow motion, it seemed, and one eye before the other, possibly. "Dunno."

"I see. Well, I'll notify your mistress of your need for rest and see what she says, then."

The doctor prodded Numo's orifices again and squeezed on certain body parts and asked him questions about how this or that felt. He left and Bollix brought water and gabbled on with exclamation points at the end of her sentences and bounded back out. Numo stared at the wooden beams and blinked. The lump of a thing in his chest turned into a massive wodge of steel and his eyes wet themselves as he realized what must have happened.

He must have hurt her.

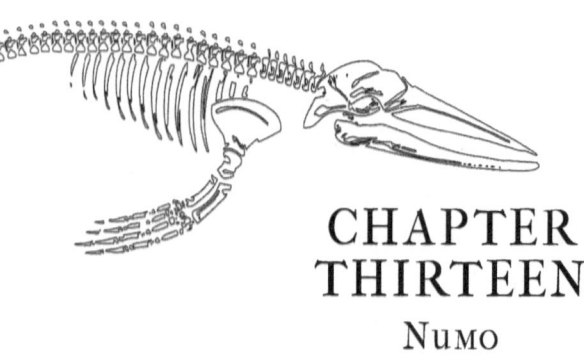

CHAPTER THIRTEEN
Numo

IT WAS DAY two of his recovery, and Numo was supposed to be doing much better—indeed, until thirteen seconds ago, he had been fine. But now he was dizzy again, and his head heavy with a feeble pasty gooeyness.

"She wants to see me?"

Bollix nodded feverishly. "Yes, brother. And then, well, I had to tell her the truth, that you weren't quite as fit as a rhino after all, took a little turn—so I said—and she was very much concerned. She insists upon it. Provided you're feeling all right. But she's getting picked up by her master shortly, you see, so it must be now or not at all."

Numo was sitting upright, but it seemed to him that he was listing to one side. He clutched at the bedsheets to anchor himself. He couldn't see her! He couldn't. He had hurt her. Couldn't remember how, exactly, but he must have, must have offended her sensitivities or dug at a weak spot or been uncouth right to her face. And yes, the doctor had disabled his servile gland, but that only meant that no physical trauma manifested in his physiology with the guilt. The emotional toll was so much worse.

"Numo? She needs an answer."

"I—I can't." He wrung the bedsheets until they were taut enough to whip himself with. "I can't."

"You're a shy sort, aren't you?" Bollix grinned. Numo wondered if maybe Bollix had a head injury as well—repeating herself so much and all. Well, but she had the dementia, he remembered. Lynchpins and shy sorts. "You feel all right, though?"

"I don't know."

"Sure you do! I see the color come back into you, brother, the rebel spark in your eyes! Fit as a rhino, you are!" Bollix patted him on the knee. "I'll tell her to come on in."

"No!" Numo tried to exclaim, but it came out as a tiny, whispering purr. "no."

Bollix didn't hear it, or the sound of the no was drowned out by her own enthusiastic yessing, and she pranced out the door with an alacrity that no one so aged should have managed. A moment later, the light around the door went dark. Claws scraped against the knob. Something banged against the hinges. The door fell over. Standing where it used to be was Hammerfist, blocking out all natural light, and somehow radiating a supernatural incandescence directly into Numo's pupils.

"Oh, madam, heavens, I should have gotten that for you!" Bollix wailed.

Hammerfist picked the door up off the ground. She wedged it back in place, gently shoving Bollix outside, leaving just her and Numo alone in a room that smelled of salves and sweat.

She, however, smelled glorious. She smelled of wood and hair and flowers and…and…

Hammerfist held up half a jar. It was broken, and most of its contents were gone. But there was just a bit of sap still inside.

91

Her neck had been sloppily daubed with it. The dandelion, now limp and almost stripped to the stem, still remained in her shampooed-white mane, and though the marigold was gone, some of its petals sat woven into the strands of the black. She didn't look hurt at all. She looked...washed. Radiant. Immaculate. Perhaps Numo had imagined his transgression after all. His jejunum flipped over in glee.

"*Hrughgla,*" she said. *Thank you.*

"You're welcome," said Numo. Hammerfist cocked her head to the right. Confusion? Or was that a smile? Numo tried to remember how to say it in her language. "*Grrahh furgh.*"

She snuffled rapidly. Laughter. That was laughter. He made her laugh. Numo beamed. Then he thought maybe she was laughing because he'd pronounced it incorrectly, and the tips of his ears and fingers went black with embarrassment.

Hammerfist handed him a piece of paper. Numo saw his own rudimentary infandus handwriting.

MY HEART IS WONDERFUL BECAUSE YOU ARE IN IT I WANT TO HELP.

Hammerfist had corrected the grammar and spelling mistakes in great red strokes. Numo wondered where she gotten the red. At the bottom, she had made an addition of her own.

I am so sorry. I hope you can accept my ------. I was not myself. It hurts me to know that I ------ you ------. The ----- tells me you will be all right, and I very much ----- so. My greatest ------ is that you would ------ me.

This ----- has moved me -------. Do you truly want to help ------? We would love your help, of course. But I wonder if you ------- it? If you value your -----, it is not ----- doing. ------ is a real -----, and I would not want you do to it if it ----- is not truly in your heart. What say you?

Numo couldn't understand half of it, not without looking up the words. Her writing was so eloquent! He assumed, anyway. The penmanship was *vigorous*, yes, vigorous was the word for it, none other. But what did it mean?

Numo scrabbled for Bollix's book on the side table and flipped through the lexicon. But oh! The lexicon was all drake to infandus, not the other way around. It would take hours to translate the words. Hammerfist was waiting for an answer, and soon her master was coming to take her away. Numo wished he could converse, to find out where she came from and how she got here, to ask her about her wishes and wants, what her favorite type of wood was, which part of a fire she liked the best (his favorite was either the blue of a very small flame, or the orangey glow left behind by a large one, he could never decide)—so many things. But if he answered incorrectly now, he'd never get the chance to ask those things. He might never see her again.

Numo let his gaze run wild over the page, and tracked along with a finger as if he knew exactly what he was looking for. He poked at a spot on the page and nodded to himself ever so slightly, like the master did when studying his tomes. His fluids crashed through his body like rapids anticipating a waterfall.

But a thought struck him. He didn't know what Hammerfist

had said, to be sure, but there was one answer he could give her that was purely and uncompromisingly true.

Numo reached for the paper and gingerly took it from Hammerfist's claw. He picked up the jam-knife that Bollix had left on the table with his bread (which was untouched) and jam (which was long gone) and he stabbed the paper, purposefully, four times over.

I WANT TO HELP.

He handed it back to Hammerfist. She cocked her head to the right. A smile. Very much a smile, it must have been. Then she pressed her face up against his and breathed into his nostrils and his brains turned to something like doughy pasta left in a bowl of water for weeks on end.

"*Ergh haraarghuh rhhhrhrrrrrgh,*" she said. *I will tell...* rhhhrhrrrrrgh. What was rhhhrhrrrrrgh?

She crinkled the piece of paper into his palm and exhaled a slow, rolling snort. Then she left, leaving Numo drifting in a cloud of confusion and the musk of pine-scented spit.

He didn't have much time before the lingering bliss was interrupted. Rawang knocked and the door fell over.

"The hell?" he grumbled. "What in Ong-Nklak's name happened to the door?"

"Oh, dear comrade! I should have repaired that!" came Bollix's voice, echoing down the hall.

"Obviously!" Rawang yelled. He stepped over the door

and propped it up in its proper space. "Bloody trap. This whole damn building falls apart in new ways every day. Am I right?"

The doctor smelled of unshowered man-sleep and that same burning yeasty smell and genereal unpleasantness. Numo didn't know what answer the doctor expected, but he supposed he should agree.

"I heartily agree, sir," said Numo.

"Now then. I came for a reason, didn't I? Yes. Very definitely. You mentioned that you are a stoker in your master's hypocaust, correct?"

"Yes, sir—stoker and wood gatherer, and kindling expert and spark-igniter—"

"Very nice, yes. The point is, you have access to a sort of artificial ventilation in an enclosed space, correct?"

"More or less, sir."

"Good. Now, Numo, Sram—Hammerfist tells me you truly want to help our cause. Do something big. Fully committed and all that. I had thought you bumbled in out of manners or somelike. Didn't seem to me you knew what we were on about. But is it true? Are you willing," he said, leveling an unsteady finger at Numo's face and getting uncomfortably, odoriferously close, "to put yourself on the line, to give your head to what's right, to take it in whatever orifices we need you to, Numo, and maybe lose it all?"

Again, Numo was lost, but if that was what Hammerfist wanted, the only answer was yes. "I am, sir."

"Very good." Rawang withdrew a tiny satchel about the size of a small mushroom from his sleeve. He pulled open a drawer and took out a surgical knife. Then he removed the flask from his hip and poured what smelled like a stinging meaty sort of wine over the blade. "Forgive the lack of professional methods. I'm in a hurry to get back to my...my activities." Once the blade was soaked, Rawang offered the flask to Numo. "Take some?"

"No—no, sir, no thank you, no very much," Numo stammered. He was not allowed mind-numbing agents such as drinking-alcohol. And, frankly, it seemed to be a substance for the lower classes: the guttersnipes, the briny beastmasters, the bar-trollers and the jackanapes, all manner of folk Numo couldn't stomach consorting with. He was starting to think that, despite his doctorly status, Rawang was one of those people, but with a cleaner shirt. Although even that was currently debatable.

"I'm about to do something to you that will hurt very much, Numo. Your choice whether you have some or not."

"No. No thank you."

"Fine." Rawang put away the flask. "I'll tell you now, then, before you're in too much pain to concentrate. Listen close. Very important you listen to instructions." Rawang held up the little satchel in front of Numo's face. "This is going to go in your body, just under your skin, right where your servile gland used to be. You are not to bump it, disturb it, smash it or pierce it. On the night of Penultimonth 30th, at exactly midnight, when the Festival of Moa finishes the initiation day and half the city's autumn-beer has flowed into the mouths of every oligarch and alchemist and wealth-sodden weasel in the city, you are to very carefully cut it out and throw it in whichever oven is attached to the largest ventilation shaft. I'd advise running like hell afterwards, as far away from the house as you can get." Rawang's one eye squinted. "You might also want to warn other slaves to get out, too. It won't affect homunculi as quickly or as severely as it will humans, but it might still be unpleasant."

"What, um, what is it, sir?" Numo clasped his hands and tried to squeeze out the anxiety building in his nerves.

"An instrument of the revolution, Numo. All the heads of the council will be brought down at once. Then the body will flail without comprehension, and we will bind it to the ground." Rawang's unscathed eye was wide now, glinting with ferocity. It scared Numo.

"Do you understand, Numo?"

No. And it was on the edge of his tongue—no, doctor, I don't understand, and I don't like that lunatic shimmer in your eye, sir, and frankly, I don't trust an alcohol-soaked cutter like yourself quite as much as propriety dictates, sir—but then he remembered he wasn't doing anything for Rawang. It was for Hammerfist. And she would not involve him in dirty misdoings that she herself would not touch.

"I'll do as you say, sir."

"Very good, Numo." With that, Rawang raised the surgical knife and cut open the incision under Numo's armpit.

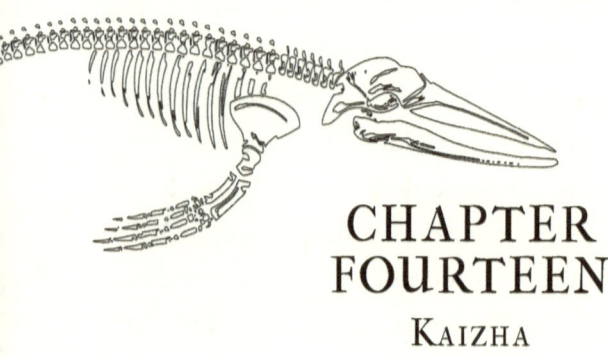

CHAPTER FOURTEEN
KAIZHA

KAIZHA WOKE UP in her illicit alchemy shack. It was dark.

The thing was still attached to her, waggling in excitement. Kaizha tried to lift the arm. It was too heavy—or else she was too weak. Was it just the pain or was the creature actually *suckling* blood from her?

It looked annoyingly contented, like it might be the sort of thing that would suckle blood and be glad of it.

She couldn't go back to her house like this. But it wasn't as if she could get the creature off her arm by herself, either.

And Kaizha didn't have much desire to know what total exsanguination felt like.

That was one thing about Mozeh. He knew how to keep someone alive. With that thing tapping right into what she assumed was an artery, and a nice channel in her arm gored out of her, Kaizha might actually need him.

She tried to stand up. Her knees seemed to be made of watery butter. Everything in her visual field lurched to the left before going spinning off to the right and she fell. Her body heaved over and over, as a pro forma reaction to the barrage of nausea, but there was nothing for it to regurgitate. At least there was that. Silver linings.

Kaizha flung out her good arm and clamped onto the edge of a floorboard. She dragged herself forward, kicking with her feet. She had to stop. Even that was exhausting.

It was going to be a long journey home.

When Kaizha finally arrived at the end of the tunnel, she was hallucinating. She'd only brought a few nebulizer vials, and they did not last long enough. The prolonged exposure to tunnel air and the triple shot of medicament made her brain gasp and show her things that weren't there; giant spiders and water deer prancing through starlight. She was clammy, coated in dirt and rat feces and, in sooth, some of her own urine. It was not the first time she had wet herself in the name of alchemical progress.

She peered up at the hole in the floor of her quarters. Pulling herself out seemed an incalculably futile proposition. But, like a whale beaching itself, she managed to fling her soggy weight onto the floorboards. Kaizha slid the trapdoor shut with her foot and kicked the batskin over it. Possibly, she fainted, but not long enough for it to merit her concern.

When the spots in her vision faded, and when she stopped seeing the batskin rug laughing at her and calling her decrepit and feeble, Kaizha dragged herself into the bed. She waited. Eventually her breathing slowed and her pulse stopped banging away at her forehead. The sweat cooled. It itched. She could smell herself and was not amused. Kaizha hid as much of herself under the covers as she could, lit the candle by the summoning-bench, and pulled down the nearest strictureweed ring she could reach.

A brief dip of the ring into the candle's flame brought a drake toddling into her room. It was Moffet, the kitchen manager. He was old as Mozeh's dick and never lifted his eyes off the ground. "Do you need something, Mistress?"

"I need you to get—" She blinked and inhaled. Talking hurt. "I need you to fetch my husband. Tell him he has my permission to enter. And tell him to bring the healing kit."

Moffet shambled back out. Kaizha lay there staring at the washbasin near her bedside, wondering if she had a greater chance of arousing Mozeh's good graces if she were less powerfully-scented, but the mere imagining of the exertion flattened any desire to try.

So she'd lay there stuck to the sheets, sorry as a bedsore. She couldn't say she didn't deserve it.

Mozeh entered as he always did when she allowed him inside—timidly, his face full of both gratitude and mistrust. But when he saw her, the hunched shoulders straightened and the nascent sniveling in his lips faded away.

"Kaizha! Oh, my Kaizha. Moffet told me to bring the healing kit—I—what has happened to you? Where have you been?" Fast turnaround from concerned to angry, that was.

"You know where I've been."

Mozeh pushed the washbasin on the bed-table aside and put down the healing kit. "Again, Kaizha? You promised this would end."

"I had to lie, sweetheart. I've told you before—you're great at practice, but you're rather lacking in the innovation department. Someone has to do it to preserve your name."

Kaizha wished she had more energy in her. Something told her that this was going to escalate, but she wasn't in any condition to properly emasculate him.

Mozeh glared at her, his broad face taut, like a mossbear's hide stretched on a frame at a tannery. He undid the hasp on the kit and banged the lid open. "What is it, then? What need do you have of me, Kaizha, so that you may be done with me and get back to the illegal embarrassments you carry on under my own roof?"

"I've told you before; it's not under your roof."

"Then where is it, Kaizha?" Mozeh's voice trembled in that way it did when he was about to scream at her. Perhaps it was time to change the topic.

Kaizha pulled her arms out from under the covers. Mozeh flinched and tottered backwards.

"My—what—goodness sakes, what is that?"

"It's…I'm not sure what it is. But it's stuck inside me and I don't know how to get it off. I think it might be inside an artery. Or a vein. Or both."

"Curse it all, Kaizha," Mozeh growled. He paced away, across the room, thumping his mechanical leg on the floor. He turned back and he pointed at her arm, as vehemently as a man could point. "It's that. It's things like *that*, Kaizha, that prove women cannot be allowed to do alchemy! Your minds are too soft! You don't consider the consequences; you don't take precautions; you don't allow for error and you don't adjust your—did you even take notes?"

"Of course I took notes. I just didn't do any of the other stuff. Caution trammels progress, Mozeh. Safety is a lack of freedom. It's all just jargon for entropy. Now can you help me—"

"No, Kaizha. Not this time."

"I don't think you understand…will you come and look at it, please?"

"I don't think *you* understand. I don't want to lose you to your own silliness, and I don't want the sanctity of alchemy to be poisoned by your womanly nature. We all acknowledge the progress that your kind achieved when they ran Moaki, but the alchemy was too dangerous and the government too martial. The very populace was a tinderbox of violence. Now we must be more civilized, Kaizha. We have peace. But you insist on more disruption. Why must you be wedded to chaos instead of me?" Mozeh bit his lip. It looked like he might cry. Now was the opportune time.

"Mozeh," Kaizha said, softening her tone, "I'm sorry. You know how strong the call of alchemy can be. I am weak. I can learn to resist it, though, if it really means that much to you."

"You've said such things before."

Kaizha sighed. She *had* said such things. She'd have to think of different things. Mostly, she had to survive. "Mozeh, look at me. I've nearly killed myself today. Or yesterday? How long have I been gone?"

Mozeh swallowed. "Days, Kaizha."

That wasn't good. The old habit of fear crept into her. She'd gone soft in her role as a dolt and let things like fear back in, although the reaction was often delayed. But—if Mozeh refused—

"I'm scared of what I've done, Mozeh." That had real emotion in it. Kaizha was almost proud of herself. "I don't want to die." A lump appeared in her throat. The fear was getting out of hand. But the wetness in her eyes was having an effect on her husband.

"All right, Kaizha. All right." Mozeh moved towards her warily, as though approaching a wild animal. He inhaled and released. "So you have no inclination of what might cause this creature to let go?"

Kaizha shook her head.

"Have you tried killing it?"

She glared at him. "And destroy the experiment? Do you know how long—"

Mozeh lifted an eyebrow.

"I mean…I…my alchemical weakness…"

He removed a knife from the kit and sliced into the creature, down the length of its body. It shrieked and the sound tore into Kaizha's ears. The world yarred and flipped over. The creature's pain twisted through her body and a scream clawed out of her mouth. Spots of grey clouded her eyes until she only saw blurry patches of light. A rough hand moistened with a sharp-smelling chemical pressed on the back of her neck, rolling the muscles and veins around, massaging feeling back into her skin.

"Kaizha—Kaizha. Stay with me. Stay still." Blurry outlines of Mozeh appeared, cradling her head, his hand clutching the writhing thing on her arm. "I'm sorry. I'm so sorry. And I'm so sorry for what I'm about to do."

The tube inside her arm shot through her palm and ripped away. There was blurry blood everywhere. Her body went slick with it. Agony seesawed up and down her arm and into her spine and her body contorted as though she was seizing. None of her body belonged to her anymore; it was all an abstract hell of pain that she happened to be attached to.

The smell of chemicals and boiled plants punctured her awareness. Tinctures heated with fire, molten metal stirring through fluxes, consecrated waters cooling their tempers, burning flesh. Comforting smells, the ones of her childhood, her grandmother setting things on fire in the kitchen. And more importantly, the sorts of smells that meant she would soon stop bleeding.

It took longer than she would have hoped. She might have passed out once or twice, and time might have melted and turned to lard for all she could tell.

When the sun was a bit higher and piercing abominably through the window curtains, the fog began to clear. The pain had dulled from a sharp twist to a thudding ache. The smell of blood and drying powders and burned skin had overpowered the urine. Things were looking up.

"Kaizha, my Kaizha," Mozeh murmured. All the vim and piss seemed to have quit him. His voice was watery. "I'm so sorry. I didn't know. I didn't know how bad it was. I wouldn't have yelled at you so. You are too stoic; you must tell me when you are so near death. You must shut me up forthwith."

Would that I could.

"This can't happen again, Kaizha. I won't lose you. I—I would rather—" Mozeh sniffed. His nostrils trickled effluvium into his mouth, as though he were a child who'd been pushed into the mud. "I would rather report your activities and see you kept safe from yourself..."

Prison? He was threatening her with prison?

Kaizha's chest lurched. If she was imprisoned, it was over. It would all be for nothing. Women caught doing alchemy were "reformed" in solitary cells with nothing to solace them but endless basket-weaving and goat-skinning.

"You would lock me away?"

"To keep you safe, my Kaizha. You're not safe."

Anger surged lamely inside her and her eyeballs throbbed with blood rushing through her head. She needed time to contrive a solution, an answer...

"I won't do it again, Mozeh. Please give me another chance to prove myself."

He held her at arm's length and looked at her with that repugnant pall of entreaty. "One more, Kaizha. One more incident, one more hint that you are involving yourself in alchemy, and you will leave me no choice."

"Absolutely. Of course. I'm so sorry for worrying you."

One more chance. One more before Mozeh's costs outweighed his uses.

She would have to shut him up before then. Permanently.

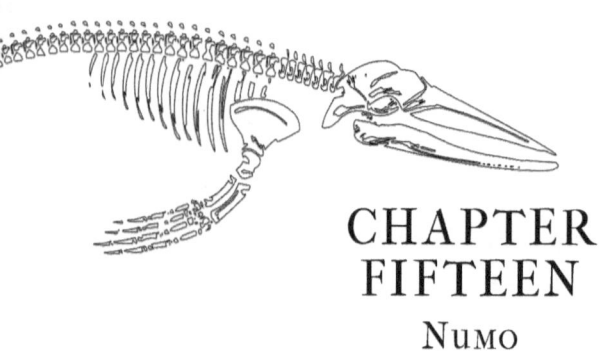

CHAPTER FIFTEEN
Numo

NUMO WAS INSTRUCTED to go home two days later. His armpit ached most powerful, and the stiff pain seared all the way down his torso into his hip. But the dizziness had abated, and though his head felt thick as smoke from moistened worm-filled wood, he could walk all right.

He trudged across the city again under the harsh sun, thinking of Hammerfist and promises and heads of beasts until he hadn't the energy to think anything at all. By the time he reached the hypocaust entrance, his legs were shaking with fatigue. He opened the door and gazed despondently at the staircase. It would take much less effort to let himself fall down the stairs than to measure out his energy on each step. How lovely it would be to let his body go slack and tumble down…

Numo took a deep breath and tromped unevenly down the stairs. Then he made his way to the back of the oven lines, slid off his satchel, and collapsed face-first into his hammock.

He was awakened by the squeezing of his collar.

"*Ungnnrrngnnnnnnnn,*" he said to his hammock. By Pyri's fiery intestines, he did not want to get back up…

But he was being summoned. There was nothing for it.

Numo dragged himself up the staircase and pushed open the little door with his forehead, so as not to bother expending the energy of raising his arms.

The Mistress Shanyang was at her woodworking bench, slowly shaving lengths off of what appeared to be the tip of an archaic wooden lance. She wore armguards over both forearms—a mode of old-timey fashion, the kind he'd seen in his book. She looked peaked, and one hand was bandaged. "Oh, Numo! I'm so glad to see you are back and sound. I hope you are feeling better."

He smiled faintly. "Yes, mistress. Thank you, mistress. Are you all right? Your hand appears injured."

"Oh, it's fine, Numo. You know me. My womanly habit of thoughtlessness does get me in trouble."

"Yes, mistress." It was not unusual for the mistress to injure herself, though it did trouble Numo so to see her aching. But it was not for him to insert himself into her medical concerns. "Did you want something, mistress?"

"Yes, yes." The mistress strode over to him and sat on the floor, fluffing out her wide pants, the red linen billowing like the sheer curtains over the windows. "My, you don't look well at all, dear. I mean, I expected it so; the doctor's messenger did tell me you hadn't responded well to surgery and needed more rest. And of course you can have it! I simply wanted to ask, my poor Numo, what you had found out from your visit? I wouldn't bother you right away, normally, but I feel it might be a matter of urgency, you see." The mistress bit a corner of her lip.

Found out? Yes. He'd found out some things. He wasn't sure which things were important to her, though. "Well," Numo began, "I believe this doctor Rawang is of a lower character than I originally perceived."

"Oh yes? I expected as much. But did you find anything out about his cure for the fall?"

"Oh, yes. He said the cure is hope."

She frowned. "Hope? I thought it was surgery. Nothing so prosaic as hope."

"Well, he said that there would be a *revolution*, whatever that is, and their pain would end, and so this gave them hope, so they wouldn't suffer so any longer..."

Numo stopped himself, remembering some sort of thing Rawang had said, something about what he must not do, but for the life of him Numo could not remember what it was. It was something the doctor said before the accident, something knocked out of his skull. He wasn't sure why he was near-remembering now. Perhaps it was just a surgical instruction. *Don't lick the incision?*

In any case, what Numo had told her was enough to give the mistress pause. The frown evaporated, the mistress's lips parted just so, with her eyebrows lifting ever higher as she spoke. "Oh my. A revolution? Is that so?"

"It's what he said. I don't quite understand it, myself. Would you happen to know—"

"Of course not, Numo. I wouldn't expect you to have any business about something as tawdry as a *revolution*." How odd. When Rawang had said the word, it sounded like a homey crackling fire. When the mistress said it, it sounded like a blight upon the crops. "Don't worry yourself about it. I wonder, though," she continued, "if he mentioned to you when this revolution was going to occur?"

"Well..." Numo's memory was so fuzzy; his brain so spongy with exhaustion and injury. Rawang had said something about next Middlemonth? Or—no, that had been when he went to that meeting. Penultimonth? Yes, he vaguely remembered it. But when? He would have to go back and ask—drat his small banged-upon fat-encircled brain!

"Penultimonth, I think," Numo said.

"Penultimonth? Any particular time?"

Numo sagged. "I don't know. I will have to go back and ask."

"It's all right, Numo. No need." The mistress bit her lip again and her forehead wrinkled. "Thank you, Numo. And, er—you do remember what I said about not telling the master? Keep on with that, yes? In fact, it is best you say nothing to anyone about this. You understand?"

Numo nodded. It hurt. The mistress was not blinking. He nodded faster, which hurt more, but perhaps she needed more reassurance. "Yes, I understand, mistress. I won't say anything to anyone about it."

"Good, Numo, sweet Numo." The mistress petted him with a pair of fingers. "You can go rest now. Thank you."

But she still wasn't blinking, and the fingers vibrated with a taut energy, and they wouldn't stop petting his head, and it was all making Numo very, very uncomfortable.

"Okay then," said Numo, and he stepped back slowly, so as not to disturb her reverie. Her fingers froze midair, and her eyes stared at the white batskin carpet. He wondered then if he hadn't made a mistake one way or another, but the wondering was so muffled and so far off, like the sound of a snorting rat under a leaf in the forest, and his poor beshredded brain struggled to make any sense of it.

Before he turned away and hurried down the stairs, he thought he saw the beginnings of a smile creep across her face.

Numo was eager to get back to sleeping, to let his brain heal and to remember whatever it was he had forgotten. But on his way to the hammock, his foot caught on his satchel strap, and he saw a corner of parchment sticking out.

The note. He hadn't translated it yet.

He snatched it up and pulled Bollix's book out from the satchel. Numo flipped through the lexicon furiously, then stopped himself. He was never going to get anywhere unless he went slowly, word-by-word.

Numo spent the next several hours poring over each entry in Bollix's lexicon and flipping back to the appropriate grammarly permutations of each potential match. His eyelids seemed to be fattening. The fog on his brain rolled on and on and painted itself thick in layers, until Numo could scarcely comprehend what he was reading. When he'd finally filled in the blanks, he blinked a few times and peered at the message again.

I am so sorry. I hope you can accept my deepest apologies. I was not myself. It hurts me to know that I caused you any pain. The doctor tells me you will be all right, and I very much hope so. My greatest wish is that you would forgive me.

This note has moved me deeply. Do you truly want to help the cause? We would love your help, of course. But I wonder if you fully comprehend it? If you value your life, it is not worth doing. Death is a real possibility, and I would not want you to suffer it if it is not truly in your heart. What say you?

Death…!

Numo had never been fond of the idea of death. The void of dying was an oppressive thing, a distant comet casting a shadow that would eventually explode him into bits. He'd often thought that nothing was worth facing the void for but his master.

But Bollix had already pegged him all those months ago, when she'd dangled the taunting-grape of the book. Now the only thing worth the void was Hammerfist.

The only thing?

Numo's eyes snapped open with a surge of dread. Did that mean his loyalty to his masters had diminished?

Numo buried his head in his hands. It ached and spit mud and spun about in a spatter pattern, making every thought mottled and not quite readable. It stuck him with little needles, saying *you needed to remember this*, but he'd already forgotten the thing he had been trying to remember. It was all just—

Wrong.

He'd chosen Hammerfist over his masters only once, hadn't he? And it wasn't likely that the two loyalties would clash again, was it? He could be loyal to both, perhaps. Rawang's scoundrel opinion didn't matter. What did the doctor know of loyalty?

He didn't understand it, but he didn't have to. If it came to losing his life, well, that was what it came to. Who was to say Numo's life was worth any more than hers? Indeed, it seemed to him that on a universal scale, just about anyone's life was worth more than his. He should be glad to give it up for Hammerfist.

Of course, that didn't mean he couldn't still be terrified.

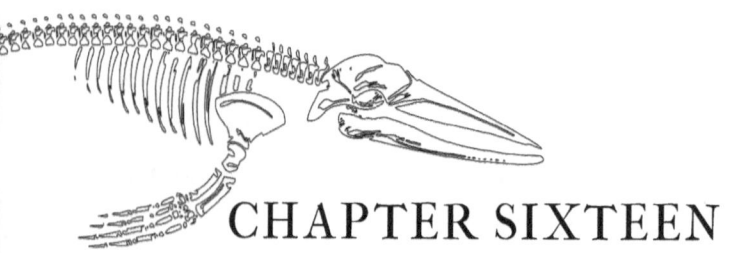

CHAPTER SIXTEEN
HAMMERFIST

HAMMERFIST WAS INSIDE her master's house. No recollection of how she'd gotten there, what she'd last done, when she had last been aware of the world around her, or what she'd last eaten, although the particular flavor of rot on her breath suggested it was hyrax carcasses.

The black gaps in her awareness were getting longer. Maybe. It was hard to know such things.

She was being led up the wooden stairs on a leash by Tungsamran's smallest slave—a little fetchthis-fetchthat infandus named Barback, who had only stared at her vacuously for a half-hour when she had floated the revolution idea a few weeks ago. He seemed to stare vacuously most of the time, as though it were a form of meditation, or as if he had no means to close his eyelids all the way.

He was in the category Rawang called "hopeless."

Barback drew her into the hearth-room, where Tungsamran sat chewing and drinking and whistling through his nose amongst an odd assortment of people. Some were familiar Moak merchants or fighter-handlers, but others had pendulous earlobes, or skin as light as off-ratio arsenical copper, or no facial hair whatsoever, or very long pointed animal teeth plaited into their hair like small horns sprouting from their scalp. One old woman had purple-bluish skin the color of distant mountains at sunset.

Why was Hammerfist standing around in front of a table of foreigners? Was she supposed to put on a show for them or something? Tungsamran liked to show her off, have her shatter the odd piece of furniture in front of people, but being so social wasn't really like him. He even seemed to have washed himself for the occasion.

"Thank you, Barback, you just tie 'er up there, and you can go till I call you," Tungsamran said, with a suspicious formality. Barback wrapped the chains of her leash around one of the iron studs in the floor, bowed, and backed out of the room.

"Well, here she is, lads and lasses," said Tungsamran, waving his arm at Hammerfist. "Saved the best item for last."

"The best, hm?" grumbled someone. A Moak.

"Yes," Tungsamran said curtly. "The best, make no mistake about that. Has held the Champion title for fifteen years now. Seven thousand and seventy wins. The absolute best."

"Then why are you selling her?" said the purplish woman.

The words hit her like a toppling crucible of molten iron. He was *selling* her?

He couldn't be. After all those years together, all the battles won for him, the money he spent on her armor implants, the vetting—she'd pretended to come out of the fall well enough, hadn't she?

"He's selling her because she's started losing," said the grumbly Moak.

"She hasn't lost a match in two months now," Tungsamran

113

said. "And before that, there were nine losses. Nine losses against seven thousand."

"She's winning, but she's not killing," retorted the merchant. "We've seen the matches, Tungsamran. She doesn't hit hard enough anymore."

Hammerfist's lungs seemed heavy enough to pin her torso to the floor. Doesn't hit hard enough, doesn't kill—the last few matches, what had she been doing, she couldn't remember—

She'd been maiming them. Hurting them bad enough to send them to Rawang. That was the plan. But she hadn't done it every time, she knew she had to be careful, and Tungsamran always liked her to win with that killing blow.

"True," said a large-bodied Moak. "She's old. She's on 'er way out, Tungsamran."

Way out? But she couldn't have…She couldn't have thrown the matches every time. She wasn't that careless, was she?

The last match, yes. The match before that. The last five matches…

Her hands shook, her claws scraping quietly on the floor. Ten matches. Twenty. She couldn't remember.

Her heart sunk further into her chest like a turtle's head slipping back into its shell. She'd lost track. She hadn't been paying attention.

"That," Tungsamran said, lighting a plain clay pipe, "is not as great a worry as the two of you make it sound. Let's face it, lads, Moaki is front and center of the circuit: the toughest, the fastest, the strongest of any infandus fighters anywhere all compete in that arena right there. No fighter in the Moaki High Matches that ain't a born-bred mass murderer. Hammerfist is getting up in years, no mistake about that, but she's still the top of that pile of meat."

"Not for much longer. You want us to buy a used-up homunculus, Tungsamran?"

"'Used-up' is a bit strong." Tungsamran frowned. "And no, I don't expect you Moaks to be particularly interested. If you saw nothing else today you liked, I have more stock to show you tomorrow. Enjoy the dinner, make merry, all that nonsense. But you all," he said, pointing his pipe at the foreigners, "damn well *should* be interested. How rough is the competition in Raeng? In Dailin? Trago? Gyatsu? Is there even an arena in Reykholme?"

A woman wearing thick fur on her shoulders grumbled. "There's no arena—no market, period. I told you I'm looking for laborers."

Tungsamran waved a hand. "All the more opportunity. Regardless, I tell you what, this girl here will blow it all out of the water. Smash them to pieces, anywhere but here."

Pendulous Earlobes clapped his hands like a child. "True! Too true!"

Hammerfist tried not to shake, not to react, not to flatten them all against the wall like doughy noodles.

She couldn't leave. She wouldn't.

"So. Enough of that. Let's start the bidding at a hundred thousand orduras."

The Moaks sputtered at the number. Fur Shoulders and Teethplaits sat unmoved. But the rest of the foreigners jumped on it. Arms were raised, hands gesticulated, numbers were shouted out; the purplish-blue woman wagged her finger like a dog's tail. It started and ended in a blur.

Pendulous Earlobes won.

"Oh, capital!" He cried. "Oh, but I only brought the hundred thousand with me, I'll have to go to the money-changer in the morning to get the rest…"

"Fine, fine," Tungsamran said, waving. "Come back tomorrow. We'll sign the papers then." He thanked everyone for their business and told them to get out.

Hammerfist stood there as the guests filed out, her hands sweating under the fuzz, slowly gluing themselves to the floor with sticky salt. Her innards quivered, her heart raced, her mind slid over and under itself like a child trying to grasp an eel. Tungsamran stared at her, smoking his pipe. Why didn't he dismiss her?

The last one slid out the door. Barback shut it behind her. Tungsamran uncorked a bottle of something-or-other.

"So this is it, old girl." He drank. "It's been a long road for both of us. You did me proud. I hope you don't think I'm mad at you or anything, sellin' you like this."

Hammerfist didn't say anything. She wasn't sure what she was supposed to say. What she was supposed to feel. Panic? Attachment? Fear?

"I thought it would be right for both of us," said Tungsamran, standing, swaying a bit before finding his balance. "Nice bit of money for me, nice retirement for you, bustin' in heads of those cheap imports they got elsewhere. Eh? Easier for you now. And I don't have to watch my greatest fighter go down the toilet." Oh god, did he actually—he looked teary-eyed. Hammerfist's mouth filled with acid spit, bile from her stomach, hatred…

He swayed towards her, sloshing the bottle around. "I am sorry it had to be him, though. Poncy old fuck, in't he? I think he told me his name was—it was *Jiminisius*." He laughed, choking on the alcohol in his throat. Hammerfist hoped he'd drown in it.

Her whole body vibrated with anticipation. Her fists were lighter, magnetized to the space between his life and his death. She'd never been this close, alone, without anyone to stop her. It would be so easy to just fold his body like a napkin and run out the door. She'd be free. Hunted, maybe, but free, out in the middle of nothing, where no one could see how twisted or disgusting she was, where no one would try to save her, and she could just fade into nothingness...

She ached for it.

But people would know it was her. They'd know she had the fall. They'd stop sending homunculi to Rawang for "surgery." Rawang himself might be imprisoned for quackery. Little Numo, and Bollix and all the rest of them—they wouldn't have their chance at being free.

The revolution would fade into nothingness with her.

Hammerfist clenched her fingers against her palms, drawing her own blood. Tungsamran stepped closer. She'd fantasized so often about killing him, feeling his skull splinter, driving a shard of his own tibia into his brain matter.

"Have a sip, won't you? A little goodbye from me," said Tungsamran, holding out the bottle.

Lightning danced through her brain

Drown in it.

One of her tongues shot out and wrapped around the bottle, taking it from his hand. Tungsamran smiled, that piss-guzzling smear of goat smegma, he actually smiled. She wrapped his body in her arms, pinning him without crushing him, careful

117

not to cut him or leave any marks. The smile vanished. His eyes widened. Her tongue flipped the bottle upside-down and rammed it into his mouth. Another tongue licked his face, felt for his nostrils, pinched them shut to cut off his air supply, forced him to swallow. She pushed him backwards. As far as her chain would reach. Shoved him into the table. The rest of her tongues went out, feeling for goblets, bottles, anything with more wine in it. One by one, she dumped them down his throat. His eyes bugged and boggled. It wasn't enough. He reached out for one of the oil lamps on the table, her strictureweed ring in his fingers, getting it just close enough to the flame for her collar to tighten. Another inch closer, and he could drop it in entirely, strangle her, and that would be the end—

She heaved against the chain and the floorboard ripped away. The ring fell out of Tungsamran's hand, disappearing under a chair. Her collar relaxed.

The two of them did a dance, Hammerfist and Tungsamran, her forcing him around the table in a tight embrace, searching out the remnants of wine and emptying them all into her master.

The doors opened. Hammerfist froze.

Barback stared at her vacuously.

Hammerfist thought she saw the wood melting and exploding around him. Her fate wrapped up in that one empty stare. Whether she'd be broken on a wheel, or have her tongues pulled out a hole in her neck, or be cut over and over again with a small shard of glass—

"More wine?" Barback said.

Hammerfist blinked. "Yes please."

The little infandus bowed and came back with a fresh case. Five bottles it took before Tungsamran slumped into her arms, gurgled, and stopped breathing.

Barback stared.

"You all right?" Hammerfist said.

He looked up at her, his unblinking eyes all bloodshot and crusty.

"More wine?"

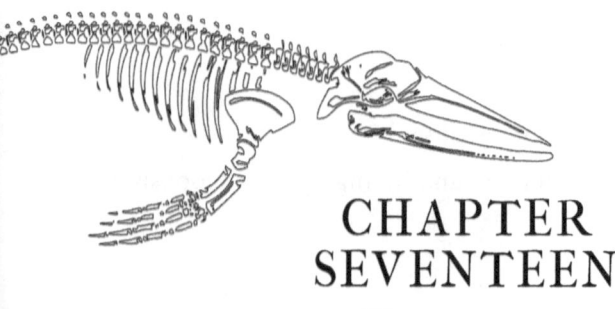

CHAPTER SEVENTEEN
HAMMERFIST

BEING OUT IN the open without anyone dragging her by a leash should have been liberating. It should have lifted weight from her, made her light and airy. Happy.

But she wasn't headed towards freedom, and she knew it.

"Do you think I brought enough wine?" Barback had two bottles in each hand. Hammerfist wouldn't let him take more because of the clinking noise. She couldn't decide if he had the fall or if he was just...like this. She couldn't even tell if he'd known Tungsamran was dead or not. Maybe that was his genius. Who was she to judge?

"Yes, I do. I think our new master will like it quite a lot," she said, keeping her voice low. They were in the tiny back alleys, it was dark, they probably wouldn't be seen—but she was, well, rather noticeable. They'd tidied up the place a bit, tried to make it look like Tungsamran drank himself to death all on his own so no one would look for a murderer, but there was no getting around the fact that they were now runaways.

"Is our new master nice?"

"Sort of." Rawang was...she didn't know what he was. But he would keep them safe. Unless he decided to cut Barback's brain out of his skull. "Can I ask you a question?"

He stopped. "More wine?"

"No, not that. I was wondering if maybe you would like not to have a master."

He cocked his head. "Haven't we already had this conversation?"

Hm. Maybe he didn't have the fall. Or maybe he was flaring into lucidity. It was so hard to tell...

"Well, you didn't seem to have an opinion then," Hammerfist said.

"I don't really understand it."

"It's like...you'd bring wine to yourself, instead of the master. Do you like wine?"

"Very much so."

She turned. His eyes were empty as always, sparkling blankly in the moonlight.

"But I like serving it more."

Her heart sank. This happened so many times. There had to be another slave out there like Numo, one without the dementia or the fall, someone who saw reason...

But what if there wasn't? What if her revolution would just set them all adrift and leave them with nothing?

To the thirteenth hell if I do, to the fourteenth hell if I don't, and taking all those innocent souls with me...

She pushed the thoughts aside. Anything was better than what they had—it had to be...

Hammerfist led Barback down through the city until they made it to Rawang's. The only safe place she could go.

She knocked. The lower peephole slid open.

"!" said Bollix. Locks tumbled, someone went *oof*; muffled

yelling reverberated from within.

The door opened.

"Sister! What a frabjous surprise!" Bollix shot through Pantaloons' legs and bounced up and down. "And you brought a comrade! Whatever brings you here at this time of night?"

"I…I need a safe place to stay."

Bollix grinned, the shadows playing a sinister light across her brow. "Why, what happened to the place you normally stay?"

Hammerfist thought. "Tungsamran drank himself to death. We chose to leave."

"We've come to see our new master! I've brought wine," said Barback, raising the bottles.

"I see," said Bollix. "Oh—" Her face fell. "I see. You need a new prison."

That was a rather blunt way of putting it. But Bollix understood.

"Well, come in here, quickly. I'll tell the doctor, if the noise hasn't already stirred him!" She gave a faint smile.

Barback shuffled in behind Hammerfist, still holding up the bottles, blinking occasionally. He stared at Pantaloons. "I like your trousers."

Pantaloons grunted.

They stood like that, Barback with his hands raised, Pantaloons contemplating his own trousers, until the doctor finally appeared.

"Oh, Sramai!" Rawang stood in the hall, looking very uncomfortable, as though not flinging his arms around her took all his willpower. Which, in sooth, she appreciated. "I'm so happy to see you! Bollix told me the situation. You can, of course, stay here, as long as you need. Don't worry about a thing." He held a hand out, withdrew it, and bit his lip. It was like he suddenly didn't know how to behave around her.

"Come in, come in. You there, go with Pantaloons, he'll take you to a room and get the nameplate off that collar," he said, gesturing at Barback.

"I brought the wine," said Barback. He placed the wine at the doctor's feet and bared his neck.

"Oh...yes. Well. It looks quite good, thank you. Run along, then."

Barback straightened and loped behind Pantaloons. "He said it was good, he did," went his voice, echoing down the hall.

"I'm getting a special room set up for you," Rawang said. Hammerfist didn't like the sound of that. "It's just next to mine, there. A proper room, now that you're not a slave anymore."

Not a slave anymore?

A spidery-legged feeling wrapped around her like a net and squeezed.

If she left the doctor's practice, she'd be captured, sold, put to death, or worse. And Used-to-be-Her-Husband was a different sort of human, but a human all the same. He wanted something from her that she didn't want to give. A promise, a service. Devotion.

She was still a slave and everyone seemed to know that but Rawang.

He ushered her down the corridor into a room that didn't seem proper at all. There was no straw in it to sleep on; just a great rectangular thing in the middle of the room, something that looked like a toilet, and another thing that also seemed like it might be a toilet, but a bit higher up than should be convenient.

"Where is the straw?"

"It's in the mattress, sweetheart. It's a real bed. For you."

"Mrhtsh." There wasn't any such word in her language.

"Try it."

She walked over to it, unsure what to do with the great rectangular thing.

"Well, climb on," Rawang said.

She did. Her claws tore into the fabric and straw spilled out. Oh—she had to get the straw out herself. That made more sense. Hammerfist tore up the fabric until there was enough loose straw for her to lie in.

Rawang looked disappointed.

"Was that wrong?" she said.

"Yes."

He sat down on a stool by a shiny reflective thing. A mirror. She hadn't seen one of those in—in—however long it had been. Why in the name of Samaak did he think she'd want a mirror? Suddenly the prospect of seeing herself ballooned up and swallowed her.

"Can you cover that?"

"What?" He turned. "Oh. This? It pains you to see yourself? Don't worry, Sramai." A broad semi-smile widened across his face. "You are hideous now, but we don't have to deal with that much longer. I've come up with a solution."

"Solution" sounded like an oozing black word. And he still didn't cover the mirror. She turned away to make sure she didn't catch an accidental glimpse. "What?"

Rawang shuffled over to face her. He gently unlatched her collar. She didn't like this. But she supposed she had to have it off—it would mark her as a runaway now.

But he kept touching her.

He took her claws in his fingers. She tried not to yank them away. This was bad. Whatever he was going to say...

"I can do surgery. I can do many surgeries. And I'm getting close, I think, with my experiments, to finding a cure for the fall. I think, oh Sramai, I think—I think I can make you human again. Or very very close!" He squeezed her claws as though she could feel anything but the ground falling out from under her. "What do you think? You and me? Like old times—"

Hammerfist swallowed and swallowed and swallowed as though it would keep the anger from spewing out. She shoved him down into the straw. Him and his damn mirrors. And the brain experiments—the experiments he'd said he was done with; he *promised*—

"Sramai—why—why are you upset?"

She couldn't look at him without wanting to kill him. It wasn't fair, it wasn't fair to him at all, but it wasn't fair to her either; this whole wretched tortuous mess wasn't fair. Hammerfist whirled and accidentally saw the mirror.

Crooked jaw. Crooked fangs. A constant line of drool. An unkempt mane spattered with brown. Pointed half-bitten ears like a street dog's. A giant hole in the face for a nose, like the nostrils of a skinless animal skull.

And he said he could make her human?

This was her. This was what she was.

"I told you to cover that *fucking* thing!" She smashed the mirror against the wall. The remnants crushed under her knuckles like little splinters of skull.

"Sweetheart—I don't understand the verb you're using, I'm sorry, I've been too busy to study more—let me get Bollix in here to translate..."

She was shaking, trembling, a wet rat shivering inside a hollowed carcass, trying so hard not to let her mind go all red and black and small, because if it went red and black and small, this man—this man who she should not hate on any sane planet, but who she hated nevertheless with the passion of a thousand stars—this man might very well have all the blood pounded out of him before she could stop herself. Hammerfist folded herself into a corner and covered her eyes with her fingers and tried to pretend she was inside a hole with enough garbage in it to bury herself forever.

Rawang's footsteps went away. Maybe this was a mistake. She shouldn't have killed Tungsamran; should have stayed with the predictable bastard who treated her like the pile of walking demon warts that she was, begged him to let her stay, pleaded with him not to sell her...

But Rawang cared for her so. And he did what he could for her ideas of revolution, even though she knew his heart wasn't in it. Indeed, he'd gone above and beyond her expectations, given how dismissive he'd been before she convinced him her life depended on this.

He'd done so much for her sake. Why should she hate him?

The footsteps came back, along with smaller, prancier ones.

"Oh, she's quite upset!" said Bollix's voice.

"Yes. Can you help me talk to her?"

"I will do what I can!"

"Sram...Hammerfist? Hammerfist, I'm sorry, I forgot you prefer to be called that," Rawang said in a soft, patronizing tone. "Please tell me what's wrong."

Hammerfist looked up. Rawang's face filled her with rage again and she buried her eyes in her fingers. She tried to think of something to say that he might understand.

"You promised you wouldn't do the experiments anymore."

Bollix did not need to help him with that, at least.

"Oh, those? But, sweetheart, I'm so close, and those poor creatures have one foot in the grave—"

"No more," she rumbled. "No more deaths on my behalf."

Rawang inhaled sharply. "But I have to finish the experiments. I have to find a cure. Don't you want that? Don't you want to be human again?"

"*No,*" she roared. Both Rawang and Bollix flinched away from her as though the wind was a small hurricane. "No. I don't remember being a human. I don't remember you. I don't *love* you. There is no such feeling in me anymore. Even suggesting I can go back is...it's torture. I just want this one chance at helping other creatures to make up for all the ones I've hurt, as a human and as this thing. Then I want to *stop existing*, Doctor. That's what I want."

Bollix took a while to translate all of this, her face bright and somber at the same time. As it went on, Rawang's face went red and taut, and droopy and dark, on and off, or all at the same time, she couldn't tell. But the tone of his voice when he finally spoke was quite easy to read.

He was angry.

"Hammerfist," he said, very carefully, "I told you before. What happened before the transmogrification was not your fault. The person who did what you did—that wasn't you. And if you still want to put all your faith in these slaves instead of me...well. Let me show you something." He stomped out of the room. Bollix stood there mashing her knuckles together. She turned her head back from the doorway to Hammerfist.

"Look," she said, "whatever's about to happen, try to keep your wits about you. The doctor is mostly a good man, but he's also a very flawed man...very very flawed...try to think happy thoughts."

Happy thoughts?

Rawang strode back in, leading Pantaloons by a leash. He took off the leash. Then he unlatched the collar. "Pantaloons, you are now free," he declared. "I am no longer your master. Go and do whatever it is you want."

Pantaloons cocked his head to the left.

"Go on, then. Go do whatever your heart desires."

Pantaloons dropped to his knees and clung to Rawang's legs, howling.

"Now, now! There must be something you'd rather do. Someplace else for you to go."

Pantaloons's eyes went wide and shaky, and the howling transformed into a miserable moan. He contorted himself into a shape of utter hopelessness.

"Fine. Would you like to be my slave again?"

Pantaloons bobbed his head rapidly.

"All right then." Rawang put the infandus's collar on once more. "There. Go back to bed."

Pantaloons frolicked away, head still tilted weirdly to the left.

Rawang turned to Hammerfist, his arms folded. "Slaves do not want to be free, Hammerfist. The revolution will help those with the fall and dementia, but they will soon die without a cure."

She shook her head, burying it back in her hands. She'd been thinking it, but she didn't want to hear it from him.

"Sir," Bollix said quietly. "I think the issues here are rather larger than you perceive..."

"Shut up, Bollix," he snapped. "Hammerfist, I will go on with this revolution for you. Because I believe you won't truly be free without it. They'll be looking for you, and I can't hide you forever. But you must put your hope somewhere else. It may not go as you wish. And I think that, if you tried, you could put your hope in me.

"You don't remember me or love me now, perhaps. But you will. I will see to that, whether you approve of my methods or not. And when you remember, we can start rebuilding our lives. The both of us, together."

The door slammed. Hammerfist peeked out.

Rawang was gone, but Bollix still stood there, rocking back and forth on her toes.

"Go away," said Hammerfist.

"I was just thinking…" Bollix said. "Perhaps not every slave will enjoy being free at first. They won't know how. But someone could teach them, and they wouldn't be so frightened anymore. And anyway," she said, rocking, "if these efforts help even one soul, well, I would think them quite worthwhile, myself."

Hammerfist's eyes burned terribly. Her nostril filled with snot and she sniffled. "…Do you really think it will help?"

"Oh yes!" Bollix said, bouncing. "I am quite sure of it! Many homunculi and people alike! Even the doctor." She winked.

Many people, indeed. She thought of Numo and his little flower. He felt it; he felt *something*; a longing for something to be fixed that was broken, so deep he was willing to martyr himself if necessary. The others would feel it too, or she should at least try to help them.

If she had to stay with them to teach them how to be free, well…she'd just have to live a little longer.

129

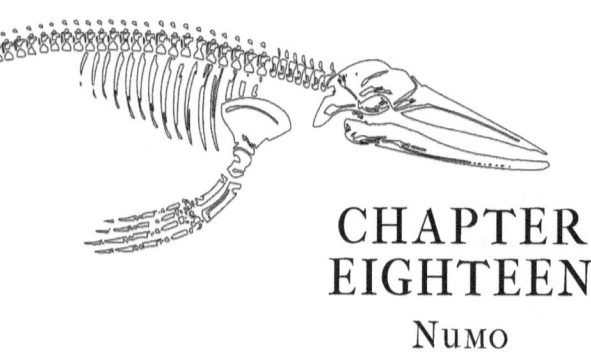

CHAPTER EIGHTEEN
Numo

Summer PASSED, AND autumn came. With it, firewood-gathering started in earnest, and the cold nights came to beg for Numo's fires. This was the season when he started to come alive again, when his purpose refreshed anew like a near-dead ember that flared yellow and white when stoked with the proper cooings and affections.

But this time, the ember in him seemed weak. The joy of gathering, burning, and hiking in the forests was numbed by a lack of Hammerfist. And, a bit, by the worry over not bursting the little satchel in his armpit as he went about gathering branches and climbing up trunks to gather flammable fungi and directing the infandi loggers to the best trees.

Now his time was not his; he couldn't go gallivanting off to veterinary practices or battle arenas, save for the one trip he made to knock at the door and be reminded by Bollix of the exact date of his duty to Hammerfist. By then he supposed his mistress had lost interest; she had never asked about it again. The rest of his time was taken up by the task of keeping the household warm during what was likely to be a snowy winter in a mountain city.

For this, he had his ovens, his woods, his resins and saps. The hypocaust was filled with ovens, each one sporting a duct leading to a particular room. These hearths were so packed into the space that the little pathways between them could not be navigated by anyone but a drake. Or a determined goat, Numo supposed. Goats seemed to be able to navigate anything.

A massive oven in the center functioned as the main hearth, whose duct went straight up through the center of the mansion. This was the fire that could never go out, and, Numo assumed, the oven into which Rawang intended him to throw his armpit-satchel, when the time came.

The walls were stacked to the ceiling with kindling and firewood. Numo had organized the woods by scent, by how quickly they burned, by color, by rarity. Indeed, he couldn't think of a nicer place to live, and if he only had Hammerfist with him, his life would be a perfect masterpiece of idyll. Only one hiccup occurred in his masterpiece—when one of the fire pokers went missing—but he had many more, and an entirety of winter to locate it before it carved out a sense of true failure into his mind.

Then, one day, out of nowhere, it was Penultimonth. Not time yet, Numo knew, but he felt it in his sweat-pores, the anticipation, the sensitivity of the satchel in his armpit forever prickling at his side.

As night fell, Numo was jolted away from his ovens with a gentle choking of his collar.

The summons was, once again, coming from the mistress's private chambers. Numo clambered up the steps, not expecting much in particular; perhaps a clearing of her ventage systems or somelike.

Numo emerged and saw his master on the floor. A fire poker—the fire poker, the missing one—had been shoved far, far into his rear quarters, and blood soaked the white batskin.

The mistress ushered Numo in. "Oh Numo! Oh, thank goodness you're here. Come, come here. Stand right here."

Numo found it hard to move. His muscles hardly knew which direction was forward or back. He sweated. His armpit throbbed. Was the master—

"Is he dead?" Numo had not seen death. But he knew it was what happened when you stopped moving, and the master was very definitely not moving.

"Yes, Numo," the mistress said, sighing. "Now come here. Stand where I told you to." She pointed. Numo shuffled forward, closer to the body. The dead body. The dead body of the master. *Oh, Nonnysteed, sweet Pig-Iron Nonnysteed—*

"There's a good boy, Numo," cooed the mistress. "Very good boy."

Numo stopped under her pointing finger, near the handle of the poker. "Um...like...like this, mistress?" Even his voice could not stay still. It breached and dove like a pteropteryx playing on a breeze.

"Exactly, Numo, just like that. Now, let me ask you—if you had to give your life to save mine, would you do it?"

Numo stared at her, wide-eyed. What was she talking about?

"Numo?"

"Y—yes, mistress, of course I would."

"My sweet fretting Numo. Thank you."

"What is it you need me to do?"

"Just stay there for me, and act in accordance with what

132

I say, dear Numo." The mistress regarded him sadly, as though he were a three-legged puppy. She stepped back. She opened her mouth. She loosed an ear-shattering scream.

"Murder! Murder!" she yelled, and then a long, brain-piercing screech, like a lance-spike to the eye. Numo winced in pain and wrung his hands in confusion and still his heart-pieces shuttled themselves frantically inside his chest-sac and his knee-blobs and his thigh-meat. The four human guards came rushing in. Infandi laborers and watchmen lolloped behind. Even a handful of house-drakes skittered into the room. All of them froze in shock at the sight before them. Their eyes landed on Numo.

The mistress pointed. "Murderer!"

Me?

The guardsmen fell on him. The crier ran outside. They clapped him in irons. They tugged at him. He was paralyzed. Speechless.

"To the square!" yelled one of the guardsmen. "To the square with him! Alert the council! The whole damn neighborhood! To the square!"

Me?

A quick jerk on the irons and he was on the floor. The men dragged him out of the room, into the corridor, letting him trail behind as though he were judged and already sentenced to the trap-drag. Perhaps a taste of things to come, Numo realized with a start. But this couldn't be happening. This was a strange fantasy that some alchemist had put in his head. Maybe one of the neighbors' laboratories had exploded in the night and thrown up airborne vision-dust and he had inhaled it and now he was delirious or bedeviled. And yet, all the while, the mistress

133

went on, "murderer, murderer," pointing, nearly fainting, falling into the arms of an infandus, recovering, taking up the cry once more, like some strange banshee had taken over her body.

The men yanked him down the steps outside the front portal to the mansion. It was snowing, only just; the flakes tiny and sharp and daggery, creating a harsh dusting on the cobbled street. Numo guarded his left armpit as he was flung out onto the stones.

The rest of the household trailed out. The throng screamed behind in his wake like a flock of howler geese. The men dragged him up the hill, towards the district square, where, he heard, festivals and punishments and disembowelings and blood-lettings were wont to happen. Numo wondered what, exactly, would happen to him. Whether he should say anything. What his mistress was doing back there wailing like a madwoman that she'd been betrayed and her drake had "slain" her husband. Numo watched the prancing of water torches and screams of neighbors as they spilled out of their fancy houses as though it were a play-act. He could only blink at the shadows.

"Murder! Murder!" the crier warbled, running up and down the street. Lights came on in the houses, torches lit, other guards and criers running out of the surrounding mansions of the alchemy district. "Homunculus murders master! Being led to the square! Common drake murders Master Shanyang! To be seen in Pillory Square for sentencing!" People darting about. Hitching up their rickshaws to their infandi. A mob gathering behind him in woolly sheepskin cloaks. Shocking how fast a quiet mountain street shed its innocuous clothes to become a scene of naked chaos.

The guards mounted the top of the hill and set Numo on

the blood-stone, a fat altar block with a pillory for all sizes attached. They latched him into the drake's slot, the rusted irons stinging against his scraped-up legs. His hands were forced into fists and shoved inside hand-shaped iron gloves that had been molded into obscene gestures. Those obscene gestures mocked Numo. His pedigree. His entire purpose in life.

It wasn't meet.

A crowd of faces murmured and shouted and pointed. Things were thrown at Numo as guards took up positions by the pillory—rotten foodstuffs, empty bottles. A child threw feces. This was supposed to be a district of sophisticates, of alchemists and reasoned men. So Numo had thought. The feces slapped against the side of his forehead and trickled down into his ear. Numo's chest heaved and his eyes leaked and his ears filled with mucous.

The mistress fought her way through the crowd. She stood on the stone just before the altar. Her hair was askew, her face puffy and blotchy, streaked with wetness. It mystified him.

"This slave!" she screamed. "This slave has murdered Master Shanyang!"

"Me?" said Numo, sadly, quietly. No one heard him. Fat droplets rolled out of the corners of his eyes, and his ears flushed purpley-black with shame. "Me...?"

The crowd fussed. The mistress went on yelling, her voice obscured by a twirl of wind and angry little snowflakes, while Numo tried to comprehend it all. He certainly didn't remember killing the master. But why would the mistress say things that were so untrue? Unless, perhaps, Numo was mistaken. Some accident of the brain had led him to go crazy. Dementia was setting in. Numo shivered in his irons, vital juices buzzing inside him like a cloud of locusts. He'd been prepared to die for Hammerfist, for his masters, but not for a failure of his own brain.

"Ahem!"

The voice was booming and bristly. Numo could hear the beard before he saw it. Master Goh strode through the crowd, with a posse of servants trailing behind. The foremost was one Numo recognized—the beardservant Reddles, in his smart-looking bandolier, whose sole purpose seemed to be carrying the end of the unfathomable reddled whiskers.

Goh marched up to the mistress, who ceased her shouting for the first time in some minutes. He bowed deeply before her.

"Is it true? Your husband is murdered?"

The mistress's voice trembled, strained and watery. "Yes, High Councilman." She bit her lip, the anger sagging out of her posture.

Goh put a hand on her shoulder. "I am so deeply sorry, madam. I will have Turian's men upon your house presently to inspect and treat the body, and we will certainly convene an emergency council, but—may I ask about the circumstances? I understand if it is too painful."

The mistress nodded, sniffling. "He and I were engaging in discourse in my chambers. I left to check on the tea we had requested—it was taking longer than usual—but I heard yelling, and I hurried back, and then I found—I found—" She put her fingers to her eyelids and squeezed. Numo leaned forward. What did she find?

"I found him," the mistress continued. "On the floor, squirming, with—with that *thing*," she said, shooting a deathly gaze at Numo, "and its fire poker, and the blood, and oh—it was too late!" A fresh burst of wailing sputtered out of her and wracked her body. She fell to her knees.

So it was. It was the dementia. It had to be. Unless—but the mistress wouldn't prevaricate so. Numo's whole face was wet now, his eyes leaking and leaking and they wouldn't stop, and it was so shameful, but he was so overloaded on shame now that it hardly mattered. Blackness was spreading over his skin, up from his hands trapped within the gloves to his elbows and beyond.

The master, the man who'd made him, and raised him, and given him a home and a duty, everything a drake needed. Numo had destroyed him.

He deserved humiliation and more. Euthanasia. Worse than euthanasia. He wasn't sure what was worse, but he was sure the humans would think of something, they being so much cleverer than he in the punitive arts.

Goh gently pulled the mistress to her feet, and, steadying her with a hand on her back, tipped her chin up to look at him. "Madam, are you saying that this drake murdered him?"

She nodded, her throat jerking and yipping with sobs. The crowd broke out again in angry yelps and murmurs. Goh held up a hand to silence them.

"Are you absolutely certain of what you saw? Perhaps the drake came in after some murdering brigand had escaped?"

The mistress only wailed louder.

"I only ask because," Goh said, turning away and facing the crowd, "I very much doubt that a drake—even if he had experienced an onset of dementia—could do such a thing. An infandus during a fall, yes, that has been documented many times, but a drake? It has never happened before. Unless any

137

of you good citizens have unreported incidents to submit?" He snatched his beard from Reddles and stroked it with long, measured movements, as though he were playing a trosan.

The crowd grumbled, looking around, waiting for someone to speak up. "No," said someone, "no, I haven't heard of such an incident."

"Perhaps it truly was some brigand?" said another voice.

"Perhaps it was Kaizha…" someone muttered.

"Kaizha! How dare you suggest such a thing!"

"Well, she's a woman, isn't she? And any woman is a snake, given the right time to strike, I say!"

"Sure, Kaizha's probably done it!"

"The lady is grieving! Shut up, all of y—"

The mistress folded to her knees again and heaved out a great howling screech. "He confessed!"

The crowd went silent. A snowflake slapped into Numo's eye.

Goh turned, flicking his beard aside, and Reddles gathered it up in a hurry. "What's that, my dear?"

"I heard him," the mistress said wetly. "I heard it…he said…he said 'down with the alchemist wolves. The revolution is nigh!'"

Goh said nothing. The crowd said nothing. Numo almost said something, but what? What could he possibly say? Dementia was the only reasonable explanation, wasn't it, unless—

The mistress hid her face from the crowd and turned. She peeked through her fingers at Numo.

There he saw something very strange. Not fear, not woe, not hate. Something like an entreaty, in her eyes. He'd seen it once before, when the master had wanted to have a great gathering for a festival but there weren't enough beds for the guests, and Numo had nearly suggested the little house in the woods without remembering that the master wasn't supposed to know, and Kaizha had looked at him like this, half plea and half threat—

Would you give your life to save mine?

Just stay there for me, and act in accordance with what I say, dear Numo.

The breath exploded out of his lungs and left them flat. The mistress a dissembler? And a murderer? And—his—but she was his mistress! His brain went blank, and his eyes and his breath, and everything and everyone seemed suspended in time and blackness, until someone slapped him.

Numo blinked. Goh was in front of him. "I said, drake, is this true? Do you mean to cause a revolution? Answer now. And answer truthfully, if you value your honor at all."

Numo swallowed. He opened his mouth. "Ah—uh—grau—" His brain was broken. His mistress was a dissembler and a murderer and his master was dead and the entire world had disintegrated in the space of an instant.

He tried again. "I—"

A young man's cry rose over the throng. "Master Zhiju attacked! Master Zhiju overwhelmed by servants in his own home!" The boy ran through the crowd, his crier cap askew, his pants falling around his hips. "Guards fighting the servants! Zhiju wounded! Servants screaming of revolution!"

Goh held up a hand to stifle the crowd, but he was ignored. "Are the city soldiers at the residence yet?"

"Yes, yes sir!" shouted the crier. "Servants being massacred!" He ran out of the crowd, shouting his way down the street.

139

Massacred...

What was happening?

Goh whirled on a Moak soldier with the neck-tattoos of an officer. "Captain Namkeng, you stay. Guard this one." He turned back to the crowd. "The rest, to Zhiju's mansion—aid in the struggle! This must be stopped!"

The throng roared and tore off down the hill. The mistress and the captain stayed behind.

"Numo," the mistress said, her voice cracking. "You will answer for this." Then the mistress lifted her ruined pants above her ankles and left, walking quietly up the hill back home.

Numo's eyes stopped leaking.

It could have been the burning inside him, the searing well of something threatening to overflow, but in the distance, he thought he saw the healthy glow of a raging fire.

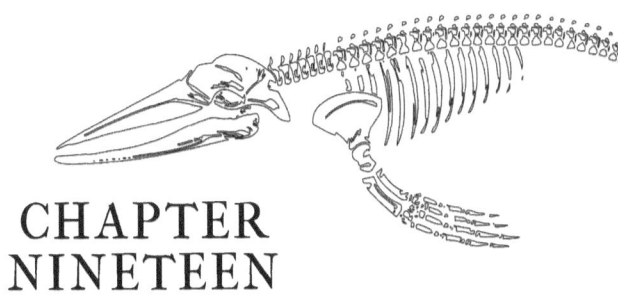

CHAPTER NINETEEN

Hammerfist

Hammerfist may have been stuck at the doctor's practice like a prisoner, but as long as she didn't set foot outside her designated areas, she was safe. Again and again, soldiers had come to the door asking about Tungsamran's missing infandi, and again and again, Bollix had made them disappear.

Hammerfist was afraid to ask how. Eventually, they stopped coming.

A few months of living with Doctor Rawang had made her forget what the outside looked like, and in the absence of anything interesting at all coming from the outside world, memories began to surface from within. The day he brought her a basket of bread and first asked to court her. The time she caught bleeding-sickness and he didn't sleep for fear that he might not be awake when she might need something. The day he brought her a pet rabbit and it shit all over the floor and he named it Turdsy.

Flashes of the day they got married. The oath she took, promising to protect and provide for him. Those were the hardest. The ones that made her want to eat her own tongues just to make herself wake up from the past.

In those memories, she loved him. But then the memory would burst into reality and vertigo would crash into her as gravity reversed and the floors turned to sucking mud. She was a different creature watching another creature's life. Any loving feelings left her for confusion and guilt. She couldn't decide if she cared for him or resented him or pitied him or all three.

She still didn't know what she had done to be transmogrified. Maybe it was for the best. If happy memories gouged her so deeply, maybe she couldn't handle the other ones.

Maybe she should listen to Rawang. Maybe she should let go...

One night she awoke from a nightmare to the sounds of children screaming. But children always screamed, whether they were having the best time of their lives or being murdered with rocks, so she tried to ignore it. Then the clanging started. Shouts of *fire fire*, the city's buglers trumpeting somewhere, criers' feet pounding the streets, their calls muffled by the hunkerwood between her room and the alleyway.

Bollix banged her door open and stood there with three watershot torches blazing in both hands, the whites of her eyes showing a fiery shade of crazed. "It's here."

"What is?"

"The revolution."

"No it isn't." It wasn't time yet. It couldn't be. What day was it?

"It is." Bollix strode towards her. "Come on. The reckoning is nigh."

What was wrong with Bollix? No romping, no joy— everything about her was suddenly sharp and dire...

"It can't be. I'm not in the right place. No one is. The

drakes haven't infiltrated the other oligarchs' houses—we're—
I'm not—nothing is prepared." This couldn't be happening. She
and Bollix had made rosters, maps, counterfeit strictureweed
collars for the few demented drakes that they had to wear as
they inserted themselves into the households of the council-
members—only half were installed, half still at the market
waiting, and…it was all for nothing.

Everyone she'd recruited, everyone she'd made promises
to—they'd all die.

Bollix stared down at her, the fire of the torches reflecting
in her pupils. "My soul is prepared. Is yours?"

Hammerfist's limbs shook and the crust in her eyes scraped
against her frantic blinking. "But—"

"No, nothing is as it was planned. But most things aren't.
We must go on with it anyway, the both of us, to find our target."

Their target was Goh. He would have been in the temple
of Moa, drinking his twentieth cup of beer on the 30th, on the
second day of the festival, too drunk to retaliate, too drunk to
direct the guard, too drunk to know they were waiting in the
shadows until he and the high priest were already captured
and ransomed for freedom.

But now—who knew?

"We must go. Now. Before the opportunity is swallowed
in chaos." Bollix reached out and tugged at her claw.

"Okay. Okay. Yes. You're right." Everything was screwed up,
but she didn't know why she should be particularly surprised.
There was still a chance she could save those she'd promised
to save. She had to fight for it.

Bollix tore down the hall. Hammerfist followed. She
thought briefly of Rawang, of Barback and Pantaloons, of the

half-dead infandi that the doctor kept somewhere, but maybe they already knew. Maybe Bollix had woken them and they were already out. In any case, they'd be all right, she was sure.

Until they got outside.

Fires were everywhere, churning smoke out of houses like mouldering butter. Burning ash mixed with stinging snow. City guards sliced into homunculi or wrapped them in chains, dragged them away, shoved axes into their necks, lopped off their feet to keep them from running away and left them there in the streets like rat carcasses.

Hammerfist tried to suck in air and choked down the smoke. If the soldiers were already down in the lower terraces, then it was too late.

No one would be all right.

"We have to go back," she said.

Bollix stopped. "What for? There's no time!"

"The others—what about the others?"

"I tasked Pantaloons with waking our brothers and sisters. Don't worry, they are in the streets, fighting the good fight—"

"What about Rawang?"

Bollix shook her head. "Couldn't wake him. The good doctor's been eating the rubbing-salves and drinking the cleansing solution again. But he's a human, sister. He's no longer part of this fight." Her eyes glittered and she grabbed Hammerfist's claw. "Do you understand me? Whatever happens, we're free of him now. We're free."

Hammerfist shook her head, her body heavy, her brain fogged like a window full of scratches, her breaths coming too fast to catch. She pulled away from Bollix. "We can't just leave him there. They'll find out what he's done. They'll kill him."

"Truly, sister, we don't have time for this. I won't force you to do anything, but make your choice now. I'm going to the upper terrace to find our target. You may join me or no."

Hammerfist's mind listed this way and that. She may not have liked him, but she couldn't leave him to die. Not after everything he'd done for her. Her chest filled up with guilt like a pleural effusion and clogged up her lungspace.

She was no one's wife. But he was still her husband.

"I have to go back." She spun away from Bollix and sprinted back inside, her knuckles denting the floorboards as she went. At Rawang's door, she pounded a fist on the wood. It snapped.

Fuck it.

Hammerfist burst into the room, splintering the wood and warping the doorframe. Rawang lay sprawled and naked on the floor, surrounded by empty containers of salve and ointment and little vials of cleansing solution. The intrusion didn't seem to bother him.

She bent down, poking at his nostril. "Wake up."

Nothing.

She roared in his face. She spat on him. She hit him. She hit him harder. She left marks. Finally, he stirred.

"Owmrbralmble," he grumbled, and rolled over.

"Get up," she growled.

"Nnnn."

"Get *up*." She yanked on his arm. It popped out of the socket. He whined in pain and went limp again. What the hell had he ingested?

Hammerfist shoved the arm back where it belonged and picked up the doctor like a sack of turnips. She started down the hallway, but someone battered down the door at the far end.

Soldiers' voices.

Shit.

She trundled Rawang down the side hall, heading towards the courtyard, trying to find anywhere to be inconspicuous, anywhere the smell of both of them wouldn't invade a soldier's awareness. Maybe she could get to the back door, maybe—

More soldiers. Spewing in through every door. Why so many? Did they know already? Were they hunting Rawang?

She held him tight and curled into the shadows of the courtyard.

"Oh, Sramai…"

She clapped a hand over his mouth.

A soldier jerked his torch in their direction.

He pointed.

He saw them.

Hammerfist tore them apart as they came. Slashing into their torsos with her fangs, impaling them on her claws, pummeling their organs with her fists, bleeding them dry. The smell of death flooded the spiral-sensors in her nostril. There was a pause in the flood of soldiers as the survivors hung back, weighing her appearance against the pile of bodies in front of her, muttering to each other about whether they should get reinforcements or keep shooting her with fire and wait for her to tire out. In this hiccup of calm she noticed something.

Rawang's body didn't have a pulse.

She moved her fingers. Pushed harder into his wrist, his

neck, to feel it, find it, scuttling her hands over him frantically—

And accidentally pierced his neck.

Hammerfist recoiled and lay him down, pressing a knuckle against the bleeding gash. Fireballs from watershot-torches slammed into her side. "Stop, stop!" She wasn't sure who or what she was screaming at, exactly, but the fire stopped coming. The torches were lowered.

Nobody moved.

Hammerfist couldn't do anything. She couldn't force breath into him, she couldn't stop his bleeding, she couldn't touch Rawang without hurting him.

"Help him! Do something!"

A soldier with the tattoos of an officer cleared his throat. "If you stop resisting and allow us to arrest both of you, we will do our best to keep him alive."

Arrest.

Yes, it was a fitting end for the revolution, indeed. *Everything I touch.*

Everything.

CHAPTER TWENTY
Numo

MORE CRIERS RAN past. An alchemist had been attacked in the street. Councilmen murdered. The founders' gate on fire, the temples to Moa defiled, the white woolly rhino loosed from the consecrated stables. The entire army called up. Homunculi slaughtered in the hundreds.

More and more homunculi were dragged up the hill and put in pillories. The night became colder. Soldiers held torches to frozen hinges, thawing the shackles so they could be clamped on wrists and necks. They soon ran out of room. Tens of infandi, twenties, maybe a hundred, and a few drakes scattered among them, shivering, chained up, and held at swordpoint by the Moak army.

So this was a revolution. It was horrible. How would this help Hammerfist? How would this help anyone? Numo's eyes leaked again and again until his body felt dry as a salted fish and his face begat a frosty crust. Namkeng stood very stolidly the whole time and twitched his mustache every so often, but even he was unsettled, shifting his torch from hand to hand.

Numo shouldn't speak, but it didn't seem he could sink much lower. "Captain Namkeng?"

Namkeng looked down at him in befuddlement. "Yes, what?"

"Why is this happening?"

"What do you mean, why? Shouldn't you know? You're the one that started it."

"I...I don't know anything." Numo didn't know what to say. His mistress wanted him to seem guilty. Maybe he should seem guilty. He said he'd give his life for her.

Not his honor. But maybe his honor was implied.

"Hmph." Namkeng twiddled his mustache. "Well, you do seem like less of a mastermind and more of a pawn, drake. Yes, I suspect you were manipulated."

"Manipulated?"

"Cheated, no? Lied to. They told you that killing your master would bring you freedom, was that it?"

"No. Why would I want freedom?"

"You don't care for freedom? Then why on earth did you do it?"

"I didn't," said Numo, in a very small voice.

"Hmph," Namkeng repeated, then he sagged in a world-weary sort of way. "Lad, I can guess why. You did it because the dementia has begun to strike your brain, and you heard some sort of fervor out there in the streets where your masters were so lenient to let you go faffing about. Something about being able to do as you please, move as you please, work only for yourself, worship as you wish, fall in love with a nice lady homunculus, perhaps—"

"Fall in love?" Numo hadn't heard the expression before. "What is that?"

"Oh, fine, maybe not falling in love. I suppose you all can't feel such a thing. The point is, you were deluded. All of that is a lie. A homunculus needs a master. To kill him is—well, idiocy."

"And that is what a revolution is?"

"What? Killing, yes. Idiocy, in your particular case, certainly." He looked down apologetically. "I'm sorry to say."

"I mean, it's supposed to be freedom?"

"Supposed to be, yes. Unfortunately it turns out rather differently, sometimes."

"And freedom would mean that an infandus," said Numo, "an infandus who had to fight in battles—she would no longer have to be hurt?"

Namkeng sighed, his mustache poofing out in the sudden breeze of his nostrils. "Lad, you aren't getting it, are you?"

Numo was starting to think he was.

By dawn, the square was full. Every decitude of standing space was taken by a chained homunculus or a soldier. But none of them was Hammerfist.

Her letter kept flashing through Numo's head. *If you value your life, it is not worth doing. Death is a real possibility...*

Numo had been so wrapped up in the idea of his own personal death that he hadn't stopped to reach his thoughts out any further. So self-swaddling was he, so obtuse, it hadn't even occurred to him that Hammerfist might be talking about herself as much as him.

She might well have been prepared to die.

And if she had, well, there was simply no point in anything anymore. His master slain, his mistress the cause, and the

150

revolution, whatever it was for...

"Uprising squashed! Revolution smashed! All upstarts in shackles or in burn-pits, blood puddles or prison!" the criers howled, running half-naked through the streets. At some point in the night, most had lost their shirts in favor of a basting of sweat. "Dr. Rosvayi Rawang in chains!"

It was over. Whatever it was.

"Now for the weather. Expect temperatures to climb today as..."

Numo stopped listening. It was over, and Hammerfist was...somewhere, the sun rising on her—through a window, he hoped; in an iron maiden, possibly; or warming her body, as dead as his master's. If she was dead, if Hammerfist was dead because of Rawang's *revolution* cure, he would—well, Numo didn't know what he would do. His imagination did not stretch that far. Something very unpleasant. It boiled in his craw and he'd never felt any fire or coal so hot as what filled him now. His hands and earlobes were turning white and red and shimmering orange, rolling over him in waves. He didn't think he'd ever been such colors before, and he didn't know what it meant. But for once, he didn't care. It seemed the whole world was full of scoundrels and prevaricators and thievers and charlatans and *fefnicutes*.

It was well into the morning before Goh and his entourage returned. Goh carved a path into the thick of the menagerie, and around the outer edges, a tired-looking crowd of humans and servants gathered.

A beefy infandus crouched down. Goh climbed atop his back, using him as a stool.

"Prisoners!" he shouted. "If you have not already heard,

151

you should know: your little revolution has ended, and quite unsuccessfully. Next time, you would do better to organize." The edges of his mustache pricked in smugness. "There are an unlucky few of you still alive, here and elsewhere. You will all be held in Mizu Jail until the festival of Kiroktera, where you will be entered in the Homomachy. Should you resist, we shall not hesitate to execute you before the games and add your hollowed-out corpse to your compatriots' toilet facilities.

"Soldiers, escort your prisoners. To the rest, thank you, and nice try," Goh said, sweeping his eyes over the prisoners and landing on the mustachioed man hovering over Numo. "Namkeng, you may return to your post. I will have a common soldier take him with the other prisoners. It seems he wasn't so important after all." Goh stepped down and disappeared.

"I suppose this is where we part," said Namkeng. He patted Numo awkwardly. "Sorry, lad. Good luck in the Homomachy. I hope the man that kills you is too inept to do it slowly."

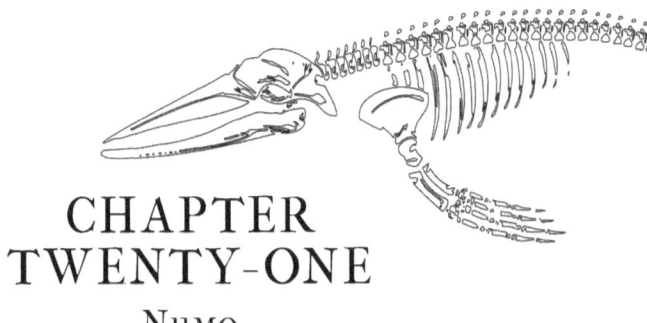

CHAPTER
TWENTY-ONE
Numo

SOLDIERS CAME FOR Numo. Two carried a huge pole between them, with several lengths of chains attached. Several other drakes were already latched to the chains by collars or shackles around their necks, and two more soldiers hovered around them uttering obscenities at unpleasant volumes.

The soldiers looped the end of one of these lengths around Numo's irons and one around his collar-ring. They shoved him in line. Most of the other drakes kept their eyes stalwart on their feet, refusing to look at him. But the drake just in front of him—one who'd had an ear ripped off—turned and stared, his eyes boring straight into Numo's. Then he looked down at Numo's collar. When he read his master's name on the plate, a smile of recognition appeared on his face, and he gave a deferential nod.

A soldier jabbed the drake with a watershot torch. "Turn 'round, you."

"Silence!" said the drake with one ear. "Dog of war, pig of purulence, blister of bung-leaka—"

The soldier snatched the drake off the ground, wrapped his chain several times around his neck, lifted him, and then let him drop. The drake dangled from the pole, his feet now just shy of any purchase, struggling, his eyes bulging, his skin turning dark blue.

The soldier nodded to his comrades, and they marched. Numo marched with them—there was little other choice. But he couldn't stop watching the drake with one ear as he hung, twirling, kicking at the air.

By the time they reached the bottom of the hill, Numo was watching a swaying corpse.

The soldiers marched them out of the city gates, down the side of Mount Barisok, and into the forest below. Numo had been to the forest many times, but not without rest or some means of conveyance. His legs gave out once or twice. If he didn't keep walking, though, he was dragged. The chain around his collar and One-Ear Deadlad hanging in front of him made sure that he always got back up.

It seemed an affront that the sun should be so bright and powerful on a morning like this. It should have been clouded and dark, the sky shrouded in caliginous mourning garb, but instead the heavens acted as though it were any other frabjous day, a day when the universe hadn't been upended and dumped all over the floor like a box of soot-sweepings. Arun the sun-goddess was shining her approval on the humans for smashing Rawang's foolish revolution.

Numo hoped there was some god watching over Hammerfist.

And another, watching over Rawang and Mistress

Shanyang, waiting for the right time to strike the gong of evil fates.

Oh! He shouldn't wish so ill on the mistress. She was smarter than he, and perhaps she had her reasons. After all, Numo made no difference to the universe whether he was alive or dead, and the mistress shouldn't be punished for employing a slave as was her right.

Right? Numo watched the dead eyes of One-Ear Deadlad. One-Ear Deadlad had died for something. Numo thought he was starting to figure out what the something was, but it kept flitting away every time he turned his mind to it.

Something was very wrong with him. Or everyone else. Or both.

The march was leading them further down in altitude than Numo had gone before. The trees themselves shifted in type and appereance, the pine varieties intermixing with some sort of pale tree with snaking roots that climbed up over the others and wrapped around the stones. Road markers were covered with them, so creeped over by creeping roots that Numo wondered how anyone read them. But, near a pile of great tumbled-over stones that might once have been a building but was now overtaken by root and moss, the line of prisoners turned.

Past more large mossy rocks they went, and then came to a stop. There was a gate ahead, with a wall stretching beyond sight in either direction. Words too far away to be understood were shouted. The gates creaked open, and the line shuffled forward.

Beyond the wall was a placid blue lake, with banks of tawny grass stretching up into the foothills, the mountains beyond reflected on its surface. It might have looked pretty, but in the middle of the lake was a gargantuan circular structure of wood and stone and iron with spikes and soldiers decking it out at every possible space, and that looked not very pretty indeed.

The homunculi were marched or dragged on sledges over the single drawbridge that led to the structure. On his way in, Numo and the others were branded with letters and numbers. Numo wrinkled his nose as his flesh burned, but he was quite used to burns. The others on his pole screamed and got kicked. The soldier with the branding iron pointed and laughed at One-Ear Deadlad.

"Headed for the toiletpannery, is he?"

"Yeh, couldn't keep his mouth shut," the soldier grumbled.

The soldiers sniggered.

They trudged onward into the building. The sunlight melted away but for a giant shaft of it spearing through an oculus in the domed ceiling. The building was arranged in circular tiers of cells on wooden platforms, with a giant pit in the middle. It was loud, cacophonous, assaultive. As they got closer, Numo saw where most of the noise was coming from.

The pit was full of homunculi. Overfull, in fact. They were piled on each other, writhing, hundreds of them, like snakes in a hole.

Brothers and sisters...

Where was Bollix now? Dead somewhere? She didn't strike him as the type to let herself get captured. But what did he know of anything anymore? Perhaps Bollix was really a talking ground squirrel in a costume.

He swiveled his head right and left. The cells all had humans in them, jeering and banging and calling out rude and incomprehensible words. Numo was headed straight. Like everyone else. Into the snake pit.

The soldiers hefted their pole onto the floor, and one by one, they loosed each drake from their tethers and flung them into the pit.

"You'll kill us—" shouted one as he went, but the soldier only chuckled.

"Plenty of comrades to break your fall," he muttered. He grabbed Numo. Without a word, he slid the chain away from Numo's shackles and tossed him over the edge of the platform.

Numo plummeted, his arms akimbo and legs splayed, falling, falling, to what surely would have been his death, had he not landed on a very broad and fleshy infandus.

The infandus grunted and tossed him aside. Numo got lost in a forest of infandus legs and feet and hands and claws and tongues. More homunculi were coming down like boulders being rolled on top of them all. He had to get to higher ground, or he'd be crushed.

But where was higher ground? He thought he saw upright boulders or somelike in the corner. One of them glinted, reflecting a particle of light. It was tall, at least, whatever it was. Numo pawed his way through the legs, taking a knee to the face here or a foot to the jaw there, clambering and falling and taking the smartest beating of his life. Finally he reached the gray shiny thing, and it rose before him as a shadow, almost as tall as a man.

Maidens. These must be maidens. He'd heard of them, but never seen—

"Numo."

"Gah!"

"Brother, calm down." Bollix leaned down from near the top of one of the maidens. Most of her was swollen and bloody, and though Numo couldn't quite tell, she might have been missing half her face. "Come up here, brother. You can do it. Climb, before you get trampled."

Someone's heel walloped him into the side of the maiden. It was iron. It hurt like iron. He grasped at the rivets in the thing and pulled himself up, straining his sore body until it burned and then straining some more. Bollix reached down and grabbed him, forcing him to keep going upward.

Numo flopped onto what he supposed was the shoulder of the man-shaped maiden and collapsed in a heap. Bollix panted, looking down at him. Yes, the eye and part of the nose gone—half the entire outer layer of muzzle gone, exposing her teeth and gums on the left side. Numo's postventricles lurched.

"Oh, Bollix," he said.

"Don't be sorry for me, brother," said Bollix. "The pain is good. It is my prize. The fight is not over yet, and I intend to finish it exactly as I wish. And that is, after all, the most one can hope for in this existence."

It was strange, very strange. Bollix was so different. No bouncing and no exclamation points. But Numo supposed he, too, might be a little less inclined to bouncing and exclamation points if half his face had been torn off.

"Now, will you help me, brother? Our sister Hammerfist is in one of these maidens—"

"Yes. Yes." Numo stood up. Energy flooded him and hope and joy and all sorts of odd feelings he absolutely should not be experiencing in a hole like this. "Yes. Let's find her."

Bollix half-smiled at him. "I thought you would say that." She slapped her hand against the head-piece beside them. "I think this one's dead already." She spit on her palm and laid it over the mouth-hole, next to a bamboo tube that ran from the mouth up to the platform they'd fallen from. "In spirit, brother or sister, in spirit." Bollix held out her non-spitted hand to Numo and gestured to the next maiden.

"What are these tubes? In the mouth?"

Bollix led him to the edge of the shoulder. "For feeding." She let go and jumped across the small gap to the next shoulder. "They put the most dangerous ones in the maidens. The tubes are their pale attempts to keep the prisoners alive, but some die anyway. Doesn't matter much to them, though they'd prefer to keep them breathing until they can kill them in whatever beastly way they find ideologically meaningful."

Numo followed her across the gap. "How do you know all these things?"

Bollix chuckled. Sort of. "I've been around quite a while. Longer than most drakes. You pick things up, bit by bit. What do you think of this one?" Bollix banged on the face panel. "Hammerfist? Sister?"

A rumbling noise came from inside. It wasn't her voice. Numo shook his head.

A great haggard moan came from fifty paces over. It didn't sound like a homunculus.

"Sramai! My Sramai, can you speak at all? Please, try again, please..."

Rawang, nakeder than Numo would have ever cared to see him, yelling at a maiden.

Why was Rawang in with the homunculi?

"Dammit," muttered Bollix.

"Stinkard," Numo said, before he even realized he was thinking the word.

"You don't like him either?"

"He's the reason we're here, isn't he?"

"No. Partially…but not the way you're thinking of." Bollix sighed. "Look. We're going to go over there. I'm really not sure how much you understand of any of this, and believe me, I know whatever you don't understand is not your fault. I've been there. I used to be like you. I had hoped—well, it was silly of me to hope. But if you understand one thing, understand this: Rawang is a better human than most, no question. But he's still a human. And he still sees her as property, just in a different way. So we can't let—"

"Bollix! Bollix, thank the meteoric phantasms you're alive, come here, quickly, I think she's here, it must be her, but she won't speak to me." Rawang shuffled over, his body hunched and stumbling. "Is that…" Rawang squinted. "Numo?"

"Now, doctor—"

Rawang lurched forward and pushed Bollix aside. He poked Numo in the chest, hard, as though he were hitting him with a small truncheon. "How dare you. How *dare* you still be alive. You stupid walking pustule of a creature! You've ruined everything! You've destroyed—"

"Now, now," Bollix said, "don't be too hard on him. He got confused."

"Don't be too hard on him?" Rawang whipped his head towards Bollix. "He completely ruined the entire thing! Months of planning. Preparation. He promised he knew what he was about. I should have known not to trust an empty sac of sheep scrotum like you!" Rawang snatched Numo off the maiden, throttling his torso. "I told you the goddamn 30th. I *told* you that!" Rawang was screaming, and he was reddening, but his own eyes were leaking. "Chaos. Complete chaos. One slave pulls the trigger too early and no one knows what to do. You are responsible for what's happened to her. What's *going* to happen to her. I hope your useless slave brain can understand that." Rawang's rage seemed to be draining out of him. His shoulders slumped. He put Numo back on the maiden, and he leaned back against another.

Numo scrunched his toes. "I didn't—sir, I didn't. My mistress did it. I wasn't the one—"

Wait.

Did I put her in the maiden?

Numo's legs went wobbly and he fell hard on his rump. Of course, not directly, he hadn't put anyone in any maidens, but—

The mistress had set it off too early.

The mistress had murdered the master and blamed it on the revolution. Used it as *proof* of a drake's misdeeds...

Numo was the one who told her about the revolution. About Penultimonth. Back when his brain was snowed under with injury and general ignorance and he hadn't realized what it meant, what *telling his mistress* meant...

Yes, he'd put Hammerfist in an iron death-statue.

He bit his lip, where the black gumline sagged under the tusk, and tried not to let his eyes leak any more. Then he'd look as sorry and pathetic as Rawang.

Bollix shuffled over and knelt down. "Well. I wasn't going to bring it up, but now you know. In any case, brother, it's all in the past, and we have another shot. You'll still get your chance." She rose and turned to Rawang. "Doctor!" she said, suddenly burbling and bouncy, "I'm so glad to see you again! Do tell me, where is she? I'll see what I can do!"

Rawang pointed, his finger forlorn and lifeless. He dragged himself to his feet. "Come on then, Bollix." He turned and shuffled away.

Numo watched as Bollix bounced over to the next maiden, following in Rawang's wake. Bollix waved for him to follow. Numo shoved himself up on his wobbly knees.

Hammerfist was waiting, always waiting. She was trapped to begin with, and Numo had only closed the walls in around her.

A short way down the row, Rawang draped his arms around one of the maidens and pressed his lips to the small opening in its haphazardly-repoussed mouth. "My Sramai…"

"This is her? Are you positive, doctor?" said Bollix.

He nodded. Numo clasped his hands and kneaded his fingers against his palms, standing well away on the shoulder of a different maiden. Bollix motioned him forward. "Numo, brother, come here."

Numo shuffled to the edge.

"No, come now. Closer."

He eyed Rawang, but the doctor didn't seem to be paying attention to him. Numo hopped over to where Bollix stood, on the shoulder of what might well be Hammerfist's maiden.

Bollix pushed him towards the mouth. Numo wasn't sure what Bollix expected from him, but he smelled her. The peaty unfettered musk. The glittering olfactory exuberations. And the breath, the unmistakable ragged breath, the exhalations like the wingbeats of the glorious bat-priestesses of Kiroktera.

"H…Hammerfist?" Numo said.

Rawang roared up behind him and snatched him away. "Don't you call her that! Stop bloody calling her that!"

Something inside the maiden banged against the iron. Scraping. Claws. And a terrible belabored hiss.

Rawang set Numo down on the maiden's shoulder. "Is that you, sweetheart?"

Sweetheart?

"My Sramai…"

A few more weak hissing and groaning sounds came out of the maiden's mouth, but they died away mid-sentence.

"I understand, er, but, my dear, that is your name, after all—"

Bollix patted the doctor gently on the hand. "Oh, but sir, you must let her have her comforts! It must be most upsetting at this juncture to be reminded of her past, you understand, sir, being so clever and all—"

Rawang choked on a sob. "Yes, yes, fine. I suppose. Whatever she wants." He slid to the floor. "I'm here, my love, when you are ready to be reminded of *your past*."

All the *my love* and *my dear* and *sweetheart* stuff sounded rather like what the mistress and master used to say in front of company. So perhaps—

Oh. *Oh.*

Oh dear.

Hammerfist used to be human. Numo kept forgetting. *How very awkward.*

"Now, sir! Don't fret so!" Bollix said. "I think the thing to focus on now is how we are going to get her out."

"It's not going to make a fourth a fuck of difference

whether we get her out or not. If we get her out, she'll still be trapped here with the rest of us. If we don't, they'll free her at the Homomachy after making her watch the rest of us die, so that she can be properly murdered for sport. There is no point."

Bollix went quiet. "Is that so?"

"Yes, Bollix, it bloody well is *so*."

Numo clenched his fists. If this man was Hammerfist's husband, he was a poor one indeed. He could see why Bollix didn't like him either. "Perhaps you would see a 'fourth a fuck of difference,' sir, whatever that means," said Numo, "if *you* were the one trapped in an iron man-mold with a moldering little tube in the mouth. Maybe you would be all right with letting her stay trapped in there until we are all set to die, sir, but I most certainly am not."

Numo swallowed. He'd thought such things about humans before, but never *spoken* to one, like this. So baldly, and unapolegetically, and—and quite angrily.

Rawang shot up and put his grimy face very, very close to Numo's, so close that Numo could see the tartar between his snarling teeth. "Do you think you can talk to me like that just because I've been thrown down here with you lot?" he hissed. "I'm still your superior, dammit. I'm still a *human*. It is a punishment to be here with your kind, you understand?"

Numo flinched, unsure how to respond. Several infandi around them scooted away, eyeing Rawang with wary uncertainty. Bollix stepped in between the two of them. "Oh! Sir! It must be awful indeed! Perhaps you should take a rest to calm your nerves, sir. I shall keep an eye on her for now and see if there's anything I can do to make her more comfortable."

"Rest, sure, take a rest in a writhing pit of brutes…"

Rawang grumbled. He sat back down at the foot of the maiden and folded his arms. Bollix stood there, stock still, without moving, so Numo did the same. Finally, Rawang began snoring, and Bollix relaxed her body.

"Look," she said, stretching her neck, "I don't like him either. He's a stinking, selfish clod who is too often sodden with alcohol and other poisonous substances. But it can be very useful to have a human ally, Numo. Keep that in mind, next time you think to provoke him."

Numo nodded. "I apologize. I was extremely impolite."

Bollix turned back to face the maiden. "Those rivets are well-soldered on there, aren't they?"

Numo examined one of them. "Yes, I'm afraid so."

"Damn. I don't suppose you have a knife or a carving tool or anything sharp on you…"

A faint few words came from inside the maiden.

"No, we will not let you die," said Bollix. "Not yet, anyway. The fight is not over. Wouldn't it be simply delicious to have our true revolution during the Homomachy? It would be downright poetic, would it not?"

A sigh. A snort of affirmation.

"Right, then." Bollix patted the metal delicately. "Numo and I promise we will help you die if this goes to hell and all hope is lost. Right, Numo?"

Numo clutched a hand to his chest to slow his heart-bits. It didn't work.

"*Right*, Numo?"

His lungs twisted up inside him like gnarled branches. There seemed to be a brick of lead in his windpipe. But if Hammerfist wanted to die, who was he to say she could not?

Her disease was saddening and deteriorateful and deadly, after all. It would be selfish of him to keep her on the earth that much longer just for his sake.

He'd put her here. He had to make it right—he had to make her free. No matter the cost.

"If that is truly what you want," Numo said, gazing into the iron mouth, "of course I will do it."

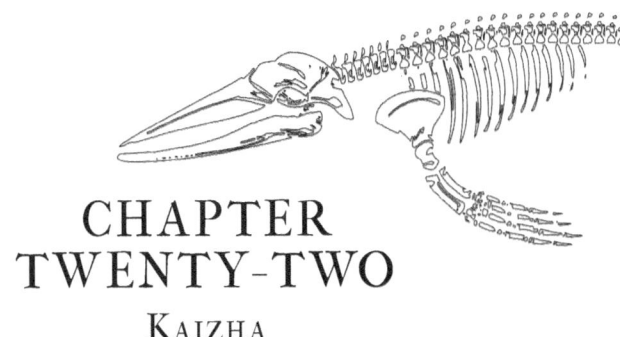

CHAPTER
TWENTY-TWO
KAIZHA

KAIZHA REGRETTED ACTING on passion. If she'd had any sense at all, she'd have killed Mozeh on the hardwood. The batskin was ruined—no amount of scrubbing and laundering seemed to get the blood out of the pelt.

To be fair, there had been a certain amount of planning. It had been necessary, if Mozeh was going to lock her up for alchemy—which she most certainly would not allow—and if she was going to have any reasonable scapegoat to pin it on, it had to be in the month of the servants' cute attempt at uprising. But her choice of that particular moment, in that particular place, well…

That, she was ashamed to say, was a result of her passion during an argument over what entrees ought to be served with which garnishes at their pre-festival dinner.

Still, it worked out much as she needed it to. And most everything else was back to normal. After nearly a fortnight of inquiries and investigations and well-wishers and mourners and Turian the Handsy Pathologist, it was over. She'd gotten rid of all the drakes, as well, and most of the infandi. Some she hadn't really wanted to lose—truly, no one could ever handle her netherbeard with as much aplomb as Curlyshears—but in the end she narrowed it down to two. She had to play into her own fearmongering and do away with the "rebellious synthetic slave-beasts," as she had professed to some investigator or another. She kept Spittle and Poison Tester Number Six, only because they were loyal as sedated dogs and she couldn't find humans who would be as discreet and unwaveringly faithful on short notice.

The house was gloriously empty. Quiet. Kaizha couldn't help but cry. With joy, at first, and then some horrible black aberration of an emotion crept in. Guilt, regret, sadness—one of those cancerous emotions that ate away at all the useful scraps of vigor in her.

She knew she'd loved Mozeh once, and in many ways he had been a sweet man. And, in other ways, a useful one. It was just that she could only take so many years of his "you've the brain of a woman" jiggery-pokery before the intoxicating nectar of love turned to hard coprolites of resentment.

In sooth, she felt worse about what she'd done to Numo. But it had been too perfect. And it was bigger than just Mozeh. It was the beginning of the end for the whole slave business. If Kaizha could tarnish the reputation of homunculi—and Mozeh's little semen-children in particular—the economy could shift in her favor. In women's favor. Moaki's slave trade was the men's doing, born of their monopoly on drake production. After the next social reformation, the business of Moaki would no longer be slaves—it could turn back to the proper dealings of war and tribute, double its efforts in the trade of alcohol and lithia water and lumber, expand the performance of religious rites and consecrations. Reinstating the holy brothels of Kuru wouldn't hurt either.

Spittle and Six had moved her equipment from the shack into the east wing of the house, where Mozeh's lab sprawled across four rooms. She'd been living there since his death. Sleeping on the floor, eating bits of bread and dried fish left in the pantry, forgetting to bathe, mixing the syntho-amniotic fluid with the distilled cane sugar juice when she ran out of food—it was like the old days. Real alchemy.

Failure included. All her tweaks to the weaponized squid-creature formula had proved fruitless—either the resulting things were inert, or they were even more violent than the first, and she'd had to stab them to death.

Kaizha opened the hatch again and prepared herself with a knife. But the weapon was unnecessary. The thing inside was ill-formed and lifeless.

She sighed and fell into the leather-wrapped chair. Kaizha removed the armguards she'd been wearing since the incident with the creature and scratched at her air-starved skin. Those armguards had earned her some shifty looks, being fashion relics from the Dreaded Time of the Matriarchy, but she had merely giggled and said something about nostalgia and fashions having a cyclical go-round and no one had questioned it. Her right arm was still discolored and crooked, weaker than it had been before. It was slowly looking less horrendous, week by week, but it was taking its sweet time.

Someone knocked at the main door to the lab.

"What do you want?"

Spittle's voice growled wetly through the wood. She was quite a difficult infandus to understand—something had gone awry with her salivary glands—but Kaizha was able to discern something about a visitor to see her.

"Tell whoever it is that I am indisposed."

There was more growling and grumbling, more insistent. Something about Goh. Goh was at her door? He'd already done the official condolences, the official investigation, the official delivery of his wife's "sorry your husband was violently murdered" sweet bean kralan rolls...couldn't he leave well enough alone?

Kaizha slipped the armguards back on and tried to arrange her hair in some semblance of order. Then she remembered that she was still technically in mourning, and she could look as disorderly as she wanted.

She opened the door. Goh stood there, him and his beardservant, peering into Spittle's mouth with his quizzing-glass. He straightened.

"You have a mild aberration here," he remarked. "Yet another case of the inexact transmogrification practices before Turian's innovations."

"Indeed," said Kaizha, who didn't much care for most of Turian's innovations—what she knew of them, anyway. "I've gotten rid of the other servants, but I couldn't fathom where this poor beast would find a home, defective as she is. Do you come on business or for pleasure?"

"It is always a pleasure." Goh tipped his head. "But I'm afraid it's official business. Unpleasant circumstances. Troubling findings, and the like."

"...Findings?"

"Yes. To be direct, the inspectors have finished the inventory of the homunculus prisoners, and there was an anomaly. A female drake."

Kaizha's breath stuck in her throat. Goh continued babbling, oblivious to the fact that her entire body had gone rigid.

"Rather aged, as well. I assume it must have been a product of some early experiment, but it won't tell us its origin. Seems to be immune to physical torment. Of course I realize that any alchemist—licensed or otherwise—might have illegally tinkered with your husband's approved formula, but I thought I would check his old records first. Would you mind allowing me access?"

"I—well," Kaizha said. She couldn't let him into the lab. Her own notes and mess were scattered everywhere. "I was just cleaning up in there myself. I can bring you his notes, if you would care to wait in the foyer?"

Goh's mouth tightened. But he didn't press. "Indeed, I would." Kaizha started to retreat back into the lab, but it seemed he wasn't finished. "Oh, Mistress Shanyang? I was curious about your fashion choice." He waved at the armguards. "I understand the wishes of a woman to return to a more youthful time, but it does seem rather inappropriate now that you're in mourning. You might consider taking up the sackcloth."

"Ah yes. The sackcloth." It was a more recent fashion. As far as Kaizha understood, there was a sort of a competition between widows in the comprehensiveness of their sackcloths. The bigger the sack, the more properly devastated the widow obviously was. And the more devastated the widow, the more social merit was gathered, which could then be used to build immunity for small transgressions, such as taking several helpings from a communal tray of baked goods or engaging in light embezzlement. Kaizha understood such concepts, but had no energy for such inefficient and fiddly social economy.

"You must forgive me. I am truly horrible at keeping up with such things. I've become much too preoccupied with my music and my basket-weaving."

"Oh! I did not know you were an aficionado of basketry. That is a grand pursuit indeed. I have some interest in the art. Do you have any samples about? I might very much like to see them."

Kaizha put her hand on the doorknob. It was time for this conversation to end. "I'm terribly sorry. I burned my basketry in a fit of impassioned grief."

Goh's lips parted again. Kaizha rushed to fill the pause. "I've kept you too long now with talk of my silly pursuits. I'll just go and get those records for you, Master Goh." She shoved the door open, slid inside, and shut it again on his smarm-ridden expression. As soon as she was alone, her mind flooded with panic, sucking up the strength from her muscles and nearly driving her to the floor with the shock of enervation.

Kaizha reeled her mind back into place. Goh was right: it was possible that some back-alley alchemist had once created a female drake of her own, back before the regulations of production were in place. It was possible that this drake was not hers. After all, the one Kaizha had made was supposed to have been destroyed. Mozeh had been extremely adamant about that.

Although, come to think of it…she never saw a body. And Kaizha hadn't been there to witness it. All she knew was that the drake had disappeared.

Kaizha breathed slowly through her nostrils, counting the inhalations. Then she set about finding those notes for Goh. Luckily, her husband had kept well-organized records. It did not take long to find the aged bundle of papers and flip through them to make sure there was no mention of Kaizha's experiment. She was satisfied with what she found. Mozeh was brilliant in some respects—he'd even fabricated a rather long and detailed lie about how he thought up the drake formula in the first place.

Kaizha handed the bundle over to Goh and bid him farewell, promising to procure a sackcloth at the earliest possible convenience.

"Very good," Goh replied. "Will we be seeing you at the Homomachy?"

"Oh. Hm. When is that?"

"On the morning after next."

Kaizha hadn't planned on it. Maybe she should have. "This is the Homomachy where the prisoners from the revolution will be executed?"

"Yes, indeed. I understand if you are still too aggrieved to witness it, but I thought seeing the death of the murderer—"

"Yes. Yes, I will be there."

"In proper mourning garb, I hope?" He winked at her. She wanted to smack that eyelid off his face.

"Of course. Thank you for coming by, Master Goh." She shut the door on him for what she hoped was the last time. Then she strode over to the desk and poured herself a full glass of amnio-alcohol. Going to such an event was not her idea of a merry time. But there could be a great opportunity there for destabilizing the oligarchy—the entire ideology. And if her drake was still alive and slated for execution, something indeed would have to be done about that.

She just wasn't sure what.

CHAPTER
TWENTY-THREE
NUMO

IN THE INTERMINABLE time they waited in the pit, Numo and Bollix had been taking turns scraping against the iron with their diminutive tusks. They always aimed at the same place—near where Hammerfist's claw would be. If they could make a slit of weakness in the edifice, they reasoned, perhaps Hammerfist could pry it open from the inside. But Bollix's tusks were already badly worn down to smooth nubs, and by her own admission, she wasn't much use. Numo ended up taking most of the work. Even though his neck was cramping and his jaw was aching and sometimes his skull seemed to get stuck in one place and his teeth itched, he kept scraping away until there was hardly anything left of his little tusks.

And sometimes, he'd feel Hammerfist scraping back. A claw, scratching faintly on the opposite side. If he could only break through, if he could only cut through those last few millitudes, they could touch. The thought sent a cascade of excitement through his lymph so powerful it near set him to shivering, though the ample body heat in the pit ensured it was far from cold. All the while Rawang was behind him, murmuring or yelling or sobbing, by degrees melancholy or wrathful or insufferably turgid.

One morning, a drum sounded above them. Soldiers marched in, brandishing longaxes and swords and meteor hammers, decked out in brilliant crimson finery.

"Guess our time is up." Bollix sagged against the maiden. "Well well. Now the real war begins."

"It's a massacre, not a war," grumbled Rawang.

"Oh sir," said Bollix, the enthusiasm in her voice muted with fatigue, "don't be so despondent…"

The soldiers came. They dragged Rawang away and shoved him in line with the infandi. Numo ducked behind the maiden's head and hid there, clinging to one of the bands of rivetry.

Bollix's harsh half-faced breathing disappeared. Numo waited for a soldier to snatch him, for a hand to close around his middle and leash him to a chain. Nothing happened. Infandi marched out of the pit in a line, and drakes on poles, but no one came for him.

Once the pit was emptied of all but maidens, a pack of infandi rickshaw-pullers were ushered in. One by one, the soldiers disconnected the maidens from the feeding-tubes and heaved them into rickshaws. Numo pressed himself tight against the maiden and hoped to the hearth-gremlin Pyri that no one saw him.

They dumped Hammerfist's maiden in on its side. Three of Numo's fingers and two toes smashed under the weight of the iron. The bones splintered like dry wood under a five-sided axe and he bit down on his tongue until it bled to keep from crying out. But at least he was squished up against the corner, hidden from sight. *Pyri giveth only what ye shall suffer for,* so the verse went.

The rumbling of the rickshaw jarred against his broken bits. The weight of the iron drove harder into his splintered fingers with every shift and shuffle. Numo buried his muzzle in his chest to smother out any sighs or illicit whimpers, tensing his remaining fingers like claws. He wouldn't abandon her. He wouldn't.

The sun was on the maiden, the heat channeling through the metal to Numo's body. For a while, it was pleasant. Then it was uncomfortable. Then it burned him.

Hammerfist moaned softly. It was burning her too. The soldiers cackled at her, at this and that, and said things like *you know which one this is* and *this the one that burned the shit out of them alchemy apprentices* and *yeah* and *well thank Kiroktera this cackpile is about to get her rectitude* and other things Numo couldn't quite hear.

The rickshaw canted, sliding him and the maiden backward ever so slightly. They were going uphill. Numo couldn't see, but the scent of pine became stronger, and the air thinner. They were going back into the foothills...

The roar of a crowd somewhere far away wafted over him. As they passed from direct sunlight to the dappling shadows of a forest, the noise grew. Humans chanting:

Homo-machy homo-machy homo-machy

Over and over, as if such a thing never got tiresome. What did it mean, anyway? He'd heard about it, of course, but homunculi were not invited to spectate at such activities, and so there had been little to hear.

The volume surrounded him as the rickshaw bobbled ahead, as though he were on an island with an ocean of noise crashing on all sides. Finally, the cart stopped. The maiden was lifted and—

"What is this?" a soldier said, peering at Numo. Numo squeezed his eyes shut and clung harder to the maiden.

Another one laughed. "Look at it! All this time, it could have run off! Sat here in the bloody rickshaw clinging on." Meaty hands peeled Numo away. His hands unclenched from the maiden and he moaned in pain as the broken bones shifted.

"But you're too stupid to run off, eh?" The soldier shook him around like a sock and his ears flapped around, slapping the back of his head. "Dumbass drake." The soldier let go and Numo dropped to the ground. His foot crackled in agony. The world went black and starry.

"Should I manacle him and take him with the others?" said the third soldier.

"Aw, hell with him. He's just a drake. He'll die here or there or anywhere." The others hefted the maiden out of the rickshaw and set it upright on the grass. They sat down on the empty cart and smacked the infandus laborer across the head. "Go on then, Peaches."

The rickshaw-infandus trotted off. Numo gingerly pushed himself up with his good hand. Around him, maidens were arranged in a sort of half-circle in a forest clearing. Beyond that, the trees, and beyond that, a cluster of drakes milling about, and beyond that—

He squinted, peering hard. Everywhere he looked there was a wooden barricade in the distance, with humans jeering and chanting in stands atop the walls and soldiers standing rigid at the bottom.

It was an arena.

CHAPTER
TWENTY-FOUR
KAIZHA

KAIZHA HAD CHOSEN one of the esteemed seats on the first tier, just above ground level. And, importantly, just above the posts where they would tie up the lesser-classed infandi. Now, though, she was regretting that decision. What she had just seen deposited in the clump of common drakes indicated that something bad was going to happen.

It was her drake. The original drake.

Bollix was still alive. Mangled, battered, aged, but she was still alive.

Bollix had been so perfect. So willing and loyal. Until she started murdering people for their minor insults against Kaizha. It was cute at first, but it had certainly made things difficult—covering up the murders, making them look like accidents or human crime—especially when it was nobility. Then Amia, the senior of the oligarchy, had called Kaizha inept. To her face. She even spat. Bollix saw it and nearly tore out her throat there in the dining hall.

Kaizha had locked Bollix up for a while until she thought the drake had forgotten. But once she was loose, Bollix slaughtered Amia's entire family. By then, of course, the drake had gathered enough base intelligence to know that she should frame some of the infandi in the household, and both Kaizha and Mozeh scrambled well enough to cover the tracks. But Mozeh insisted the drake had to be destroyed, and Kaizha… well, she was in a weak state of mind then. So young, and so in love, and a little too fancying of makhat. Mozeh paid off some wine-wastrel city guards to take Bollix out of the city and kill her. That was the last Kaizha heard of it.

Had those low-born sots failed? How could a slew of armed guards fail to kill a drake?

Kaizha suspected she was about to get a demonstration. Another very pertinent suspicion was that she should not be anywhere near the arena once that demonstration began. But she had to ensure that the Homomachy went her way.

She would have to sit there and wait and hope to the firmament's edges that Bollix did not do anything murderous. At least until after Kaizha left.

Thank Kuru's loins she had worn the sackcloth. It was thick and uncomfortable and proved a significant hindrance to proper breathing, but the drake wouldn't see her face. The black, billowing robes of mourning had also proved useful in other ways: several packets of alchemical fire, a vial of white phosphorus in water, ten vials of nebulizer—in case she needed more oxygen for the phosphorus—and a small skin of water were hidden in the folds and sleeves. The whole outfit even came with gloves, which would probably come in handy for handling all the fire she was about to start. Who would have thought that Goh's ridiculous suggestions had merit?

Xiongnyao was coming towards her. Kaizha sat demurely, silently, hoping that an invisible aura of aloofness would repel the insufferable woman. Xiongnyao was like a cat. The scent of someone's aversion to her was an irresistible lure.

"Mistress Shanyang!" she ejaculated, the words burbling out of her like a sulfuric spring. "Is that you? I haven't seen you in ages!"

The younger woman came and sat in the box adjacent. Thankfully, there was a short wooden partition between them. Less-than-thankfully, that partition was very thin.

"I hope I'm not bothering you," Xiongnyao said. "I know you're still in mourning. And rightfully so. Master Shanyang was a great man; a brilliant man. The sort of man I wish my husband was. Oh, but I shouldn't speak ill of him either. Turian is a great infandus-maker, and a decent pathologist besides. I only mean to say that Shanyang was something special—a mark above the average man. It must have been an awful shock."

"Mhm."

"Especially for him to go like that. A drake killing a man! Who ever heard of such a thing?"

"Most unexpected. But then, I suppose you can't trust any of those creatures, can you?"

"Oh, it was very odd for me to imagine! I would trust all of my slaves with my life. And besides, those drakes have such short little arms. Most unthreatening statures, the lot of them."

What an odd thing to say. Kaizha ground her teeth. "Mortality is a fragile thing. One needn't be threatening of stature to take it away."

"Well, I suppose." Xiongnyao's voice dropped. "But I would also suppose one might need be of a certain height to be able to thrust the entire length of a fire poker through a man's backside at a certain angle, and one might need a certain amount of physical strength to twist that fire poker around and pull it out whilst the man is writhing in agony, and perhaps further physical strength might be required to ram it back in twice more for good measure. I suppose."

Breathing through the sackcloth became very difficult. Kaizha reached up inside the mask and inhaled a nebulizer vial. She counted her inhalations, slowly and deliberately. The threads of the cloth stuck to her drying lips. This was a massive blunder. She had counted on Turian being too thick to question her story, assuming he would equate the general locale of the wound with the short height of the assailant and leave it at that. And he had.

But she hadn't even thought of his wife.

"I'm sorry. I don't understand what you mean."

"Don't despair, sweetie. You're not the only woman who has made her husband's success possible."

Kaizha couldn't see her face, but in a strange moment of quiet, she heard the spit shift across Xiongnyao's teeth as she grinned.

"I do know something of what it's like, though my talents lie in other areas. I was not fortunate enough to be born in the era before the social reformation, and am horribly ignorant of alchemy. But I can tell something of the body. My husband is not so astute. His specialty is in the creation of the infandi; his knowledge of pathology and bodies is secondary, and his common sense is perhaps a bit wanting. He doesn't know what I know. No one does. I can keep it that way. For a price."

Kaizha's mind raced. She'd never been in this particular position. "What on earth are you insinuating? I hope I oughtn't truly be insulted, Mistress Haishing."

"It's fine. It's quite a shock! I understand. Have yourself a think. I'll be here. Let me know if you have evolved a different reaction by the end of today's entertainment. If not, I'm sorry to say, there will likely be severe consequences."

Xiongnyao went quiet. The woman started tittering and yammering again when her husband joined her, resuming her usual drone of inanity, leaving Kaizha in a cloak of confusion.

It was not that Kaizha had never thought that perhaps some of the other oligarchs' wives play-acted as she did—in fact, she was hoping for it, even if it was too dangerous yet to seek them out—but she had never suspected it of *Xiongnyao*, of all people.

The Homomachy was about to begin. Kaizha had a lot of decisions to make by the end of it. At least there was one thing of which she was certain: the end would come sooner and bloodier than anyone expected.

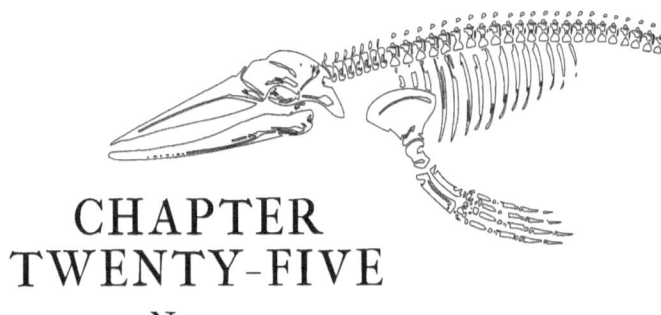

CHAPTER TWENTY-FIVE

Numo

NUMO KNEW VERY little about arenas, but he knew enough to know he did not belong in them. They were places of contest. Bleeding. Battle. The sort of place Hammerfist might know better…

He looked up at the maidens around him. One of them had a deep gouge in the side. Hammerfist was trapped, still. And what could she do from in there? How could she defend herself?

And if she couldn't…what could a small thing like himself do?

His bladder constricted.

A gate creaked open. The crowd roared louder. A small naked-headed man rode a grizzled woolly rhinoceros into the center of the arena, waving his puddingy arms. His face was painted in black and red and white. The patterns around his mouth styled his expression into a horrendous demonic grimace. His poor rhinoceros steed looked to be a million years old, its matted hair hanging from its belly like clumpy chandeliers.

"Quiet down, quiet down," he shouted. After several such exhortations, the humans silenced themselves. The man turned his elderly steed around in a circle, sweeping his arms dramatically. His belly was tattooed straight down the middle in vertical strips of sacred script, and he wore a necklace of black bird wings. He must have been a high priest.

"Spec-tators!" the priest yelped. "Welcome to the great sacrifice of Kiroktera, God of Rectitude, Lord of Order, Grand Architect, High Judge of the Cosmos!"

The soldiers rattled their swords in their scabbards and the crowd banged their feet on the wooden stands.

"Long ago," the priest said, lowering his voice to a mysterious hiss, "the great lord Kiroktera sat *homo sapiens* on top of the pyramid of the earth. Above the Neanderthal, above the apes, above the animals that swim and the pteropteryxes that fly, the goats that pull and the snowflies that die, the masters of his earthly realm, as stewards of the gods' creations—the representatives of the holy ones on this lowly planet.

"Since then, the gods have gifted us with even more servants to fall under our mastery. Moa's alchemy has granted us the homunculi, to serve us, to entertain us, to protect us. But there are times when the beasts forget where we, the humans, rightfully sit.

"And we rise to the challenge!" the priest roared. The crowd woohooed in approval. "After all, we must continue to prove our worth to the gods! To prove that we are still worthy of acting in their stead, masters of their earth! And if not, let the gods strike us down and enact a new order!" The priest jiggled his arms in a flourish above his head, startling his rhino out of its geriatric reverie before it went back to staring at nothing.

Numo shrank behind Hammerfist's maiden. She was growling inside, muttering something, seething and raging under the metal. Whatever was going to happen was bad, very bad. Numo wondered if he might shut the priest up by marching up to the podium and agreeing. Of course humans had mastery; this was a given.

Though—should it be?

Clearly some were stinkards. Those who threatened innocents, who mercilessly strangled One-Ear Deadlad, who put Hammerfist in that maiden with naught but a tube for her survival—the uncouth class, they deserved no mastery. In fact, they deserved less. A sound beating, perhaps.

But what of the mistress?

Much as he could think blasphemous things about stinkard-people, the thought of his own mistress's actions filled him with a sensation not unlike locusts filling a jar to the point of cracking. He swallowed the jittery buzzing in his craw. *The mistress must have her reasons,* thought half of him, but the other half solemnly shook its head at the first, like a mother at a foolish child.

"So we prove ourselves to Kiroktera on this day, the day of the Homomachy!" The priest's voice ripped out into the air with tremendous violence.

"First round," the priest shouted, "drakes and greenhorns. Those who have not participated in the Homomachy before— don't think yourselves untouchable because we pit you against mandrake-borns. We've provided supplies to even up the odds." He swept his arm towards a gate, and in marched a band of soldiers, carrying pikes and spears and slings and cudgels. They dropped the pile of weapons in front of the cluster of drakes.

A yelp of excitement came from Hammerfist's maiden. "*Nmmmhhaa!*"

Numo. That was his name. When she said it, it sounded like the sigh of some celestial being garbed in glittery starry drapery, and he almost forgot where he was.

"Nmmmhhaa! Yraghr fherhfah galalrhag!"

Numo, you have to get...something. What? The weapons? The weapons.

They were pointy, by gum! Sharper than his tusks, to be sure, and the groove he'd made over the past couple of weeks was so close, and if he could only get his hands on a dagger or a lance, or something with a blade, he could free her, yes, she could finally be free—

"Soldiers, unfetter the drakes! Contenders, enter! Let the Homomachy begin!" The priest thwapped the reins against his steed's shoulders and led the trudging creature out of the arena. Soldiers unshackled the drakes and retreated to the stands. A band of young men and women entered through the gates, armed to the teeth, some of them no older than twelve and all of them no older than seventeen, naked and painted with elaborate markings in crimson and white.

They took their places. No one moved. Numo wondered if now was an appropriate time to fetch a pointed blade of some sort. But it almost seemed rude to disturb the quiet.

A girl howled. The humans charged at the drakes. The homunculi scattered, snatching up weapons, running unevenly, climbing trees, hiding, attacking, snarling, barking.

Numo'd had no idea drakes could bark.

The humans gave chase. A few spears and knives were left sitting on the forest floor. Numo darted out from behind the maiden. He zoomed across the grass like a libidinous dragonfly, wobbly legs pumping, broken toes throbbing agonously, a powerful mess of hot desperation.

He snatched up a spear in one hand and a tiny knife in the other and darted back. No humans saw him. None on the ground, anyway, and who knew what the spectators were clamoring about. He sprinted back to Hammerfist's side in several blinks of a drunken eye. Furiously he worked the knife into the groove with his good hand, attacking it again and again.

"*Arg, harfrghha aghrgh! Glarha hsshe!*" Hammerfist yelled. *No. Keep the knife. Defend yourself.* Numo hesitated. He wanted to do as she commanded, but the notion of defending himself was preposterous. Perhaps she didn't understand just how useless he was, and just how certain death would be, and if he died, he couldn't fulfill any of his promises or duties to her...

It would be a bad death indeed.

Numo rubbed the knife harder into the groove, so hard that the metal bent. He threw down the knife and picked up the spear.

A drake burst out of the forest into the clearing.

"Brother! Arm yourself!"

Bollix barreled at him, blood-spattered and wounded, carrying a severed finger. Behind her, humans spilled out of the forest. They saw him. They pointed. They were coming.

But he was close, so close now, he could feel the metal thinning and weakening under the point of the spear, if only he had a minute more—

"Brother!" Bollix clapped a hand over his wrist. "The time has come. We must defend ourselves." She raised the broken tip of a knife. The hilt was gone, and she gripped it by the blade, her hands a shimmery purple mess of blood.

Numo decided he'd had quite enough of being handled

roughly. He pushed Bollix off, cracked fingers screaming at him from the strain, and kept sawing at the metal with every ounce of strength in his intacter digits. "There is no myself. There is only her."

Bollix stared at him funnily. "What do you mean by that?"

The humans were close now, yelping and screaming and raising their spears and swinging meteor hammers. Stones with sharp edges carved on all sides whizzed past them.

"I mean I'm getting her out or I'm dying in the pursuit." The gravity of the words barely inflicted themselves on his consciousness, but by Nonnysteed's ovenous maw, he meant them.

A spear flew into his buttock and he made a nasty howling noise that he didn't know he could make.

"*Hrararhghr!*" the maiden screeched. *Get away. Run.*

Numo sawed harder. He'd never been so disobedient and so contrariwise and so delirious with purpose. It was glorious. It was horrible. It made his bladder quake until he thought his pelvis might crack. The humans hollered. They were close. He would die. Bollix stared. They would all die.

A great scraping hiss filled up the forest. A few of the young humans paused in alarm. The hiss became a screech.

It was coming from Hammerfist's maiden.

Numo felt her claws through the metal, scratching and tearing like an anteater destroying a termite mound. A finger split the metal where Numo had been working. It pried open a gash. The metal groaned and squealed as Hammerfist's entire hand sawed through the weakened fissure. She grabbed both sides of the ripped metal and tore, rending the maiden nigh in half. Hammerfist emerged, a bloody emaciated scythe-wielding butterfly from an iron chrysalis, and all light in the world turned to ambrosia-flavored flintsparks.

The young humans stopped in their tracks. People in the stands screamed. Some of them threatened to overflow over the wooden barricade. Soldiers held them back.

"Humans will prevail over the homunculus! Have faith in Kiroktera!" yelled the priest from somewhere high in the stands.

The humans stared at Hammerfist. Hammerfist stared at them. Numo wrung his hands around the grip of the spear.

"Now we're in it." Bollix grinned. "Now we're bloody well in it…" She raised her broken bit of knife, her half-face snarling involuntarily but looking every bit appropriate for the occasion.

Yes, they were in it, whatever it was. They were in it and how on earth would they get out?

Hammerfist roared. Numo's skin crawled. The trees rattled. A bough creaked and cracked. It sounded like tarpine.

Tarpine?

He looked around. Just inside the walls of the arena, and stretching in denser concentrations outside of it, were trees of a familiar specie—the flora of the middling-low mountain reaches outside the city. At this time of year, and at this altitude…

He hadn't noticed before. So alien was everything up until this point that he'd overlooked the familiar.

Numo grabbed Hammerfist's finger. "We have to go."

Hammerfist glared down at him. She pushed him behind her and snarled at the humans. Numo clutched at her finger and pulled. "This way, this way. Now."

Hammerfist turned. He ran, dragging the spear, and she followed, lumbering behind at a slow jog on her knuckles with Bollix at her heels. Humans shouted in confusion behind them.

Feet padded, weapons clanked, slings twirled. Numo snatched up the broken tarpine bough with two unbroken fingers. A javelin neatly missed his ear. Hammerfist grabbed the spear from Numo's fist. She scooped up Numo and Bollix, stuck them both in her one cockeyed jaw, safe behind the cage of her fangs, and galloped off at full speed.

"That way, that way! To the north!" Numo shouted.

Hammerfist plunged forward, leaving the humans behind. Her feet tilled the dirt as she went, leaving a trail of plowed earth in her wake.

"Stop, stop!" Numo yelped. Hammerfist skidded. Numo leapt out of her mouth and thumped to the ground, barely registering the pain of the impact in his cracked toes. Here it was—a beautiful swathe of black amado fungus, shining in the cruel goddess's sunlight. Natural tinder; highly useful for quick and impressive flames.

And very good for awakening the flammable qualities of tarpine.

"Numo," Bollix said, climbing carefully out of Hammerfist's jaws, "what exactly are you doing?"

Numo pulled up a roundel of the fungus. "Gathering tinder." Many times he'd used the black balls to catch a spark from his flint and steel. But he didn't have anything that would spark this time. He had only the spearhead.

"Tinder?"

Numo blinked at Bollix. "You want me to explain?"

Bollix waved him on. "No, no, go on."

He flumped down on dirt and motioned for the spear. Hammerfist handed it over, eyeing him curiously, cocking her head this way and that. The spear shaft was light—easy to throw, easy to break. Numo took a breath, snapped off the spearhead, and yelped only a little in pain at the force he'd just juddered through his injured hand. He waggled his toes. The mighty calluses on his feet were, well, mighty, and if anything handy would burnish the metal…

Numo rubbed the flat of the spearhead on the ball of his best foot, so hard and fast he wondered if he might actually light his own feet on fire. Secretly he thought it would be beautiful and impressive to go bucking about with his heels alight, but that was rather silly of him.

The spearhead came to a nice shine. The shouts of the young humans rang through the trees. They were catching up. The spearhead would have to do. It would have to.

Numo aimed the metal just so, and the sun's rays caught on its edge. He beamed the light at the black fungus. He waited.

"Is that supposed to do somethi—"

Hammerfist growled at Bollix. Bollix snapped her mouth shut.

The fungus burned. The ember was lit. A small thing, a neonate, beautiful—

Humans erupted from the trees. *Pyri's back fat.* Numo held the ember against the bits of sap on the broken tarpine bough. Hammerfist punched the humans away, knocking them aside like rotten timbers, roaring, screaming, daring them to come near. The bough caught fire. Numo stared at it. It was glorious.

"By Ong Nklak's spiracles," Bollix laughed. "The boy's done it! Come, come, the wall is this way—"

"The wall? No, the wall is hunkerwood. It won't catch a fire this small…" Numo scanned the forest. Where was the tarpine? There! Just there, beyond the runny oaks. He grabbed

Hammerfist's claw and tugged, and the three of them set off for the cluster of trees, Hammerfist howling backwards at the few remaining youths to keep them away.

"Second wave!" someone shouted. It was the priest. More noises. Numo couldn't think straight with all the noises. The creak of a gate opening somewhere, shouting, feet pounding, metal pointy things smacking up against each other.

"Running out of bloody time, Numo," Bollix panted. She was starting to annoy him. Would she have him go hold a pitiful flame against a wall of hunkerwood? May as well hold a candle against a rock and wait for it to turn to dust.

Finally—tarpine. Numo held the bough aloft and folded one hand behind his back, as was proper for an announcement. "Ladies and gentlemen," he shouted, turning towards the stands. "I am about to light this forest on fire. I would request that those of you who are not of the stinkard class would kindly exit the stands at this ti—"

"For gods' sakes, Numo," said Bollix, and snatched the bough from his hand. She held it up against the tree and waited, as if something would happen.

"No, no, that will take too long," said Numo. Larger humans were running at them now, meaty ones, adult ones; the kind with hair on their faces and chests and legs. Hammerfist turned towards them and planted her fists into the dirt. He forced his attention to the tree, searching. He found a dried drip of resin on the trunk and held up the bough. The fire shimmered to life, skated up the tree, and enveloped the wood as it hugged against the flame. Tarpine was good for that, embracing flames, but it also burned quickly. It would need to spread fast.

Hammerfist roared at the humans. They slowed, eyeing

the burning tree warily, some of them stopping entirely, and who could blame them? The fire was glorious, and Hammerfist against the backdrop of it all was an apparition from the empyrean hearth of the gods; a creature of luminescent white smoke; a being of purest—

The humans threw javelins at her.

One of them sank into the middle of her face and she cried out in agony. The sound shattered Numo to the core and ate into his bones like a spray of poison. He screamed. He charged. Inexplicably, he barked. He ran at the nearest human with the burning bough, the flaming part of which was only an ell from his hands now, burning up fast. He drove it into a young man's groin. The man gurgled and screeched, and by the blood-spattered testes of his mistress's god, Numo enjoyed it.

But the others soon fell upon him. Blades pierced him in the foot, behind the knee, between his shoulders, before a cage of swordlike claws slammed down over his body.

Hammerfist drove her free fist into the nearest human. The woman's body broke in half before she went down. Again and again, Hammerfist whirled around Numo's prone body, cracking humans in pieces, pummeling their heads into concavities, punching their organs out their backs. Finally, they were left alone, and turned to see three whole trees aflame.

"Help me!" Bollix shouted, holding a burning little twig up to a massive tree trunk. It wasn't even the right tree. Batter-oak. Numo sighed in exasperation.

Hammerfist scooped Numo off the ground and charged at the nearest burning tree.

"Third wave! Third wave! Take her down!" shouted the priest. "*Sapiens* will prevail!"

Hammerfist struck the tree with all the weight and velocity she could muster. The trunk creaked in agony. She rammed it again and again, with one hand or a shoulder or even her beauteous face, and the trunk kowtowed to her unparalleled thew and sinew. It croaked its way down, whispering the eulogy of fire as it collided with the next tarpine, and obligingly the standing tree burst into flames.

Numo had never been more smitten.

Again and again, Hammerfist struck at the tarpine. He could hear humans coming, cheering, pounding their feet on the stands and howling, hunting. Hammerfist was tiring, her arboreal assaults weaker. But now there were only three trees left—three that would go down into the wall, three that could feed enough fire to the anorexic hunkerwood.

One down.

Two down.

The wall was still not alight.

The humans were close enough to sling their stones and throw knives. The fire was big enough to slow them, but it wouldn't stop them. They'd go around. They'd come all the same.

It would take too long. The wall wouldn't come down in time. They were going to die.

"Numo. Numo!" Bollix looked up at Hammerfist, who was straining against the last tree and trembling with exhaustion. "Drop him."

Hammerfist opened her hand and peered blearily at Numo as if she were surprised to see him there. She placed him on the ground and snorted up a deep sigh before colliding her shoulderflesh with the trunk once more.

"Numo, do you still have that packet Rawang gave you?

194

He probably stitched it into your body somewhere..." Bollix patted him down. Her face lit up when she got to his armpit. "Yes! Here we are. This is going to hurt, Numo. Sorry." Bollix flashed her nub of a knife and slit Numo's armpit open.

He didn't feel it. But then, he had many other such incisions in his skin at the moment, and the others were deeper, and rather taking up more of his attention, and come to think of it, he felt quite awful and shaky and unwell, rather like a bucket of ox feces set to a slow boil...

Bollix saluted Numo with the little packet. "Godspeed, brother." With that, she barreled off in the direction of the humans and the now-sizable flames of the burning tarpine, ululating at the top of her lungs like an overmuch-excited gibbon and waving the knife like a pennant. She disappeared in a shroud of smoke. A glimmering explosion of white ballooned into the air from the traces of her wake. Particulates kicked up and spread like volcanic tephra across the atmosphere.

Hammerfist flung herself into the last trunk. The hunkerwood wall was charring uselessly, mocking Numo, mocking him and his smittenness and Hammerfist and the dregs of her considerable might. He ran at the wall, pounding on it, screaming at it, calling it by the most inappropriate monikers he knew, the impropriety streaming out of his mouth like dragonfire.

"Empty-hearted applejohn! Beslubbering turtle-hemorrhoid! Fen-sucked bumbailey! Muck-witted—"

He was several words in before he noticed that someone else was screaming. Many someones. Lots and lots of them. The humans clutched at their throats, drooling with rather more colorful spittle than he was accustomed to seeing, tumbling

195

out of the stands and thumping heavily on the spongy mat of the forest floor. The men and women warriors stumbled out of the smoke, limply heaving throwing-axes in their direction, but the weapons fluttered like pressed paper into the grass. Blood ran from their eyes and their lips went blue. They fell to their knees. Still they pawed the ground and clambered towards Hammerfist. Numo went to kick them in the face, to give Hammerfist those few more seconds. They bit at his feet but they were too slow, their eyes unfocused and spidered with red.

The tree groaned. With a final heave, Hammerfist tore it down. It crashed into the hunkerwood planks. The charred whorls in the wood caved to embers. The wood went up in reluctant conflagration. Though it was a mealy and ugly fire, it was the most welcome of Numo's life.

Hammerfist panted, her breaths straining against her ribs, and watched the wall splinter and flake. She swayed on her feet, but so did Numo. In fact, everything and everyone everywhere seemed to be listing and twirling. Numo, satisfied the human warriors were not going to get up, sidled over to her elbow. He fumbled for her hand and patted it with the fingers that still worked. "There, you see? Everything's all right."

But then, somehow, he was on the ground, his body frozen, seeing nothing but the backs of his eyelids.

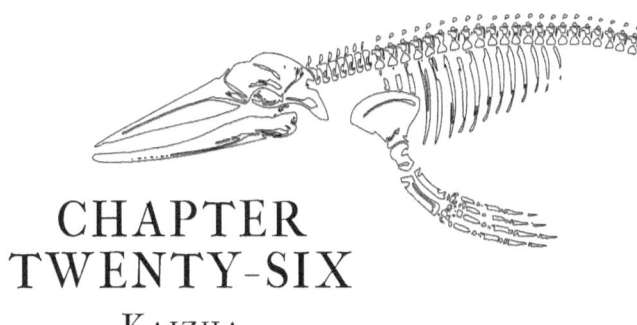

CHAPTER
TWENTY-SIX
KAIZHA

KAIZHA'S EXPECTATIONS OF her old homunculus had been borne out, though in a somewhat different manner than she expected.

Bollix had killed five initiates with a small knife and flung some sort of powder into the fire spreading around the arena. Panic was spilling over in the stands, and where there wasn't panic, there was an impressive sweep of swift and toxic death.

It would have been gloriously perfect if she weren't sitting in the middle of it.

Wisps of smoke were already curling into her lung-hairs. Kaizha should be running. But, though lovely little Bollix had unwittingly given her the gift of artful chaos, there was yet more to be done.

Everything had to happen at once, and Kaizha was going to need the oxygen from her nebulizer vials to get through it. Unfortunately—or perhaps the reverse—that meant inhaling a thoroughly unadvisable amount of makhat.

She tightened the sackcloth around her neck, leaving just enough space for her to get two fingers inside. Next to her, Xiongnyao's husband leapt over the side of the wooden barrier between the arena and the stands and reached up to help his wife over. Kaizha fingered the vial of white phosphorus chunks inside her mourning-robes. She unsealed the vial and poured the contents into her gloved palm, curling up her fist.

"Xiongnyao!" Kaizha wailed and screamed like a vengeful ghost, lurching over the side of the stands. She grabbed onto the neck-collar of the woman's dress as she straddled the wall. "Help me!"

"Get off!" Xiongnyao shoved against her. Kaizha dropped the phosphorus inside her cleavage. Xiongnyao's husband drove his bony little hand into the side of Kaizha's head and she fell over the side of the stands.

She collided with the cold ground and her back flooded with pain. The fire was racing closer to her section and she was too near the wall, but she was stunned like a lizard in a sudden frost. The only consolation was the sound of Xiongnyao screaming as the phosphorus in her bosom melted against her skin and, gods willing, burst into flames. Kaizha gasped for air. She reached into her sackcloth and uncorked another nebulizer.

The infandi tied to the poles were only a few feet away, along with that veterinarian. Some of them had to escape in order to properly frighten the old bastards in the council—they couldn't just burn there. Perhaps they needed a push.

She forced herself to roll over and crawled closer. The creatures screamed and yowled, clawing at the chains that held them. The veterinarian sobbed quietly, his hands covering his face.

Kaizha took a packet of alchemical fire from her robes and wet it. It immolated in her palm and burned her before she managed to lob it at the nearest hitching-post—the veterinarian's. The post burned. Once he was free, the veterinarian robbed a dead man of his clothes, wrapped the shirt around his face, and skittered away like a cockroach, leaving the other prisoners helpless.

Useless bastard.

She lobbed another flaming packet at a little crooked-headed infandus's post. Once it burned and fell, thankfully, the homunculus grabbed the flaming splinters and lit the remaining posts on fire, freeing the rest. Kaizha could turn her attention to other things.

Like standing up.

The powder cast a thick white smoke over the arena. People were bleeding out their mouths, choking, falling, dying. Whatever it was, it had a majestic effect. Kaizha would have to ask Bollix—

Bollix. Kaizha staggered to her feet and released another vial into the sackcloth. She could not allow her drake to die. She'd only just found her again. Her first breakthrough. Her first great experiment. The only drake worthy enough to be made of a woman; to carry the spirit of a woman. Her poor drake; her poor mutilated long-suffering Bollix...

Am I this intoxicated already?

She managed to take a few steps before that familiar delirium of too little air and too much makhat imparted itself into her mind. If Bollix died now, when Kaizha had been given a miraculous chance to save her, she'd never forgive herself. She'd never do alchemy again. She'd cater the buffalo weddings. She'd lollop across the desert on all fours wailing like a mouthbeast. She'd—

Kaizha blinked. She was on the ground. When had that happened? *Air, you need air...*

She fumbled for another vial and released. Her brain wheeled back to reality. She was in the middle of the arena.

The powder was starting to enter through the eye-holes in the sackcloth and her throat felt like blackened wood. Bollix's body was a hundred paces away, lifeless and half-scorched.

Kaizha stumbled forward and shoved her own body upright. Her knees shuddered threateningly under her. She wobbled towards Bollix, lifted the drake's tiny battered body, and slung it over her shoulders like a herdsman carrying a lamb.

Now she had to get out.

Kaizha limped and bobbled and fell her way out of the arena, plowing through the vials faster than she should have. The exit was choked with dead bodies and live ones clambering over them. Kaizha groaned. She was not in a climbing mood. The lack of air made her brain soft and her resolve softer. Kaizha had become a silly woman, just as she'd always feared. Worthless. Tears spilled out of her eyes and soaked the sackcloth, making the tiny bit of air inside wetter and fouler.

She watched as one of the clamberers dropped into the pile of the dead. A man reached down, pulled her up, dropped her again. He left. The woman's dress had been ripped off and her chest smoldered. It was Xiongnyao.

At first, Kaizha was delighted. But then her brain twirled the opposite way. Her heart lurched and her blood surged. Xiongnyao was just like her. A woman stuck in the new woman's place. Forced to hide her talents. To provide insight for her husband when he was too thick to generate it himself. To act like an insufferable boob. The pain of thirty years of repression walloped down on Kaizha's cheese-soft core and ignited a flare of anger in her.

No more.

A thrill of euphoria and wickedness and cardiac

overexertion and adrenal paroxysms vibrated through her body and covered her in a dripping film of sweat. She screamed in frustration at the mound of flesh in front of her and clawed, pounding down anyone who got in her way—men, women, twelve-year-olds, infants, they all deserved it, the doughy-hearted shrivel-balled sinners. Kaizha dropped the last few nebulizers into her underwear, gripped the skin of water, and ripped her mourning-garb from her body. She charged, the remnants of the dress billowing from her grip like a mighty flag of defiance.

Xiongnyao was murmuring and groaning, with a hole in her chest still smoldering as the phosphorus ate through her body. Kaizha ripped free a bit of cloth, soaked it in water, and plugged up the hole in Xiongnyao's bosom to smother the insidious flame. She wrapped the half-dead woman in her own robes and pulled. The body slid easily over the others—surprisingly so. But maybe it was the adrenaline. Maybe it was the anger. Maybe it was the mind-blitzing amount of makhat turning her into a fiery drug demon.

Kaizha dragged Xiongnyao pell-mell over the mound, out of the arena, and into the forest. Bollix's own body bounced around behind her neck like a soggy mountainous tumor. Kaizha was strong with insanity. She was like a panther, a river dolphin, an exploded star; she ran until she was clear of the arena and tore off the sackcloth. The forest was weird and spinning and dark, even though it was broad daylight.

It was a long way yet to the hidden shack. She inhaled her last three vials for good measure and barreled away from the crowds, hoping no one noticed she was going in the opposite direction of the city gates.

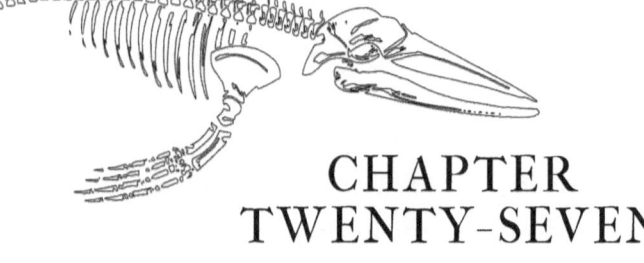

CHAPTER
TWENTY-SEVEN
HAMMERFIST

HAMMERFIST TRIED—SHE TRIED to hold on to sense and keep her brain afloat. But everything was on fire, and the smoke was choking out rational thought. She knew she'd been more human before, when the Homomachy started, but air was poisonous now, and the chaos was confusing, and the noise made her brain as comprehensible as a mosaic with half the pieces missing. Bollix had run off, and no one was there to remind her of what she was supposed to be doing, or who she was supposed to be.

No one but Numo, and he wasn't moving.

Numo—

She snatched his limp body off the ground and sprinted out of the arena's burning walls. Hammerfist ran and ran and ran until she realized she had fallen down and was just flailing her legs. Blood flooded out of her nostril but that didn't seem too out-of-the-ordinary. She licked it and swallowed it and remembered that eating her own blood made her stomach upset but there was no other way to get it off her face.

"Numo?" she said. She poked him. A pearl of blood appeared. She'd poked too hard. "Wake up, Numo." She clambered to her feet and fell over again. Wherever she tried to go, the ground would follow. She licked Numo's body over and over. Maybe if she licked him enough he'd get irritated and wake up. She'd annoy him to life.

Someone coughed. Other someones crashed through the sticks and foliage of the forest. "Sramai? Sramai, thank the gods..." More coughing. It was the doctor. Used-To-Be-Her-Husband, the lower half of his face wrapped in a shirt, his chest spattered in blood and soot. Behind him was a crowd of infandi trying to put out the little fires in their manes. "Are you all right?"

"The ground won't get off me and Numo won't get up," she said.

"What? I can't hear..." The doctor did not look well, yawing as he stood, an ill-constructed paper boat with scorch marks. More infandi spewed out of the hole in the wall. She hadn't gotten very far at all. The fire was spreading.

"We have to go," the doctor said, laying a hand on her shoulder. "Come on. Get up." He tugged and nearly fell over. Another infandus lifted him. More hands grabbed hers.

"Sister," someone grunted. She looked for Bollix, but it had been an infandus, someone she didn't know. The infandus helped her to her feet. She bent over to scoop Numo up, but the doctor batted a limp hand at her wrist.

"Put that thing down."

"No."

"We have to leave. Now. Put the fucking thing down."

"Shut up." She bent over again and rolled Numo in one of her tongues.

"Sramai—"

"I said no," she growled, and smacked Rawang in the face with the back of her wrist. He went down. She took him by the ankle and put Numo in her mouth. They would all get out, together, whether they liked it or not.

"Let's go."

They stopped when dusk fell. Rawang woke up at some point and started yelling and protesting, but she didn't let go of him and let him walk on his own until he went quiet.

The others had already started collapsing from weakness or injury. The little clearing seemed as good a place to stop as any. Hammerfist placed Numo in a soft spot with her tongues and shoved a bunch of leaves over him to keep him warm.

"Why do you care about him?"

She looked up. Rawang stood there, his arms crossed over the brown stain on his chest, his beard crusty with blood.

"Why care about anything?" she said.

Rawang pursed his lips and shook his head although he had water in his ears. "I can't understand you." He took a few trembly steps towards her. "Do you care about him more than me?"

Hammerfist let her haunches fall against a tree trunk. They burned terribly. "I don't know what I care about or why or how much. I'm too tired. I don't care about anything. I hate everyone. Please shut up."

He paused, his eyes tracking the dirt in thought. "Did you say you don't care about anything?"

She grumbled in assent.

His breath came out in a hoarse burst of stale air. "Of course you care, Sramai. Don't try to lie to me. I can see..." He panted, little wet droplets of blood spraying out of his mouth.

"Can we please just rest?" She scratched under her belly. There was blood there. Everywhere. It was so itchy. Inside and out.

"I don't understand it. I don't." Rawang shook his head and smiled the kind of smile that, Hammerfist had learned, meant someone was about to jam a broken goat bone in your armpit. "I've given you everything. I've done everything you've wanted. All he's done is ruin it."

"How?"

"He's the reason we've ended up here, Sramai. He's the reason your revolution has failed."

"...Failed?"

"Yes, indeed. You see them?" The doctor swept a finger across a small group of infandi, blinking at her expectantly. "These are all the survivors of your revolution. No more. No one left to fight. The oligarchy is still in place. Goh has escaped. Whatever damage we've done will be reversed. We've failed." He erupted in a coughing fit and bent over his knees.

Hammerfist heard herself breathing, air slicing in and out of her like the sound of a knife through a blighted radish. It had failed, hadn't it? Because she touched it. Like when she touched Rawang and almost killed him, twice, and when she touched Numo and poked a hole in him and made him bleed.

As she exhaled, her mind clubbed itself into a mute daze. Her heartbeat slowed to a dull shamble. Her eyelids slid over her eyes, once, twice, and pressed on her eyeballs with their heaviness. The mouth of the infandus inside rose up behind her, poising to swallow...

Rawang's coughing died down to a gritty panting. "The revolution's done and gone. Now there's only me. Us." He took her hand. She didn't feel it. It didn't seem like part of her body. "We are still free, you and I. It would make me—and Numo— and the others—very sad to lose you now. There is still hope. You can come with me and we can make a new life." He smiled weakly. "What do you say, Sramai? Give me a chance."

It was incomprehensible. Muffled words behind a glass pane. She looked at them dancing around in the air, and they looked back at her, stroking their beards in puzzlement. On her side of the pane was blood; on theirs, Rawang. There used to be something else in between, but it was dead now. Redemption. Lying there with its guts out like a butchered duck.

She could choose one or the other. But choosing would mean doing something.

She only knew what she was made to do.

Her brain went black.

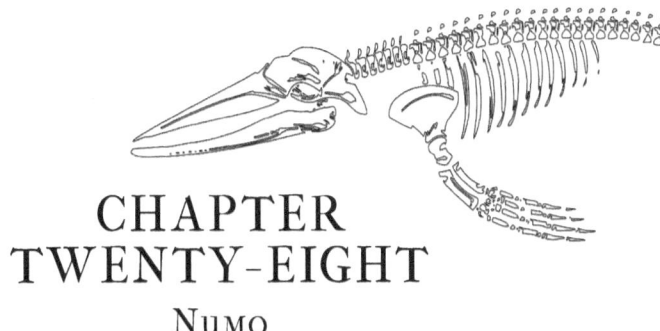

CHAPTER
TWENTY-EIGHT
Numo

Numo HONESTLY COULDN'T say if he was awake or not. It seemed to him that he was, and indeed the feeling of rough skin lifting him off the grass and dragging him and dropping him seemed quite real. Hot coals had been dumped into the spongy holes in his bones and fresh cat urine was coursing through his body. Parts of him seemed to inflate or shrink or abrade—all sorts on the spectrum of molestation.

And the things he heard: a rough voice saying *put that thing down*, and grunts and growls, and another command to *put the fucking thing down*, and a hard smack and something heavy being dragged…

Then, refreshingly, the rawness of reality dropped away, and Numo was not aware of much but a vague wetness on his skin.

Later, the wetness disappeared, and all that touched him was dry and scaly. For some reason this was so disconcerting that Numo's eyes opened and his body worried itself to life.

It was dusk. Gray. Cold. Leaves covered him. An uncountable plethora of eyes stared at him. A thrill pulsated through him as he recognized the volcanic luminescence of Hammerfist's gaze.

She was alive.

She was writhing.

Rawang strained against a rope tied around Hammerfist's wrists, pushing his foot against her chest as she lunged and flailed at him. "Calm down, calm *down*—" His words ran together, as though something was wrong with his mouth. A wide spatter of dark stained his chin and the front of his neck. Somehow he'd been dispossessed of his shirt.

Hammerfist shrieked at him. Hot saliva sizzled into Rawang's face. "*Hrgrhaghr rrrrahhha! Hrgrghrhgar erarrrash! Frghrhassc!*"

I'll kill you. Let me die. Saucepan.

Saucepan? That couldn't be right. Numo wrapped his arms around himself. The screaming chilled his insides. Hammerfist was in pain. The kind flowers wouldn't fix. He didn't know what to do. He searched the grayness of the forest for something, anything, an idea, relief. A small throng of infandi watched in similar helplessness. Lost, desperate, Numo decided to say the first words that came to mind and hope someone listened.

"You two," he said imperiously, "stop it."

Hammerfist turned to him. Her eyes were like fire with no center. She had that look, that thoughtless wild base-minded look, like the time right before she flung him into the wall and—

Hammerfist lunged. Her claws came down before Numo could move. He squeezed his eyes shut. A great wind bore down on him, all the air above his head compressing on him like a paper press machine. The skin on his forehead sliced open. And then, as suddenly as the tip of the claw entered his face, it shredded its way back out.

Hammerfist howled. Numo opened his eyes. Rawang

and the other infandi heaved on the ropes tied to her wrists, wrenching her arms around in horrific-looking unnatural angles. Numo's chest constricted. Part of him wanted to visit fisticuffs on Rawang's soiled face. The greater part of him was too terrified to move. His brain could only say one thing over and over, as though rocking and sobbing inside its protective fat-sac.

Hammerfist…my Hammerfist…

Rawang finally forced her back against a tree. He wrapped the rope around the trunk of the poke-birch and commanded the others to tie her. Once she was strapped to the poke-birch, wailing and squirming and spitting, Rawang flopped to the ground.

"Thanks for all the help, asshole," he panted. He pulled a long strand of dark gooey saliva from his lips and flicked it away. The man was pale, sweaty. Unwell.

As were they all.

Numo swallowed and looked around a bit, as much as his neck would allow. He didn't recognize this part of the forest. It smelled different. It smelled feral, somehow, even though he wasn't quite sure what that meant. "Where are we?"

Rawang's voice was strained. "Forest. Halfway to the lowlands now, I imagine. We ran as far as we could dragging your dead weight—at Sramai's insistence."

"All right then." Numo didn't like this. He'd never been this far outside the city, and out in the wilderness, he'd heard, were things like megalobats and water deer and plaguemice, and horrendous legendary things besides. "And how did you— we—em. Escape?" Numo ventured.

"Dunno about you. I was tied up to a post. Someone tried to burn the infandi, but burned the restraints instead. I ran.

Barely made it—just got my shirt over my mouth in time. You had to go and trip the powder and poison everyone in the damn place. Still corroded the tip of my bloody tongue. Thanks for that, too, you sack of piss."

One of the infandi burst into hysterical laughter. Rawang dragged himself up and slapped the infandus until the laughter died down into quiet hiccups. Hammerfist's shoulders tensed and untensed, and her jaw clenched and jolted ever so infinitesimally from side to side, but she didn't move.

"Don't mind that." Rawang sat again, caressing his palms as if repeated slapping had made them sore. "That's just Fustilugs."

Numo surveyed the homunculi. No drakes to be seen. "Where is Bollix?"

Rawang rubbed his pallid cheeks. "I don't know, Numo. Couldn't find her; couldn't wait. Doesn't matter. If she's alive, she can take care of herself. If she's dead—she'd have wanted to die that way."

Dead! She couldn't be dead. "But what if she—"

"Enough with your questions, Numo. I need you to answer one for *me*." Rawang was breathing hard, swaying. The exertion did not wear well on him. He leaned in close and leveled a finger at Numo. "I need to ask you what the hell you're doing here."

"Um. Me? I'm...well, I don't know how I got here, sir."

"No, not here. I mean—I mean, what are you doing here. With us. It's become clear to me, these past weeks, that you are not clever enough to understand what *we* are doing here. So why are you with us? Why do you continue to show up in my life, Numo? And don't give me that propriety nonsense; we passed propriety half an age ago."

Numo opened his mouth. He made a sound that was not

210

a word and he shut it again. He tried to think and it seemed that it was only wind whistling through his ears. In between, the glare of Rawang's face sluiced on him like a flood. Numo couldn't help but think that this was a face of a man who already knew an answer to a question and didn't like it. But, even if Rawang knew, Numo was still somewhat in the dark. He'd done it to follow Hammerfist, but why?

"I suppose I don't rightly know, sir," he said.

"You're lying," Rawang growled, lurching upright. "I've seen it. I've seen it in your eyes and your gormless expression and your leering slack-jawed compliments. You *think* you're in love with her. But let me tell you now, you malformed purulence, it's not love. *You* can't feel love. You've only transferred your blind slave-devotion to her. For what reason, I have no idea. Some sort of glitch in your brain. Maybe the beginnings of your dementia. But you're no more in love with her than you were with your master. What she and I have," Rawang said, his voice rising to a high cracking pitch, "*that* is love." He grabbed Numo's torso and held him up to his face, so that Numo could smell every dizzying expectorated syllable. "And I won't have you confusing her with your misguided slavishness. Do you understand me?"

No. No, he didn't. This was all new to him. Numo supposed he'd heard of that type of *love* before, between humans, but he really had no idea what—

"I said *do you understand me?*" Rawang shook him so hard Numo thought his neck might snap off.

"Yes, yes, I understand, sir, yes, I understand!" Numo said, over and over again, until the shaking stopped. Rawang put Numo down. Numo wobbled and fell over.

"Good." The doctor's eye darted around the forest. He wiped his mouth and took a deep, wet breath. "It's getting dark. Can you walk?"

"Me?"

"Yes, you."

Numo was uncertain. He could feel his legs now, and move his toes—the ones that weren't broken—but he was wobbly and exhausted and his body hurt powerfully. But the man was obviously unhinged; not one to be crossed in weak moments. Numo had to please him, for now at least, until he could get Hammerfist away to safety. "I think so, sir."

"Marvelous. You can go look for food then." Rawang jerked his head towards the previously hysterical infandus. "Take Fustilugs with you."

Was Rawang serious? He certainly looked serious. "In the darkness, sir?"

"Don't have a choice, Numo." Rawang grinned. His teeth were dark like his spit. "We need what we need when we need it. What can I say. Fustilugs will protect you—as long as his wits stay about him, anyway."

Numo looked to Hammerfist. She looked so hateful and yet so baleful and limp and wan. Yes, he could be brave for her. He could march out into the darkness to get her food. Scary beasties be darned.

Numo stood up, leaning his weight on the foot with no broken bones. He smiled at Rawang. The doctor might try to lose him in the forest or get him killed by megalobats, maybe, but Numo would give all his dying breaths to any half-formed bung-witted scheme if it had a chance of making Hammerfist safe. And it wasn't like he had any better ideas.

"Yes, sir. Right away, sir."

Numo took Fustilugs by the hand and strode lopsidedly into the encroaching night.

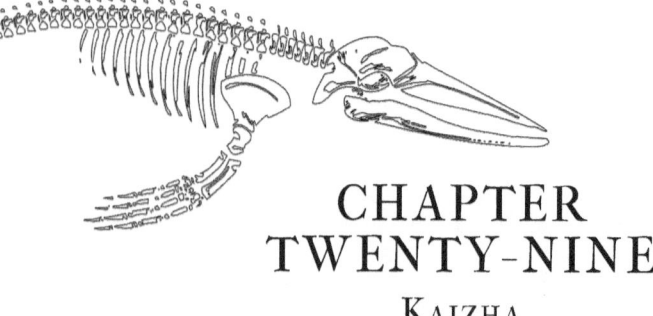

CHAPTER TWENTY-NINE
KAIZHA

KAIZHA'S THROAT FELT like it was full of burning straw, with someone stuffing more and more in with every breath. But the other two were much worse. She had to get them stable, before she ran out of the little handful of backup nebulizers she had taken from the shack and had to rely on her own ineffectual body for breathing.

She kind of wished she hadn't killed Mozeh—he'd have been good at this sort of thing—but then, he would not have approved. Probably would have refused to help. Typical.

They'd made it into the shack, through the tunnel, and into the lab in the main house. Kaizha released Bollix's body and laid it on the table. She had to deal with Xiongnyao before the phosphorus in her chest re-ignited. The lab had a system for running water, thank the gods. Kaizha left Xiongnyao on the floor, stuffed her chest-wound with a new bundle of soaked bandages, and sealed it with strips of plaster but for a small opening. Then she jammed a water-fed tube into the hole.

"Don't move. You understand? If you move, and that tube comes out, then the bandages will dry and the phosphorus will re-ignite. It'll burn through what's left of you. You understand?"

She seemed to be talking at supersonic speed, but she couldn't help it. Xiongnyao looked pained and puzzled and not terribly alive. Kaizha forced herself to talk slower, to repeat everything two or three times. Xiongnyao finally nodded, faintly grasping the tube to hold it steady against her shuddering wheezes.

Kaizha turned to Bollix. The lower half of her body was blackened and burned beyond all hope. She wasn't breathing.

My drake. My poor drake.

Kaizha ground her teeth. It was thoughts like *that* that got her in trouble in the first place, that made Mozeh convince her she couldn't handle creating drakes. Too attached. Too emotional. Too womanly. But she couldn't help it. Her drake was dead.

My only.

Kaizha sank in a chair, trembling, mashing her face with her hands. She couldn't let her go. Bollix had been too perfect— and too flawed. She was too loyal, but too independent. Too much mind. Just enough murder. Bollix, in fact, would have been the perfect weapon, if only—

Kaizha gasped. *If only.*

Distilling alcohol made it stronger. Why couldn't she do the same with a homunculus? Aside from the obvious, of course—

Well. She was in no mind for the obvious.

Kaizha rummaged in the lab for the scalpels. She found a fat knife. It wasn't quite as fine as she'd like, but it'd have to do.

She fired up the incubation tank and popped open the input chambers. She raised the knife over Bollix's abdomen and pushed down before she could hesitate.

It didn't go deep enough. It was too dull. She raised it up

again and hacked at Bollix's skin and organs until she made a hole big enough. Her slave—she was slicing up her slave and she couldn't even do it properly. Heavy tears rolled down into her nostrils. Messily but effectively, she hacked out Bollix's sterile withered uterus and ovaries from her body, then her brain and heart, the purple of the drake's blood messing her hands and crusting across her palms.

Leaking bloody mucous out her nose, Kaizha put the organs into one of the input chambers. Then the squid eggs, and the acid, and the amino-conductor and the rhino blood and the nitrogen and all the rest of it, heating and cooling the chamber at the precisely-timed intervals, shooting it through with electricity at the appointed temperatures. It took over an hour for Bollix's remains to liquefy, and when the time came for Kaizha to seal the incubator, she'd almost gotten used to Xiongnyao's increasingly loud whimpering and forgotten about her.

"Kaizha—please—" Her wheezes found words. Kaizha whirled around. "The pain. Please. Something," Xiongnyao said.

"I have alcohol and makhat. Both will probably make the bleeding worse." Kaizha paused. She tried to do as her mother told her and think what she would want if she was in Xiongnyao's position. "Oh, hell." She poured out some of her most recent batch of distilled alcohol and tipped it down the woman's throat. Xiongnyao coughed and spluttered and a chunk of something red came out of her mouth.

"What—what was—"

"Distilled fermented cane juice mixed with water. I don't have a good name for it yet. You'll like it; just give it time. Meanwhile, do me a favor and take a deep breath." Xiongnyao choked and glared at her. "Well, as deep a breath as you can manage." Kaizha sprayed her in the face with a nebulizer. She only had two more pre-made vials left, but she needed to alleviate the guilt from what she was about to say.

"I was quite set on letting you die earlier. But I think we can do better than that, can't we? And I think both of us are sick of being the backdrop to our husbands' fake successes—you just haven't bothered to kill yours yet. So why can't we work together on this, hm? Be friends?"

"On what? Friends? What are you talking about?"

"I'm working on a certain project and I could use your help. Perhaps your anatomical knowledge?"

"Fff—fie," Xiongnyao breathed.

"If this project succeeds, it will reverse the social reformation. I know you're too young to remember it. But I can promise this: you will not have to support your husband anymore. You can pursue your own whims. You can be as smart and vicious as you desire. Would you like that?"

Xiongnyao gaped. Maybe because she was impressed. Maybe because she could hardly breathe.

Kaizha smiled. She felt a childish little thrill inside her at the prospect of having made a friend. Sure, said friend had a hole in her chest and had no other option but Kaizha to save her life, but—

"Oh! Saving your life. Yes. Very important. Have the drugs kicked in yet? How are you feeling?"

Xiongnyao swallowed with difficulty. "Worse, but less concerned."

"Good. That's good. Have some more of this." Kaizha poured more of the alcohol mixture into Xiongnyao.

217

"Stop that," Xiongnyao coughed.

"Sorry, but what happens next is going to hurt."

Xiongnyao's brows furrowed and her face twisted. "You have to debride the wound."

Kaizha grabbed the sleeve of scalpels. "Yes. Then we have to…replace…the missing flesh with something. How do you feel about having a piece of your buttock removed? I know it's awfully flat down there and you might not have much to work with but—"

Xiongnyao shook her head. "Shut up. Shut up. Just—just do what you have to do. Don't tell me about it. Just do it."

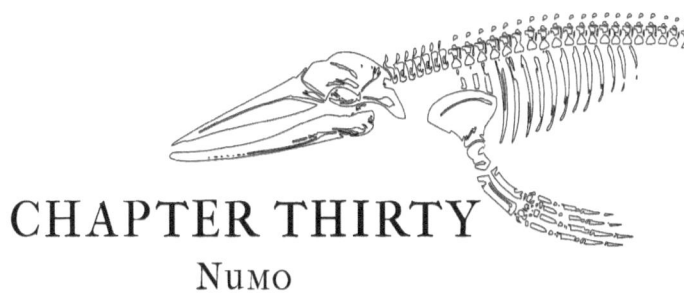

CHAPTER THIRTY
NUMO

FUSTILUGS WAS LEAN and wiry, and he was smaller than Hammerfist, in all his apparent parts. There were dangerous-looking claws, but they were diminutive in comparison to hers; there were fangs, but they almost looked precious. He had very little mane, but he did have a great many gossamer white whiskers along his crooked jaw. He moved like a baby muntjac, prancing unsteadily, freezing every so often to stare at the forest. Little chortles erupted out of him at strange intervals. It was hardly stealthy. Numo hoped that finding food did not involve hunting. Fustilugs would scare away their quarry.

Quarry. Numo smirked at himself. As if a drake could have *quarry.* What would he do, throw a stick at a rat?

Numo sucked in a surfeit of air to puff out his chest, like he'd seen the soldiers do. Then he wondered why puffing out his chest should make him any braver or stronger. Truly, it just seemed that his lungs were bloated and his nipples jutting too far into the atmosphere. He blew out the air and sagged.

"Forget to breathe, did you? I have that problem sometimes selfwise-the-same," mumbled Fustilugs. Numo tripped over his own feet and gasped in pain at his toes.

"You speak the human tongue?" And in nearly-coherent sentences, at that.

Fustilugs snorted. He had two nostrils instead of one glorious Hammerfist-shaped nose-hole. Snub-nosed. Kind of like a bat, really. "I am human, arter all. Just a bit squidgy. Twirled-up, like." Fustilugs spun a finger through the air.

"I thought infandi couldn't—"

"Aye, for most, the mechanics are impossible, true enough. Mouths mutilated. Tongues ripped out and flipped. The alchemist that did me wasn't so furrow."

Numo blinked. "Furrow?"

"Furrow! Diligent-like. Didn't cut up my tongue enough. See? I still almost got half a lip." Fustilugs pointed proudly.

"I…I see. Well done."

Without warning, Fustilugs smacked Numo across the back and knocked him into the dirt. He pressed Numo's body into the earth, hard, as though squeezing the juice out of a melon. Numo's breath *squee*d out of him and his lungs flattened. This was it. This was how he was going to die, in the name of—whatever it was—under the palm of a bat-faced maniac. His obligations unmet. His priorities in shambles. His Hammerfist—

"I must tell you some-what," whispered Fustilugs. "You must keep close. So furtive. The furtivest."

"'Kay," Numo rasped.

"I've had the fall for a long time now. I remember most of my talk, now, you see. I remember who I was, too. Don't tell the masters; they'll try to have me kilt again. But I think—I think it's done in my head." Fustilugs giggled, then smacked himself in the face and twisted a claw around his half a lip. "Don't tell the masters."

"No—no—wouldn't."

"Good." Fustilugs released his grip. Numo inhaled and sucked in the humid earthy air. His lungs were not pleased. He coughed and hacked until finally he coughed up a wad of blackish sputum and his chest stopped spasming.

"Love, you'll chase away the prey," said Fustilugs.

Numo sat, wheezing. "Sorry." At present, he didn't care. Something Fustilugs said had planted deep dark seeds of ominousness inside him. "You have the fall? Still? Did Rawang not cure it?"

Fustilugs chuckled, rounding off with a pained braying noise. "No cure for the fall, love. No cure for the fall." The infandus froze and his eyes flicked skyward. Numo stared at the statue of a creature. His wispy beard billowed against the hairs slick with drool. His eyes were blank and frightened, his muscles twitching and beaded in sweat. This was infandi's fall.

Hammerfist had the fall. The revolution was supposed to be the cure, Rawang said.

The revolution had failed.

Numo's face twisted. His eyes leaked. He was a fool, a foul abortive mank of a dung-smear.

The revolution—it was his fault...

But the mistress...

The thought started strong but died in his head without a sound, like a moth swept away in a river. Numo tried to think that thought again, for it seemed very important, but the words smashed into a wall and disintegrated into gibberish.

Fustilugs came to and pranced a few steps into the forest. "Come now," said Fustilugs. "We have a mission, yes? We must find some prey."

The prey, whatever it was, was not forthcoming. The forest also seemed frustratingly bereft of berries and edible fungi. Numo gnawed quietly on a twig. Fustilugs pranced and chortled.

Numo wondered about him. He said he remembered being a human, didn't he? He might know about some things. Well, one thing in particular. Something that was bothering Numo terribly, and Fustilugs had already used the word a few times, suggesting some degree of familiarity.

"Sir, can I ask—do you know what *love* is?"

Fustilugs's face drew itself out to a most serious length. The purplish-black balls of his eyes glared with gravity. "Oh yes. Yes, I do. Love."

"Can you explain it to me? I've been—I've been accused of it. I don't understand."

"Accused of love? Yes, me too. Accused, convicted, sentenced. Transmockrified. My advice is not to transmockrify."

"Er...yes, but what is it? What does it feel like, I mean?"

"Oh, what it feels like!" Fustilugs yelled. Foliage rustled as small things scurried away. Birds scattered. Numo was doing horribly at his job.

"The prey—mind the prey," he said.

"Never mind the prey. The prey cometh! The water deer love the noise of a gibbering fool."

"Water deer? If the water deer come, *I* am the prey."

Fustilugs appeared to mull this over. "Oh, what it feels like," Fustilugs said, more quietly. "Love is the most holy thing. The highest order cometh from the primordial whim. Greater than a god or a demon. It is pure. It is—it is the common song of the heavens."

Numo's ventricles swelled, and he wondered if it was rather silly, but he couldn't help it.

"Love," continued Fustilugs, "is when you feel you must be with her, or him, or them, or it, you see, this other thing, it clams onto everything, your skin and your air. It pulls you. You cannot escape it, and you must not be without it. It is your planet, your star. It is when you sing, you must create songs for it, or your tongue will go blind and your stomach will shrivel up dead. It is music."

Numo swallowed. "I see. Well. I feel most of those things. Except the singing and the music—I don't—I've never sung a song before. Or had music." It was improper for a homunculus to gad about singing, and especially improper for him to engage in music. Music was a human art.

"Oh, but you must have music! You are in love!"

"I am? Do you think so?"

"She is your planet?"

Numo bit his lip. However he looked at it, he couldn't see a way forward without her. Maybe that was sufficiently planet-like? "I suppose."

"Then you must have a song. A love song. A song that births from your heart-pumps." Fustilugs thumped his chest and unhinged his jaw. "*Yes, we have no bananas, we have no bananas today…*"

Somewhere in the forest, a twig snapped. A fat twig, by the sound of it. Numo swiveled his head. Fustilugs was being very loud. Any predator in the forest would know they were there. Did water deer attack things as large as an infandus?

223

They certainly attacked men. Numo had heard enough stories to know.

Numo turned back to Fustilugs. "Do you—"

No one was there.

A leaf rustled. Numo brandished the stick he'd been gnawing on. It was pointy enough to kill a bee. If the thing in the forest was larger than a bee—

They erupted from the trees. Deer, shaggy, wild, each as large as a hunting dog, with long curved fangs jutting from their mouths. Prancing. Galloping. Bounding towards Numo like a plague of silent death.

Numo waved his stick at the nearest water deer. "Off! Back! B—"

It pounced. Its hooves went into his chest and knocked him to the ground. Its fangs punctured his windpipe. Numo grasped at the thing's head, but it was too large for his hands. Water sluiced out of the fangs into his trachea, gushing into his lungs, drowning him slowly in the middle of a forest. More deer on top of him. More fangs into his neck. More water in inconveniently fatal places.

A blur pelted across his vision. The fangs ripped out of his neck. Bodies thumped to the ground next to him. Water deer scattered, as quietly as they'd come. Numo coughed and rolled over, spewing water and black phlegm, trying desperately to see what had happened but too busy with the labors of breathing.

When he could finally come up for air, Fustilugs sat on top of two dead deer, merrily eviscerating them, ripping out their tendons and other stringy bits.

"Oh, you must have music, you must have a song," he murmured. Numo's eyes went hot. His chest felt like cracked glass, hard and friable and likely to shatter at the slightest provocation. Fustilugs grinned as if nothing had happened. "You know," he said, "I used to be a minstrel. The finest minstrel. I could sing in four languages." He grabbed a long stick, bent it, and strung a tendon across to make a bow. "Properly this ought to be dried—properly I ought to have a many-stringed instrument—properly," he chortled. He wiped his paws up and down on the tendon, caressing it. "A resonator. Oh, no resonator. You will have to be the singer. My mouth will resonate. Are you ready? To sing what is in your heart-bits?"

"What? No. I've just nearly drowned, actually, thank you. Having a bit of a bother with—with my lungs," Numo wheezed. Blood dribbled out of his neck when he tried to breathe. Fustilugs did not seem to notice.

"Nonsense. You will sing," Fustilugs said.

Numo plugged up the holes in his neck with his fingers. "I can't."

"You will sing," Fustilugs growled. His face darkened. The light went out of his eyes. His bloody claws twitched inside the deer he murdered.

Numo thought perhaps he should sing.

"Think of your gravity," Fustilugs said. "Hear the music. Give us a song for her. Or him. Or them." Fustilugs put one end of the bow in his mouth and gaped, his half a lip curling. He picked up a stick with one hand and whacked it rapidly against the bow. The claws of his opposite hand fluttered up and down the length of the string. The tones of the string echoed inside Fustilugs's mouth. It was oddly enticing. Rather frantic. Perhaps frantic was fitting.

Fustilugs looked at him pointedly. Numo supposed he

ought to sing. Something. A *love song*. But it would help immensely if he wasn't bleeding from the neck...

Numo stood up. He wobbled, his head going spotty. There had to be a resinous tree somewhere. He blundered towards a tree trunk, patting it, trying to find oozing sap. Nothing.

The music stopped. Fustilugs whipped a furious glare at Numo. "*Sing*, or I put my claws in your internals and clap my hands."

The music started again.

"Oh...oh something," Numo sang, blood slowing his tongue. Fustilugs closed his eyes in satisfaction. Numo staggered to another tree. What else had Fustilugs said about love? Maybe it didn't matter what Fustilugs said. It only mattered what Numo knew. *No sap. Next tree.*

"When she looks at me
I wither like a drying snail
My juices burble in my head and..."

Numo couldn't think of a single word that rhymed with snail, though he knew such words existed. He wondered if "burble" was really a word that belonged in a song. *Still no sap. Still bleeding.* Numo pressed harder on the holes in his neck and thought hard. His song was not going well. Did that mean he didn't love her? What was it, if it wasn't love? What if Rawang was right and it was just his slave-brain tricking him?

He went on to the next tree and the next, stammering.

"and...and...I'm bleeding out my neck
But I care not for my bones

I'd rather drown in blood and deer
Then leave her all alone..."

"Oh!" Fustilugs cried. "That's beautiful. That is straight from your soul that is! Keep going!"

Finally, Numo found a tree that was oozing. A...a knotted...he could hardly think well enough to remember what kind of tree it was. He swiped at the sap and smeared it across his neck.

"and if I should die of puncture-holes
My greatest of regrets
Is not that I didn't live
But that I didn't know her yet..."

Numo sniffed and pressed his fingers against his eyes, trying to hold back the leaking. It felt like wooden screws were winding behind his eyeballs, inside his chest, in his throat. His knees sagged underneath him and he sat, sadly pasting the punctures over with tree sap, making a contemptible mess of himself. Numo wanted to curl into a ball and pass out. He might not die now—or he might yet—but he suddenly felt that someday soon, he would die trying to love her, without ever having really known her.

The music stopped. "Oh," Fustilugs said mournfully, "a good love song, that is. Bravo, little meat-nugget. Whatever-your-name-is." He daintily extracted something that looked like a bladder from a pile of deer organs and ate it. "Have you died yet?" he asked casually.

"No. I think I may live for the time being."

"Oh." Fustilugs picked at his teeth. "How long will it take you to die, do you think? I'm not supposed to come back until you're dead or lost. Oh, perhaps you could be lost instead? Less of a nuisance for all involved!"

Numo felt waves of heat shoot through his ears, changing their color. The stress-mucus in his head made it hard to hear—maybe he hadn't understood properly—

"Who said that?"

"Oh, the man. The no-shirt beard-face one, you know the one I mean, that one. Perhaps I should have asked you first, which you intended on being, lost or dead? Verminous me!"

Numo plopped himself on the ground, listening to the soft gurgle of fluid shifting in his eardrums. He couldn't muster the energy to be surprised by such a thing. It was unsurprising, wasn't it? The doctor was upset with him. Humans killed the things they were upset with. Still, his profound misery profunded further, expanding into all his extremities, intoxicating them with inertia. And something increasingly familiar.

That blasphemous anger at human beings.

"I'd prefer not to be lost or dead, if that's all right with you, Fustilugs."

"Hm." Fustilugs froze and stared up at the trees. "Scoured," he finally whispered. "All scoured. Not a heartbeat in sight."

"Would it be all right if we went back to the camp now?"

"The beard-face said not to."

Numo paused. "If I'm lost or dead, I can't sing my song to the lady I love."

Fustilugs gasped. "Lolly-balls!" He smacked his hands on his cheeks and tore little lines into the sides of his face. "I did not think of that, in sooth."

"…Does that mean we can take the deer and go back now?"

"It must. I can't have the little loveless meat-nugget die without his song."

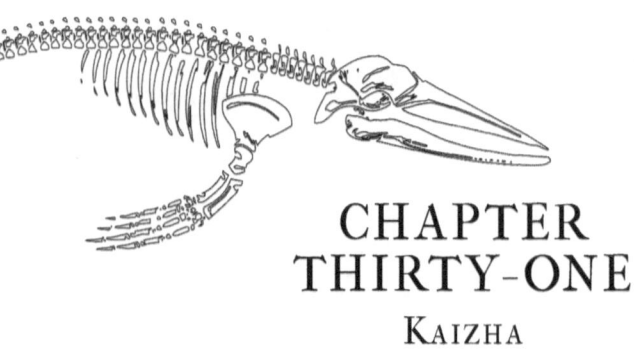

CHAPTER THIRTY-ONE
KAIZHA

KAIZHA WOKE UP on the floor of the alchemy lab with a scalpel stuffed down her breast-restraints and a bottle of thrice-distilled alcohol in her hand. Xiongnyao was crawling across the floor. Her pained grunting was probably what woke Kaizha. Inconsiderate woman.

Wait—what was Xiongnyao doing crawling across her floor?

Kaizha rolled over and struggled to sit up. Her hands burned with pain when she set them on the floor. The change in position angered her lungs. She hacked and spat up viscous pink effluvium before she could manage to speak. "What are you doing?"

"I'm—I'm trying to find more of that—that stuff you gave me for the pain. Before. Earlier. That stuff. Where is it?" Xiongnyao breathed in violent, wet coughs. She pulled herself up on the desk and wailed, gritting her teeth.

The woman was in her underwear. She had bandages wrapped around most of her torso and a patch of plaster spackled on her buttcheek. It struck Kaizha that she was similarly attired. Her head felt like some poltergeist was trying its damnedest to beat her head back down to the floor and claw her viscera out of orifices that were much too small. Blood stained the floorboards and part of the lab seemed to have flooded. The little water pump dripped off the desk.

Vague memories emerged wetly like gas in a swamp. They filled her with roughly as much pleasure. The Homomachy had gone wrong, and Xiongnyao had said something, and there was phosphorus and fire—

Oh sweetest gods tell me I didn't. Tell me I didn't let her live and then bring her back here and tell her...everything...

Kaizha swallowed. Her throat seemed to be coated with festering snake guts and coarse sand. She wondered how much Xiongnyao remembered. If she could make her remember less. "I have it here. But I'm not sure how much is...healthy."

Xiongnyao let go of the desk and collapsed on the floor. She rolled over and dragged herself to Kaizha. "Oh who cares... give it to me...please..."

Briefly, Kaizha wondered if she could get Xiongnyao to drink enough of it to kill her. But it was probably not palatable enough...

She handed it over, evaluating other options for ridding herself of this particular problem. The desk had sharp objects on it, but it seemed so far away, and her body hurt so badly, and her head spun terribly...

Xiongnyao took a swallow of the liquid. She hacked it up and spat it all over the floor, grabbing her chest. "Oh—oh—fie— fie on everyone and the stinking putrid world—my chest..."

"Try it again. Small sips."

Xiongnyao tried several more times and eventually forced down a serviceable amount. After a few minutes, her ragged pathetic attempts at breathing slowed and she stopped writhing around like a panicked worm in a rainstorm. She clutched the bottle as though it were her baby and curled herself around it.

"Try more, if you wish. I don't need the stuff," Kaizha prodded.

"No...no more..."

Damn.

"Do you know how long I've been asleep?" Kaizha asked.

"No. I was asleep, too, until the pain woke me."

"I see." Kaizha took a breath. It was exhausting. Maybe she didn't have to kill Xiongnyao right this moment. "Do you remember what happened before that?"

"I remember fire. I remember being burned. I remember Turian dropping me and leaving...I remember bits and pieces," she finished vaguely. Tears ran out of the corners of her eyes.

"Uh huh." Kaizha wasn't sure what to do. She thought about strangling her, but the thought of the effort made her want to melt in a puddle. Instead, she patted Xiongnyao's head awkwardly. The woman grabbed at her hand and let out a noise that sounded like a constipated muntjac. It took Kaizha a moment to realize she was sobbing.

"Turian...he *dropped* me. And you were the only one who bothered to save me!"

Kaizha let out a breath. It was possible that Xiongnyao didn't remember the less favorable things.

Then Xiongnyao stopped wailing.

She snapped up like a cobra striking and slammed the bottle down on Kaizha's elbow. Kaizha cried out. She collapsed on her arm. Xiongnyao rolled on top of her. She smacked the bottle against Kaizha's shoulder, her head, her ear, until it shattered on her jaw. The crazed woman held the jagged edges against Kaizha's neck. Kaizha could feel her own pulse beat against the glass, against her eyeballs, against her ear, searing through her body.

"I also remember you dropping something into my breast-restraints, and I remember that something burning my chest and catching fire. I remember Turian tearing off my dress because it had already spread to the fabric. I remember that something worming its way into me. I remember it wouldn't stop burning. I remember that you as much as confessed to killing your husband, and I remember you doing something that looked very much like alchemy. And I think that Master Goh would find this information extremely interesting." For a woman slurring her words and shaking like a volcano about to crumble into smoke, Xiongnyao was more frightening in this moment than Grand-Mum-Ma had ever been. Saliva spilled out of Kaizha's mouth like a baby's spit-up. She wheezed through the leakage in her throat and gasped.

"But you—but you said—"

"That I would go along with your insane plans? I was dying!"

"So you want to go back to your idiot husband and uphold his idiocy? Stay where you are forever?"

"Yes, my husband is not the most intelligent person. Yes, he has incurred tremendous debts—which is why I felt the need to blackmail you, shameful as that is. But he is my family. This world is unfair, but it is my home. And I'm not about to go around murdering our own people to change it."

Kaizha's breath stuck in her throat between in and out, clinging to her uvula.

"Which is why I'm not going to kill you." Xiongnyao took the bottle away from Kaizha's neck for an instant. Kaizha should have moved. But her brain was too slow, too stupefied, giving Xiongnyao the chance to drive one of the bottle's shattered edges into Kaizha's eyeball.

Kaizha screamed and curled over on herself. Xiongnyao leapt off her body. Off-kilter footfalls thumped across the room and the door opened and shut again. Her eye was burning, full of knives and flame and venom, boring into her skull and carving a bigger hole in her head. She yanked out the shard. She was half-blind. She was bleeding out of her face and her head was full of hammers and demonorrhea.

Worse, Xiongnyao had escaped. And Kaizha was helpless to do anything about it.

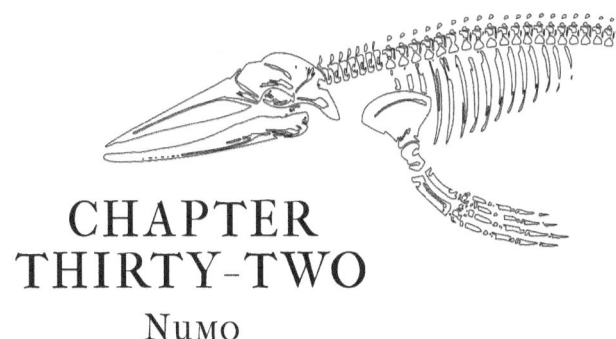

CHAPTER
THIRTY-TWO
Numo

FUSTILUGS ENDED UP having to carry Numo part of the way, dragging the deer carcasses with one free hand. The sap stopped the bleeding and sealed the holes, but imperfectly, and Numo's lungs were weak and withered. Plus, part of the way was uphill. Numo never did get along with hills. It was part of what made living on a mountaintop quite challenging.

The camp was still in its original place, much to Numo's surprise. He'd have thought Rawang would try to pack up and lose them both. Instead, he was yelling, swearing, messing around with Hammerfist's ropes, and sweating like a fever-patient. Maybe he couldn't have left even if he wanted to. Oddly, though, Hammerfist was now calm, no longer writhing and violent. Most of the chaos was coming from the doctor himself.

Rawang grunted at their arrival. He blinked at Numo and growled at Fustilugs, but was too sweaty and breathless to say much more. He ripped off a chunk of deer and handed it to Hammerfist. She chewed. Bits of debris fell from the mess of her slackened attempts at mastication. Aside from the half-hearted gnashing of her jaws, she was quiet as a corpse, her face vacuous and unblinking. Rawang occasionally poured water into her eyes.

"Is she all right?" Numo asked.

"It takes time to recover from an episode," Rawang grumbled. "I'm doing the best I can."

"I didn't say you weren't, sir," said Numo. He had no doubt Rawang was doing the best he could. He also had no doubt that Rawang's best was not very good. "But perhaps we ought to see if we might find an alchem—"

"Infandi's fall can't be cured," Rawang snapped. "Not by me, not by alchemy. I'm doing the best *anyone* can do." He lowered his voice. "She's much better than she was. She has hope. Had. Before you, anyway." He looked sidelong at Fustilugs. "You and I are going to have a discussion later."

Numo hesitated. He probably shouldn't say anything. "Sir?"

Oh, Numo, you dratted boot-scrape.

"Yes, Numo?"

"Er. Well, Fustilugs—I bootbla...I mean, I blackmailed him, sir."

Rawang squinted his best eye. "What do you mean, Numo?" he asked softly.

"I...I *blackmailed* him," Numo said, adopting, he hoped, the certain and dauntless air of a person who knew completely the meaning of the words he was saying and how to use them in a sentence. "That's why he didn't do it. It's not his fault."

"I really don't know what you me—"

"I won't tell her, sir. I won't say anything."

Rawang's lips tightened. "I don't know what you're talking about, Numo. Perhaps the dementia is starting to get to you." He turned back to Hammerfist.

Numo swallowed. His throat still tasted of blood and dirt. He thought about things, about the puzzling conversations, the trodden tang in everyone's voice, the empty gaze in Hammerfist's face, stuck there like painted doll eyes. Perhaps Rawang was right. Perhaps there was nothing that could be done.

But these things weren't hopeless until they were. And Numo would keep trying. Even if he had to stomach a scummy man like Rawang.

Numo ate what he could of raw deer flesh—very little, he found—and curled up next to a sweet-smelling nectar tree. He might yet think of something—something to help, something he had simply overlooked. For now, he desperately needed to waste a few hours on his own exhaustion.

A twig snapped. Numo's eyes popped open. Well, mostly. One of them was half-swollen.

Rawang? Surely not even a stumblebum like Rawang would come and kill him in the night. Early morning. Whatever-it-was.

Water deer.

He wrapped his hands around his neck. It was crusty and sticky and offensive to every sensibility he'd been brought up with. But it was intact.

Another stick destroyed. Rustling in the woods. A lot of rustling.

Numo braced himself against the tree trunk and pushed himself up, poking his head around the thickness of the bark.

Rawang was asleep, along with the others. Fustilugs was curled at his feet.

237

Hammerfist was still tied up. Like bait.

Numo launched himself off the ground. There was no thought or reason until approximately three seconds after he'd done it. By then he was in a full limping lopsided semi-injured gallop and it was too late for reason.

He thumped his body into Hammerfist's thigh. She snorted. Her eyes stared open, blinking slowly.

"Hammerfist," Numo whispered, prodding her buttock. "There's something—something in the woods." His breathing was loud. So loud. The rustling stopped. Numo winced. Whatever was in the forest must have heard him.

She turned her head vaguely and stared at an area above Numo's head.

"I'm going to untie you." Numo swallowed. It might not be the best decision. But she'd be a target if she stayed wrapped around a tree.

He set himself on the rope. The knots were tight and blood-encrusted. Wrenching at them took time, but at least it was a quiet activity. The rustling in the woods started up again. It migrated. It came closer.

The ropes slipped off. Hammerfist didn't move.

"Go. Hide." Numo shoved her leg. He poked her. She looked down at him.

She screamed.

Hammerfist scooted away, falling over herself, and shrank back against the tree trunk. She covered her eyes and quivered.

"What's happening?" Rawang stumbled blearily at them. "What are you doing to her?"

Numo kneaded his fingers. "I—I didn't—there's something in the woods and I had to—"

"You untied her? Are you stupid?" Rawang paused. "Yes. I'm sorry. I keep forgetting."

Numo shuffled up to Hammerfist. She flinched. "It's just me," he said.

She lashed out. The tips of her fingers raked Numo's arm. The others were waking up, gathering around. Hammerfist's eyes darted between them. She growled.

"Back off!" Rawang yelled. "Everyone back off!"

"Sing her your song, meat-nugget," Fustilugs murmured. His half a lip had been split open. Numo fliched. Was that his fault?

No. It was Rawang's. That…that…matty-haired wankdog… "SING."

Numo looked up at Hammerfist. She trembled. So odd that she should be afraid of the smallish puniness of him. He cast his eyes away and he knelt on the ground, so he wouldn't look threatening. Softly, slowly, he sang.

"I'm bleeding out my neck
But I care not for my bones
I'd rather drown in blood and deer
Then leave her all alone…"

Hammerfist stared. She'd stopped shaking. *"Nmmmhhaa?"* *Numo.*

"That was beautiful," said an unfamiliar voice. Numo raised his head. They were surrounded.

CHAPTER THIRTY-THREE
Numo

A HORDE OF INFANDI encircled them. Branded ones—with a slew of maker's marks, master's marks, and finally, Moaki's seal burned into their bodies. Exports. Traded out to other cities on the continent.

Why were they in a forest?

"Um, thank you," said Numo.

"It was not beautiful. It was sickening," Rawang spat. "Get away from my wife. You're scaring her."

The infandus who'd spoken peered at Hammerfist. "I apologize. Victim of the fall?"

Though his pronunciation was strange, and his *v* and *f* sounds were closer to *b*s and *p*s, he was oddly well-spoken, for an infandus. Perhaps Fustilugs was not the only one with pieces of a lip or most of a tongue still intact.

"Don't worry. We are all victims, sir. We understand." The infandus yelled something to his comrades in their language. The horde retreated.

"I am sorry for interrupting. We saw the lady in distress and had to see that she was all right, you see. Brothers and sisters must stick together."

"Thank you for your concern," Rawang said, not sounding very thankful at all. "Who are you? What are you all doing here?"

"Merely seeking a way back." The infandus was smiling, in a snarl-faced toothy sort of way.

"Back to Moaki? You're insane. They'll kill you for desertion."

"Most of us are insane, yes. But Moaki is just a means to an end. What I meant is, we seek a way back to human form."

Rawang crossed his arms. "Impossible."

"Perhaps, perhaps not. There is an alchemist in Trago, where we come from. He has surpassed the alchemists in Moaki and discovered a way to reverse transmogrification."

"There are no alchemists in Trago," Rawang said, but he sounded uncertain. "It's still occupied; alchemy is outlawed…"

"There are no *legal* alchemists in Trago. But as long as they don't flaunt themselves by creating homunculi, Moaki does not notice.

"This alchemist has promised to un-transmogrify anyone who brings him the head of a Moaki oligarch. If we bring them all, he will perform the procedure on us all. So," said the infandus, "we are going head-collecting." He nodded at Hammerfist. "You may want to consider the offer yourself. A human does not suffer the fall."

Rawang said nothing. Everyone said nothing. Hammerfist made no indication of acknowledgement.

Numo trembled, his brain creaking and crashing.

"Tell her, when she comes to," said the branded infandus. Then he called for his group to move out. The infandi rustled their way back into the forest and disappeared into the dusk of the coming morning. Numo listened to them until the sound died and there was nothing but a dissonant calm, as though Numo's head wasn't full of coals and fire. As though he hadn't just been faced with the prospect of chopping off a man's head.

It was a ridiculous proposition. Numo couldn't quite take it seriously when he turned it over in his mind, as though he were trying to puzzle out a way to bake very tiny bread inside someone's navel.

But it seemed it was the only solution.

"It would be a death sentence for any of the rest of us," Rawang said. "You're small. You can go unnoticed. As long as you don't wave a fucking flag that says 'kill me please.' You do understand you're not to do that, Numo? That the humans will kill you if they realize who you are? Not that dense, are you boy?"

Numo's anger rose in his throat like an ugly fungus. Grumpy improprietous words greedily clambered to escape his mouth, words like 'clotpole' or 'spleen-addled rudesby,' but he remembered what Bollix said about being proper to the man.

Numo glanced back at Hammerfist. She was still staring at the forest. Her mouth moved thoughtlessly, almost unnaturally, like a puppet's limbs. Numo had to do this. Even if Rawang was only sending him away as a convenience, hoping he'd get killed again, he was still right—it had to be Numo. "No, sir. I understand, sir."

"And the rest of us?" Fustilugs chirped. "The rest of us try as well, for our own sakes?"

Rawang's lip curled before his expression reverted to its

normal artless form. "I have no say in your fates. You are free now. That is for you to decide. But it is my opinion that if you go back, you will die."

Fustilugs snorted out a high-pitched squeak. The other infandi tittered and hooted and grunted and cocked their heads. "Dying is not so grievous a thing," Fustilugs said. "We will get ourselves a head, eh?" He whistled, chortled, and gamboled into the forest. The others shambled after.

Numo grabbed one of Rawang's meaty fingers. His hand slipped off. So much dirt-lathered clamminess. Numo wrinkled his nose. Still, it did not fail to get the doctor's attention.

"What?"

"Won't Hammerfist be—won't she be most upset if the others die?"

Rawang furrowed his brow. "I don't understand you at all. How can you grasp things like that, but you can't grasp—never mind. Hell with it." He blew out a stenchful clot of breath. "She will be sad that they die, but she will be happier that they had the freedom to choose to die. That's all she wants…um. For—for them." Rawang swallowed. He blinked rapidly. His eyes even looked a bit wet. "You'd better go now. You'll want to get back to Moaki at the same time as all those infandi. They'll at least provide a distraction."

"And—and you? And her? Where will I find you afterwards?"

Rawang gazed somewhere else and sighed. Probably wishing he could make sure Numo never found them afterwards—but then he wouldn't get the head. Suddenly Numo was important. Funny old world, it was. "We'll be here, unless we're found out. Then I daresay we might try our luck in Trago.

Now get out of here before she comes to. She'll be mad as hell when she finds out you're gone."

Numo clasped his shaking hands together. "She will?"

Rawang snarled. "Don't be excited about it. It's a bad thing."

Yes, it was a bad thing. A bad bad thing. But some primordial gibbering part of Numo's brain wailed *she likes me she needs me she likes me.* And even as he trudged back in the direction of Moaki, the city that had nearly killed him, he could not stop grinning like a buffoon.

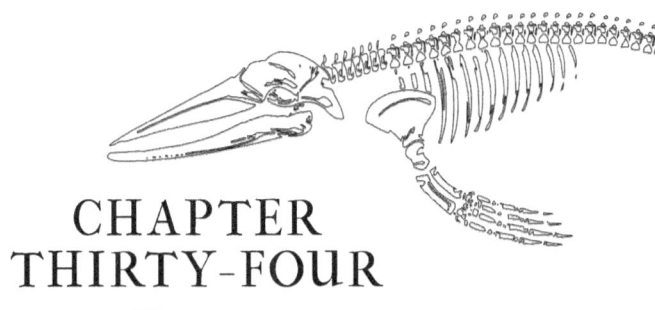

CHAPTER
THIRTY-FOUR
KAIZHA

KAIZHA HAD SPITTLE and Tester Six move her equipment and notes back to the shack in the woods while she tried to get her eyelids to stop bleeding and drink enough of what little alcohol she had left to forget about the white-hot hellstorm in her eyeball. Xiongnyao was injured, she told herself; she wouldn't move fast. And the whole city was probably still in some degree of chaos after the Homomachy, so retribution might not be swift. Still, how long did she have? Hours? Days?

She could run. Kaizha could prep a few important vials, grab her notes and whatever was left in the pantry, and light out to the wilderness.

But there was one thing she couldn't take with her.

That incubation box, with all of Bollix's salvageable parts inside. It was still burbling and broiling. She could disconnect it for a short time, but if warmth was abandoned, and the sluicing of water irregularized by inconsistent plumbing, and the holy writ ignored, and the rhino blood depleted, then the contents, if they were living at all, would die. And she'd lose Bollix and her wonderful perfection for good.

Part of her thought herself silly for caring, but really, it made very good practical sense to reuse such well-begotten material. That she still thought of Bollix as hers, as an essence too valuable to be lost, was just an unrelated fact.

Kaizha sat heavily on the floor, her head accumulating heaviness like old furniture collecting dust. She carefully plastered a patch over her eye. Her hands still shivered. She'd need to disconnect and reconnect the incubator when the infandi moved it, fuel it again with more packets of alchemical fire and lithia water—hell, she was low on lithia, she hadn't gone to the market in so long—and remake the amnio fluid, prime the pumps in the shack, heat the spigots...

The idea of walking anywhere, let alone down a long tunnel into the woods to do manual labor, filled her with the ghost of nausea to come.

The bell hanging outside the front door rang. Kaizha didn't move. It rang again. Whoever was ringing it was not going away.

"Six! Spittle!" Kaizha forced herself to run to the incubator, which felt very bad indeed. She began disconnecting the attachments and disassembling the smaller components and *where the hell were the infandi?*

The bell rang again. Kaizha yelled for the slaves again. She shouldn't have gotten rid of all the strictureweed rings; after all, who was going to look that closely—

When they didn't come, Kaizha tried lifting the incubator herself. It slipped out of her arms and banged into the floor. The sealant held, thank the gods. She shoved it across the floor, rolled it, pushed it with her toes—anything she could manage to get the thing over to her old quarters.

Spittle and Poison Tester Number Six popped their heads out of the trapdoor. Six made that sound he made that almost sounded like "yes miss?" mixed with the chattering of a fox.

A horrible crack and splintering noise came from the front of the house. They were forcing their way in. It might take them a minute to search the house and find her, but...

Oh sweet gods, give these wretches enough brain to understand what I'm about to say.

"Take this," Kaizha ordered, shoving the incubator towards them. "Take this to the old shack and place it on the black stand above the burner. Find the water pump near the burner; pump it twenty times or so, and open the sluice-line. Set the burner to a mid-high flame. Then...then..." The instructions for what came next—it was all too complicated; they wouldn't have a chance of understanding. "Do either of you read the human tongue?"

Spittle nodded.

"Oh thank you, thank you, blessed creature—find my book of notes, and in the very front of it you'll find instructions for hooking up the incubator—just go do it, now, and *do not come back here.* Do you understand?"

The infandi nodded and grabbed the incubator. Then they ducked into the hole and disappeared. Kaizha kicked the rug over the trapdoor. Footfalls pounded closer to her quarters. Her heart thrummed with anxiety and pain, but not for her imminent arrest. She'd just ordered two thick-as-snot slaves to go carry out rudimentary alchemy on their own.

She was going to lose what was left of Bollix. Her experiment. Her future.

Someone knocked at the door.

"Yes? You may enter," she called, propping herself up against the bedframe.

Goh strode in. His beard, though still uncommonly long, was much shorter, the ends blackened and singed. The left side of his neck was pinkish from a burn. The beardservant Reddles held just the tips of the whiskers that made it past Goh's knees, walking with the depressed gait of a slave who had failed his duty. The drake's face had been swathed in black bandages up to his eyes, with two little nose-holes poked in them for air. One of his ears seemed to have been burned down to a nub.

"My, aren't his face-dressings somber," Kaizha remarked. It was the most inane thing she could think of. Goh appeared confused, briefly, then latched on to the hooks of familiar vapid conversation.

"Oh, yes. He insisted, in his own way. Can't talk anymore, poor fellow, but he seems set on being in mourning. He nearly had the whole of his face burnt off trying to save my whiskers. Performed valiantly in the course of his duties." Goh peered down at his servant with a grim little smile. "Anyway, Kaizha—I apologize about our forced entry into your abode, but I was concerned after your health, given the horrific events that transpired...are you badly injured?"

"Moderately."

"Are you in need of medical attention?"

"I..." That hadn't really occurred to her. "I've attended to myself, thank you."

Goh offered a hand to help her off the floor. Kaizha had no desire to get up, but it was dizzying to look up at his face, so she allowed it. He led her to the edge of her bed, and then went to sit on the bench near her bed, where the slaves' rings used to hang.

"Unfortunately, I do have an ulterior motive in my visit,"

he began. Kaizha tried to look flaccid and unconcerned. "I have just finished an audience with the Master and Mistress Haishing, who wish to bring some charges and evidence against you, pertaining to offenses old and new. Now, I'm unsure of the validity of some of the Mistress's charges, frankly, but some other assertions and evidentiary revelations are rather more disturbing."

"Oh?" Kaizha wished she had a cup of tea to sip in an unconcerned manner. Instead, she clasped her hands in her lap.

"Yes." Goh removed a bit of paper from his sleeve-pocket and held up a quizzing-glass to his eye. "Mistress Haishing formally accuses you of purposefully burning her with the intent to kill, and of practicing alchemy. She also submits that she heard you confessing to killing your husband. Master Haishing reinforces this claim, having done another inspection of his reports on the autopsy, and confirms that the angle of entry and the amount of force used to attack Master Shanyang excludes the possibility of anyone under the height of five feet being the culprit." Goh put away the paper in the folds of his sleeve. "How would you like to answer these charges?"

Kaizha's pulse banged away behind her eye, as though it was trying to squeeze it out of the socket. "Oh dear. I'm afraid the Mistress has allowed her imagination to run rampant..."

Goh nodded. "Go on."

"I did see the Mistress at the Homomachy, with her clothes removed and her chest badly burned. Her husband had left her for dead, I believe, but I—possessed of some odd surge of womanly passion!—entertained such a conceit as to think I could help her with my husband's far-famed healing equipment. I brought her back to his lab, and I am ashamed

249

to admit I did commit basic alchemical procedures to treat her wounds. But I was quite panicked, you understand. Being in mourning for the love of my life has spilled my reason-beans right out of the canister. And, I confess, I was being haunted by the monthly ovarian imps at the time, bleeding me dry and making me dizzy..."

She was going too far. It was time to shut up.

"...At any rate, I must plead guilty to the alchemical charge. As to burning her on purpose, I'm not sure where she got the idea. Perhaps the smoke and fear twisted reality in her mind."

"She claims that you used a strange substance on her chest that would not be extinguished."

"I'm not quite sure how to answer to that, Master. The poor woman must have been delirious with pain."

Goh nodded. "I did inspect the wound and it seemed like Mozeh's healing methods. Indeed, you may have saved her life. I'm sure that may fall under the clause of extenuating circumstances. But you understand I cannot let such a thing go entirely unpunished—there will be a fine."

"Of course, of course." Kaizha's eye seemed to be growing, swelling, taking on a life of its own, sprouting jaws and biting itself. She wished desperately for some ameliorating substance, but it was such substances that had begun the trouble in the first place.

"I am more concerned about the charge involving your husband's murder."

"Yes...I..." Kaizha swallowed. Her whole body seemed to have opened up its sweating-pores and saliva pooled in her mouth. "I'm afraid I don't know how to answer that either. I already stated what I know to have happened. As I said, I did not see the murder itself, only the immediate…aftermath."

"Yes. It seems that you and the drake were the only ones who witnessed anything at all." Goh crossed his legs. "Had the drake shown any signs of dementia prior to the event?"

"I didn't pay much attention to the peripheral slaves, Master Goh. He was only a hypocaust stoker."

"Supervision of the slaves is a duty that must befall a wife, Mistress." Goh arched a reddled brow. He stared at her as if he expected some response, but then he took a sharp breath and switched the subject. "Had you noticed any infandi about the place, Mistress?"

"Hm?"

"Had you noticed any infandi, or human persons, in the immediate vicinity, upon your discovery of the body?"

"Well I…I don't know." Kaizha thought. "Yes, I suppose Mummerhat was close by, since Mozeh does not like to be long without his jester, and Scrubtongue was in the hall doing the floors, and Bushtickler was just outside at the flower-beds…"

"But could any of them have gotten to your husband in your brief sojourn for tea-fetching?"

"Master, I could hardly know such a thing."

"Indeed, I suppose you couldn't." Goh stared into space. Kaizha briefly fantasized about hitting him in the head with a fire-lamp, but that would require very swift movement. Her head would almost certainly strike her down with vertigo.

Finally, he stood. "Mistress Shanyang, I will not officially place you under arrest. I don't believe the charges have enough merit to warrant it as yet. But I do insist you remain in this house until I have finished investigating them. I have brought a large contingent of the city guard, and I shall install them at all major access points of your home. They will bar the exits, as well as access to your husband's lab. If you go beyond this room, you must be escorted."

"Escorted? In my own home?" Kaizha tried to keep the mindless smile plastered across her face.

"You will be brought food and drink and comforts, but I'm afraid I can't let you leave until I have gathered enough evidence to convince myself either way."

"You mean to place me under house arrest, then."

"Unofficially. But…yes. You understand. I have a duty to uncover the truth in all things." He stroked his mustache. "By the by, where have all your slaves gone?"

"My slaves? I got rid of them, of course, for my own safety. It is difficult for me to believe that everyone in the city hasn't done the same. What need do you have of them?"

"Ah. Hm." A snowfly buzzed somewhere against the window, marring the awkward silence. "How have you been maintaining yourself and the house?"

She paused. "I…well, I simply—do things."

Goh looked incredulous. "You collect and make your own meals? Stoke your own ovens? Boil your own water when the pumps freeze?"

"Um. Yes?" Well, technically, she'd had Spittle and Tester Six do some of that, but she wasn't about to confess it.

He sighed. "Restricted as you'll be, I will have to lend you a few of my own servants for basic necessities, then. But that wasn't why I asked—I feel that perhaps the truth is somewhere in their heads. You had them taken to the auction grounds?"

Kaizha nodded faintly. Her eye *wob-wob-wobbed* harder and faster. The slaves? He was going to question the slaves?

Who had ever heard of such a thing? It was simply not done.

Goh swept aside his robes and strode towards the door. "My men will be stationed outside the door of your quarters. Let them know if you have need of anything." The door closed on her.

A torrent of panic crashed over Kaizha. The unused scraps of Bollix's body—the parts she hadn't already put in the incubation chamber—were in the trash heap just over the city walls. She'd only managed to get the infandi to carry it away from the house, thinking she'd dispose of it later. There hadn't been time. She hadn't cleaned out the liquefying compartments in the lab, either, and there were almost certainly residual oils and fluids from the homunculus, and possibly even blood. And it was only a matter of time before Goh tracked down all her slaves and discovered certain incriminating things, if they were not smart enough to keep their mouths shut. Questioning the slaves! The very height of impropriety.

Kaizha went through the trapdoor and pulled it shut, trying to wiggle the batskin across the top as best she could through the gaps underneath. She hurried down the tunnel. The air was even more infectious than usual. Her chest felt like it was full of porcupine quills. She wasn't sure what she would do. She could run, but that would be admitting guilt, and everything she had worked for would erode like a flimsy mountainside in a rainstorm. She could finish her experiment, and perhaps sell her technology to another city-state, and come crashing back down on Moaki with an army of her own weapons in the hands of foreigners. But Moaki was the holy city, her family's home for generations upon generations, the birthplace of alchemy. She'd wanted to restore it, not destroy it. Her lungs caught on her heavy staggering breaths, filling and seeping as uselessly as engorged ticks with holes poked in them. Everything she'd loved was gone or transformed into something she didn't recognize. And some of it she'd destroyed herself.

Kaizha emerged from the tunnel into her shack. She looked for a nebulizer, or even some dregs of makhat, but there was nothing left. She'd used it all and not bothered to replenish her stores. So she stood there, wheezing, staring at Six and Spittle as they fiddled with her incubator. Shockingly, they seemed to be handling it with aplomb. Spittle read from the book in wet growls and grumbles, and Six would make a tiny adjustment here or there. The nozzles were already connected and the flame underneath was the exact color and size it should have been. Spittle looked to her and nodded with a customary neck-exposing bow.

Kaizha smiled and sank to the floor to catch her breath. She had no proper chairs in here anymore. She had no proper anything, really. Her warped brain decided that this was a metaphor for her whole life, and depression soaked into the spongy outsides of her mind.

A commotion sprang up outside. The megalobats shifted and tittered, their wings roiling the air. Someone was coming. Whoever it was would likely die—Kaizha had made the slaves build the shack in the territory of a megalobat colony for just that reason. But all her muscles went taut. This couldn't be it. She needed more time, time enough at least for the experiment to incubate, for her to make something of what was left of Bollix. *Please, Moa, Kuru, anyone, just give me time—*

Something tiny crashed through a windowpane, followed by the gnashing teeth of a megalobat's face. The bat snapped its jaws inside the windowpane until it could get no further, then gave up and left.

The tiny thing that had crashed through the window stood up, haltingly, blood trickling down its leg. It had some minor burns, smeared blood all over its neck and chest, and mud spattered up its belly, but Kaizha would recognize that face anywhere.

"I'm terribly sorry for my—my inappropriate entrance," Numo panted. "But I'm afraid I have desperate need of your counsel, Mistress."

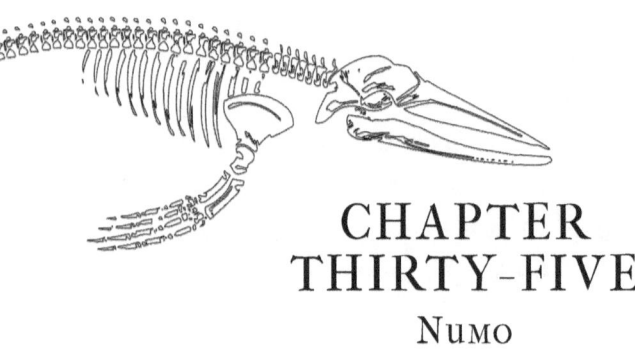

CHAPTER
THIRTY-FIVE
Numo

THE MISTRESS LOOKED to be in a very bad state. Apparently she was not even capable of operating her own equipment—infandi were playing at the bellows and flames of some great stonemetal box. But Numo had just sprinted through a hive of rhino-sized megalobats who had been asleep when he started and not-so-asleep right at the end, and was therefore far too adrenaline-sodden to delay his purpose for her sake.

"I need the head of an oligarch," he said.

The mistress blinked at him with the one unplastered eye and crinkled her brow. "What?"

Numo sighed. His neck hurt most powerful. "There is an alchemist in Trago who will transform Hammerfist if I bring him the head of an oligarch and it's her only chance at hope and life and curing the fall, and if she has no hope left she'll want for me to help her kill herself otherwise and I simply don't know if I can bear—"

The mistress held up one hand. It was covered in fresh burns. She gestured for him to come closer. He shuffled forward, barely caring at this stage in proceedings how unseemly he must look. If he was unseemly, so was she; this whole place was unseemly. It was like he'd entered some other dimension. He wasn't even sure of the proper way to speak to her anymore.

"You must pardon me, Numo. I've had a rough—um. Period of...time. Night? Morning?" She pressed her fingers against her temple. "I don't know...am I hallucinating, or are you saying actual words? Are you even alive? *How* are you alive?"

Numo blew out a shaking breath. His nerves were still strung taut from the megalobat encounter. "My...my great friend saved me from the arena."

"Your great friend?"

It didn't sound right to him, either. "Hammerfist. She is an exquisite being. And she is in desperate need of help."

"An exquisite being, is it?" The mistress's eyebrow arched. "Is she a homunculus, Numo?"

"An infandus. Yes."

"Infandus...well. And you have a strong desire to serve her, do you?"

"I—I don't know..." Numo set his jaw and his neck muscles sparkled with twangs of white-hot pain. "I composed a song about her."

"Did you now? Why did you do that?"

"It is, I was told, the thing you do when..." He paused. "When one is in love. I was told I'm in love with her." He paused again. The mistress seemed incredulous. "I was also told I have transferred my slave-devotion to her and my feelings are not real." He found himself unable to ask her the question on his tongue. But it occurred to him that she, of anyone currently living, must know...

The mistress leaned down, resting her elbows on her knees. "Well, Numo, which do you think it is?"

"I wouldn't presume to know such a thing, mistress," he murmured.

"Is the difference important to you?"

Numo's throat suddenly felt swollen and wet, like repeatedly rained-upon sticks that had been stripped of their bark. "Very, mistress."

She inhaled slowly, and coughed once or twice, before leaning back on her stool. The two infandi at work beside her finished their project, whatever it was, and sat back on their haunches. They stared at him as though he were a performing monkey wearing a priest's paint. The silence between them all grew so ponderous Numo could almost feel it pressing on his empty belly.

"Oddly, it is important to me as well. I find that most fascinating, actually…" The mistress stared at the floor, her gaze unfocused.

"You mean you don't know?"

"Well, of course not, not without some experimentation. However, the experimentation could prove fatal, and then we wouldn't be able to see the results, would we? So I suppose… no. I don't know."

Numo could feel his ears changing color. He was actually getting impatient with the mistress. That hadn't happened before. But in sooth, she seemed like a different creature to him now.

"Never mind it. That's not what I came for, anyway. I came because I need to obtain the head of an oligarch to help her. And frankly, Mistress, I don't know how to go about it. But I thought—well, I thought perhaps you would have some ideas."

"The head of an oligarch, eh? My sweet fretting Numo

wants someone beheaded." She gave a small fraction of a smile. "I haven't seen that desire in a drake since…hm." Her eye wandered to the stonemetal box, but it didn't stay, and she didn't finish her thought, which Numo was rather glad for, as he did not, at present, care. "You've changed, Numo," she said.

"I don't know that either, Mistress." But he did. He was different, and she was different, and the whole world had gone darker.

"How will the head of an oligarch help her?"

Numo tried to explain again. The mistress was quiet for some time. Then she said, "Transforming an infandus is impossible. Well, it is at least inconceivable. But then again, as Grand-Mum-Ma always said, alchemy is the bridge to the inconceivable…"

Numo's head was spinning. "Can you help me or not?"

The mistress gave a faint smile. "Would you like my head, Numo? I am technically a member of the council. And how you must *hate* me. I did horrible things to you, Numo. I wouldn't blame you for it."

Numo's mouth was dry and gummy. He coughed. "I am… still very confused. About what happened; about what you did, and why. But it's past now." He shuffled his feet, wondering if, even after all this, he could ever bear to remove his mistress's head, a head he would have not so long ago given his life to keep attached to its blossoming dewlap. "I don't want your head, mistress. I would fain take the first seat on the council."

"Goh?"

"Yes, Mistress."

"My head isn't lofty enough for you, Numo?" She smiled cheekily, as though she were making a joke, which he didn't quite understand.

"It's too lofty, Mistress; all heads are, for I am small of—oh." A pun. Numo did not appreciate puns. "You mean valuable." He looked at her jovial smirking expression and wanted to lance it through. She was taunting him, was she not? It was all games and jolly-winks for her, here we go round the butterfly bush, tralala and giddy-merry. He curled his fists and released. Calmly he said, "No. It is not."

The mistress's expression wavered. "That's all right, Numo. I am quite happy to help you exterminate Goh. To help you plan it, anyway. You see, I'm unable to leave my quarters—well, they don't know about this place. The point is, I can't go faffing about town for you. You will have to do the work. But I can help you figure out what that work should be." She pursed her lips and crossed her arms. "And you need to survive this assassination, yes?"

"Yes. I must bring the head back. Out of the city. I must leave here with a head and my life."

"Hm. I see. Give me a few moments." The mistress stared at the floor, her brow crinkled, the wrinkles around her eye deep in squinted contemplation. Numo sat, his legs weak. It occurred to him that he hadn't had much to eat or drink since his last feeding in prison. He nearly asked the mistress for something, but he didn't dare interrupt her thoughts.

The Mistress looked up at him, her eye bright. She pressed two fingers against her lips. "How do you feel about getting your left ear burned off?"

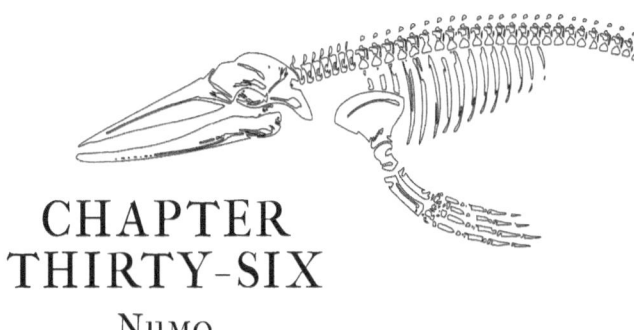

CHAPTER THIRTY-SIX
Numo

Numo did not care for the mistress's plan. Completely aside from his ear being burned off—and he had to admit he was becoming rather tired of his physical person being burned, lacerated, broken, partially drowned, and otherwise molested—the whole thing sounded, well…

Odious.

But it was, after all, murder. He supposed there was no getting around it being odious. And the mistress assured him that, if he did as she said, he would get away with the deed, and no one would come looking for him. In sooth, he had no ideas himself, and she was better versed in murder than he, and, after all, he was desperate.

She sent the infandi to gather makhat first. "For the pain," she said, since she was going to light his ear on fire. While they were gone, she went to the house to fetch food and water, and materials to make something called a *nebbelizer* or a *nobby-blazer* or something of the like. Numo fell asleep on the floor. He woke to the sounds of the mistress bashing the juice out of the makhat leaves. It was dark again. Night, though he didn't know when. He wondered if Hammerfist had recovered from her episode yet. If she was angry at him for leaving. If she was trying to figure out how to kill herself. If Rawang would stop her.

The mistress fed Numo, watered him, and dosed him with the makhat. Numo would have argued in the old life, when it was wrong to consume the holy plants of men, but the mistress promised it would not only numb the pain, but also give him strength and courage for what he was about to do. Numo decided he very much needed those things. He didn't like to think about it or admit it, but the idea of cutting off Goh's head—really imagining the act, not just saying the words—made him trembly and sick inside.

Then again, the makhat was starting to produce a similar effect.

"Do you feel odd?" the mistress asked.

"Yes."

"Good." She grabbed his head and pulled his ear out straight. One of her hands held his chest back as she pushed the ear over the flame burning under the stonemetal box. Numo felt it, the pain was there—but he wasn't nearly as perturbed by it as he might have thought. The smell was far more disturbing. The scent of burnt hair and charred meat and cauterized blood turned Numo's wobbly guts. He gagged.

"Don't throw up," the mistress said. "Don't you throw up, you hear me? If you waste my good makhat…"

Numo struggled to make his throat stoic and unresponsive to the desire to expel everything he'd just ingested. Instead, he started laughing. He couldn't stop it, he couldn't control it, and he certainly didn't think anything was funny, but everything seemed entirely laughable all the same. The mistress smacked him in the jaw. That stopped it well enough.

The mistress jerked him out of the fire and covered his ear with a damp cloth. It felt much smaller than before, and it smarted awfully. The mistress spread some foul-smelling chemical over it, saying it would prevent demonic infection.

"Now, take this," said the mistress, handing Numo a bit of black cloth, "and wind it around your face, so that only your eyes are showing."

Numo did as he was told.

"Good. Now, the beardservant has had his face burned off and can't talk anymore, so you mustn't speak either. Just go in, drug Goh and his wife, take the head, and get out." The mistress dropped a few vials into his palm. "Open these right into their nostrils. It's a mild sedative and stronger paralytic, but neither will last long, so you'll have to be fast. Don't inhale when you open them."

The mistress took a long breath. It caught somewhere in her throat and weltered its way back out in a fit of coughing. "Damn. Ugh." She spat and thumped herself on the chest. "So. You know the way to Goh's house? If you don't want a scuffle with the megalobats, you'll have to take the tunnel to my room. Go straight from my room to your hypocaust—do not go anywhere else in the house, do you understand?—and leave from the drakes' passage down there. And I suggest you go in and out of Goh's residence the same way. Security is up everywhere now, extra guards on any infandus-sized doorways and certainly the main floor, but my bet is that Goh doesn't have his guards on the drakes' underground service entrance."

Numo was skeptical. After all that had transpired at the Homomachy... "Why would he not?"

Kaizha shrugged. "Despite my best efforts, no one seems to believe that drakes are truly capable of deliberated murder." She gave him a horrible, pained smile. "Yet."

Numo might have had some emotions about that statement if he weren't so busy vibrating and imagining his arteries might be full of millipedes.

The mistress went on to give him instructions on making sure that Mistress Goh saw him in the act and suggested some objects he might find in the household to behead someone, but Numo's hearing seemed to be getting blurrier and his head filled with nonsense noises. His vision got so sharp that the details were deafening—er, disorienting. The taste of honey soaked his tongue, even though he hadn't had any. He wasn't sure if he was in real life or in a costume-play.

The mistress stopped talking and Numo was ready to launch himself into the air. Or run, whichever was more prudent.

"Are you ready, Numo?"

He jerked his head up and down in an attempt to nod.

"Good. Off you go then."

Numo's feet pattered softly against the cobblestones. The moon was a bare sliver. The streets looked very different in the dark without an angry mob to light them. But he knew to run uphill, at least.

As the highest seat on the council, Goh had the highest house in the city. The wealthy neighborhood of alchemists folded into the highest altitudes of the terraces of Mount Barisok, the street winding narrower along sheerer rock faces until it reached its summit: the temple of Moa, right where the terraces ended and the great crags of rock began. Goh's house was just next to the temple, so it would not be hard to find.

It was, however, a great pain to run to.

Guards were tightly packed around the human and infandus entrances. But, as with his own house, no one bothered to watch the drake's entrance to the hypocaust. Here it was merely a small door in the ground—one of those tunnel exits. Numo allowed a few minutes for his lungs to wheeze and clatter themselves into calm submission. His neck hurt—one of the holes had opened. Numo daubed at the hole with his finger until it stopped bleeding. He must look composed and proud. From what he'd seen, Reddles was ever thus, although he might be forgiven for being marginally less composed after having his face burned off.

Even so, excessive seepage was unseemly.

Numo strode into the tunnel. The warm glow at the end beckoned him like a moth to a lantern. He imagined that when he reached the end, he'd burn up and die. His feet slowed.

Hammerfist needs this.

The thought of her rekindled his energy and the dose of makhat burbling around in his blood. He puffed out his chest. Yes, he felt bigger and braver and more intimidating. He could do this. Goh deserved it, after all, didn't he, with his great self-important swagger and—

"Reddles?"

Numo was standing in the middle of the ovens. He must have walked much faster than he thought. In front of him was himself. No—another stoker. Numo had never met another stoker. He supposed most of them didn't get out of the hypocaust much. This one smelled wonderful, like ovens and fire and sap. Numo's eyes burned and his blood-tubes surged with longing. It was like home.

"Reddles, is that you? What are you doing down here? Is something the matter?"

Numo swallowed. His mouth was dry and his throat was crusted with aging blood. Most unappealing.

"Oh—I've forgotten," said the stoker. "You can't speak anymore, can you, poor creature." He slapped him on the back.

Numo nodded.

"Well, can you mime something? I do want to help you, sir, with whatever-your-needs."

Numo nodded. Then he shook his head. Nodded again. His head seemed to be bobbing around of its own accord and his nerves moving him like a shadow-puppet.

"I'm afraid I don't understand."

Numo thought. He rubbed his arms and feigned a shiver.

"Cold? The servants' quarters are cold?"

He shrugged.

"Odd. I only checked the fire for the servant's quarters but a short time past and it was of standard size and temperature."

Numo stared at him.

"I suppose I should check again. Perhaps I was mistaken, or there's something wrong with the vent..." The stoker shuffled away and disappeared in his own forest of ovenry. Numo missed it, his little maze of fire and metal, his wall of wood, his jars of sap...

He needed to focus. The head. Goh's head. He needed something to cut it with. The mistress had said this would be most prudent, that a drake running through the streets with a sword or somelike would draw too much attention, but how he wished he didn't need to make such decisions on his own.

Numo hurried over to the wall of logs. In the corner by the end, as in his own hypocaust, was a little rack of tools for wood-shaping, but the rack was woefully deficient: it contained only a hatchet and a hacksaw. It was artless hypocaust-keeping, to be sure. At least it narrowed his choices. But which one? Numo seemed to float up out of his body as he watched himself ponder which instrument was meet for the decapitation of a man in his bed.

"Reddles? Where'd you go?" The stoker was calling for him. Numo decided the hatchet looked a bit dull and went for the saw. He ducked low and crept along the wall. Eventually he should come to the doors that led up to the main floor, shouldn't he?

"My hacksaw! Reddles, did you take my hacksaw?" the stoker called. "What are you doing?"

Numo looked up from behind an oven. The stoker was wandering around yelling. He hadn't seen him yet. There was a door to a stairway a few paces away. Numo darted into it, hoping the steps led up to the master's quarters, or somewhere close by.

It didn't.

At the top of the stairs, he found the servants' quarters. A pile of sleeping homunculi, drakes and infandi, bedded in musty straw spread over the floor. The walls of the room were studded with doors that led to other areas of the house, with labels in human and infandus languages. Naturally, the one that led to the master's quarters lay diagonally across the room, through a clotted jungle of sleeping bodies that might strangle him if they woke up and realized what he was doing.

"Reddles?" A thumping footfall sounded from the bottom of the stairs. The stoker was coming. Numo had to go. Now.

He tiptoed around the sleeping bodies, carrying his hacksaw high above his head so as not to smack it into anyone. One of the infandi stirred. Numo froze. The stairs thumped. He ducked behind a large infandus and bid his muscles to stay still as logs.

"Reddles?" The stoker was at the top of the stairs now, peering out into the sleeping quarters, panting wetly.

"*Shhhtthhhaa*," mumbled an infandus.

"Beg your pardon," the stoker whispered. "It's just that I think Reddles has made off with my hacksaw. I don't quite understand it. But it seems to have happened nonetheless. Odd, isn't it? Wouldn't you think it odd?" He paused. "Does it seem cold up here to you? It doesn't seem very cold up here to me—rather the standard appointed temperature, I daresa—"

"*Hgrhaarr flsh.*" The infandus rolled over and shoved the stoker down the stairs.

Numo gasped and clapped a hand over his mouth. The stoker cried out after the first thump, but the rest of the thumps were devoid of any voice. *Thump thump bump bumblethump* he went, and with every sound Numo's alary muscles pounded into his sides until it seemed his ribs might crack.

And nothing. It was quiet.

Was he dead? Was Numo responsible? Had he just killed a fellow stoker?

Numo couldn't risk moving or calling out to make sure. He listened, for a time, but heard only a terrible nothing.

Numo wrung the handle of his hacksaw, his fingers

trembling. What was he doing here, if he was to torment and—by the gods—kill fellow drakes? And Reddles—

It hit him. In all his blind panic and disgust over the assassination itself, he'd missed it. What he was doing to Reddles now was not only odious, it was exactly—*exactly*—what the mistress had done to him.

Time stopped, briefly, while his head thundered with the magnitude of how thick he was.

Perhaps, if he begged, the mistress could find some way to save Reddles from the spindly hand of punitation—but why would she, even if she could? And what if Reddles was tortured or put to death…well, Numo thought, there was no "if" about it; it was more or less a certainty, unless Reddles had some way to escape before being captured.

He would have to wake Reddles on his way out and warn him to leave. That was the only thing for it. It was nothing for a homunculus to die, really, but Numo would not have anyone die on *his* behalf, not after the contemptible mess he'd already made. Not after Bollix…

The stirring infandus rolled over and sighed. Numo decided he must put the stoker behind him—after all, the drake might not be dead, only quiet, or too far away to be heard. He would check on the drake on the way out, and perhaps bring him to the mistress if he required alchemical treatment.

All would be well, he told himself, painfully aware he was using a very loose definition of "well."

He put the hacksaw in his mouth and crawled towards the master's door. Just outside of it was Reddles—or who he presumed to be Reddles, with most of his head blackly bandaged—sleeping upright against the wall. Numo opened the door slowly, carefully, so as not to wake him just yet. Then he trod on all fours up the long twisting stairway to the master's quarters.

After a very long plod that spent his breath, Numo arrived at the foot of Master Goh's bed. Unable to step forward, and unable to step back, he slid his hands up and down the blunt side of the blade.

Numo took a deep breath and fingered the vials of paralytic. If his love for Hammerfist wasn't real, then what he was about to do was the gravest sin he could commit. But if it was—if it was, then anything he did with her in his heart was exactly as it should be.

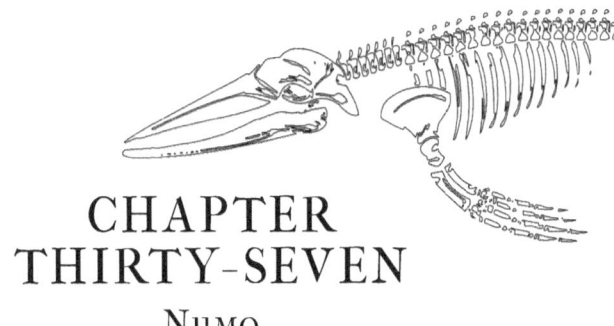

CHAPTER
THIRTY-SEVEN
Numo

RELEASING THE VIALS of mist was calm and uneventful. Master Goh snortled at it, and then sighed in his sleep. The Mistress Goh simply inhaled it. Numo counted in his head, as the mistress had told him to do. He was meant to count to one hundred. By twenty, his hands were shaking most powerful, and he had to put down the hacksaw atop the bearskin to avoid dropping it. By forty, Numo could hardly breathe. Black phlegm slid up and down his throat and plugged half his windpipe, but he didn't dare cough. His legs tingled. Eighty nearly had him puking on Goh's chest.

One hundred.

Wake the mistress.

Numo shook her. He slapped her. Her eyes cracked open in two foggy-looking slits of sentience.

Make sure she's neutralized.

She didn't move or speak; she barely seemed to notice him.

Sever the head.

Numo laid the hacksaw over Goh's neck and threw his body weight on top of it. He sawed. Blood gushed out in tiny founts, spewing out at Numo with every touch of the man's pulse. Goh's eyes opened—those same two foggy slits. Numo sawed. He coughed up the black phlegm. He sawed. Blood sprayed up into his nostrils and he sneezed it back out onto Goh's face. He sawed. The saw got stuck in bone.

Numo's eyes leaked. He tried not to whimper, but desperate and weird sounds came out of him. He threw himself on top of the saw again and again. He pressed so hard that his arms went numb. Goh opened his mouth. It was dark and black and wet inside, dripping like a cave.

"*Auuarghhh*—"

The spine gave way. The head came free. Numo threw up and the bandaging on his face kept it stuck there. His body went purpley-black with shame and his fingertips throbbed and all of the sick words in his sick brain seemed like poison.

He grabbed Goh's head by the beard and leapt down from the bed. He ran to the door, dragging the head in his wake.

Numo wrapped the beard around Goh's head, covering the dark death-filled maw with less morbid reddled hair. Then he tied it off and dragged it down the stairs behind him. *Thumpety thump thump thumpety thump thump.* It would wake up the servants, but his arms were weak. He couldn't carry such a ponderous thing. His legs barely kept him upright, wobbling like soggy noodles under his weight. *Thumpetybump.* Numo wished he could fling himself down the stairs. Just tie off the beard to his waist and not have to make such a percussion to announce his grievous misdeeds.

But then Hammerfist wouldn't get her head, and she wouldn't get transformed, and she wouldn't get healed.

He sucked in his breath. This head was his. He shouldn't be ashamed of it. It was a badge of his love. Fustilugs had said that love was higher than the gods, the song of the heavens… it was pure.

Numo did not feel pure.

He arrived at the bottom of the stairs, just before the door to the servants' sleeping-quarters. He took a moment to unwrap the bandages and wipe away the liquid disgorgements on his face—finding, perhaps a bit gruesomely, that Goh's beard was more absorbent than it looked—and then he recomposed himself, to the extent that he could manage such a thing, which required utterly forgetting that he'd just wiped his stomach contents off his skin with a beheaded man's facial hair.

He took a breath. He opened the door.

The homunculi were still asleep in their straw. Peaceful. Quiet. As though nothing had happened.

He still had to warn Reddles. Reddles would be quiet. Reddles was proud and dignified and serene. And his mouth was burned off besides.

Numo shook him awake. The drake blinked at him.

"Hello," Numo whispered. "Sorry for waking you. But I must tell you that you have to quit this place forthwith."

Reddles blinked.

"Your master is dead and you will be accused of murdering him. You must leave."

Reddles narrowed his eyes.

"Okay. Well then." Numo stood up. Reddles didn't move. Why didn't he move? Numo had been perfectly clear. Perhaps he was waiting for Numo to leave first. Polite-like. Of course. Reddles was gentlemanly and dignified. Numo nodded in deference, and then lifted the head above his own. It was heavy and horrible, and his legs trembled already, but he couldn't risk dragging it.

Reddles' eyes widened. He stopped breathing. Poor fellow—the shock of the thing must have been hideous.

"Terribly sorry," Numo whispered, and made his way across the room with great care. He was at top of the steps leading down to the hypocaust when he heard a stirring behind him. He turned.

Reddles collided with Numo at a dead sprint. The two of them tumbled down the stairs, becoming tangled in Goh's beard. The head hit the ground first and Numo bounced off Goh's cheek. He tried to stand but his feet were caught in the whiskers. Reddles pounced. He bounced Numo's head into the floor over and over.

Oh Nonnysteed, sweet Nonnysteed!

Numo rolled. He kept rolling. Reddles chased him, scrabbling to catch some body part. Numo hit something solid. He looked. He shouldn't have.

The stoker's body was warm—but then, he was next to an oven. His neck was warped and squashed, crammed partway down into his shoulders, like a crumpled paper puppet with a snapped frame. Numo squeezed his teeth together to keep from crying out. Reddles grabbed him by the arms and wrenched. Numo lashed out with one stumpy foot and clubbed Reddles right in his wounded mouth.

The drake squealed in pain, his hands fluttering over his face. Numo grabbed Goh's beard, pulled two hanks of hair over each shoulder, and ran. The head smacked into the ovens as he went, *clank clank thumpety bump bang*, with Reddles' feet pummeling along after. The head almost didn't fit through the exit, but Numo's muscles surged with newfound panic. He pulled and strained and the head came loose with a floppy sucking noise. Numo tore down the side of the street in the shadows of the mountain crag. Reddles was still squealing, still running, but the footfalls were slow and the exhalations so loud and belabored that Numo could hear them even above the by-now-tiresome bumping of the severed head.

A commotion clattered from Goh's household. Lights fired up behind Numo, casting shadows in front of him. Reddles' shadow grew longer and grayer in the warm glow. Then it fell away entirely. Before they were even far enough from the house...

Numo didn't care to be maimed to a doughy pulp, but if Reddles didn't keep running, he'd surely be caught and killed.

Numo turned. Reddles had sunk onto his knees in the middle of the street. He met Numo's eyes for just a flicker of a second. The misery in that flicker was heavier than any drake could bear.

He pulled out a large razor from his bandolier of beard maintenance instruments and flicked open the blade.

"Stop!" Numo disentangled himself from the beard and galloped back to Reddles. The drake stared at him wetly and drew the razor across his belly. Numo dove. He smacked the razor away and knocked Reddles to the ground. Shouts rose up from the house. Running footfalls. Man-boots. They were coming.

"Get up get up get up get up!" Numo yanked Reddles to his feet. The beardservant had cut himself thoroughly from under his ribs to his middle. Blood gently cascaded down his leg. There was no time to halt the bleeding. Numo pulled. Reddles crumpled.

He hesitated. Reddles was making the saving of his life quite difficult. Perhaps it wasn't even something that wanted saving. Perhaps it was more merciful to leave him.

But if Reddles was merely a victim of momentary passion—

Numo didn't know. There was no time to puzzle it out, and besides, he'd already caused the death of one innocent drake that night. He couldn't stomach another.

He dragged the drake bodily to Goh's head, tied him up tightly in a skein of beard, and wound the whiskers around his own chest. One deep breath and he could hear the guards grunting mere decitudes behind him.

He ran.

His legs were starved for rest, and his broken toes were stabbing into his feet, and his lungs felt like they were full of sand and hammers. But all of it was coated in a veil of panic and shivering desperation that kept his joints swinging and his blood shoving oxygen through his body. Through the town, through his depressingly ill-kept hypocaust, through the house, through a tunnel, into a shack, until the mistress put her foot in front of his body and he splatted on his face.

"Thank you, Mistress," he gasped. He tried to get up, but his arms went limp and his legs fizzed with numb unresponsiveness. His whole body was its own pulse, throbbing in time with its fruitless gasps for air. The mistress was saying something, but Numo's ears may as well have been full of spider silk. His vision faded. Something wet sprayed in his face and his throat bucked backwards like a goat bouncing off another's skull in rutting season. His airway untrammeled itself somehow and he coughed up blobules of phlegm, gulping down the sweet air between.

Numo finally managed to force himself upright. The mistress straddled her stool, fiddling with something on the table, and her two infandi hovered around her. Goh's head was staring at him. Reddles—Reddles was the thing on the table being fiddled with.

Numo sidled up to the mistress's feet, dragging his much-pummeled bad foot like a stump on a chain. "Is he alive?"

"For the moment."

"Can you help him?"

"I'm not sure, Numo—Mozeh was always better at such things, and his equipment's not available to me—well, I'm not sure, Numo." She paused. "Is that why you came back here? Running through the whole city and risking getting caught just to save him?"

"I didn't want—I didn't want to do to him what…" He wasn't sure how to finish the sentence.

"What I did to you."

Numo didn't answer. "Can I see him?"

The mistress gave him a sad look. "You're sure you want to do that to yourself?"

Numo nodded. The mistress picked him up and placed him on the desk, just under the chin of the bearded infandus. Reddles was pale, almost greenish. The mistress had removed the cloth that was over his face. She'd put some bandage or plaster over his gut, but it was still bleeding. He had hardly any life in his eyes, but the pupils aimed themselves at Numo. Reddles raised an arm, the wrist limp. He reached up. His arm suddenly seized into a rigid thing, his fingers going clawed, their stained tips pawing upward in desperation. His eyelids snapped back so far they seemed to recede into his head. Numo flinched, but he stood his ground. The drake would tear his face to tatters and he deserved it. Numo might have had the same impulse if someone other than his mistress had killed his own master, and if he were a gentleman, he'd wait for his comeuppance and let his face get shredded into a lace-patterned mess.

But Reddles' hand shot past his face. The drake shoved himself upright to reach the larger infandus's beard. The mistress opened her mouth as if to object, but instead her mouth twitched, and she merely pressed harder on the drake's bandaged gut. When Reddles' fingers connected with the grizzled black and white strands, his mouth twitched and his eyes leaked anew. His fingers twiddled around in the beard, and his eyes marveled and sluiced as though he were looking at Nonnysteed himself, or whatever spirit was dearest to a beard-servant's heart.

Numo knew that look. He knew it because that look was palpable on his own face whenever he was around Hammerfist. He could feel it in Reddles—whatever caused that look. It was inane and inexplicable and ineffable, and utterly confusing.

And Reddles, who had only minutes earlier ripped himself open with a razor for love of his master, was deep in—in *something*—

Reddles drew a razor from his bandolier and whipped his hand in a line just under the infandus's chin. The infandus howled and flinched away, patting at his face as if to check for blood. Reddles clutched the liberated beard to his chest, nuzzling the whiskers, taking deep, shuddering breaths of euphoric relief.

A viciously adhesive malignancy grew on Numo's chest, clogging up his internal pathways. Could the love of a slave for his master be so easily transferred? To *beard-whiskers*, of all things? Could something so profound be that wanton and senseless? Did it really mean anything if it could jump from thing to thing like a flea?

That was all it was, the slave-love. A flea. A parasite. Some disease of his brain-folds. It wasn't real.

Reddles gave a last heaving breath and flopped backwards onto the table. The mistress pressed a finger under his armpit and his stomach and his groin, where his pulses should have been.

"I'm sorry, Numo…" The mistress coughed and sat herself upright. Numo stared at her. She seemed so different, like a well-groomed mountain rhino degenerated into a diseased skeleton. As if he'd descended to the twelfth hell, where all good things turned into their opposite; where ice burned you and fire chilled you and honor was a fungus that rotted your innards. Was his love for her a flea or a song of the heavens? And Hammerfist…

His duty to her would never change, not after what he'd done. But he had to know. He had to know what was real. Hammerfist did not want him a slave, and a slave he wouldn't be.

"Mistress," he said, his voice deep and sure, and seeming to come from some other voice flaps than his own.

"Yes, Numo?"

"You mentioned an experiment that might determine whether I felt real love for my—for Hammerfist. Whether or not I am still merely a slave to a different mistress."

The mistress nodded. "I also mentioned that it could kill you."

"Yes. In that instance, I would expect, since you have

done her so many wrongs, that you would act in my stead and bring her this severed pate, so that her life may yet be saved. I would expect you to do this because I believe you still have some honor and feeling left in you."

The Mistress looked astounded. Galled, even. "Numo, I've never heard you speak this way."

"I know." Numo's body was shaking, but his mind was steady, as steady as it had ever been, as though cold water had been thrown over it. "It does not matter. I want to do this experiment, but I must have your word this head will be delivered into the hands of Hammerfist, come what may."

"Hammerfist."

"Yes."

The mistress's nostrils flared. Her eye darted left and right. Her body seemed to go weak, and for a moment Numo thought she might fall. Her mouth moved soundlessly and formed words that may have been "I had no idea" or "amenorrhea" or somelike. But she recovered, and her face hardened.

"Tell me what she looks like and how to find her, and I promise I will do as you say."

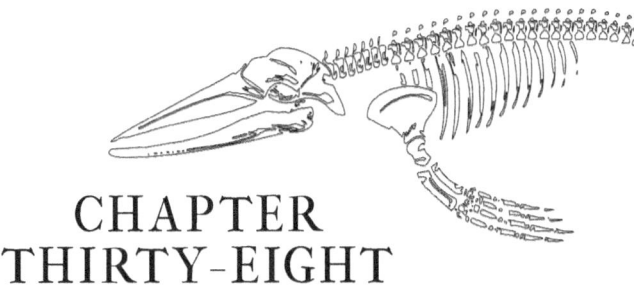

CHAPTER
THIRTY-EIGHT
HAMMERFIST

Hammerfist's body was weak, but Rawang was weaker.

It was easy to outrun him, but not to lose him. He'd find her trail. She couldn't help but destroy everything in her path, tearing up the grass and scraping the rocks and snapping branches and leaving bits of her mane behind as the trees tore out her hair. It was simply the nature of this miserable body. But she could still get there first, and really, it was much better for him for them to be apart.

She'd nearly killed him when he told her. When she finally woke up from the pall of blackness that her brain spread over her and found out everyone was gone—that Numo was gone— and that Rawang had sent Numo to collect a *severed head* of all things—

Numo was not a murderer. Numo was a poor innocent thing. And if she didn't get to him in time, he would die for some pointless exercise in getting her brain back.

Hammerfist crashed into a ditch and caught a snoutful of dirt. Numo's scent trail vanished from her senses as she sneezed and spat. To stop moving for even an instant sent her heart careening into a frantic sputter and she had to count her breaths to keep herself from hyperventilating. With the dirt gone, she snuffed the scent back up—tree sap, dried drake blood, dirt, and that lingering smell of ovens and burning wood.

She ran for hours. It was dawn when she found herself sprinting into a hive of megalobats. The ones that were awake screeched in alarm and woke the whole pack. They swooped down from the trees and tore at her hide, drawing bits of blood, pinging off the armor on her shoulders and arms, scraping their claws against the eye-protectors that flared out from her skull. Hammerfist crushed a few, separated some limbs from some bodies, but kept her eyes and nose to the ground, her heart fluttering in her throat. If Numo had come through here, he'd be dead, almost certainly—poor sweet Numo couldn't defend himself, not against these things—but the trail kept going straight through the megalobats' territory.

A bat tore a chunk out of her back leg and she stumbled. She wasn't quite sure how to respond except to tear the bat's head from its body and fling it at one of its pack-mates.

The cloud of bats in front of her dissipated for an instant. A tumbledown shack came within view. But Numo's scent trail went around the side of it.

It ended. She stopped. She huffed, sliding her breath in and out, trying to find where the trail had gone. She heard a human inside saying, *Spittle, will you go see what that commotion is.*

The trail went up the side of the shack, hovering around a window. She looked. Numo was inside. But there was a human inside, too.

A drooling infandus popped its head out of the window and glared at her. It opened its mouth as if to say something.

Panic surged in Hammerfist's brain and the world went red. She shoved the infandus's face back inside and crashed through the window, enlarging the hole by several degrees and taking some chunks of the wooden wall with her. The infandus struck out, but she was smaller. Much smaller.

The red in Hammerfist's eyes fizzled darker and darker, her vision receding into a tunnel. She'd kill this infandus, this thing that dared to challenge her. She'd bash in her skull and use the shards to carve up the brain-meat. She'd smear her on the walls and use her skin as a snuggling-blanket. She'd—

"Hammerfist!"

Numo.

He was strapped to a table. A well-dressed woman held a thin dagger or a needle or some tiny blade to his face.

"Let go of him," Hammerfist said. Nothing happened, but maybe the woman didn't understand; she couldn't tell if she was high-born enough a human to have learned to understand infandi. She tried to speak human, but it only worked out to grumbles and growls. Damn her mangled jaw. Hammerfist lumbered towards the woman and drew herself up, rolling her shoulders back, and tried to make it very very clear. "*Let go of him.*"

"It's okay, Hammerfist," Numo said. The woman said nothing. But she didn't lower the dagger. "It's okay," Numo said again.

Why in the spotted dicks of the eighth hell would it be okay? Hammerfist glared at the two of them. There was something odd in Numo's expression.

"Is this your mistress?" Hammerfist said.

Numo nodded.

So that was why. Numo, poor Numo, still a slave, still stuck with his collar and his slave-thoughts and his horrible artificial devotion, was going to allow his mistress to stick a knife in his face simply because she was his mistress.

"Allow me to fix that," said Hammerfist. She pounded her claws into the woman's torso. The woman's back slammed into a stonemetal box. The box fell off its stand and the boiling contents spilled over parts of the woman's body. She screamed. Something white and shimmery writhed out of the box and onto her arm. Sickening cracks and ripping noises came from inside the woman's body. Before Hammerfist could turn and help Numo down from the table, a flail of muscley tendrils pounded into her.

Hammerfist was crushed into the floor, the wooden boards cracking under her. Her lungs flattened and her breath left her gasping and choking. She'd never felt anything like that—no other infandus had ever managed to hit her that hard. Not even the whippings laid her so low. An entirely new kind of pain juddered through her spine and scrambled her brain. She tried to move her arms but her toes waggled instead. She tried to force her legs upright but her tongues shot out and searched over the floor for purchase. She tried to blink and her arms flexed.

Numo was screaming—at her, at his mistress, she didn't even know; her ears seemed to be turning all the words backwards as they received them. The woman was wide-eyed and gasping like a fish on a dry beach, her skin giving off the smell of boiled chicken and mineralized hot springs. Numo clambered off the table and grabbed Hammerfist's arm, but she felt his fingertips in her chest. He tried to move her. She was too big. She was huge and monstrous and he was small and sweet and had part of his ear burned off. When had that happened?

A man crashed through the hole in the wall. Rawang. Rawang had found her. The bad half of his face twitched.

"What happened? What did you do to—to her..." His eyes traveled from Numo to Hammerfist to the woman panting and gasping and groaning in a puddle of odd-smelling fluid with a many-tendriled white thing stuck to her arm. Her eyelid—just one, for the other was plastered over—fluttered as though she were fighting to stay conscious. The two other infandi in the room shrank back. Hammerfist hadn't even noticed the second one.

Rawang walked over to something hairy and lumpy on the floor. He picked it up. It was a severed head with a tremendous beard. Snowflies orbited the mouth.

Numo had cut off a man's head. For her.

Not for some glorious cause, but for her.

Oh gods... The nausea burbled up and down inside her with the acid tang of fodderless bile. She wasn't sure when she'd last eaten.

Rawang tromped over and grabbed Hammerfist's arm. "Are you hurt?" he asked.

Hammerfist tried to speak. Instead, her arms pushed her off the floor. She was in a crouch, somehow, but she wasn't sure how to go from there.

"Are you hurt?" Rawang repeated. Hammerfist didn't dare move. Rawang grabbed her arm and yanked her upright. The effort instantly rendered him breathless.

"Come on," he gasped. He pulled her forward. Her feet

stumbled automatically.

Hammerfist's body seemed to be recalibrating. But she couldn't make it resist him; she couldn't make it pull backwards. She tried to speak and her tongues waggled soundlessly. Numo was still standing there, staring at his mistress, at a book on the table, at the thin dagger on the floor.

"Are you all right?" she heard him say. From the corner of her eye, Hammerfist saw the woman's mouth twitch. "I hope you don't mind if I take these," he said. He tore out a page from the book and picked up the dagger. Why? What was he doing? Was he going to kill himself too? She couldn't have that—not for her, not on her behalf. She'd yell at him the moment her voice worked again.

Rawang dragged her out, the head dangling from his wrist like a bangle, and picked his way across the clot of dismembered megalobat bodies. Numo followed behind, plodding, dragging the dagger at his side, and staring rapt at the piece of paper. When the sun lanced through it properly, Hammerfist could almost see what was drawn on it.

It looked like a diagram of a brain.

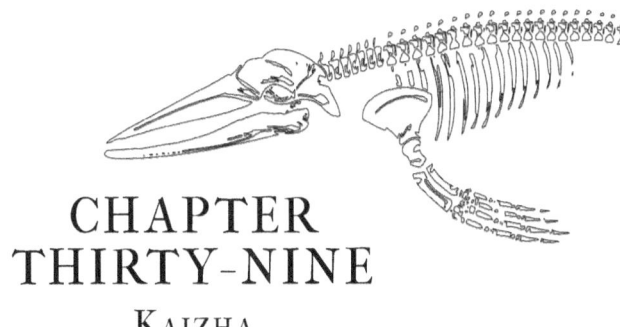

CHAPTER THIRTY-NINE
KAIZHA

KAIZHA COULDN'T BREATHE or see or speak or think. That could have been partially a result of getting her whole upper body punched by a huge battle-infandus with enormous badger-claws, but most of the pain was erupting out of her arm. Like sulfuric gas being pumped directly up her nostrils, it overwhelmed her senses and drowned her.

Six's bony infandus hands wrapped around her shoulders and lifted. A stool was put beneath her. Her head fell and thumped on the desk, in the middle of the sticky purple drake blood.

The thing's veiny little tendrils had not only shot through her palm and her arm, but wrapped around the inside of her shoulder and seeped into her chest. Into her mammaries. It was sucking at her but there wasn't anything there. Yet. There was an odd tingling and her breasts ached. Her entire chest felt inflamed and swollen, as if there was barely any room for her heart to keep beating. And everything below the chest was flattened—ribs smashed and poking into other organs, or so it felt like. She slumped out of the stool and lay on the floor. She waved the infandi away with some fingertips that still worked.

Her body was warm, full of fervid biting heat, draining.

Fury wracked her head. *This* is how it would end? One punch from an infandus. And at the one time she wasn't even doing anything *that* morally questionable. Before she could save Moaki from itself; before she could restore her city to what it was; before any of her work was done. Her whole life would culminate in senseless murder and a soiled silk dress, having done nothing and no one but her husband and pointless musical instruments.

And Bollix...

As if it felt her thoughts, the monstrosity on her arm twitched and tingled. Sadness flowed from it. Pity. Sympathy, even. And then something more substantial.

More tendrils inside her, like branches of nerves, traveling down her chest and into her ribs. Wrapping themselves around her broken bones and her wasted lungs. Moving them—

Kaizha screamed. She dug her nails into the floor and flailed and the infandi came and held her down but nothing could keep her from full-bodied writhing. The creature was rearranging her broken parts from the inside, welding her back together with white searing agony. When it was done, she spasmed over and over as if she were in the final throes of blood-fever. Maybe she was.

A moment passed. She didn't die. In fact, she felt rather improved. Exhausted, half-dead, but much improved, rather like she might have felt after a protracted and violent episode of the flux.

It was morning. Goh's guards would be knocking at her door soon with some pointless thing like breakfast. She had to get back to the house.

With some difficulty, she managed to create enough words that the infandi could understand her. They lifted her delicately and began taking her back down the tunnel, but the bastards stopped every time pain registered on her face, which was every other second or so. Still, they were most of the way down the tunnel when she heard the faraway tinkle of the bell inside her room signaling someone at her front door.

"Run!" she commanded.

The infandi managed to race the rest of the way, deposit her on the floor of her room, and disappear back into the tunnel before the guards at the door of her chambers grew tired of knocking.

"Mistress, I must insist you answer; if you do not, we will be forced to enter…"

She had nothing in her to get on the bed or look presentable. She was smeared with blood and had a wriggling white tentacled creature stuck to her arm sucking desperately at her throbbing breasts from the inside like some kind of teat-leech.

This would be quite difficult to explain.

The door hinges creaked. Kaizha yanked the bearskin cover off her bed, spread it over herself, and shut her eye.

"M…Em, Mistress Shanyang? Are you all right?"

Kaizha let her eye crack open and inhaled as deeply as she could, as she'd often done upon waking. But inhaling deeply resulted in coughing and a horrible tear of pain whipping across her body.

"Oh." The guard ran to her side and knelt down. "Mistress, are you hurt? Are you ill? Shall I fetch a doctor?"

"No. I mean yes, I am ill, and hurt, but not in any novel

way. I was wounded in the fire. Bit of a fever from demonic infection, I gather…"

The guard laughed nervously and shuffled away a bit. "So I—should I get a—"

"No. I don't need a doctor. I just need to be left alone."

"I see." But he didn't go away.

"What?"

"It's just that I've been told to summon you. Mistress Goh is at the door and she has need of you. She seems very distraught. She said it was an emergency."

"Sooth and balls…" Kaizha murmured.

"I'm sorry?"

"I can't come to see her. I am ill."

The guard finally seemed to accept this and left. Kaizha moaned and rolled over. There was no side of her body that it didn't hurt to lie on, but she could at least shift the pain around. Her breasts felt swollen to bursting. She could feel liquid percolating up her chest and into her shoulder and down her arm through the infinitesimal foreign tubes in her body. Some bestial instinct wanted to claw the things out of her own flesh.

The guard came back. "I'm sorry, Mistress, but—"

A small woman in mourning-garb barged past him. She whipped the sackcloth off her head. "I am very sorry for the inconvenience, and for being so inappropriate in my behavior," she began. "Are you quite unwell?"

"Quite, Halin." Halin Goh was small and shrinking and quiet, normally. Today her voice seemed to be vaulting out of her.

"I am so sorry to hear that. And I am so sorry to intrude,

but—can I help you to your bed?"

"No." Kaizha drew the bearskin tighter. "No. Getting up is not something I want to do."

"I am very sorry to hear that indeed." Halin rubbed at her neck. A nervous habit she had; something she did quite often when she was forced to appear at parties.

"Stop apologizing," Kaizha said. "Why are you here?"

"All right." Halin stood there and fiddled with her gloves. Then her head bobbed back up. "My husband was murdered last night."

"Gods have mercy on us," said Kaizha, hoping she sounded dramatic enough. "I'm so—"

"Please don't." Halin stared emptily at the bedpost. "Sympathies are painful for me to endure right now. We must look to the practical matters at hand. The city is imploding. My husband was not the only one murdered last night. A band of fallen infandi stormed Bianfu's house—most of them exports. Escapees. One or two got away. Most of them were killed by the guard but—but not before they murdered Bianfu."

Well. Kaizha certainly hadn't planned for that.

"Our first, second, and third seats are murdered. Huli and his wife died in the fire. Fourth seat gone. And the human race did not exactly secure a victory in the Homomachy."

Kaizha forced herself upright, leaning against the bedpost and pulling the bearskin around her. She tried to look the opposite of delighted. Her stare fixed on the whorls in the floorboards.

"You understand the severity of the situation," Halin continued. "We must have an emergency meeting. What remains of the oligarchy must convene, to find new leaders, to restore order. I am sorry to say that even us—us wives—we now are essential attendees. Our numbers are much diminished. We must find a way to bring this under control or we will lose Moaki." Halin bent down and pulled Kaizha's chin up, forcing her gaze away from the floor. The woman's eyes were practically vibrating out of their cubby-holes, wet and worried and raw, but full of measured fire. Kaizha would almost be titillated if—well, if there were very different circumstances. "You must come. The guards will escort you. Namkeng is in charge of the city guard now; he will bend the terms of the house arrest for me. You must come."

This was it. This was the day that Moaki's future would be decided, and all Kaizha wanted to do was pass out on the floor in a soiled dress. But she had to go. Kaizha had to convince the rest of them. "I understand. Give me a few minutes to compose myself. I will come to your home as swiftly as I am able."

"Oh, no, not my home. My home is—it is tainted." Halin's eyes puddled up with tears and she rubbed them angrily. "We are meeting at the house of the fifth seat. The only seat left." Halin sniffed and inhaled sharply. "Thank you. Thank you for agreeing to come. Excuse me now—I have to go get the others."

Halin swept out of the room, pulling the sackcloth back over her head, and the guard left Kaizha alone after that. She slid back to the floor, her head swirling. The house of the fifth seat. She had to go to the house of the fifth seat.

The fifth seat was Turian. Xiongnyao's husband.

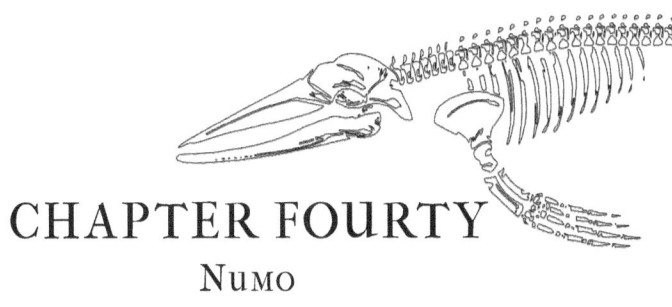

CHAPTER FOURTY
Numo

NIGHT HAD FALLEN again before Rawang would stop. Numo supposed it was for the best, but they'd passed two perfectly good streams—or perhaps the same stream twice—and he was desperate to fling himself into some body of water, so as to rinse the dirty sullied impurity from his body. Bloody beard-hairs stuck to his skin and he couldn't seem to peel them off. All the while Hammerfist glowered at him from Rawang's side as he dragged her, as if evaluating Numo, or reviling him, or puzzling over him, or possibly even fretting. He had no idea. He had done many foolish things, and now a gruesome thing, and yet she had come for him. But he didn't ask—even if he could find the words, he couldn't make them. He couldn't even ask if she was all right. After the mistress's drugs sweated out of his body, he hardly had the life in him to stay on his feet, and his lungs hurt awfully. He imagined air burning up inside them, shimmering with heat like his ovens in a snowstorm.

When they did stop, there was a small pool of water nearby, but Rawang wouldn't let him bathe. "We need to drink out of that," he said.

Numo flopped to the ground, his legs too weak to lower

him properly. Hammerfist's eyes glowed in the twilight. Smartly, deeply. Full of—of something. She hadn't spoken to him, either. But she might not have had control of her tongue. Her body seemed discombobulated, though eventually she'd managed to move under her own power. Numo wasn't sure what the mistress had done to her. If whatever it was turned out to be permanent, well, he would be extremely cross at the mistress about that.

Extremely cross.

He looked at the head sitting at Rawang's feet and imagined it was the mistress.

His throat jolted. Had Numo become *that sort* of creature?

Rawang handed Numo a handful of berries. "I found these earlier. I don't know if they're poisonous or not. Want some?"

Numo shook his head. He gasped to suck in more air. There never seemed to be enough these days. He cleared his throat, opened his mouth, and prepared to say—

"*Nmhhaa*," said Hammerfist. Her eyes smoldered. "What is that paper and *shrrr* for?"

Numo's mouth snapped shut. A weight fell upon his throat as though he'd swallowed a stump.

Rawang glanced over at her. "What did you say, sweetheart?"

Hammerfist repeated herself. Her voice rose higher and louder at the end, and Numo felt he was shrinking, smaller and smaller, wishing he'd disappear, and not quite understanding why.

"Paper? What paper?" Rawang whipped his head around to Numo. "Let me see it."

Numo stiffened. He tightened his fist around the roll of paper. Rawang would call him stupid again. Rawang would yell at him and call his love a lie and call him a brain-deficient slave. And he'd had enough. Numo was taut as a wire, worn as a cliff face, tired as a beermonger on the solstice. One more gust of wind and he'd snap like a shoddy laundry-pole.

"Come now. Let me see it." The good half of the doctor's face softened.

"Let him see it, Numo," Hammerfist prodded.

Numo held out the paper. Rawang took it from him gently, squinting, turning it this way and that until his expression lit.

"These are diagrams of a drake's brain. An alchemist's diagrams! These are…I've been looking for a reference like this for years."

"Why do you have it?" Hammerfist growled. She loomed up over Numo, blocking out the moon.

"Well, I—I wanted to test my own brain."

"What do you mean *tsshhhh?*"

Numo glanced at Rawang. His face had grown very serious again. "Yes, Numo. What do you mean?"

Numo cleared his throat. His body was twitching and prodding him to shy back from Hammerfist, to run and never speak of his sordid brain again. But Numo found himself sidling closer. He took the end of her claw and patted it, wondering if she could feel it.

"I feel—certain things—for you," he began. "I feel that…I feel that my greatest happiness would be your happiness. I hold you in my thoughts even when I don't know I'm having them." Hammerfist's body stiffened and her finger tugged away, but he clasped it harder, digging shallow cuts into his palms. "I would throw myself on a fire to warm you and I don't know why. *He* says that it is a trick of my slave-brain. That I've only bound myself to you as I would to my master—that my brain has malfunctioned and switched its object of devotion.

"But—but someone else has told me that it is love."

Hammerfist flinched away, yanking her hand from his, gouging a deep slice into the meat at the base of his thumb. Numo's mouth went dry and phlegmy at the same time. He swallowed and ahemed. Hammerfist said something, grunting and bellowing and gekkering so rapidly he could barely understand her—something about "don't" and "I'm lost" and "don't" again. There were many "don't"s.

"I just want to know which it is," Numo said, batting his knuckles together, kneading his fingers to keep them from trembling. "So I asked the mistress, and she said there might be a way to—to kill the slave part of the brain. With a very small dagger. And brain diagrams..."

Hammerfist howled a terrible, wordless howl. Birds fluttered away in twittering clouds. She snatched the paper away from Rawang and stuffed it in her mouth.

"No!" Numo ran to her, not knowing what he expected to do when he got there. He stopped. He dropped his arms and stared into her eyes. "No. Please. Please don't."

Hammerfist chewed once.

"Please! I—I—don't you understand?" The panic trilled in Numo's head and drowned out his sense. The words he meant to be saying were banging around his brain like tiny swallows trapped in a bronze bell.

He clutched the sides of his head and squeezed, then let go.

"You wanted to die to escape being a slave," he said finally. "You would die. I agreed to help you, if that was what you wanted. I agreed to help you die. I would do anything to help you be happy. And now, when—when I finally understand what it is like to want to be severed from it myself, and *you* wish to prevent me…" His breaths pronked and pitched and seesawed through him and he couldn't talk anymore. He could only put his face in his hands and try to stop up the wetness spilling from his eyes.

Something poked his shoulder. Numo looked up. Hammerfist held out a chewed and sodden wad of paper.

"You're right," she said slowly. "It's your choice."

"Now hang on," Rawang said. "It's not fair to let him do such a thing, if it's only about you, darling."

"It's not," she said.

"But it is. Perhaps we weren't listening to the same speech? I understand you do get confused, sweetheart. You had a muddle of a head even before the transmogrification."

Hammerfist was quiet. Her head sagged a few millitudes.

"You should know by now, Numo, but your brain is rather small and slow and fat-sheathed, so I shall make it plain," said Rawang. "When we take this head to Trago, and the alchemist reverses the transmogrification, your Hammerfist will cease to be, and my Sramai will return. She will be my wife again. I can give her that. I can give her another chance at a normal human life, and a family. You—you won't be a part of that equation."

Hammerfist's lip raised in a snarl. She rumbled, but she didn't lift her head. Her shoulders seemed to be receding into her, her body wilting in Rawang's shadow.

"Well, not much of it, anyway," Rawang added. "I suppose you're still welcome to pick flowers, drop them at our door— whatever silly things you do. But a drake and a human together who are not slave and master is wrong, Numo, and I know you know it is so."

It was so. It felt like a river-python crushing his chest and collapsing all his organs into fine sand, but it was so. Numo plopped his rump on the ground and stared at Rawang's shins. He'd never felt so small.

"I do hope you understand. Being a human again is her chance to be happy. The fall will be gone from her head, and she won't have to be burdened with the hell of being an infandus anymore. She'll be happy, Numo. But she'll be happy whether you truly love her or not. And, personally, were I you—under the circumstances—I'd prefer not to know which it is."

Numo gazed up at Hammerfist. She gave a quick bow of affirmation. "I'm sorry," she said. "I'm not good for you, and I just want the pain to stop, I just want to make up for the things I've done, *gglrhss*, I need *tshkii*, another chance..."

Numo suddenly felt as though he were underwater, looking up at a rippling image shadowed by the glare of the sun, moving in slow motion. He nodded, his head floating up and down. They were right. They were both right. It hurt worse than the megalobat scratches, worse than the burns, worse than his fingers and toes breaking and worse than seeing his master's dead body and worse than the mistress saying he was the cause of that deadness and worse than killing Reddles.

But it was meet. It was certainly better than Hammerfist killing herself. And Numo would see it to the bitter end.

"Yes," he said. "You deserve to have your pain gone and to be as you once were."

Hammerfist sagged and her body heaved with a powerful grunt. "I'm so sorry." She let loose another rapid-fire barrage of sounds and words that Numo couldn't follow. Something about how he'd suffer anyway, how she was violent and sick and bad, how she was a monster and not okay and none of it was okay, and a slew of other things besides. Her voice got higher and hoarser and by the end she could barely say anything between the snorts and grunts and huffs and the mucous pouring out of her giant nostril. Numo didn't understand entirely, but he understood that she was very sad, and he was very sad, and Rawang stood there grinning like a demon who'd just farted into the soul of a newborn child.

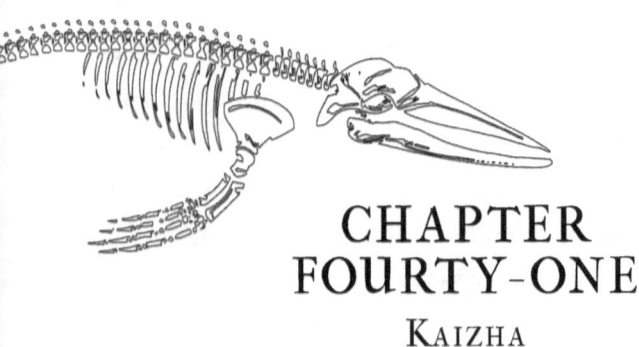

CHAPTER FOURTY-ONE
KAIZHA

KAIZHA MADE HER way down the hill in the back of a goat-drawn trap. The distance was not far, but she didn't dare trust her own feet, and when she'd asked a guard to pull a rickshaw he'd looked at her like she was sprouting nostrils in her eyelids.

"Don't you have slaves?"

Clearly her message of terror hadn't gotten to the lower classes yet. It made her nervous. But, she reasoned, no one of the lower classes would be at the meeting.

The trap joggled over the stones, stabbing her thorax with fresh hell. The teat-leech on her arm wriggled underneath the bandages she'd plastered around it, jostling in the sling she'd cobbled together out of Mozeh's summer pants. Thankfully, almost no one had seen her since the fire, so it wouldn't be difficult to pretend that the arm had been hopelessly injured.

Except for the troublesome complication of Xiongnyao.

Kaizha's head was a jungle of beasts and their incessant howls. She hadn't even processed the incident with Numo yet, or tested out the creature suckling at her teats, or contemplated what fraction of that creature was Bollix and if that fraction should love her or hate her, or, on a related note, determined if she was going to die or not. And now she had to figure out how to shut Xiongnyao up without killing her in front of several witnesses. More importantly, she had to figure out how to get the surviving council members to see what she saw—to want to bring Moaki back to its former self. To reverse the social reformation. To end the sullied business of slavery and bring back war. To do what Xiongnyao had roundly rejected doing, even though she was exactly the sort of woman Kaizha would think ideal to the task...

She felt quite dejected about it, still, when she had a moment's peace to feel anything.

In any case, it all had to be done. And done with, she hoped, more planning and foresight than what she'd attempted with Xiongnyao before. But trying to tear out a single strand of thought to formulate a coherent plan of attack was like trying to find a droplet of spit in a lake.

Now she was out of time. The goats came to a halt before a modestly-appointed house.

The Haishings' residence was much smaller than her own, and some of its clay roof tiles seemed to be on the verge of disintegrating. Kaizha dismounted, tried to steady herself, and knocked. A drake answered.

So Xiongnyao was stubbornly hanging onto her slaves, even after all the fearmongering. It was not what she had hoped, but about what she expected.

Trust my slaves with my life, indeed. Infandi too, from the looks of the servants darting about in the shadows with trays and brooms. Fearmongering or no, there *had* been an attempted revolution and a firm majority of oligarchs murdered—and it was plain lunacy to place that much confidence in anything created by Turian. What a good wife Xiongnyao was, trusting her husband's abilities like that.

Disappointing.

The drake led her into the dining-room. Turian was at the head of the table, sipping his drink. Xiongnyao and Halin were on either side of him, talking too low for Kaizha to hear. The former appeared wan and tremulous, with a faint slick of sweat upon her face and a ridge of thick bandaging underneath the bosom-area of her dress, but unfortunately nowhere near death's door. Bianfu's wife, Matang, stared ahead vacantly. Across from her was some young woman Kaizha might have seen once or twice but didn't remember.

Halin raised her head and gestured to the empty seat next to her. "Thank you so much for coming, Mistress. Take a seat, please."

Kaizha sat.

Xiongnyao nudged her husband. He swallowed and set down his drink. Kaizha had only rarely heard Turian speak, and whatever he said was never memorable.

"Ladies," he said. He gazed around the room, his laryngeal prominence twitching up and down. "I am so sorry for your losses." His eyes landed on the unfamiliar young woman. "Who are you?"

Xiongnyao's mouth hardened. "I told you when she came in, dear…that is Lili, the representative of the Huli house. Their only child."

"Right, yes, you did tell me. I'm sorry, dear. Welcome, um, daughter of Huli."

Lili nodded. Her eyes didn't betray much of anything.

Turian took another sip of his drink and tapped the empty

cup on the table. A slave scurried out to refill it. "We are facing a crisis. I think we are all aware of this crisis. This crisis has taken its toll on all of us. And we must find a way to handle this crisis." He sat back in his seat and folded his hands over his belly. "Em. Discuss."

Xiongnyao exhaled sharply. "Tell them our idea, Turian."

"Oh. Yes. Our idea. Our idea is that…is that *women*," he said, squinting at Xiongnyao curiously, "should be allowed to assume proper seats in the oligarchy. Right?"

"Temporarily. Because of the dire nature of the situation, yes. Yes, Turian. Well done," said Xiongnyao.

Kaizha was taken aback. Perhaps her drug-addled implorations hadn't gone completely to waste, after all.

"You can't be serious." Lili's voice was small and her eyes weren't looking at anyone, or even in the general direction of anyone. "We can't be trusted with something like that."

"I agree," said Matang. Her nose twitched. "I'm not even sure why we're having this meeting. Turian ought to call upon the living males of any alchemist or priestly families to create a temporary council to handle this. Or hand-pick candidates from the Holy Academy. Proper ones."

Halin sniffed. "How odd that the first two of us to offer an opinion say that women shouldn't be allowed to have opinions."

"Of all things a woman should have an opinion on, it's when her opinions are not needed." Lili folded her arms and continued to look out the window.

"Makes sense, I'm sure," Xiongnyao grumbled. She rubbed her face wearily. "So that's two against, three in favor. Mistress Shanyang?"

Kaizha blinked. For the immediate future, it almost seemed

303

as if…as if Xiongnyao, together with Halin, was her best hope.

It was extremely depressing.

"In favor," she said.

"Sure, all the old people…"

"Lady Huli, if you don't feel comfortable offering any opinions, you are free to leave," Halin said.

Lili sat still.

"Old people!" Xiongnyao snuffed. "Mistress Shanyang is the only one here who remotely fits that description."

Kaizha tried to keep her swimming head focused. "That's true. And as the only really *old person* here, I have a few other proposals, based on what has worked in the past."

"Turian hasn't asked for other proposals yet."

"I believe he said 'discuss.'"

Turian licked the sides of his empty glass and nodded. "Discuth."

Xiongnyao shot him a look. "Turian…"

"I think it's reasonable. After all, Mistress Shanyang is the most senior member of the oligarchy, now." Halin gave her a deferent nod. "Let's hear what she has to say."

"Thank you." Kaizha felt very out-of-it, as though she were inhabiting some other plane of being where it made sense to beg a room full of salted slugpates to listen to something reasonable. "I think that not only should women be allowed to assume seats on the oligarchy, but they should take it back in full."

Halin's brow furrowed. "Well, now, I don't know about—"

"I think that alchemy should once again become the bailiwick of women. I think that we ought to abandon this shameful business of making and selling slaves. Making them do our work for us makes us soft, vulnerable. We don't even earn our own existence anymore. Humanity is losing its honor, its strength. And the gods know it. We lost the Homomachy, for heaven's sake. Our economy can be sustained through martial effort and sales of nonliving goods—"

"Hang on, hang on!" Halin grabbed Kaizha's hand. The creature on her opposite arm flinched in indignation. Kaizha hoped no one saw the bandages pulsate.

"No, no, you must listen—I'm quite serious. Please…" Kaizha's own voice was getting faint against Halin's warbling.

"Wait now," said Halin, "I'm not sure you understand what you're saying." She glanced around the table. "Mistress Shanyang is very ill. She could barely make it today. It is probably delirium."

"It is not." Kaizha gently removed Halin's hand from hers. "I know you all are too young to remember what it was like before the social reformation. I know this sounds insane to you. But it is the most natural thing in the world. Human beings were meant to work and suffer and war—it is what makes our lives so precious. And the slaves are more human than we think they are. The gods can see it. That's why the Homomachy was lost."

"It sounds insane because it *is* insane," Xiongnyao said.

Kaizha fell back against her chair. She was too tired for this; too weak and limp and pale and bloodless and aching. It was like trying to teach a bucket full of lobsters how to read. Why had she bothered? Why would she think anyone in the room would listen…

Maybe she *was* delirious.

"Well, now, Kaizha does have a point about the slaves," said Halin. "Clearly we've underestimated the homunculi. We've long been aware of the dangers of infandi, but always insisted the benefits outweighed the risks. And now not only are they rising up to kill us, but the drakes are turning against us, as well."

"They are not," Xiongnyao said. "Mistress Shanyang commanded her own and—"

Halin banged a palm on the table. Her eyes burned like Kaizha had never seen them. "Mistress Haishing. Please do not tell me that you are about to dismiss what I saw with my own eyes."

Xiongnyao's face tightened, her temporal muscles straining all the way to her eyelids. "No. Of course not. I was merely about to say that one incident, or even two, do not make an epidemic."

"A thing does not have to be an epidemic to be a problem, Mistress."

"Yes, and problems abound, and we must select which ones to address—"

"And how many more will die before—"

Xiongnyao's fingers wrapped so tightly around her cup of tea that they turned white. "You would do well to remember that you are no longer the wife of the first seat, Halin."

Halin sat back in her chair, her jaw muscles clenched.

"Look," Xiongnyao continued, forcibly unclenching, "I agree that the current way of things is imperfect. But Mistress Shanyang's antiquated views of how society should function are also imperfect. That's why the social reformation happened in the first place: things were unequal. The revolution was supposed to correct the imbalance, but it got into the hands of the extremists and merely swung the imbalance the other way. We must bring things to center. *Peaceably.* Without warring or any of that nonsense."

It was the greatest load of steaming sheep scours Kaizha had heard in recent memory.

Lili and Matang snorted.

"Women will always create chaos when they can," Lili mumbled.

"Yes, look at how chaotic we are right now," Halin said. "My stars, I think I might have spilled a droplet of tea; everything goes to hell in a woman's hands, doesn't it—"

"You know what she means," Matang snapped.

Halin huffed and leaned forward, staring at Xiongnyao. "And what about the economic considerations? You would have us continue the production of homunculi?"

Kaizha looked at Halin, admiring her. This was the sort of woman who could be converted. Who could lead. Who could be, with some work, the future of Moaki.

Matang started crowing again, ruining her good mood. "We ought to sell our baskets. Baskets and pilgrimages. Moaki is already the holiest city on the continent; I see no reason why we cannot remake it as a grand center for the art of basketweaving—"

There was a knock at the door of the house. Before a slave could answer the call, Namkeng, the captain of the guard—and now, Kaizha realized, the only functioning commander of the entire defensive force—marched into the dining room. His gaze went straight to Kaizha.

"I am so sorry to interrupt, Master Haishing," Namkeng said. "But we have just come upon disturbing evidence in some of our ongoing investigations."

"I see," said Turian, rubbing his mustache.

"It pertains to the case of Master Shanyang, and the claims of yourself and your wife."

Kaizha did not make eye contact. Her heart twitched

faster. The teat-leech vibrated with nervous energy.

"I see," said Turian.

"Would you like to look at the evidence and follow your own action protocol, sir, or would you like to confer upon me the responsibility?"

Turian nodded. "Yes, yes, go ahead. Do what you need to do. I am simply a humble anatomist. Just because I sit in Goh's seat doesn't mean I know how to act in his stead."

Namkeng turned to Kaizha. He held up a little bit of paper. The writing on it looked like hers. "Mistress Shanyang, we have proof that on the third of Hindermonth, you requested that the veterinarian Rawang—who was since convicted of treason for his role in the Penultimonth revolution—should remove the servile gland of the same homunculus you later accused of murdering Master Shanyang." He spoke in rapid-fire syllables, so fast she barely had time to process what he was saying. "You did not request permission to do this from the Homunculus Regulatory Commission, nor did you register the surgery with the Commission. You, in effect, physically enabled a drake to carry out orders to murder a human being unbeknownst to the Regulatory Commission of Moaki."

"Please." Kaizha snorted, hiding her sweaty palm and twitching monstrosity under the table. It was becoming increasingly agitated under its bandaging. "His gland was overactive. It was done entirely for medical reasons. I am—I was the wife of the second seat. I do not need writs from Regulatory Commissions; my station—"

"Your station does not exclude you from the law," Namkeng boomed.

By Kuru's throbbing testes.

She'd ripped up her original excuse for sending him to spy on the veterinarian. Anal gland expression. Simple, innocuous anal gland expression. But Numo's gland had genuinely been bothering him…

Fuck. *Fuck.*

"This act," Namkeng said, "together with Mistress Haishing's accusation that you plotted your husband dead, and the corroborative testimony regarding your character and the drake's character from your released slaves, gives me cause to place you under arrest, and charge you with the murder of Mozeh Shanyang."

Kaizha's breath funneled through her nostrils in little fits and starts. The creature on her arm swelled with an indignation she could feel in her pulse. The tentacles strained against the wrappings. The sling was moving of its own accord, warping and wriggling with the struggles of the creature, its crude knottings coming undone.

Bollix was attempting to return to her, at exactly the wrong moment. She had to think; she had only to think, to salvage her standing, to warp the interpretation of the evidence—

"You may come with me now, peacefully, or I can call my guards from outside to take you."

Tremors crackled through Kaizha's skin. The sling came loose from its knots. She left it on the floor, then got up from her chair, hiding her arm behind her back. Panic rose with her. Rage flooded in from the creature on her arm. The bandage ripped audibly.

She couldn't think of a way out. She couldn't think of anything at all.

"Place your arm where I can see it, please," said Namkeng,

his hand resting on the hilt of his five-sided axe.

Kaizha tried to raise her arm, but a surge of something white-hot and metal-heavy kept it paralyzed. The raging teat-leech strained against her own will, both exhausting the other. The creature took a huge gulp from inside her chest and Kaizha nearly collapsed.

"Place your arm," said Namkeng, readying his axe, "where I can see it." He gave a signal to a man at the door. The man scurried outside and yelled. More guards poured in. Kaizha's chest felt like it was going to fold in on itself. She bent over, crouching on her knees, willing herself not to fall, her mind paddling desperately through a sea of numbness.

Namkeng raised his axe. "Your arm!"

She gave in.

Kaizha's body jerked upright without her wanting it to. Her arm shot out from behind her back. Tentacles erupted from the wrappings, growing longer and thinner as they exploded from her hand. They plaited themselves around each other and slammed down on Namkeng like a massive whip. His skull cracked against the table and his neck twisted to a disturbing, unnatural angle. His eyes went dead. He slid off the table and thumped to the floor.

Kaizha wanted to explode and eat her own tongue and rip herself apart. Instead she stood there, her whole body thrumming and birring, her breasts two orbs of twisting fang-sharp pain.

There was a brief moment of staring. Shock. Disbelief.

Then the guards came after her.

The teat-leech jerked her to the side and hammered its tendrils on the nearest guard. His body snapped in half. The tendrils came apart, exposing glittery hooked barbs on their fleshy undersides, and wrapped themselves around the nearest five men. The tendrils pulled away. They peeled skin off like rolled paper, exposing bone and flesh.

"Kaizha, stop!" Halin yelled. The tendrils braided themselves and whipped the small woman into a wall. Her neck seemed to turn to rubber, the bones inside pulverized into soggy powder. Kaizha retched and dry-heaved and watched her hope for Moaki lie there dead.

Kaizha finally got a grip on her legs and bolted. The tendrils threw guards out of the way as she went, crushing them, smashing their spines down into their own pelvises, sucking her dry with every exertion. She ran out into the street. Where was her goat-trap? The valet—the valet would have taken it to the stables. There was no time to find it. She had to get out. She had to get out now.

She ran uphill, towards her own house. Her lungs began to fail before she made it a hundred paces. Her limbs had no strength left in them. When was the last time she ate real food? And with that leech suckling away, her body was wasting. She slowed. Even as the tentacles from the creature reached out at cobblestones and rocks and the corners of houses to help pull her forward, she felt the rest of her giving out. Soon her body collapsed and the creature was dragging her up the stones alone. Thoughful, but painful. Bollix never did have a mind for evaluating consequences…

The guards were getting closer. There were only three left, but they had fired their emergency flares into the air—there would soon be more.

She had no hope of getting home.

Kaizha pushed herself to her feet. The creature let her.

She turned and ran downhill. The guards flinched away, stepped out of reach of the creature's tendrils, and raised their watershot-torches and axes and slings, the flare-stones inside them shuddering with alchemical fire. A stone crushed into her shoulder as she ran past, sizzling into her flesh. Kaizha stumbled. She fell. She rolled. The tentacles forced her back up. The sound of blood flooding through her head drowned out the shouting around her. Sensation and strength in her body faded away like a distant hum. Her legs gave out again. She tried to get up. There was no getting up. Even the creature was getting weak. Kaizha's breasts had gone dry, and neither her nor the leech could sustain each other anymore. Her head spun and her vision mottled. She couldn't get enough air—there wasn't enough air—

Shadows drew around her. Men in a circle, twirling their slings. Too far for the tentacles to reach.

"*Stay on the ground!* Stay on the ground or we loose!"

Kaizha let her head fall back against the stones. She shut her eye. She had no breath in her to respond.

So this is how Moaki will die, she thought.

A soft tentacle wrapped around her hand. Feeling looped in from the creature; a distinct mixture of guilt and sorrow. As if to say *I tried*.

They both had, in their own way. Chaos and violence didn't always work, perhaps. Kaizha smiled in spite of the irons being clapped around her extremities.

Bollix had always been too much like her.

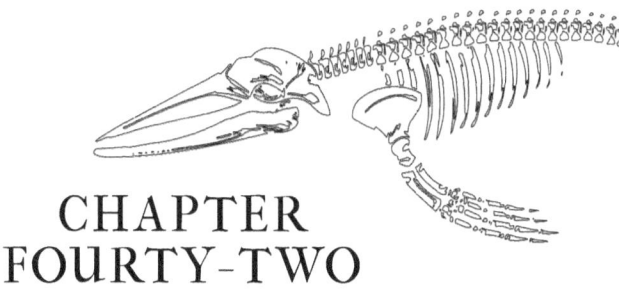

CHAPTER
FOURTY-TWO
HAMMERFIST

HAMMERFIST HAD NEVER been outside of Moaki, as far as she remembered; or at least, not beyond the reach of its foothills. The landscape, and indeed the air itself, shifted slowly as they descended further and further into the lowlands. The cold and the dry gave way to a moister and warmer air, somewhat like the inside of the stables in summer before they were cleaned. It was greener, and Numo found distraction in wondering at the trees as they changed in size, shape, even color. As they traveled closer to the coast, though, the trees became rarer and rarer altogether, then were replaced by scrubby things no taller than Hammerfist's elbow, and the grass changed color once more. The air was still wet, but saltier and breezier. They passed farmlands, flat and expansive and elevationless, quite different to the terraces of Mount Barisok.

After days of traveling, or weeks perhaps, Rawang stopped and said rather undramatically, "There it is."

She looked, and not far ahead, the ground ceased to be.

Rawang pointed downward. Hammerfist turned her head, and there, down a great wide path struck into the side of a cliff, was Trago: a city carved into the foot of the cliffside itself, the whole thing like an enormous lovingly-hewn cave. It sprawled out onto docks here and there between the black sand, the piers full of mongers and criers and eelers and shipbuilders, spanning a long shore that turned to rock and spray as it stretched into the ocean.

The bloody *ocean*.

It was enough to tear her mind away from Numo and enough to stop the invisible screw that had been boring into her chest. Temporarily.

Her mother had talked about the ocean, probably—it caused faint ripples in her memory—but the sight swallowed her in shock, like some great mythical lizard of the heavens sitting just below her and waving hello. The glorious emptiness of it made her think of drowning.

The shadows of sunset were deepening into night, outlining the dips and waves hammered out of the cliff into buildings. Pteropteryxes wheeled about, sojourning out and returning to their nests. The facades of the rock-cut buildings glinted in the white of the creatures' guano, layered thick onto their faces like plaster and carved into great sweeping arcs and whorls. Music pounded through the air—drums, mostly, vibrant and thumping, a pulse for the whole city.

The smell of salt and the whitewash of guano overpowered her nostril, and some other smell of fetid rot besides that seemed to be coming from a great bloated corpse on the beach. A sea-creature, she thought; her very first sea-creature that was not some salted fish, even if it was very very dead. A small thrill went through her dulled nerves. Her body shook. She'd like to think it was from wonderment, or relief, but she knew it was because of darker and less pleasant things.

It had been a long trudge from Moaki. There was once a river in the valley that led to the ocean, so Rawang said, but since the dam had been built to provide irrigation for Moaki's terraced farmlands, there was nothing but a trail of mud. The trudging had been fueled by very little food and mostly brownish water. They'd avoided the towns dotting the major road, which meant taking the long way around. Hammerfist was exhausted, her body still reeling from that woman's strange whip, and the other two were useless for hunting.

Rawang was sickly: pale, trembly, barely able to eat anything and keep it down. She couldn't smell the certainty of death on him yet—it flowed in and out, waxing and waning, but Death always had one hand on his shoulder, prepared for him to give in. As for Numo…

She swallowed, and the spit seemed to gain gravity as it went. Her chest felt like it was full of wooden cogs with teeth that didn't quite mesh, grinding away with stops and shudders and little catches of apnea. Part of it was weakness from hunger, but most of it was her heart spurting black hell into her like a leaking octopus. She hated what she was doing to Numo. His face, his gait, his stooped shoulders—everything about him looked utterly heartbroken, no matter how hard he tried to keep his voice upbeat and determined, no matter how he pretended to be interested in the coastal scrub-bushes and admire their "humble kindlingishness."

But it was for his own good. If he continued to care about her, he'd only end up miserable. Or dead.

At least Rawang was already miserable.

"All right. Finally," Rawang said. He readjusted the bloody deerskin that he'd wrapped around the oligarch's head.

"Remember, now; you two are, as far as Trago is concerned, my slaves. The place is still occupied, technically; there are likely to be plenty of Moak soldiers around. I don't know that they do much aside from making sure the tribute payments are on time—clearly they're crap at preventing illegal alchemy—but we must be careful. Keep to the cliff wall and get into the darkest tunnels. If we get separated, we meet at the pub."

"What pub?" said Numo.

"There's always a pub."

"What if there is more than one?"

Rawang scowled at him. "Then we will meet at the one I am drinking in."

"Ah." Numo paused, then glanced up at Hammerfist. "But won't people notice that she's wearing a prison shackle around her neck instead of a proper collar? Or that we're all covered in burns? Or that you have no shirt and look poorly and decrepit? Or—"

"No, they won't. Not if we keep to the dark and don't give ourselves away." Rawang glared at the drake. "You wouldn't behave in a manner that would give us away, would you?"

Numo's one and a half ears swiveled and purpled. "No, sir."

Rawang regarded him warily. "On second thought, you may have something, Numo."

"Might I?"

"Yes. After all, what is a poorly and decrepit wretch like myself doing with two slaves? That in itself is quite suspect, is it not?"

Hammerfist's wrist-hairs bristled.

"Perhaps you'd better go into the city separately, Numo. Alone."

"*What?*" Hammerfist loosed a snarl that seemed to echo off the entire cliff wall. Her fists curled in anticipation, knowing they might get to punch something, trembling with want. She planted them firmly in the dirt. It wouldn't do to break Rawang's skull, and yet he seemed to be forever goading her.

"He has brought up the point himself, and a very valid point it is," Rawang said. "We don't want to wander in like fattened prey into a den of water deer."

Numo's gaze seemed to wander off into the ether. His mind was clearly no longer on what Rawang was saying. What was he thinking? How much did he understand? Hammerfist puzzled and puzzled over him with all the mental strength she could assemble that was not already dedicated to keeping her bestial nature firmly tamped underfoot, but in sooth that wasn't much at all.

"...We mustn't draw attention to ourselves," Rawang kept babbling. "And Numo will be most inconspicuous, being small. No one really bothers about drakes. He'll be safe without us."

Hammerfist's claw raised itself up, springing open, ready to smash Rawang's face into the cliffside until the stone turned pink, before she stopped herself. *You are to be human. You are to be his wife.* It still seemed like such a faraway and fantastical notion, like a warped dream that threatened to fall out of her head in her waking hours if she didn't cling to it tightly enough. *And lovers don't smash each other.*

But...you don't love him.

"It's all right," Numo said. He patted Hammerfist's toe. Hammerfist lowered her hand, her body relaxing, shame flooding through her at the realization of what she'd been about to do. "The doctor knows more about such practical matters than I," said Numo. "And I think he might be correct. You two will look less suspicious. I will be all right regardless. I am utterly small and inconsequential, after all."

"Not to me," Hammerfist blurted. Rawang's face went taut. Numo smiled.

"We will meet again. At the...the *pub*," he said, as though he were saying "at the *bansptfthphlat*" or some other nonsense, and Hammerfist was about to ask him if he was sure he knew what a pub was, but then he perked and added, "Or, if not, then at the alchemist's quarters. I should most certainly be able to find the alchemist's quarters."

Hammerfist swallowed. It boggled her mind how she could always have saliva spilling out of her mouth and yet have a dry and cracking throat. "Do you promise this?"

"Of course," Numo said. Hammerfist considered him and looked for signs of any insincerity, but it occurred to her that Numo had no idea how to lie. He truly believed what he was saying. And if he believed it, shouldn't she?

Hammerfist cocked her head in assent. She tried to make her face smile, because that's what the others did, but her jaw dangled crookedly and did little else.

Numo squeezed her finger. "Farewell, for now." With that, he skittered off towards the path that cut into the cliffside and led to the city below. She watched him bobble away until he was well out of sight, lost in the descent and dusk.

"Okay?" Rawang said, gently placing a hand on her elbow. "Are we ready?"

Hammerfist wasn't sure. She looked down at the path. A precipice, like the gods had built her very own metaphor for this exact moment. If she went to Trago, it meant she was throwing her hope, once and for all, on Rawang. On her human life that was as distant a thing to her as a story written by someone else and dropped in the water till its pages bloated to obscurity. On something that might be a lie. And she'd have to leave Numo behind.

He deserved a chance at freedom. Around her, he'd never be free.

"Sramai? Are you ready?

Hammerfist began to bow, and then remembered what a human was supposed to do and nodded instead. "Ready."

Trago was bustling in the eventide. People were lighting torches—torches that smelled of woody fire and fish oil instead of alchemical fumes—and shouting in a jumble, repeating some word that sounded like "ale." Rawang kept close to the cliff wall and Hammerfist followed, trying to sink into the haze of twilight and shrink away from the crowd on the beach. The Tragans yelled amongst themselves.

"Why burn it? We ought to just shove it back out to sea."

"And have it float right back to our shore? Fucking brilliant!"

"If we burn it, it'll smell up the town for days."

A man in Moak garb interrupted. "I think that's a consequence we'll all have to accept regardless of—"

"Ai, shut up, Moaker! When we have a problem with mountain goats, we'll give you a shout."

This seemed to rouse a slew of Moak soldiers from the crowd. Rawang pulled Hammerfist into one of the alleys carved into the cliffside. As they went, she had the stiffening feeling of being watched, but—perhaps she was being watched, after all. There were people here, and people sometimes stared.

A short walk brought them away from one throng and into another—a clot of loiterers giggling and farting into torches just outside one of the smaller buildings.

"I knew there'd be a pub," Rawang mumbled. He led her towards a rudely-carved cave glowing with lean firelight and buzzing with drunken noise. She made but a few lumbering steps before a hand clapped on her elbow.

"Just a moment, there," a man said. He spoke in a Moak accent. She turned. He wore a Moaki uniform and had the tattoos of a soldier.

Shit.

Rawang gently removed the soldier's hand. The soldier didn't seem to appreciate it. "This is my slave, sir," he said, his voice tempered by some thick-tongued attempt at a Tragan accent.

"Maybe," grunted the soldier. "Maybe not." He lit a water-torch with a packet of alchemical fire and drew a *nwa*-sword—a medium curved blade finished with the sorts of barbs and hooks that did not leave the flesh without eviscerating something important. "You got a matching ring to prove it?"

Hammerfist went rigid. Her instincts flamed through her with septic familiarity, and her muscles spasmed as though they were committing suicide from the existential agony of not killing the man with the sword. She must remain frozen. If she killed him, they'd know—the city would know who they were.

Moaki would find them.

"Well, no," Rawang said. "Not on me, at the moment—I must have left it at home."

"Well. Let's have a look at this collar then, eh? I'm sure it's got the proper marks on it, at least…" The soldier began lifting the torch to Hammerfist's face, scattering the shadows this way and that. Rawang stopped his hand.

"Sir, please; we're late for a meeti—"

The soldier shoved him away and aimed the water torch at Rawang, keeping the sword at Hammerfist's neck. "You touch me again, I'll tear this slave's neck apart and set your cock on fire. Understand?"

Blood surged through Hammerfist's head. It didn't matter anymore. She had to kill—

There was a scream from the beach. People rushed through the alley towards the commotion. Soldiers barked in Moak. An emergency flare went up. The soldier tilted his head and lowered his sword for an instant. In the confusion, everyone's eyes drew away from Hammerfist. She pushed the soldier into the shadows and quietly snipped his carotid with her talons, shoving her fist in his mouth so he wouldn't make any noise as he bled to death.

Rawang dragged her back. "Dammit, Sramai, I told you not to do that stuff anymore. It's not you. You must fight your foreign nature…" He sighed. "Well. What's done is done. Thank you for being discreet, at least."

Hammerfist's hackles stood up.

"Right, well, the pub is here; if anyone knows where an illicit alchemist is, it'll be the drunken scum of society." Rawang winked. "Come on, let's—"

The din from the beach evaporated. Even Rawang hushed at the sudden void of noise. All Hammerfist could hear was Numo's voice screaming madly into the night.

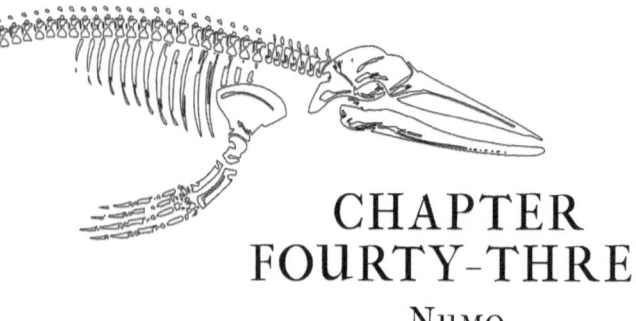

CHAPTER
FOURTY-THREE
Numo

NUMO HAD HOPED it wouldn't come to this.

He'd been watching them, Hammerfist and Rawang, and the soldier that had followed them into the shadows. The fire. The glint of the sword against her neck.

So Numo had to become the prey in a den of water deer to draw the predators away. As Fustilugs had said, they love the noise of a gibbering fool.

"Get back! Back!" Numo's hand shook on the grip of the water torch, the blood making his hands slippery. The pointy end of his tiny dagger wavered in the torchlight. It still had little bits of the soldier's tendons dangling off it. Numo had no idea that the tendons in a soldier's heels were so fat and clumpy-looking. He hadn't meant to do it, but no one was listening to his ravings…no one important.

Numo backed against the carcass of the great sea-beast. The stench of the thing closed over him like a blanket and squeezed leakage from his eyes, wrapping its miasmatic arms around his lungs with odor of engorged organs and rot. The soldiers pulled their tunics up over their noses and came closer.

"No one touches the beast!" Numo screamed. "No one

touches the fallen beast of the heavens! It has been vomited forth like a blessing upon our shores! To disturb the great gift of the gods is a…a baby's wet stain upon the rump-cloth of the earth!" He made the water torch spurt out a jet of fire, but it didn't reach far enough to constitute more than a weak threat.

Numo had no way out. He hadn't thought that far ahead. But at least the soldiers were all focused on him now. People were gathering like a storm cloud about to burst over him and kill him with fat hailstones. It was what he wanted, he told himself. Absolutely perfect, he insisted inwardly, as his whole body trembled and gimbled in the darkness. Hammerfist was safe, now that he was profoundly and irrevocably unsafe. So it was all right to die.

"Get back or in sooth I shall slay you!" Numo roared, drowning out the sound of his pulses whumming in his ears.

The soldiers swung their fiery slings over their heads, grinning. "Stupid drake."

Numo darted inside what he assumed was the mouth of the beast. The explosive wads of fire sailed at him, colliding with his shield of festering flesh. Numo gagged, and could barely see for the water in his eyes, but the creature seemed to be immune to the fiery projectiles. Its skin flared in little pockets of fire and sizzled, but the thing would not set alight.

The soldiers stopped pelting things at him and drew their swords. "Well shit," one of them grumbled.

"I know," said another.

"I don't want to go in there."

"You'd rather let it get away?"

A grumble. Then they advanced on the beast's mouth.

"Stay back! No one touches the pristine regurgitants of the

gods!" Numo coughed on the lack of breathable air and shrank further into the creature's mouth, towards the throat. Even worse smells fumed up out of the hole and he couldn't make himself go further. He threw up on his feet. It was a very odd throw-up, he thought, all pasty and phlegmy, with nary a food item in its folds. He was one of the exciting people with exciting vomit. And yet, Numo regretted being quite this exciting.

The soldiers got down on their knees to follow him, wincing, their eyes dripping and their throats heaving. One of them was nearly inside the cavernous mouth when there was a faint "squish." His eyes popped open. He screamed. And then he was dragged away.

The soldiers seemed too slow to react. Tearing noises made the air heavy—ripping, crunching, snapping, sprays of blood flinging across the torchlight. When Numo poked his head out, Hammerfist was leaning heavily on her knuckles, crushing the last soldier's chest into the beach as though she were kneading bread. The rest were…in various states of disarray. Dead. Very definitely dead.

Rawang screamed and flailed, trying to keep the crowd at bay. "She'll kill you!" he yelled, "She's got the fall; her mind's turned inside out; she'll kill you and not even know what she's doing!" It seemed to be effective enough. But then the big man came. A big, big man, striding out of the crowd, his Moak robe whooshing around his legs and his chest exposed to reveal tattoos that went from his neck to his breast. He surveyed the scene without expression, raised his hand, and threw a knife into Hammerfist's neck.

The beach seemed to tilt sideways. Numo's body shimmered with colors he couldn't keep track of. Rawang flung himself at the Moak officer, screaming, and the big man punched his soggy pale body again and again until Rawang was on his knees and pawing madly like a sheep with its rear legs hacked off. Hammerfist roared, blood oozing out around the knife and down her chest. She started forward. Numo was suddenly in front of her, though he didn't remember moving his feet.

"No," he said. "No. Lie down."

Hammerfist growled. Her body trembled.

"Lie down," said Numo. The volcanoes in her eyes were already erupting, and Numo had never heard of a volcano sucking its lava back in. But there was blood—so much blood—flowing down her chest, matting her breast-fur, dribbling down and puddling in her navel—she wouldn't stop. She wouldn't stop until the big scoundrel was dead and she was dead and his world was over.

"Lie down!" he screamed. He hit her in the knees. "Lie down!"

She didn't. She advanced, her body listing on her knuckles as her balance crumbled, but she kept going all the same, and Numo pedaled backwards yelling and yelling and she didn't hear him.

Numo took as deep a breath as he could muster. He opened his mouth. He sang. The crowd went silent.

Hammerfist stopped.

"Lie down," Numo said.

She lay down. Numo glanced over his shoulder. The Moak officer was still pummeling Rawang, who, though clearly losing the fight, refused to stop flailing at him. There wasn't much time. Numo climbed on top of Hammerfist and stared at the knife. *In or out? Out or in?* Well, it couldn't stay there, could it? He pulled it out.

Blood spurted into his face and stung his eyeballs. Hammerfist's chest lurched with a gasp of pain. Her muscles stiffened. Numo clapped his palms against the wound and pressed his pathetic body weight against it. So much blood. It wouldn't stop. He grasped the edges of the sliced skin with all his might and pulled them together and held them there.

"Rawang!" he yelled. No, Rawang was too busy losing a fight. Who then? Nobody? Anybody? Numo's heart pounded so heavily it stomped the breath out of his lungs. An alchemist. There was an alchemist here somewhere. A scan of the crowd revealed nothing but a blur of confused faces. Numo wasn't even sure what an illegal alchemist looked like. There was only one thing he could think of to do, and it might be nonsensical, but all was already lost…

Numo stuffed his paper of brain diagrams into the wound and leapt away. He ran towards the crowd, towards Rawang, towards the felonious dastard who'd stabbed his—who'd stabbed Hammerfist. Rawang had dropped his deerskin and it sat like a melon in the rocky sand. Numo hoisted it up and unwrapped the skin.

"Where is the alchemist?" he screamed. "We have brought you a head, alchemist! We have brought you a head of the first seat of the Moaki oligarchy, as you demanded! Help her, alchemist, to get your head-payment!"

The big man shoved Rawang to the ground, stomped his head into the sand, and glared at Numo. His eyes lit on the head and widened, the whites flickering in the torchlight. Then he swiveled his head and shouted at the crowd.

"Sangja!" he hollered to no one in particular. "Sangja, is this your doing? You little asshole! We'll have your head and your fingers and your damned leather ballsa—"

A shadow skittered through the crowd. Something metal flashed. The Moak officer's head lolled off his shoulders and plopped onto the beach.

A smallish person strode grumpily towards Numo. He—or perhaps she?—Numo couldn't quite tell—was human, perhaps thirteen or fourteen, with hair cut short to the scalp and fine white scars crisscrossed over their chest. Studs and spatters of metal dotted the old incisions, embedded in the skin. The wiry little person wore only pants, with a pouch dangling from the hip. They dragged a shoddy-looking bladed thing, in roughly the shape of an adze.

The person grabbed the head from Numo's fingers and peered at the mealy face. It had not fared well during the journey, but the reddled beard still dominated it. The person huffed as though put out.

"Well. I guess we're starting this now, then."

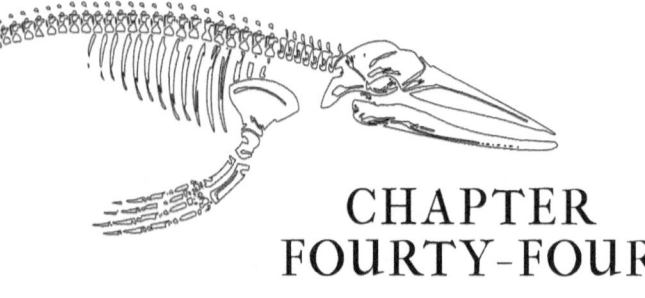

CHAPTER
FOURTY-FOUR
HAMMERFIST

HAMMERFIST FOUGHT HARD to keep her mind from receding into that tiny pinprick of bestial mindlessness, but it kept shrinking nonetheless, and she was vaguely aware of a desire to fall down even though she was fairly sure she was already horizontal. The pinprick dilated every so often, when Numo would slap her or yell or sing, or when the scarred boy without a shirt stabbed into her neck with something that looked like wire. The boy held up a vial of a wet silvery substance and let it drip, drip, drip into her neck wound, and it sizzled and burned. It hardened. The blood stopped its constant sluicing. The boy sewed her neck shut.

"She got the fall?" He had a high-pitched voice for a boy. Unless he wasn't a boy. Everything was fuzzy…

"What?" said Numo. "Oh. Yes."

"Right. A precaution then." Hammerfist saw a flash of something thin and shiny going into her neck, but she barely felt it.

"What are you doing?"

"Knocking her out."

Hammerfist's neck felt as though a metal rod was growing

inside it. It hurt like the poison of the centipede-demon that wormed through all of the seventeen hells. Numo squeezed her hand and she tried not to move because that was what Numo wanted...but where was Rawang?

Hammerfist raised her head. Rawang was dead. Or unconscious. Something surged in her chest. She had to go to him. Her body jerked upwards, much to everyone's protest, but standing up turned out to be a poor choice. She was down again before she could even feel where her limbs were.

The boy was shouting, "Trago is locked down. No one in or out. Clean this mess up. Take them to my quarters. Get the hell out of my way. And don't touch that whale." Short declarative sentences. Imperatives. And people appeared to listen. Odd. The boy couldn't have been more than fourteen or fifteen, surely?

Then she was lifted, and Rawang was lifted, and she couldn't hear Numo any more for all the shouting and stomping of the crowd. Her mind eroded away again, softly, and there wasn't enough pain or singing to bring it back. But this time, when it shrank to nothing, it was almost peaceful.

Numo was singing again.

"Will you please *stop* that," Rawang grumbled.

Hammerfist blinked, and it was as though the world shifted from black-and-white paper-scribblings to colorful sculptures. Her human mind wasn't back yet, but her infandus one was withering. Her eyes were bleary, as though she'd slept, but she didn't remember waking—well, that was hardly unusual. The infandus in her didn't have much of a short-term memory. Her neck tingled. She tried to bite at the itchy place on the side of her throat, but she couldn't reach it. Then she remembered she had claws.

"Well, she's moving now," said Numo.

"Yes...yes, I suppose she is." Rawang gently pushed her claw away from her neck. "Don't scratch, love."

They were inside some sort of darkish room carved out of stone, lit by hundreds of fish dangling from the ceiling with burning wicks stuffed into them. Hammerfist couldn't stop staring. They were shiny, the burning oil of the fish and the reflection of the brownish glass jars they were crammed in—it was so strange. Dead things made to give light.

"Lampfish," said the boy with the shaven head. "You like them? They're full of fat. Great for burning; not great for eating. Taste like the inside of an ass abscess." He sat on a cushion on the floor. They were all on the floor, it seemed, which was fine with Hammerfist, but it was quite odd to see humans there. She supposed she understood, since every surface in the room seemed to be covered with vials, burners, flasks, wires, fluxes, plants, remnants of dead creatures, bits of broken glass, and heaps of battered weaponry that smelled of old blood and urine, though she wasn't sure why people would piss on swords. An entire wall was dedicated to fire—an open hearth and several ovens, their doors of varying thicknesses. The odor inside the room was a confusing mash of plants and fire and fish.

"I'm Sangja," said the boy. "This is my...uh, my craphole, I guess. I'd offer you something, but I'm sort of low on most things you could safely put in your mouth."

Unsure how to respond, Hammerfist bared her neck.

Moving her neck made it itch worse. Hammerfist tried scritching at it again and Rawang and the boy yelled at her. She yelled back, wetting the boy's face with spit. His face looked curious with a slick of mottle-colored saliva all over it. His lips were shiny. Who was he, anyway? Why were they here? Rawang and Numo seemed like they knew what they were doing, so she tried not to make a fuss, but the panic of confusion made her fingers twitch across the floor.

"So," Sangja said, "I take it the infandus is not exactly..." He stuck his hand next to his head and made a seesaw motion with his palm.

"Her name is Hammerfist," said Numo.

"Her name is *Sramai*," Rawang snapped.

"I don't give a fuck if her name is Shitbubbles, 'kay? What I care about is if she's sentient enough not to kill us if a fart startles her. So?" He looked at her expectantly.

"Almost," Hammerfist said. She wasn't there yet—her brain was full of the desire for a knockwood; it had been so long—but she could feel herself coming back through the dark, like a tiny squeaking bat coming to squirt rabies into her neck.

"All right. But you understand me."

"Yes."

"Good." The boy leaned back and snatched a half-eaten dried fish off the table. He gnawed on its head. "So your friends have told me why you came. Given me the head and all that. It's very impressive, the first seat. Y'all have caused some— additional problems for me, and we'll get to that. But a bargain's a bargain, and I am a man of my word."

He spat out some thready bones on the floor. "Anyway, I wanted t'give you the stuff directly, since it's very valuable and

I can't trust these hagfish-fuckers." He nodded at Numo and Rawang. Hammerfist almost snorted out loud at Numo being referred to as any variety of fucker, but she restrained herself. "Nothing personal. I just don't trust people I don't know, and I don't pay people who don't deserve it. In my position, I can't be too careful. Of course, now you all have put me in a rather less careful position than I wanted…" His mouth screwed itself upwards.

"Which brings me to my next point. In saving you, certain plans I had for the…progression of things, let's say, have been mightily fucked. In Trago, we repay those who do us favors, and whose plans we fuck." He looked at the three of them pointedly.

"We have no money," Rawang said.

"There is more to life than money. Like bodies." Sangja looked directly at Hammerfist when he said it. His eyes leered—unsalaciously, but disturbingly all the same. "I need bodies for this war. Moaki will hit back at us—sooner than I was planning for—and the numbers aren't on our side. They've got a bigger army. I mean, they've *got* an army. We got the whole town, but it's still not enough. I've been stalling for more time to build it all up but…" He waved at the three of them and made a "fprthtph" noise with his tongue. "Now there is no more time. The lockdown I just called won't last long. Word'll get out, and they'll come for us. Thanks to you."

Hammerfist scraped at her claws harder and looked at the floor. Something inside her was blowing up, a burst of black smoke that started from her guts and curled up around her lungs. *Fear*, said the human voice. Was that what fear was? She wanted to run. She wanted to kick that boy in the face so hard he didn't get up and then run away. But that was bad…

Rawang scoffed. "Look, if you want to go after Moaki, now is the perfect time. We've personally slaughtered the first two seats in the oligarchy and I'm willing to bet that more died in that fire at the Homomachy. People are questioning the government's place of favor with the gods because they lost the Homomachy for the first time *ever*. The place is as confused and inefficient as it's ever going to be. Thanks to us, I might add. If you waited, you might have missed your window."

Hammerfist glanced at him. "Thanks to us?" That wasn't what she remembered. She remembered Numo doing almost all of it.

"Yes. Us." Rawang glared back. Numo pretended to play with his toes. He picked a swathe of dead skin off his feet. He seemed to be concentrating very hard on not looking at anyone.

"Well," the boy said, "without *me,* at least two of you would be dead right now. Probably three. So I don't consider your contributions—if they are even yours—to be all that impressive."

Numo cleared his throat. "Actually—"

"I told you not to speak," Rawang said.

"Hush your swamp-maw, sir." Numo paused to breathe heavily, as though saying such a thing had taken great exertion. Rawang's brow knotted and he sputtered in shock.

Sangja laughed. "Your slave's got a mouth on—"

"And you too. You hush," Numo barked. "...Sir," he added, as though he couldn't help himself.

Sangja's mouth quirked, and he looked very amused. "Well, go on then. What have you got to say?"

"I...um." Numo wove his fingers together. "What I have to say is, none of these—these other *fuggers* did much of anything.

They are useless. If you want to win your war, you don't need them. I am the…I am the one you want, the soldier of butchery." He paused and looked uncomfortable, as though he'd just passed gas or broken someone's dishes.

"You're telling me *that*"—Sangja pointed at Hammerfist— "is useless?"

"She's got no mind for work anymore, sir. The fall, you see. But I can help you. I killed my master. I set the arena on fire. I cut off Goh's head. I am a murderer." Now he looked like he was about to cry. Hammerfist was stricken with a desire to hug him, but she was afraid to move. "You need only me. I will murder whoever I am told to murder. Evidently."

"You don't have dementia? Your brain isn't rotten?"

"No, sir."

"Then how do you murder, exactly? I thought they stuck things in slaves that poisoned them to death if they even thought of it."

"I've had the servile gland removed, sir. But I retain my slave-lobe, and my need to have a master. I would give myself to you, until your business with Moaki is finished." His good ear twitched.

"You? You are tiny. What can *you* do?"

"Exactly. No one suspects me until it is too late. I am like the biting-insect that no one sees until it causes a welt. Only… only with killing people instead." Numo forced his fingers to unweave and ball into fists. He puffed out his chest and let loose a little snort. The black smoke inside Hammerfist purled up into her brains. She could register what was happening, almost—and it was awful, it was a monster in the dark about to turn a corner and leap into her face and tear her jaw off the bottom of her skull, but she still couldn't see, and it was maddening. She gnawed on a claw. *Sharp sharpen sharpety sharp.*

Sangja looked to Rawang, who seemed stunned into silence. "Is this true?"

Rawang blinked rapidly, many more times than seemed normal. "It is."

Hammerfist looked up from her spit-covered hand. "Numo doesn't know how to lie," she stated proudly. Numo gave her a wavery smile.

Sangja leaned back and rested his head against a table behind him, sighing. "It's true no one notices a drake." He bounced the balls of his feet on the floor. "But, of course, I have no reason to trust anything you say." More bouncing. "What was your occupation, drake, before all of this alleged murdering?"

"I am—was—I was a stoker. A hypocaust-slave."

Sangja's feet stopping bouncing. "What is a hypocaust? Some rich Moaker thing?"

"I made fires, sir. In ovens, underneath my master's house, to make heat. To keep it warm."

"Fire, hm. So you know how to smell out a combustible, eh?"

"More or less, sir; I'd grown quite skilled at it before— before I developed other skills."

"I see." The boy squinted at the ceiling in thought. "Fine," he said suddenly. "I take the drake, you take the elixir, we'll call it fair. Deal?"

"Deal," said Rawang. Sangja lifted himself off the floor cushion and went to rummage around in the bric-a-brac on one of the tables.

Hammerfist's brain was on fire. Take the drake? What

did that mean? Numo? Was Numo leaving? She glanced over. He seemed sad, his eyes pinched as though wincing at some invisible hurt, but when he saw her looking he smiled again.

Then she remembered—he was supposed to leave. He was good and she was bad and he couldn't be near her. She'd hurt him. He was so small and so perfect, and she was so big and bloated and toxic. Hammerfist squeezed one hand with the other as they cried out to punch the wall or punch the child or punch Rawang. But punching things wouldn't fix it. Nothing would fix it.

Maybe the elixir would fix it.

Sangja came back and leaned down, flashing a big glass bottle with a wooden stopper in her face. There was a blue liquid inside. It sloshed around shinily and she found herself reaching out to take it.

"Be very careful with it," Sangja admonished.

She tried to be careful and take it by the fingertip, but her claws slid off of it. So instead she unrolled her tongues and wrapped them around it. The bottle drew into her jaws, and she was very careful not to let her teeth scrape the glass.

"Good. Now, I want you to drink half a fingerling of that every morning and every night. Until it's all gone. It might take a few days for you to notice a difference. Once it's gone, the effects will be permanent."

She gazed up at Sangja. "What's half a *fgrglnngg*?" she said with her other tongues.

He sighed, spread apart two fingertips, and spanned half of his finger. "You know, a fingerling. Use his hands to measure, not yours."

Rawang rose from his seat and took Sangja by the hand,

jostling it up and down. "Thank you. Thank you so m—"

Sangja yanked his hand away and wiped it on his pants. "Th'fuck? Is that what you all do in Moaki? That's disgusting." He looked at Rawang pointedly and banged his fist twice against his chest.

"Oh." Rawang mimicked him. "Thank you s—"

"That means goodbye, *ai nyo*."

Rawang smiled, gave a quick tip of the head, and grabbed Hammerfist's wrist. "Come on, dear, let's go."

They got up to leave. Numo didn't. The black smoke inside Hammerfist's head exploded.

She was leaving him. She had to leave him. For his own good. It was good. It had to be.

But it still felt like her skin was being torn off her chest.

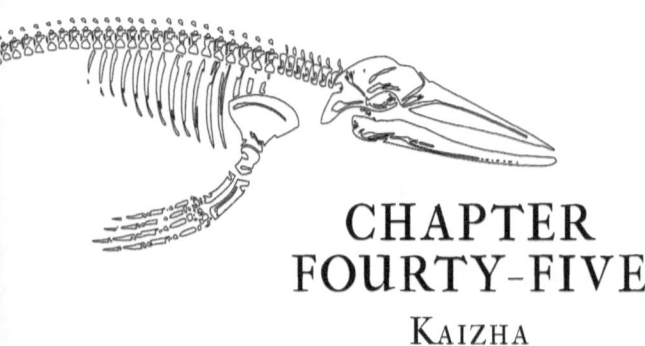

CHAPTER
FOURTY-FIVE
Kaizha

KAIZHA VAGUELY REMEMBERED being told she was arrested. There was a gap after that, then the sensation of Moak soldiers clapping two sides of an iron vessel over her hand and welding it shut. At her condemnation hearing, the jug began to crack, and they wrapped layer upon layer of spider silk over the jug. And when she was sentenced to transmogrificaton, and the creature began straining at the spider silk, they wedged a metal bar into her shoulder that immobilized the arm and pinched at the creature's feeding-tube, though she couldn't imagine they managed that last effect on purpose. Why nobody simply cut off her arm, she didn't know.

At first, Kaizha thought the worst thing about Mizu Prison was the noise. It was constant, ear-splitting, pulverizing. It seemed to Kaizha that nobody ever slept—they were too busy banging on the bars of their cells, screaming, singing songs about the Three-Bosomed Barmaid from Baru. The noise irritated her rage like a child picking away at unhealed scabs, and it bled everywhere; it seemed to fill her face and her toes and her fingers and lodge right at the base of her skull to congeal into a knot of pain.

This wasn't how it was supposed to end.

In three days, she was moved to the transmogrification chambers. And, a short while after, she longed for the sounds of horrible, obnoxious life.

The chambers were deep under water, down a single vertical tunnel. She was shut into a dark box that only ever saw light when someone came in to drop off a jug of watery nutrient, or tie her down to the wall-wheel, or flay her skin, or, in the case of a particular stooped-over infandus who came in to clean up after, eat the bits of skin that got flayed off.

Her mind warped disconcertingly whenever she drank the liquid filth that was her only sustenance—as though time was stretching out and multiplying every time she took a breath. It contained far more awful substances than water, she knew, but there was water in it nonetheless, and she was so damn thirsty.

Her anger stopped burning and became a long, inexorable sheet of ice.

She wanted so badly to hate Xiongnyao, to blame Goh, to sit there in the dark and plan the deaths of everyone at that meeting she hadn't already killed. But the anger only veered away from them. Magnetized to her chest and sat there, freezing inward, stalactites of icicles growing into the cavern of her chest.

It was her. All her. She hadn't covered her tracks. Had thought she was above covering them, or forgotten about them entirely. Gotten Halin killed. Rushed in with an uncontrolled experiment. Spit in the face of alchemy for the sake of alchemy. Turned into the brainless old hag with brainless old ideas that everyone told her she was.

Time and space disintegrated. Every day, the guards who brought her the nutrient asked her how long she'd been there, and every time, she became less and less sure. When she said "I don't know," they made her guess. Five days. Twelve days. Three weeks. A month. She didn't know. Nothing ever happened when she answered, until measures of time faded from her memory completely, and all she could say was "I don't remember how to answer the question."

That was when Turian began his part of the work.

Kaizha never would have dreamed she could be afraid of a man, let alone Turian. With his heavy-lidded eyes and his bored face and his slack-jawed affect, Turian had been, in all civilized contexts, a bland stump of a thing. But in the distasteful art of transmogrification, he was another creature entirely.

In her previous life, Kaizha hadn't given much attention to what he did here in the prisons. She only knew she didn't like the fashion of making an infandus as large as a man or larger—it was hardly a proper *homunculus* anymore—and Turian had defended it. He'd insisted, with some uncharacteristic effort and a great deal of stammering to find the right words, that the term "homunculus" should more properly refer to the shrunken mutilatedness of the humanoid essence, rather than the physical size.

Kaizha, for her part, had thought anything about something's *essence* sounded far too poetic and wispy to be meaningful; that it was a flimsy excuse to bow to the economic demands of the battle-arenas.

But Turian, she now understood, had been talking about a phenomenon as definite and precise as a dagger's slice into a femoral artery.

The dim light from the door flashed. "Good morning," he said.

Kaizha flinched instinctively at his voice. It wasn't much of a flinch—she'd been glued to the wall-wheel with acidic pricking-gum, twirling and twirling, unable to move much of her own accord. But that "good morning," as familiar as it was by now, was still jarring as a funeral bell tolling in her ear.

"Now—how are you supposed to respond?" he said.

She paused. Something in her withered. "Good morning, master," Kaizha gurgled. He'd been applying various hooks and stretching instruments to her mouth and throat, but she could yet speak. Somewhat.

"Well done." Turian stepped inside, dragging a cart behind him. "I've thought of another possible name for you. What do you think of Murdersquid?"

Kaizha thought nothing of it. Her name was Kaizha and she'd force herself to remember it. It had been many years since her alchemy training, and she'd never been too involved in the creation of infandi—but she thought she remembered that the first sign of the growth of the slave-lobe in the brain was forgetting the name. But of course, she had just called him "master" and not wanted to drive a sharpened wheel axle through her head, hadn't she?

"No, hm?" Turian fiddled with some instruments on the cart, banging metal against metal. The door clanged shut, and he lit a water torch, throwing deep shadows across his face. "Xiongnyao didn't care for it either. Said it was too violent." He sharpened something against a whetstone.

"Yes, master," Kaizha said, before she was aware she'd even thought the words.

"Yes, she—oh hell. Stop that spinning. It's giving me a headache." Turian leaned outside the door and shouted something. The wheel stopped and Kaizha was stuck sideways across the wall like a shelf. At least, she thought it stopped. Her head continued to twirl.

"Better," Turian continued. "Anyway, she's quite anxious to have you. You and that thing on your arm. You'll fast become her favorite slave, I'm sure." His voice became tired and disdainful. "She does so enjoy curiosities. Wasteful, if you ask me."

Kaizha blinked. Now that the spinning had stopped, she had started to wonder, as though the thoughts had time to accumulate instead of sliding out of her ears. "How long have I been here?"

Turian laughed the kind of laugh that took the least amount of effort, a bare staccato of air in his throat. He poured a boiling substance into a flask and swished it around. A mild explosion poofed out of it.

He always ignored her, but it was a question she'd grown accustomed to thinking of every time she saw light from the door, and though she didn't know if she could understand the answer, she couldn't let it go.

Kaizha blinked again. She seemed to have more eyelids than usual, even though she only had one eye without a bandage stuck to it. "How long have I been here, master, if you please."

"You say that a lot," he said. "You know, Xiongnyao says that you've whined about the lack of innovation, with men and alchemy..." He rubbed something that smelled like oil and sulfur over a metal instrument. She didn't recognize it from her own training. It must be new. After her time. "I've made quite a lot of contributions to the art of transmogrification. But no one notices, really. People want their slaves faster, the prisons fill up; they asked me for higher turnover. So I made it faster. And yet, for you, it's longer. Torture can't be done without at least the illusion of a very long time. So," he tapped the side of his head lazily, still not bothering to look at her, "I've given the public what they want, and enhanced the art at the same time. How often did you or your half-wit grandmother manage such a thing?" he asked, as though he were half-asleep and asking a fellow meadow-napper what the shapes of the clouds reminded him of.

Kaizha tried to remember and couldn't. She couldn't remember anything—the lobe was growing—her breath juddered out of her like shutters slamming against the windows in a windstorm.

"Yes, that. That's what we're going to fix today. Xiongnyao wants you in the best possible condition. So we're going to break you open and try to do something with those lungs." He went to the wall and moved a lever around. The wooden cogs under the floor creaked and clanked. The wheel she was stuck to moved down the wall, bent at the joint in the middle, and flattened out on the floor, becoming a horizontal platform.

"This is...this whole thing...it's..." She tried to remember the word. "Asinine. Moaki can't still want infandi after everything that's happened. You can't still—"

"Oh, no, Xiongnyao's fixed that as well. The problem isn't infandi; it's the fall. The earliest an infandus has ever succumbed is their tenth year of service. So from now on, every infandus is to be destroyed after its ninth year. Problem solved. We may have to expand transmogrification sentencings, but aside from the criminals, everybody will be happy." Turian lifted the oily metal instrument. It looked like a cross between a harpoon and a mallet. "She's very smart, you know. Happy happy happy." Turian sighed, took aim, and cracked Kaizha's chest open.

343

After a while, she forgot her name.

After a longer while, she came to learn to measure time again—by the appearances of the master. One day to the next was marked by Turian, and Turian alone, though he told her that soon she would have a mistress, to be marked nearly as important as himself.

She could hardly wait. And one day, there was no more waiting.

She was taken out of the chamber, up through the prison, and into the light. Though at first she could hardly see, she was led into the back of a rhino-drawn cart, and from there the brilliance of colors softened into her vision.

Today was her introduction day, the soldiers told her. They'd washed her to make her look nice. The master had taken out the rod in her shoulder. He said he'd leave the metal contraption covering her arm for the mistress to remove. The thing under the metal contraption was anxious to be free, and glad to have full access to her bosoms once more, or so it told her. Today was a happy day indeed.

Today she got to go home to live with her masters, the Haishings, the greatest alchemists in the city, first seats of the oligarchy. Masters of Moaki! She was undeserving, but they wanted her, somehow. She trembled—fear, anticipation, cold, all at once, wracking the fibers of her jerking skin.

The mountain got colder as the rhinos pulled upward and her hot breath plumed out of her mouth. The humans pointed at her, saying something that sounded like "Shanyang," which sounded faintly familiar but too vague for her to remember. A lot of things were like that. She almost asked what they meant, but she forgot she couldn't talk anymore, and had no permission besides. Instead she looked at her hands—one a big pawy thing with sharp ends, the other still covered with a metal jug—and tugged at her floppy goatish ears. She didn't quite recognize her own body parts, either, and she felt lonesome and lost, like a baby bird fallen from the nest. But it was going to be all right. Her masters would give her a new identity. It was going to be all right.

The cart stopped at the very end of the road, almost halfway up the mountain, it seemed, right before a great looming temple. The house was great and beautiful, in the shadow of so many great and beautiful things. This was where she was to live! She couldn't imagine her ugly body touching such purity. But the soldiers led her to the door, her great un-fine paws shuffling across the fine wood of the entrance-deck, sometimes on all fours and sometimes on twos—she hadn't quite figured out how many feet she was to use when she moved.

They knocked. Another infandus bowed and let them inside. She waited in the hallway, trying not to touch anything. Then her mistress came flowing out of one of the rooms like a shimmering waterfall.

"Welcome, welcome! Oh, let me get a look at you." The mistress looked her up and down with a broad smile. "Turian has done a magnificent job. You are impressive." She wrinkled her nose. "Except for that." She pointed at the metal thing. "We'll have to get that off of you…" She murmured something to an infandus and he loped away.

"I'm sorry." Her words sounded strange. Wrong, somehow,

more full of consonant-type sounds than she remembered.

"Now, now." The mistress's smile returned. "I'm sure you're wondering what your place here will be. Most infandi I receive are most anxious to get their first orders. Luckily for you, I have a very important job I think you'd be perfect for."

"Yes, mistress?"

Xiongnyao went to a table, picked up a scroll, and unrolled it. A map. "I want you to go to Trago." She pointed. It didn't seem too far from the dot that said *Moaki*. "We've stopped getting reports from our military outpost, and yesterday we heard a rumor about escaped revolutionaries holing up in the town, but no one seems to be forthcoming about what happened. Turian is already getting the army ready to march on Trago, but after recent events, they need some time to prepare, and he is unused to getting things done in an efficient manner. I feel this needs some immediate response."

She grinned.

"I want you to go there ahead of the army and find out what happened to our officer and who's responsible. See if you can track down the revolutionaries. I obtained permission to omit your servile gland, so you are free to kill them and whoever else has slighted the rule of Moaki. If dead, bring their bodies back to me with your report. If you manage to take them alive, drag them here in chains. Either will please me." The mistress took her hand and squeezed. The infandus she'd sent away came back with a torch and some kind of saw and began working away on the metal stub on her hand.

"Oh! And I nearly forgot…" The mistress went to a table and picked up a beautiful silvery strictureweed collar, the nameplate imprinted with the marks of the house of Haishing.

Her skin shivered as the mistress put it around her neck and clicked the latch into place. Her muscles were jumping like agitated fish. Her first orders. Her first collar. And—

"Your name…your name. I've had a hard time thinking of one. But…" The mistress stroked the ends of her floppy ears. The infandus working with the saw cracked open the metal stub and the creature on her arm waggled its tendrils in glee. The mistress's lips got twitchy. "I have it. Oh, I have it." Amused snorts rolled out of her nostrils and she clamped down on her lips with her teeth. "You shall be Floppacles."

It was grand name! A glorious name! And so beautiful in the mistress's honeyed voice! Floppacles cocked her head to show her pleasure.

"You like it, do you?"

"I like it very much," said Floppacles.

"Mhm," the mistress giggled. "Moltnips, fetch your engraving tools. We shall need her new name engraved on her collar-plate for all to see."

The infandus with the saw nodded and flew off into the house again.

"Very well. My husband has done well with you. I'm quite pleased. I trust you have no problems with your task?"

Floppacles shook her head. "No, mistress."

"Wonderful. Oh, and I forgot—once you get outside the bounds of Moaki, you are free to dispatch anyone that gets in your way. If that means destroying the entire town, well, they will have brought it on themselves." She smiled. "Godspeed, Floppacles."

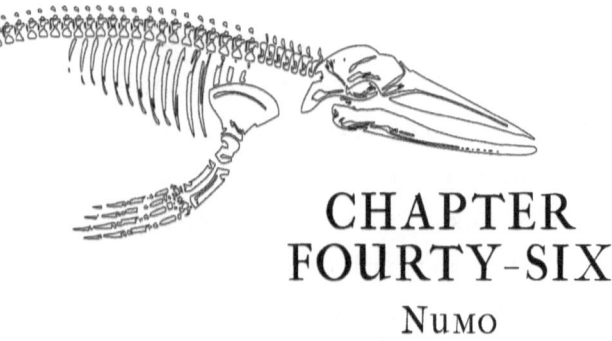

CHAPTER
FOURTY-SIX
NUMO

SANGJA HAD OFFERED Numo a cushion on the floor to sleep on and a bushel of dried-up "waster-fish" to eat. Numo didn't know what a waster-fish was, but they tasted foul and were full of tiny thready bones. Still, he couldn't complain; he had a place to be and a person to serve, which was where he should feel right.

Only he didn't.

Sangja gave him shelter and orders to fulfill, but he wasn't a master, not really. He didn't feel like one. He was a stranger, an odd one at that. Numo's primary orders from Sangja, for the past two weeks, had been to "fill that dead whale with lamp-fish and guano and anything you would put in your ovens." Which was quite vague. Which oven? Which season? Fodder for a quick burn when the nights got cold after warm days, or a slow massive fire to keep the place warm through steadily freezing temperatures? Sangja didn't know and seemed to get irritated when Numo asked. So Numo stopped asking and went about collecting a random assortment of everything.

Sometimes Sangja would ask him to fetch other things, all manner of things, as long as they were strange and useless-looking. Dead spiders, rotted cereals and discarded rice from the fields of farmers who tended lands above the cliffs, scrap metals, tossed-out meat and plants from food stalls, anything that washed up on the beach and hadn't yet rotted, trinkets and coins that drunkards dropped in the tavern, kore-seeds, beer, and *harlots*, which, Numo discovered, were *persons of a very agreeable nature*, and not at all in the class of stinkards as he had once thought. Numo quite liked the harlots, actually; they were merry and made Sangja merry and he wished sometimes they would stay, but they never did.

The boy claimed to be an alchemist, but was nothing like any alchemist Numo had known. While he seemed well-versed enough in healing arts to treat many of Numo's wounds and pains from the previous days, he otherwise seemed to be a knave and a brute. He was leery-eyed and crude and unkempt and hardly ever wore shirts, and he smelled of sweat and the sea. His quarters were worse than the mistress's cabin—cramped and small and dim, the floors slick with molten fish fat. Even though Sangja did, surprisingly, hang fresh clusters of some sort of pleasantly fragrant sea-plant around the walls with some regularity, it did little to improve the atmosphere. As much as Numo now hated the world he came from, he longed for home.

But that was the least of his longings.

He tried not to think of her. Truly he did. But thinking of her happened anyway, like the muscle contractions of his intestines; unbidden and unconscious, they moved thoughts of her into the foremost digestive-sacs of his mind. He wondered mostly if she was all right. If she was happier. If Rawang was kinder. If she looked or smelled more like a human than herself. If the glimmer in the shoestrings of saliva that hung from her mouth like wet pendants had gone dull, or if her teeth had grown stunted, or if her mane had ceased to grow or been cut down like barley. If she could still growl in that particular way that felt like she was sending little ghosts into his body to lick his bones from the inside.

All these things and more he thought of. He did, however, stop himself short of hoping he would see her again.

Numo trudged up the road and out of Trago one day on a whale-stuffing excursion. He was tired of gutting fish and scraping off bits of pteropteryx poop, and longed for the more familiar burnables of a forest. Even the twisty rock-swallowing trees of the lowlands were quite far from Trago, but he could at least find something, he supposed, in the shrubby bits of barked plant life they'd seen on their way to the coast.

Leaving the cliffside also got him away from the jumbly bustling excitement of the town, which he no longer found all that exciting a thing. Nothing was particularly exciting anymore, or good, or meet, or within any of the bounds of order that he knew of; he was only waiting to fulfill his obligation to Sangja. And if he survived, then what?

Well. He probably wouldn't have to worry about that.

Numo pulled the empty carrying-hammock close around him. The air was cold with sea spray. The sky was bright and piercing and the sun irritated him. Piercingness reminded him of her hands, and he told himself not to think about her, which naturally led to thinking about her again. He tried to imagine her in a nice house, whittling at a woodworking table as his mistress used to do or whatever pursuits women fancied—but he couldn't. Hammerfist was Hammerfist, not Sramai.

Hammerfist wouldn't exist anymore, and that was meet.

It *was* meet, darn it all.

So why did Numo feel like his body was slowly being ripped in half from scalp to sacrum?

He still had that paper he'd stolen from the mistress. It was covered in blood, and he could barely read it, but read it he did. Every morning, every night, puzzling and wondering. The more he thought about it, the more sure he was. Numo had to make the pain go away, make the thinking-about-her stop. If it was all a trick of his slavish little lobe, then stabbing it should fix the problem.

If it wasn't, he supposed he was doomed. Oddly, the prospect of a blade inserted into his brain was a more comforting thought than love.

Even if he wanted to proceed, though, Numo couldn't stab his brain by himself. He'd never felt so completely alone, wanting only someone to stab him in the head and having no one.

He dragged himself across the nearest cereal-field. Numo dragged himself everywhere, these days, or trudged; his feet were simply too heavy. He supposed he ought to have followed the paths around the farms, if he cared at all about propriety anymore. But cutting through the field seemed the quickest way to the shrublands, and while he suspected farmers didn't enjoy slaves tromping across their stubs of sheared barley, no one seemed to be around to take notice.

Just as he was thinking this, a strange snuffling sound whuffed from behind some row of withered stalks. Numo stopped. It didn't sound human. It didn't sound like a beast, either, though admittedly Numo was not well-versed in the noises of coastal wildlife. But the growls and rolls and snorts sounded rather infandus-like.

His breath hitched and his legs got lighter and the sunlight didn't seem so awful and his mood leapt into the air like a pronking goat. Numo put a hand on his chest as if to keep his organs from leaping out.

It isn't her, he told himself. *It isn't her.*

But what if it was?

Numo bent down on his knees and peered through the stalks of whatever-crop-this-was.

It was Fustilugs.

The infandus's head swiveled to meet Numo's gaze. "Crenellate me," he murmured. His body was crumpled into a ball, and his face was lost and frightened, as though he had no idea how to unfold himself.

Numo stood and pushed through the barley. "Fustilugs? It's me, Fustilugs. Numo."

Fustilugs pointed a gnarled finger at him with bright, glossy eyes, his hands still stuck up around his breast. "You have arms. Buxom? Help." He cocked his head into the dirt and managed a crooked attempt at smiling, though Numo had no idea what he was smiling at.

"Oh, dear." Numo grabbed his finger and pulled. The arm straightened. Fustilugs giggled in wonderment. He waggled his other fingers. "Trembletrembletoos."

Numo slowly pulled out all of Fustilugs's limbs, until the infandus was lying straight out on his side. He sighed in relief.

"Oh, small lover. Thank you."

"You remember me?"

Fustilugs chuckled. "I remember! Small lover. Terrible storm in the mountains." He stared up at the sky and his face went blank.

"Fustilugs?"

No response. His body was still, devoid of the rise and fall of breath. Numo did the only thing he could think of. He pounded his fists into Fustilugs's chest.

"Oh, meat bean! Thank you." Fustilugs turned over and splayed out, waving his arms happily and playing with an imaginary string.

The fall must have worsened. Numo wondered if this was what it looked like when an infandus was close to death. Mangy and emaciated, his ribs prominent through snowy white body hair. The others must have left him behind when his sickness became too far advanced. Although how he got here, exactly, was a bit of a mystery. "Are you all right, Fustilugs?"

"Wonderful! Glorious! Bonafacial! Alimentary! And yourself? Did you garrulate your song to your love?" Fustilugs rolled over, hunkered down, and put his chin in his claws, gazing at Numo with eyes so lifeless they might as well have been rocks stuck on his face.

"No. I couldn't be with her. It wasn't meet."

Fustilugs's face crumpled vaguely. "Fuck?"

Numo nodded, and pulled the carrying-hammock tighter around his shoulders. "It hurts, if that's what you mean."

Fustilugs pounced on Numo. He wrapped his claws around his little body and stuffed him into his wiry-haired armpit, folding him in an embrace that smelled like onions left to rot in the mouth of a cat with dental disease. "Oh, fleshbean," he murmured, "nubbin of passion, whelp of freesongs and throbbing! How I know the twisting barb of love unmade!" He removed Numo from his armpit and shook him roughly in front of his gaze. "You must tell me if there is anything I can do to help. How can I help? Albumin. Allspice. Ah! I have it! We shall make wine from our urine! Come, let us—"

"No, no, thank you, Fustilugs. Thank you ever so, but no."

Fustilugs bit his lip. "But I must do something."

Numo regarded him a moment. His eyes—they were dead and alive all at once. His body swayed just a little, and some of his toes waggled around in an uncoordinated jumble. Poor Fustilugs had somehow made it out of the mess in Moaki alive only to disintegrate.

But he was here. And he was the only one in the world who seemed to understand the ache that inflamed Numo's brains.

"There is something you can do," said Numo. He pulled out the blood-encrusted wad of paper and the thin dagger. "You can pierce my slave-lobe."

"Ah, a euphemism, is it?" Fustilugs asked.

"No. What? No." He unfurled the paper and smoothed it out carefully. "This is the slave-lobe," he said, pointing. "It is in the front part of the drake brain. Just behind the tops of the eyes."

"What is this line?"

Numo held up the little dagger.

"Mustard." Fustilugs gasped in awe.

"It goes right between the top of the eyelid and the brow, you see, just under—"

"Okay, yes! Yes! I understand perfectly! I have it!" Fustilugs snatched the tiny dagger from Numo. It looked like a thread in his wide fingers. "Lie down, small lover."

"Well—I wasn't thinking of doing it right here, and precisely this moment, you see, more like—"

"I said *lie down!*" Fustilugs rammed Numo in the chest

with his forehead, flattening his lungs and exploding the breath out of him.

"There. Perfect." Fustilugs laid a claw on top of Numo's torso, pinning him to the ground. He pushed the point of the dagger up against the top of his eye socket. "Hold still."

"But—I—"

Fustilugs's hand wavered and the dagger slid around over the skin of his eyelid.

"Wait. Wait—"

"Time does not." The infandus squinted and forced the dagger in.

Numo remembered the front of his face erupting, and the world dissolving into colors and then black, and hot purple blood welling up over his eye and running down his face and into his mouth, and he screamed and Fustilugs screamed, and then, thankfully, there was a gap of weird space that wasn't quite nothing and still wasn't quite anything. He didn't remember waking up, either—if ever he'd fallen un-awake—but when he came back to himself, he was in a pit, having dirt thrown on his face.

"Stop?" he requested, weakly, without much confidence in the matter. "Stop," he tried.

The dirt stopped. Fustilugs leaned over the little pit. "Hello, dead body?"

"I'm not dead..." He wasn't quite alive either, but he felt he was not dead at all. One of his eyes was crusted shut.

"Oh no," Fustilugs groaned. "I have failed. I have failed!"

He disappeared from the pit, wailing and gnashing. "Even as a human, I cannot stop failing!"

Numo's ear pricked. A human? Did the fall make infandi think they were people? *Advanced stages, perhaps.* He tried pushing himself up and the surroundings got all twirly. Numo sat heavily, squeezing his head, imagining that he was pushing more blood out of his eye socket, which smarted horribly. After a minute or two, the world stabilized. Numo pulled himself out of the little pit.

The sky looked strange, as though it had changed colors without changing appearance, faded blindingly to the color of a corked hiss. The air trembled with Fustilugs's anguished wailing and made Numo dizzy again. He flopped to the ground. "Will you *quiet down*," he barked. The noise came from deep in his gut. Odd, foreign, but somehow natural.

Fustilugs sniffled, but did as told.

"What are you keening about?" Numo said, his voice cracking and squeaking.

"I failed at killing you."

"But you weren't meant to kill me. Not this time, anyway." He was very tired, his head-muscles constricting around his brain-fat with crushing vigor, his eye socket throbbing as though his pupil contained one of the chambers of his heart.

He wondered about Hammerfist, bleakly, blandly. There was something there, still something, but it was far away.

"No?"

"No."

Fustilugs's face broke apart into an uneven grin. "Oh! Spectacular!" His face lit up and his finger stabbed at the air, waggling like a baby goat's tail. "Since you're not dead, would you like to be my slave?"

"What?"

"Humans, you know, they have slaves. I finished the elixir yesterday, so I am permanent human, you see, but they still don't seem to take me as one of them—perhaps it's because I have no slaves. With you to be my slave, though, they will be convinced! And I would be the grandest of masters, I promise."

Numo's head hurt. "The elixir?"

"Yes, the elixir. The alchemist gave it to me, after I gave him a—a—what was it." Fustilugs frowned. "A lucky foot, or somesuch."

Numo's numbness dissolved into dread. "A severed head?"

Fustilugs gaped. "How did you know?"

Numo didn't answer. He couldn't—the words were fast and oozing, like mucus in a sneeze, spattered and dribbling all over his thoughts. Fustilugs had made it out of Moaki with an oligarch's head. He had gotten the elixir. He had finished it. And he was still a dying infandus with a brain disease rotting him from the inside.

What would become of Hammerfist?

The Something about Hammerfist burst and washed over him in a lukewarm gray tide. It had changed; it had shifted its gravity. He wasn't inexplicably drawn to her anymore like a bug crawling into fire. She wasn't a star that captured him with her divine ebullience. She wasn't an avatar of some goddess with amnesia floating across the earth.

She was a…a person. A person who had made a mistake and trusted a slave-brained fool and a selfish knave.

He no longer wanted to throw himself in a fire just to warm her, and he might not want to chain himself to her wrist and twirl about her as though she was a planet, but he also didn't know if he knew her well enough to feel such things properly. What if he had time to know her? Could he love her then? Or did he love her already?

What if Fustilugs had been wrong and he still didn't understand?

He raked the dirt softly and looked at the sky. It didn't matter if he loved her or not. He had to warn her. She needed him. By the hearth of Pig-Iron Nonnysteed, he still cared for her, and she needed him.

"Small'un?" Fustilugs tapped him and ended up shoving him over. "Small'un, I asked you a question. I don't remember what it was. Do you remember?"

Numo stared at Fustilugs. His wasted body. His vacant eyes that flashed occasionally with sentience like a spark in a stuttering breeze. His toes that wouldn't stop dancing.

"No, sir. I'm sorry."

"Sir! Fine thing, that. A human for a whole day and he's the first to call me sir." Fustilugs grinned at nothing, staring somewhere above Numo. "Sir! Sir indeed."

"Sir…I wonder if you might accompany me to—" Numo stopped. Fustilugs's toes had quit dancing. His entire body had gone rigid. There was no breath. No life.

"Sir?" Numo grasped him by the back of the knee, feeling for a heartbeat. The infandus collapsed at Numo's touch.

Numo leapt upon his chest. Slapped him. Hit him in all the places where a drake's ventricles were situated before he realized that infandi probably had their heart-chambers in different places. Where was a human's heart? He didn't know. Why didn't he know such things? Numo's eye was bleeding

358

again. He kicked Fustilugs in the face one final time, so hard he thought he'd broken his toes again.

Nothing happened.

Fustilugs was dead.

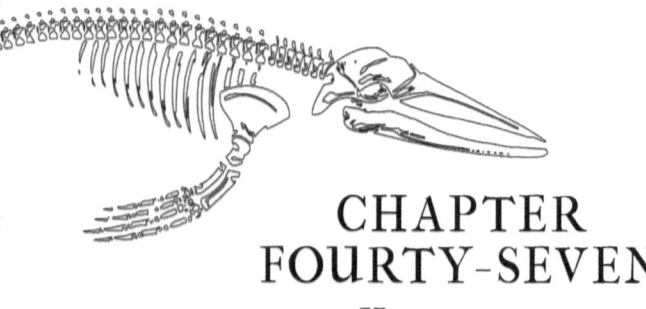

CHAPTER
FOURTY-SEVEN
HAMMERFIST

HAMMERFIST—SRAMAI, SHE HAD to remember—had drunk almost half of the elixir over the past two weeks. And she was happy. Sort of. She couldn't quite remember what happy was supposed to feel like, and it seemed to be a slippery term, she thought, that probably related most to a transitory mood rather than a constant state of being, though people seemed to use it differently, which was very confusing.

But the elixir made her stop caring. It was such a relief to not want to die that she didn't mind so much about the particulars, and it was only in that saggy middle between doses that she remembered about not being happy.

Rawang had found them an abandoned farmhouse to live in. He made a family shrine to Samaak, "just like before," he said, and made her a bed big enough to sleep in. After that he spent most of the time trying to fix the roof, though she didn't much see the point; she was used to all forms of weather dripping or blaring or snowing down on her head. But she supposed it was the principle of the thing. Humans, after all, had roofs.

He had her in charge of hunting and finding food, though

they had no implements to hunt with. "But I'm turning human," she'd said, "I can feel it. Soon I won't be able to hunt without weapons." He just smiled sadly and suggested she take a sharp stick if it made her feel better. But she always ended up breaking the sticks somehow, and the field sloths of this climate seemed more squishable than the ones in the mountains, anyway.

Memories had started to come back more steadily now. Sharper, clearer. They came soon after she drank a dose of the elixir and faded slowly until the next one. Retention was spotty. But she remembered having regular hands so well now that she could almost feel them. She could see her claws receding into human fingernails. Feel the fleshy softness erupting over the calluses and fur and keratin. Most of the memories were simple things like this—hands, lips, being a child, being something called an "apprentice" and banging a hot piece of metal against a larger chunk—and most of them caused her no pain, but every so often she'd get a flash of something hotter, piercing, dark and unbearable. But flashes only, skipping by too fast to burn into her thoughts.

Until the fifteenth day.

On the fifteenth day, Rawang came running into the house, sweat-smeared, all atwitter. "Sramai! Sramai, I found you a present." He beamed at her lopsidedly, hiding his hands behind his back. "Would you like to see?"

She nodded. Gods help her, she was even a little excited.

Rawang swung his arms forward, presenting her with a big thing with foldy leather in the middle and two bits of wood on either end. "Voila! For you, sweetheart. For when the elixir has finished its work."

She stared. "What is it?"

"Well—well," Rawang stammered. "It's a bellows." He turned it over in his hands, his expression deflating. "I'm going to make you another forge. You were always happiest when you were at work. And this is the first part..." He held it out to her, his smile gone. "It's a bellows."

"A *brraaauughohh*," she said. Why didn't her words sound like his? Her mouth felt normal now, but she still made awful noises, and Rawang didn't understand half the things she said. Maybe it was poor muscle memory?

She took the bellows from him and turned it over in her fingers. The wood and leather electrified them. The heat lanced up her hands and her spine. Her fingers remembered. And then *she* remembered.

The last time she held a bellows, she had been fracturing a man's skull with it.

Sramai dropped the thing. The house shifted and melted around her. Rawang was bending over her somehow—was she on the floor?—calling her name, he was calling her name and his voice was far away, but his face was far too close. His half-burned face. Sramai saw herself, in the orange glow of her old forge, knees pinning Rawang to the ground. He was screaming; the other men were screaming—she'd beaten them with hammers and tongs and yes, the bellows—and she pressed a great hot glowing sword against his face, harder and harder until the smell of his burning skin had seeped into her nose-hairs, and the soldiers came and lifted her off of him, and they took her to the jail and into the chamber and strapped her to a wheel—

Sramai couldn't breathe. Her lungs were like wooden boxes inside her chest. Inert. Rigid. Flammable. Rawang shook her. Her spit was pooling in the back of her throat, blocking the airway. He rolled her over. She blinked furiously, gasping, threads of saliva sailing across the floor. The pain in her chest was like nothing she'd ever suffered in the arena. It held her to the floor like an anvil sitting on her ribcage.

She'd known that she was a monster as a homunculus. But she hadn't imagined what a monster she had been as a human.

Sramai lay like that for some time, forcing air in and out, though she wasn't sure why anymore. She had done all this to escape one horrible existence and jump headlong into another. She was forced to kill as a slave and a homunculus, but she'd been free as a human. Free to not kill anyone. And she'd done it anyway. Why? Would her mind convert back into that murderous state once she was herself again?

She couldn't allow that.

It was all pointless. All for nothing. And Rawang...

He rubbed her back, making gentle hush-hush noises as the whimpers creaked out of her body. What did he think he was doing? Did he remember what she'd done?

"Why?" she said finally.

"Why what?"

"I tried to kill you as a human. So why do you want me to become human again?"

His brow sank. Rawang glanced at the bellows. "Oh," he murmured. "So you remember it, I suppose..."

"Yes."

"That wasn't—I didn't think...I had hoped you wouldn't. I had hoped..." He swallowed. "But surely you also remember that there were other circumstances. Things that made you behave that way. Things," Rawang said, "that...that *I* did, to make you do something like that." His face pinched.

Sramai slowly pushed herself off the floor. Her nails got stuck in the floorboards and she accidentally wrenched out one of the planks. She shook it off, leaned against the wall, and clutched her body so that she wouldn't destroy anything else. Her fingers trembled, the nails sawing into her skin as they jiggered back and forth. "I don't remember that."

"Oh." Rawang looked at the floor, and then rubbed her arm. She flinched. "Just know that it wasn't your fault. Please just... just forget it ever happened."

Forget?

She shoved him away with far more force than she meant to. His body skidded across the room and thumped against the opposite wall. "I *can't* forget. And I won't inflict myself on you or anyone else. Not as a human, not as a homunculus. I can't do this, Rawang. It's over..." Her voice cracked and fell away, as though its knees had been cut out from under it.

"Don't talk that way." Rawang scrambled to get up. He took a step towards her, then stopped when she bristled. "Please. It wasn't your fault."

She stood up and knocked her head on the roof joists. Bits of thatch and dust tumbled down. She wanted to scream, to tear apart the house, to tear her own skin to shreds. Instead she bit down on one of her tongues so hard it bled. Why did she have more than one tongue, still? "I'm going back to Trago. I might at least be of some use there in their war before I die. Please—forget about me. Go and have a happy life."

She turned, but Rawang ran in front of her, his hands raised, a vein standing out in sharp relief from his forehead. "I can't have a happy life without you, Sramai! Don't you think I tried? I couldn't. Please. If you don't believe me, I'll tell you—I'll tell you what happened. But you have to remember I'm not the same as I was. I was terrible then, a monster, a garbage person. I'm not a perfect man now, but I used to be horrible. I deserved what I got, and I've changed."

Sramai tried to swallow back the saliva gathering in her throat. "Changed from what?"

Rawang dropped his hands and his face sagged. "You... we. Um."

"Go on, then."

"Okay." He took a breath. "We wanted to have a child. You got p—you got pregnant." His throat was hitching, all the muscles in his neck twitching and bulging as he tried to keep his voice even. "But the midwife said that it was dangerous. That your womb was not safe for a baby, and that the pregnancy would not go well. She told us the best chance of survival was the seahorse method—that I should carry the baby in an artificial womb. We went to an alchemist to discuss it. But I wanted a second opinion.

"...You have to understand, this was years ago, when the social reformation had just begun. Men were finally allowed to do alchemy. I was so excited about apprenticing, making something respectable of myself..." Rawang sat on the floor, looking very small. Things he was saying pinged against her memory, lighting up dark little sections. "Excited about apprenticing" was an understatement, she remembered. He'd wanted to be an alchemist so badly that he started meeting with the back-alley practitioners after he got rejected from the schools. She'd hated it. She'd told him not to bother, that her blacksmithery was enough for the

365

both of them. But he'd said it was about his freedom…

"My mentor said there was another way. That I shouldn't let you force the baby on me; that carrying a child was a woman's lot and women had been too long enslaving men with seahorse pregnancies or some nonsense. Nonsense I believed at the time. So when he said there was a treatment that would make the pregnancy safer without transferring the baby into some implant in my guts, I insisted on it. I refused to transfer. And you were so…"

Angry. She'd been furious. Taking a treatment from his charlatan of a mentor was the most dangerous and ridiculous thing he'd ever suggested to her. She understood that he was trying to get out in the world and make a way for himself, but she wouldn't take a chance with their child, or with her own life, and hadn't understood why he would.

"Unreceptive. You were skeptical. Of course you were skeptical. You were always smarter than me. You were right." Rawang paused, swallowing. "But I didn't see it. I thought you were being unfair to me and didn't believe in my work. So I put the treatment in your food. In your water. All the while we'd keep talking about the transference and I'd say, let's wait a little longer, keep the baby from experiencing such trauma until it's more viable, trying to sound reasonable, when in fact I was…I was out of my mind."

And she hadn't seen through it. That was the most infuriating part. She'd let it happen. The thought that Rawang would be capable of something so horrible didn't ever cross her mind. Until the day she found a vial.

"Then you caught me out. You were—you were upset."

Another great understatement.

"I told you I'd go through with transference the next day.

Instead I called a meeting of the apprentices to try to come up with a way to force you to go along with the alternative route. While I was in that meeting, you had a miscarria—"

"Stop, for the love of all that's holy, stop." Bellows. Fire pokers. The hot half-formed sword. She remembered it, she remembered why, and gods, the fury—it crackled up through her body now as though it were splitting her bones from the inside.

He's different now. He's sorry.

"Sramai. Things will be different this time. You'll come back to me, and we can be as we were. We can try to have a family again."

Thoughts of the angle at which to strike his skull to make it snap in half traced across her brain.

He knows he was wrong.

It wasn't even the loss of their child. It was what he did to control her. Without her knowing.

"I need you. I need us to try again. I need to go back."

Her fingers could practically feel the flesh colliding...

He's already suffered enough.

But what if she didn't want to go back?

Her whole body shook and sweat poured down her face and slathered her chest hair and she could smell his blood, his weak pallid blood, imagine it inside her mouth. She had to get away from him or she'd hurt him again. Sramai shoved him aside and raced out the door. Her shoulder banged into the jamb and tore off half the wood. She was faintly aware of him stumbling after her. But she couldn't stop; her whole body had been jarred awake and it couldn't stop until it had his throat on the outside of his body, so she kept running, down on her knuckles again, why on her knuckles still—

She tripped.

The thing she tripped over yipped and skittered back into a clot of brambles. Sramai kept running. Some rabbit or a dog or a small bear. She stopped. She needed to tear something apart. Her body ached for it. Her nostril flared as she smelled it coming. Yes, it was the only way to release it; the only way to stop feeling it. The creature's footsteps tracked up behind her. She whirled on it, digging her nails into its soft little body, and oh, the blood, the mealy lilac blood, it was pathetic but it was something, and her body shivered—

"Hammerfist?" the thing squeaked.

Numo.

She dropped him. He bounced.

"I told you to stay away. I told you I would hurt you. I told you I would only hurt you!" Her whole face was on fire. Her eyes were boiling. She slapped her hands over her face and it bled.

"But I'm all right," Numo said, pushing himself up, staggering. "It's just a little blood...I'm fine..."

Rawang came huffing and puffing up the hillside.

"You too!" Sramai growled. "Get away from me. All of you! Stay the hell away—"

"Calm down," Rawang panted. "Please, Sramai. Calm down." But he didn't come any closer. Instead, he glanced over at Numo and scowled. "Why can't I get rid of you?"

"I'm sorry," Numo said, his eyes glassy and distant. "I know I said I would leave both of you alone, but...there's something I have to tell you."

The wind shifted. Numo kept babbling about something, something about the elixir, but Sramai's senses filled up with scent instead of sound. The world went gray and a bright aura of a familiar odor drew her to it like a flower following the sun.

It plumed out of Numo's nostrils as though he had a furnace in his belly, snorting great columns of smoke the color of half-clotted blood. It steamed up from his eyeballs and oozed out of his ears and it all drifted into her nostrils—nostril—and her mind gorged itself on it, calculating, aiming, wanting, even as her heart shriveled and her muscles went slack.

It was the scent of death.

CHAPTER
FORTY-EIGHT
Numo

"I'LL KILL THAT kid! I'll *kill* that goddamned kid!" Rawang stomped away at a dizzying rate. Numo toddled after, unsure why his feet seemed stuck to the earth and his limbs so boggy in general when something so important was going on. Hammerfist yelled something at him, but all the noise and commotion was very muffled for some reason, and in slow motion, as though the entire fabric of reality was drippy with molasses. He couldn't remember when things had gotten this way. It had taken him some time to find Hammerfist, days, but he'd lost track of how many, and now time was a pool of wax under an unsteady flame, softening and melting and hardening and melting again.

Hammerfist caught up to Rawang and grabbed his arm to whip him around. She left claw marks. She glared at her hand, and she growled and grunted, pointing at Numo. "Something's wrong," she was saying, her voice floating like a corpse drifting down a river, "something's wrong with him; you have to fix it."

Rawang staggered back from her, holding a bleeding arm. "Why? Nothing's wrong with him. Look at him. He's fine."

"I'm fine," Numo repeated dully.

"He's not fine," said Hammerfist. "Please look at him."

"Why the hell should I? I don't owe him anything, and neither do you. In fact, I'm pretty sick of him. Why is he even here?" Rawang spun on Numo. "Why are you still here? You going to tell me you love her? I've told you before, it's a lie. It's not real." He turned back to Hammerfist, softening, pleading. "It's not real."

"No…" Numo cleared his throat. It seemed to be very lumpy and hot, and the words in his head all boiled and mashed into a creamy soupy mess. "No, I don't love her. You were right. It was my brain." Hammerfist blinked furiously at him, her shoulders tightening so knottily that they clumped up around her neck. "It was my brain. I made sure of that. But I still care very much what happens to her, if it's all the same to you."

"What do you mean, you made sure of that?" Hammerfist growled.

"I performed an experiment. On my brain." Numo's voice seemed to plod out of the water in the nearby rice field, coming from the scenery instead of his mouth.

Rawang stared at him wildly. "And you don't love her."

"I don't know her well enough to love her properly, sir. I don't feel the same as I did. But I still…" He peered at her, peering back at him, a mirror image in expression, and Numo felt they swapped places for an instant, and had to squish the ground beneath his toes to make sure it was his body that was talking. "I care about her. Sir."

"Please." Hammerfist's voice rumbled, a distant snowstorm of a sound. "He needs help. It doesn't matter who loves who or what or why…"

Rawang's face collapsed like a building, the stubble turned

to rubble, and smoke went up around his eyes. "It may not matter to you. It matters very much to me. I will make you see. I will make it matter." He whirled away in the direction of Trago. Hammerfist's muscles coiled, but something stopped her. She stared at her hands. At her massive claws. She felt the outline of her crooked jaw, the fangs, the serrated teeth jutting this way and that.

"*Nmhhaa*," she said softly, "do I look like me?" Her words twirled down on him lazily, burning trails of charred bark wafting about from a fire, scattering here and there for Numo to piece together.

"You look very much like you." Numo nodded. "Very definitely like you."

"I could kill him, couldn't I? If I touch him? I could kill him without even meaning to." She stared after Rawang, her voice dropping to nearly nothing, footfalls on soft grass, dew sliding down a stalk of wheat.

"I suppose you could."

"And I suppose the alchemist might be just as *skrr'shlaghdeh* to treat a homunculus as a *kraoslehsh.*"

"I suppose so," said Numo, who didn't truly understand, but if Hammerfist was supposing it, it was probably correct.

She swallowed. "Then I think we must follow him."

It seemed she understood. Or that, at least, she was willing to go back to Sangja. If that charlatan of an alchemist didn't have a real cure for the fall, then Numo would persuade him to invent one, then and there. After all, he was a soldier of butchery. A murderer. And he'd prove it.

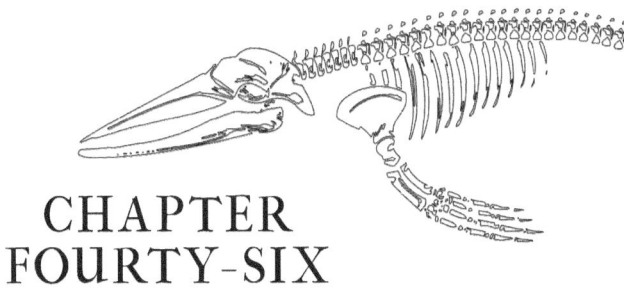

CHAPTER
FOURTY-SIX
FLOPPACLES

THE ROAD TO Trago was longer than the map made it seem. But Floppacles didn't mind. It was all for the mistress and the master. And it was possible she was just awful at reading maps.

She didn't have to kill anyone until she got there. "No one in or out," the guards said then, but they didn't seem like real guards at all. No armor and only titchy little harpoons. Scrawny necks. Easily broken.

After that, people swirled around her like a panicked swarm of gnats whirling in harmony with the pounding music in the air, *foom-ts-foom-ts-foom-ts*. She swatted them aside when they got in her way, and they seemed very afraid, but none of them would answer her questions.

"Where are the revolutionaries? Where is the Moaki guard?"

Buzzing, buzzing like insects, fast and slow. *Foom-ts-foom-ts-foom-ts*. It annoyed her. It made her brain full. So she grabbed one, let the tentacles loose upon its spine and watched them wind around its body, almost—but not quite—crushing it into pieces.

"Tell me," she said. "Answer me."

The man wrapped up in the teat-leech's tendrils said nothing. His neck went purple. He gaped. Still nothing. She almost killed him out of frustration right then, but her thoughts were interrupted.

"Master!" An infandus loped through the madness of the crowd towards her. "Master! Oh, don't hurt him, don't harm him so!" She was small and thin. Floppacles could crack her open like a crab.

"I have orders. No one will tell me what I've been commanded to find out. They must learn there are consequences."

The infandus clapped her hands over the sides of her face and pulled at her skin in anguish. She was missing a few fingers. The others were knobbly. She must have come cheap. "Okay. Okay. What do you want to know? Maybe I can help? Would you like that? Then you don't have to kill him! Right?"

Floppacles squinted at her. Spit burbled at the sides of the man's mouth. "I need to know where the revolutionaries are and what happened to the Moaki guard."

"Well I—I don't know what revolutionaries are. But! But I know that a man and a drake and an infandus were here and they killed the Moaki guard."

"Killed them? All of them?"

"Well, no, ah, um, they didn't kill the officer. That was the alchemist."

Floppacles's mind wandered from the man, and the teat-leech loosened its hold. It was quite good at that—anticipating her whims, sensing her states of fury or calm, whipping those she wanted whipped and leaving well enough alone when she just wanted to sleep. But it wouldn't let the man up. Floppacles was not yet satisfied. "An alchemist killed an officer? How? Why?"

"Oh! With an adze. I'm not sure why. I'm so sorry. I don't know. Please, please don't kill the master. I can show you where the alchemist lives! Maybe you can ask him!" the infandus squeaked.

Her heart thumped. Maybe she could ask him. Maybe he was one of the revolutionaries. A traitor. She'd drag his dead body back to the mistress and she'd be so delighted. She'd laugh again, that perfect laugh, like music twisting through her organs—

"Please! Oh, please let him go!"

Floppacles blinked. She'd forgotten about the man. She released her hold and he gasped, bluish, eyes wide and red, clutching at his neck and his breast and everywhere, as though he wasn't sure where it hurt the most.

"Take me to the alchemist," Floppacles said.

The alchemist's den was a hole in the rock face, hidden back in one of the cavernous alleyways. It was loud inside. Someone shouted "you lied, you lied" and someone with a higher voice shouted "I never said it would make her human" and screeching and growling from the homunculi—a drake and an infandus.

They were all there. Just as the knobbly-fingered slave had said. Stuck in a hole like ants in a tree. All she had to do was reach in and take them.

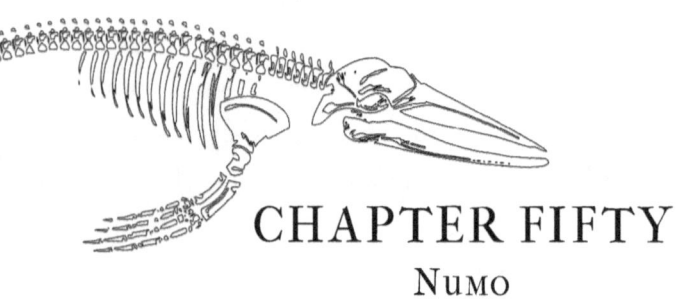

CHAPTER FIFTY
Numo

Numo couldn't get anyone to listen. But then, he didn't suppose he blamed them. He could barely hear his own voice.

"The elixir makes them think they're human. I never said it actually *made* them human," Sangja was saying—er, yelling? His face contorted, reddening, matching the wide fury of Rawang's own expression. "Gurry-sucking Moaker! What cocksloughed scab takes the word of a bunch of brainsick slaves?"

Rawang lunged at the boy's neck, and the boy dove under his legs, slicing at the flesh behind one of his knees with the adze. Rawang cried out. Hammerfist tackled Sangja, impaling his arms with her fingers, pinning him to the floor, roaring; the whole place a visual swirl that Numo couldn't make sense of. A horribly fast dance, too big and sweeping for him to comprehend. He blinked, trying to parse out a meaning. Hammerfist might kill Sangja. Rawang might kill Sangja. But if anyone had the cure, it was Sangja.

Numo drew a breath. He had to insert himself into the dance. He moved.

And then the door splintered into a thousand pieces.

Bits of thick black striaewood exploded into the room

like box social party confetti. A great dun infandus with black points and floppy ears strode in, hiding one arm behind its back. She was almost as large as Hammerfist, almost as terrifying, almost as beautiful, but with a heavily-scarred eye.

"Is this the den of the revolutionaries?" she said.

No one moved. No one spoke. The infandus shifted.

"No," said Numo.

"Oh. Hm." The infandus scratched its chin. "I'm sorry. I suppose the question was more of a pleasantry than anything." She withdrew her hand from behind her back. It was full of tentacles and tendrils, twisting, knotting, screwing around themselves. Numo strained to think where he'd seen it before and his brain bumbled down the stairs and crashed into the floor with a stomach-sucking jolt.

It was the mistress.

Shock kept Numo still even as the giant whip of a thing came swooping down on him. The mistress. The mistress was a homunculus? The mistress was here to—

Hammerfist rushed in front of him and struck out at the whip. The whip and the fist of claws collided. A quiet little crunch ate into Numo's earmeat. Hammerfist howled and reeled back, clutching one arm to her chest. The mistress struck out again, but Hammerfist lunged, pummeling her body into the mistress's. The two strived against each other like rutting rhinoceroses.

Hammerfist slammed her good claws into the mistress again and again until her ribs cracked and her handsome coat became an ugly smear of blood.

Then the tentacles got a hold of Hammerfist.

They lifted her into the air and hurled her into the floor.

Hammerfist writhed, trying to get up, but she was like an upside-down beetle. Discombobulated. Twirly. Helpless.

Love or no, homunculus or human, mistress or malefactor, Numo couldn't abide it. The mistress had hurt Hammerfist far too much already, and it simply would not do.

He grabbed on to one of the tendrils as it flew backwards in preparation for another strike. His little dagger in hand, he struggled to hang on, to see anything at all, but the world turned into a swirl of hellish chaos as he was tossed about in space. Numo stabbed once, twice, over and over again, missing more than half the time, desperate. The tentacles were thick and fibrous. They didn't seem to mind being stabbed. Where was Sangja? That wilty-hearted poltroon! Numo thrust down, impaling one of the tendrils, but it wasn't enough, by Nonnysteed it wasn't enough, and here it was speeding back down to earth, back down on top of Hammerfist, and gods only knew how many strikes even she could withsta—

The tentacles struck Hammerfist like a giant's cudgel. She cried out, a muffled crunchy awful cry. Numo was tossed to the floor, his dagger sliding across the oil-slicked wood to the other side of the room. He pitched himself up to his feet, now weaponless, and unable to get to the knife with Hammerfist's claws and the mistress's tentacles slinging about. His skin was hot and sweaty and tingly, and every time anything touched his flesh, it felt like a hammer striking hot metal.

The tendrils had already reared back, preparing to strike again. Numo climbed on top of one of the tables, to do he-didn't-know-what, searching for anything at all, picking up a large splinter of wood, putting it down again. Everything seemed useless. He was too small to stop the mistress.

He looked again at the splinter. And it reminded him of something. A diagram of a brain, and a line going through the front of it…

But the splinter was too short—it would not go through her skull—if only he had a moment to grab his dagger—

A cough interrupted. Rawang leaned against the table, drooling a brownish drool. He must have been wounded in the scuffle with Sangja.

Numo got an idea. A ghastly, inappropriate idea.

Or was it?

Humans did it to those who made them upset, and Rawang had made Numo upset many a time. Tried to get rid of him, in fact. It was only meet. Besides, Rawang would want this. Rawang said he loved Hammerfist and if he meant it, he wouldn't mind. He wouldn't mind at all.

The fat living whip came sailing back down. Numo picked up the giant splinter, ran the few paces down the length of the table, aimed at the back of Rawang's shoulders, and whacked him as hard as he could manage.

The doctor stumbled forward and tripped over Hammerfist's fists, landing on his hands and knees in a crouch over Hammerfist as she tried in vain to right herself. The tendrils cracked into his neck.

Rawang plopped back on his knees, looking confused. He swayed lightly. His head seemed slightly tipped-over, as though it were a decanter about to pour his brains out of his ears. His eyes went dark, then light, then nothing. His body toppled like spilt jelly.

Numo could not spend the time to absorb the horror of what he'd just done. He slid himself across the floor in the time it took for the mistress to re-calibrate her tentacles and grabbed the dagger. She was already preparing for another strike.

Rawang had only bought a few seconds of shielding, and the mistress showed no signs of slowing.

Bloody carbuncles.

Numo wrung his hands about the little dagger. This was it. He was smallish, his weapon tiny, his existence mostly pointless at this juncture. But by Nonnysteed, by Pyri—by Moa and Ong-Nklak and all the humans' gods, why not!—this was it. All of it, whatever It was, wrapped in a flicker of time, slippery and cold as ice.

He clambered up onto the table. He barked at the mistress. He chattered and hissed and made all sorts of horrible guttural noises he didn't know he could make.

"Come closer, you sack of rot-pudding."

She glanced away from Hammerfist.

"Closer! Scally-wagged nightsoil-bedded caitiff-snuggler!"

She took a step towards Numo.

"Yak-scented flux-licking fopdoodle!"

The mistress cocked her head. She was amused by him. Amused!

She took another step. Numo launched himself off the table at her head.

He pawed at one of her ears, grabbed onto a floppy bit, and swung at her face with the dagger. He bounced off her snout and into her mangled crusty eyelid, clinging to the scabby knolls of skin. Numo took aim and thrust the weapon directly above her eyeball, into her head, and, he hoped to any god that gave a wether's withers, right into her slave-lobe.

The mistress stopped moving. For a second or two.

She roared—the type of roar that vibrated through Numo's throat; the type that shook all the lampfish and rattled the bric-a-brac; but not, apparently, the type he could hear very well. Tendrils wrapped around his tiny body, their muscles thicker than his whole torso. They had rough barbs on them, too small for him to see before, but very prominent as they scraped away at his skin and slowly degloved part of his foot. Numo found his mouth open and his breath rushing out as if he were screaming, but no sound—

A small hand clasped her throat from behind. A boy whose name he couldn't remember appeared in the broken doorway. The hand it belonged to plunged a little metal rod into the mistress's neck.

Her arms went limp. Her knees buckled and smacked onto the floor. The tendrils loosened and Numo fell, thumping dully onto the ground, his lungs flattening on impact. He tried to gasp for air, but none came. The spray of sparks inside his skin gutted his joints and spinny glittery lights twinkled in his eyes.

The mistress looked at him blandly, but her gaze went far past him. Her mangled eye-socket turned into a turnip and her good eye became a lizard crawling out of her face. Hammerfist beetled and bobbled and turned into a puddle of liquid iron. A flatulent noise tooted from the ceiling, and a limpid voice burbled from the underworld as the boy came stotting out of the darkness. Numo tried to blink but his eyes got stuck shut. Hammerfist had puddled. And he'd turned his mistress's brain into lizards.

Numo thought, in that moment, that he should really stop attempting to do anything at all, and his brain, in compliance, dissolved into oblivion.

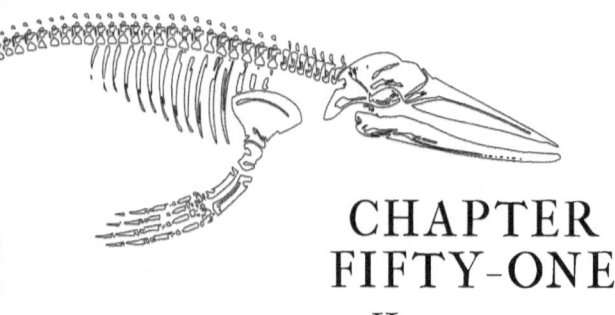

CHAPTER
FIFTY-ONE
HAMMERFIST

Hᴀᴍᴍᴇʀғɪsᴛ ᴄᴏᴜʟᴅɴ'ᴛ ɢᴇᴛ up. The boy was yelling something at her, or at everyone, maybe, and at the other infandus especially, but she could hardly care.

"Is Numo dead?" she tried to say, but her tongues licked her eyes instead. She reached for Numo with her eyelashes, which were meant to be her hands—her body parts seemed to be all mixed up and malfunctioning, like the time before. But it was worse now. Even her senses crossed wires. She could smell death, and she could smell impending death, and she could smell life, but everything was so muddled she couldn't tell what smells were coming from where. Rawang lay next to her, his eyes blank, his skin blanching as any dead skin might, but she couldn't know for sure; she could never tell until she smelled it. "Is Rawang dead? Is Numo dead?" she licked.

They certainly looked dead.

But she couldn't let herself entertain such notions yet. There was still a chance. Until she knew, until she could smell them, or someone more knowledgeable could tell her—

The boy-alchemist ignored her frenetic lickings and bent over the other infandus, examining the thing in her eye.

Sramai—Hammerfist—whatever-her-name-was-supposed-to-be tried to scramble, to catch his leg and force him to pay attention, but her elbows banged into the floor. He pulled out the thing in the creature's eye and asked her questions. The infandus murmured answers drowned out by the yelling inside Hammerfist's head. Then the infandus slumped over and her eye went blank, her nostril rumbling with jagged snores.

Feeling returned to one of Hammerfist's fingers. She rapped furiously on the floor.

The alchemist turned. "What? What is it?"

She pointed at Rawang.

"Dead," he said.

A great massive iceberg piled in her throat. Her husband was dead. She was supposed to protect him. She was supposed to provide for him. She was supposed to be his wife.

She was no one's wife.

Only one thing left that mattered. She pointed at Numo.

The boy huffed at her, but he didn't say "dead." He clambered over to Numo and prodded his neck and armpits and knees. He paused. Then the boy scooped Numo off the floor and shook him. "What did you do to the infandus?"

Hammerfist recoiled, nearly snarling but spitting instead. Numo was alive. Numo was alive and hurt and the little smear of a human was molesting him. She should have killed him when she had the chance. She should have killed everyone. Killing everyone would have been so much simpler.

But surely that was just the infandus in her?

Surely...

She bit her tongues. Two of them bled. It made her feel more even-headed for some reason to have blood in her mouth.

That couldn't be good, could it? She had tried to be good, to purify herself, to cleanse the beast in her, but it had only gotten stronger and invaded her human brain…

It was hopeless.

"What did you do?" The boy—Sangja, she remembered now—sat Numo up on a table and stared him down. "Say something!"

Numo's sweet voice cracked and broke like splintering wood. "Same thing I did to me," he mumbled.

Sangja furrowed his brow. "And what did you do to you?"

"Stabbed me in the slave-lobe."

"With what? When? Where?"

"Cabbage tubercles. Biscuit vittles. Tenderness," Numo said, and he went limp in the boy's hands.

Something boiled inside Hammerfist. It trembled up through her guts and grew, gaining momentum, like she was throwing her own fist through the center of her body.

It was a scream.

Such a noise came out of her that Sangja dropped Numo and scrambled backwards into the wall.

"Is he dead?" she roared, her tongues finally at work, "*is he dead?*"

He couldn't be dead. He was the one person she'd never wanted to kill. He was Numo. Her Numo. *My Numo*—

"I don't…I'm not…" Sangja stammered, his face rearranging itself back into a hard look that Hammerfist could so easily shatter and stir into a fine mash. Hammerfist plunged her fingers into the stone floor and dug in hard, gouging furrows into the rock. She pulled herself forward by her claws alone. Damn her legs, damn her arms, damn her breasts and abdomen and thighs and everything else that refused to take her to Numo—her claws would get her there. He couldn't be dead. He couldn't be. Not after everything he'd done, not after all this. But the smell of death spilled out of him—or Rawang—it filled her nostril like gas—she couldn't tell. She couldn't tell if only one had gone or both. She had to know. If Numo was dead—if he was dead—

Numo's pale besweated body lay in a tiny puddle of moistness and spilt honey. He wasn't moving. His eyes were empty.

Hammerfist's heart seemed to stop beating and her lungs quit the business of breathing, but her fingers, gods bless her fingers, they kept dragging her onward, even as the crucial parts shut down and gave up in shock.

She pulled herself to his side. She peered at him, looking for his chest to rise and fall, but she couldn't see anything. Hammerfist traced a claw down his chest, hoping to feel something, a heartbeat, a breath. There! Or no. Maybe not. Was she imagining things? She was.

He was dead. Numo was dead and it was her fault and she couldn't save him and there was no point anymore and—

His eyelids fluttered. "Hmrfs?" he whispered.

Hammerfist's whole body jolted as though struck with lightning. "Numo! Numo, you're alive! You must stay that way, you understand, you must—"

"You can use her," Numo muttered, and then his eyes rolled back again and stagnated.

What? Use her? Use who?

"Are you dead or aren't you?" she shouted.

"I don't think he's dead. Yet." Sangja came and picked up

385

Numo's little body, cradling his neck. "But I think he might have jammed this into his brain." He held up a blade the size of a large needle. Hammerfist tried to take it between her claws, but it was too small for her to handle, and it clattered to the floor. Stains were smeared all the way to the hilt, with little bits of meat dangling off it. "He's probably gotten sick from the contamination of the blood. He'll need spider fuzz if he's to have any chance at all."

"Spider fuzz?" What the hell was spider fuzz?

The boy leapt over one of the tables and went rummaging around in some interstice near the stoves. When he came back, he carried a handful of dead spiders with some sort of bright blue fluff growing on their underbellies.

"It's not a great name, admittedly. I'm not great at naming things. Still, that's what it is. It only grows on the dead ones." Sangja pointed. "I don't know how, but it can sometimes help with contaminated blood."

Hammerfist stared at them. Blue fluff. Dead spiders. Indeed.

But anything else was just as likely to work. Or not. And she couldn't let Numo just slip away.

She grabbed the spiders out of Sangja's hands and mashed them into Numo's face.

"Easy! Easy. Birdshit-headed infandus," the boy grumbled. He snatched the spiders up off the floor from where they spilled out of Numo's mouth. He glanced over at the stunned infandus that had tried to kill everyone. "She'll need them too."

"Her? Why not let her die?" Hammerfist would have killed her by now if her legs worked. "How is she better alive than dead?"

"Did you not hear him?" The boy's brows lowered into a straight angry line of black fur. "He's right. We can use her. At least, I can."

"For what?"

"For the war."

Hammerfist was too awash with fury to respond. Use her? Who cared about her? They could use swords and hammers and spears, too. What was one infandus? Especially one that had killed her husband and deserved to die? Her husband who had sacrificed himself to save her—

Rawang. Dear Rawang. He had given up everything for her. She had let him die for it.

Sangja kept babbling because he was an asshole who didn't care.

"Besides, it has side effects, and you can't just go around stuffing dead spiders into people's mouths. It has to be prepared. And he must have the right dosage." He paused. "And, of course, someone must pay for it."

Hammerfist swung at him. He leapt away like a little rabbit and perched on a stool far out of reach. She dragged herself, threw furniture at him, but he was far too quick for her mess of a body. "Asshole. Fucking *asshole*!"

"Yeah, I am!" he barked. "I didn't get where I am by being nice. So yeah, I'm a fucking asshole. Sorry." He stared down at her, his dark brows shadowing his eyes. "Will you pay or not?"

"Pay with what? I have nothing."

"Like I said before: I need bodies."

Hammerfist thought. The revolution. It wasn't dead yet. Yes, it was more of a war against all of Moaki now, and it had ended disastrously before, and it probably would again. But this time it wouldn't be her fault. And at this point, she would be glad of some disaster that wasn't her fault. "Yes. Fine. I'll fight for you."

"Not just fight for me. Stop taking the elixir. Be my slave. Until one of us comes to a bitter end."

Hammerfist glanced up at him, grinding the only two of her molars that occluded properly. "You know I have the fall."

"I expect a bitter end to come fast." He grinned. His front teeth were sharp—maybe artificially so; she couldn't tell.

Hammerfist wanted to squeeze her own head until her brain popped out.

This was supposed to have ended.

She was supposed to have her revolution, free the afflicted slaves, cleanse herself. But she only got a lot of people killed.

Then she was supposed to turn it all back. Become a human. Fulfill the duty to her husband that she'd fallen down on. Get time to make up for what she'd done. But that had been a lie. And she'd gotten Rawang killed.

So now Sangja wanted her to murder again. More. Again. On and on forever. She'd never redeem herself. Her family god would turn away from her forever.

To hell with her.

Something broke inside. A blister. An abscess. Fluid leaking into every bubble of air, filling her up and draining her dry at the same time.

She was lost. There would be no redemption. There was only Numo.

"Fine. Just save him."

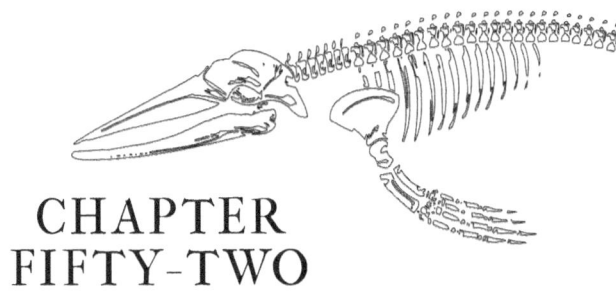

CHAPTER FIFTY-TWO
FLOPPACLES

FLOPPACLES AWAKENED TO a skull-pulverizing headache. She was tied up. The teat-leech was pinned under a great metal stove and its tendrils knotted around each other.

Someone pulled at her eyelids. She flinched.

"Don't move!" said Someone. Her eyelids were stretched, yanked down and up again. Then Someone squirted something into her eye.

It felt like a march of knives parading through the center of her pupil. She tried to claw at her face but she couldn't move her hand. The stove clattered and shifted as the teat-leech tried to come to her aid—"aid" how, she wasn't sure, maybe it'd pluck out her eyeball, and just at this moment she was all right with that idea—but Someone yelled "get more weight on that stove" and someone else did. So Floppacles writhed and moaned for some time before realizing how strange it was that she was in this position at all.

When she opened her eye, the world was blurry, blue, and utterly pointless.

She tried focusing on her breathing. Slowly and carefully, she breathed. For some reason, she was surprised that her lungs worked, but she had no memory of why she should be surprised.

Her memory, in fact, seemed like the dot-puzzles Grand-Mum-Ma had given her as a child. A great big box full of small paper dots of different colors. One dot was nothing but hue, but when the dots were all arranged in a particular way, they made a picture of a High Alchemist riding atop a white rhino, just as Grand-Mum-Ma did on festival days. The snippets of knowing were there—like the thing about her grandmother and the dot-puzzle; where had that come from?—but trying to recall any memory in particular was like dumping that box of dots on the floor and trying to see the picture.

"Stop struggling," Someone said. She hadn't realized she was still straining against the chains. Floppacles peered up at him. Her. Him. A boy with great white scars on his chest and blood-smeared pants. The room smelled like fish. A huge infandus with massive arms sat on the oven, her eyes steadied on a drake wrapped in a blanket on the table. The clutter of it all bothered Floppacles and she closed her eye again.

"I didn't say to stop being awake." Someone kicked her lightly in the forehead. "We need to discuss some things."

Floppacles opened her eye and stared at the floor. It reminded her of bats, for no discernible reason. "What?" she muttered. Her voice sounded strange and unnatural.

Someone bent down over her. He stank of the docks and beer and leather and decaying organic matter. He breathed in her face, so she did the same. She could taste the rancid meat and unfortunate centipedes on her breath. Why had she been eating centipedes?

"You may be wondering what's happening here. Your deformed head is probably sore, so I'll keep it simple. My name is Sangja. I'm an alchemist. Your brain has been contaminated and you need my treatments if you want a hope of surviving."

"There is no proven treatment for contamination of the brain," she murmured.

"And how would you know?"

Floppacles couldn't answer. "Just one of the dots," she said.

He raised an eyebrow.

"I just know."

He brought a bottle to his mouth and sucked down the last of the contents. It smelled beery and salty at the same time. "You're right," he said finally. "There is no proven treatment. There are experimental ones. That's all I have here. Experiments. Because your goddamn oligarchs won't allow the study of alchemy outside your stinking mountain wart of a city. So I've had to take what knowledge I can steal and make up the rest."

Floppacles felt a weird swell of admiration. The word "experiments" lit some sort of fire in her. She wanted to do those. She very much liked those. If only she could remember what they were.

"Formal training is not everything," she found herself saying.

"I agree," said Sangja. "So do you want my treatments or not?"

Floppacles thought. He could be lying. The "treatments" could kill her—but then he wouldn't be asking permission.

"What do you want in return?"

He smiled. "An intelligent infandus? They must have screwed up your making somehow, didn't they?"

Infandus? Yes. No? Was she supposed to be an infandus? The question stoked an angry black smoke inside her chest. The teat-leech on her arm went hot with anger. It wanted freedom. It wanted to rip off this boy's smug mouth. But her breasts were empty and it was weak. "Answer me. What do you want?"

"Fine. I want to know some information."

"What information?" She was getting tired of this. The light bothered her eye.

He bent over, putting his hands on his knees. "I want to know who sent you, and I want to know why."

Floppacles tried to think. Should she tell this boy anything, even if she could remember? Well, of course she should; she didn't want to die. Or did she? Somewhere inside, she wanted to die. It pressed on her chest, that black smoke in her. Odd. She couldn't remember...

"Who is your master?" the boy prodded.

"I need time. My memory doesn't work right now."

"Fine. I'll wait."

He did. He sat, then got up and fidgeted, relieved himself into an empty bottle out of a prosthetic leather penis, shifted through a pile of bottles to find a full one, came back and sat again. Floppacles's mind cranked along, maddeningly slow. Tatters of things came to her, all out of order and jumbled. A bird getting loose in the house. Having sex with a man. Having sex with a woman. Grand-Mum-Ma showing her how to play *ro-chgai-chgui*, and then showing her how to play dirty. Whittling an idol of Moa. Finding a dead bug in her hair. Getting a toenail ripped out by a goat's hoof. Somebody putting a fire poker in somebody's rectum. Somebody lighting somebody on fire. Somebody gouging her eye...

Bollix. The teat-leech. The arrest.

The transmogrification.

Rage shuttled through her, up and down her limbs, whirling about her heart. The teat-leech wriggled around under the oven and the infandus clambered off of it to clasp the tentacles in place with her fists.

Floppacles. Xiongnyao thought she was so *fucking* funny, did she?

"I remember," said Kaizha. "I remember now."

Sangja sat there and listened. They had a long conversation. Much of what she said to him was true, and some wasn't, and some she couldn't remember. By the end of it, she had ideas. Big ideas, ideas that frightened her with their blasphemy, but she had to prevent larger blasphemies still, and couldn't think of how else to manage it. She didn't tell him about those.

At the end of it, Sangja leaned back on his little pillow, took a drink from his third bottle, and said, "It seems to me like we have a common enemy."

"Oh? Who?"

"Moaki, of course."

Kaizha didn't think so. It was the hoary thost currently running Moaki she had a problem with. But she nodded anyway. Her mouth was dry and she was getting shaky; the pain in her head swelled like a beesting. Maybe the boy hadn't been lying about the contamination.

"So I have a proposition." He scooted forward. "You go back to your masters. By whatever means you deem necessary, you get them to let go of Trago. Independence, that is. No more policing us, no more soldiers stationed here, no more tribute, no more laws about who can or can't do alchemy. And I'll give you the best treatment available."

Trago independent and alchemy outside of Moaki. Quite the sacrilege, and a blow to the cash flow besides. Of course, what she was contemplating doing to her "masters" was also quite a sacrilege—but that was on a much smaller scale. This was treason against Moa. But there was nothing keeping her from lying to him about it. It would be the least of her wrongdoings.

"You want me to give up something like that for an experimental treatment for an always-fatal condition that I may or may not have?"

"Well, of course not. That would be ridiculous. I've also poisoned you."

She blinked. "You've *what?*"

"Slow acting. It'll be a little bit before it starts to overwhelm your organs."

Kaizha wanted to smirk at him but wasn't sure she could manage it, with whatever face she presently had. "I'm supposed to believe this, why?"

He shrugged. "It's up to you. But I'll give you both the anti-contamination treatment and the antidote to the poison if you do what I say. Plus, I'll give you some other presents. I'll take out what's left of the Moak army, so if you decided, let's say, to stage one of your little revolutions"—he waved his hand—"or something, there wouldn't be much to stop you. I'll also throw what's left of our militia behind you."

A little revolution, no. A coup, maybe. She very much liked the sound of that arrangement, but...

"How exactly do you plan to take out the Moak army?"

Sangja gave her a funny look. "Come on. I have complete

faith in you to do things that no homunculus should be able to do. Can't you at least do the same for me?"

"I have a monster." She nodded at the creature, at Bollix's legacy. "What do you have?"

"I have Trago."

She stared at him. He stared at her. The smells of the room amplified her nausea. She sweated and drooled. She didn't realize how badly she was shaking until she heard the claws on her toes clacking together.

"Fine. I agree. Give me the medicine and I'll be on my way."

Sangja smiled. He went to the table and grabbed two vials, but he only handed over the smallest of them. "That one will keep you alive for the next week or so, but you'll need more than that to kill off the contamination and rid yourself of the poison. I'll give you the rest when I come to Moaki to co-sign the proclamation that declares Trago independent."

"You?"

"Don't be fooled," said Sangja, waggling a finger. "In Trago, I'm the closest thing to one of your stupid oligarchs as we got."

Kaizha grumbled. "And if I can't get it done in a week?"

"Take your chances, if you want," Sangja said. "But I'd hurry, if I were you."

She kept her mouth shut. It didn't matter. He had the high ground now, but she'd soon find a way to make the earth shift.

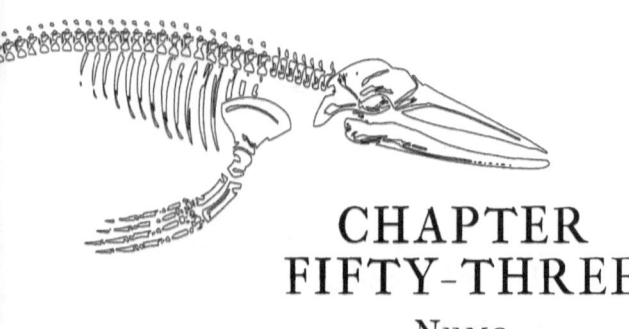

CHAPTER
FIFTY-THREE
Numo

NUMO WOKE UP on his back inside a glass bulb.

At least, it seemed like a glass bulb. Light was distorted. Sound was muffled. There was an invisible wall between himself and everything outside.

But then Hammerfist poked through it to feel one of his heartbeats.

He reached up and grabbed her claw and it was real and she cocked her head at him and that was real.

Why did everything seem so much more real than before?

Hammerfist said something to him. He could hear a rumble like a distant earthquake coming from her mouth. But he couldn't make out the words. It was as though she had a pillow-sack jammed in her mouth.

"What?" he said, but he couldn't hear himself, either.

She kept saying things and he kept saying what and not hearing any of it until finally her face fell and she went away to get Sangja. They talked over Numo, not to him, and he kept saying what, and finally Sangja wrote something on a piece of paper.

Can you hear anything, it said.

"Mumbles 'n' bumbles," Numo murmured. He hoped that's what he said anyway. Or something like it.

Sangja scribbled something else. *I think the contamination in your brain might've screwed up your hearing.*

Hammerfist's head drooped low against the table. The very image of the word "crestfallen."

"Contamination?" Numo said.

F-f-s went Sangja's lips.

Sangja wrote for a while and held up the paper. It said Numo had been a "fucking twit" and "jammed a dirty knife into his brain" and contaminated himself and he might die. Hammerfist read it, too, and then batted it away when she got to the end and made rumbly noises at Sangja, who made higher-pitched rumbles back at her.

"It's okay," Numo said. "I knew it might kill me when I did it."

Sangja finished rumbling and chucked the paper in the air. He stomped away out of sight. Hammerfist tried to pick up the paper and the pen, but the pen was too small and she punched holes in the paper. She stopped and took a deep breath, staring at the ceiling as though begging the lampfish for patience. More calmly, she dipped a claw into the inkwell and began writing.

Why did you do it if you knew it might kill you?

Numo blinked. "I had to know if it was real."

What?

"My feelings. For you." But sooth, his head hurt something awful. He was hot all of a sudden. Smotheringly hot. "Everyone said I was a slave and had slave feelings and I wanted to know the difference."

You shouldn't have done that. Not if this was the consequence.

397

"You wanted the revolution, didn't you?"

Hammerfist cocked her head—to the left this time. Confusion.

"The revolution. You would have died, wouldn't you? You would have died in order to not be a slave and know what was real and help others know it too."

Her head clicked back into the regular position. She scribbled furiously, then stared at it, ripped it up, grabbed a new piece of paper, scribbled and scribbled and ripped it up again. She blinked over and over and over. Finally she wrote

I understand.

Hammerfist sat back on her haunches and stared at the floor. Numo wondered if he could sit up. The lights were blinding. Maybe he could at least roll over—but the crashing pain in his head—it hurt. It really hurt. He'd never felt pain like this. Not because he'd never been in that much pain, but because...well. The world seemed more opaque. Feelings were sharper. He thought of his own mortality as a mechanism to make the world beautiful, which was strange, and not something he had contemplated in any great depth before, and the pain was his body angrily slapping away the ghosts of his own dissolution. It was quite pretty inside.

That must be why Hammerfist was the way she was. To be something truly beautiful and perfect, there had to be pain. And impermanence. Like an eclipse, or the short dance of two slugs dangling from a branch in a mating-knot before dropping harshly to the ground.

Hammerfist tapped her claws on the table, pointing at a sheet of paper.

So what is real now?

"You are beautiful," Numo murmured.

Still delirious?

"No..."

You said your feelings for me weren't real. Back there...

"I did? I did." Numo didn't remember it, but it seemed like something he might have said. "It's hard to explain. Before, I felt...I felt drawn to you. Like I would to the mistress. Or the ma—well." The master was dead. Numo felt nothing upon remembering that fact. How very peculiar. "Just drawn. No rhyme or reason or wherefore, as though I was built to be drawn to you and devote myself as I might to an alchemist. But now I—I feel—differently." He smacked his lips, trying to get some wetness in his mouth. Hammerfist poured a bit of water in, but she could only grasp a big jug, and ended up sloshing it on Numo's face. He didn't mind. He felt disgusting and unkempt. How long had he been lying on that table? Days?

Differently? Hammerfist wrote.

"I still find you beautiful. I still care for you, as a friend might care for another." Numo tried to smile, but it seemed all the muscles in his head were utterly focused on constricting his skull and pressing in on it. "But I still don't know enough about you to be...to feel...em..."

Love?

"Love. Yes. From what I understand, that is. And I wouldn't expect you to love me, either. We haven't known each other long...It was silly of me. Very silly." He patted the tip of her claw. "But I'd very much like to get to know you. So I can do it properly this time."

All this talking was exhausting. And the more he talked, the worse he seemed to make things. Hammerfist looked deflated, half-melted, sagging; sadness was painted all over her. Or regret, perhaps. Maybe embarrassment that Numo had confessed he ever fake-loved her, or discomfort that Numo desired to real-love her still, when she felt nothing in—

A sonorous growl came from her mouth. She wasn't saying words, not real ones. Just long, honeyed hums. A deep and bone-hugging noise. She rumbled and grumbled in sweeping arcs of vibrating sound for a minute or two before Numo realized he recognized the tune.

She was singing his love song.

Numo still drifted in and out of sleep like an uncatchable wisp of fiery ash floating in a pneumy heat. He had no awareness of time, or how much of it was slipping away. At first it didn't seem to matter. Hammerfist was there with him, and she was singing for him. She, singing for him! He could hardly think it was real, but it seemed unlikely he would have the same fever-dream over and over again. Especially when his fever-dreams generally consisted of water deer biting into lowermeat and leaving him to bleed on a batskin rug.

But there was still something wrong in her. There was too much pain in her eyes. It took him far too long to remember why she might be so sad.

He'd killed Rawang.

Numo bolted upright on the table in the middle of the night. Sangja snored, clutching a dead shark. Hammerfist slept on the floor, curled up in a ball like a lumpy hillock.

I killed her husband.

Numo had done it as freely and guiltlessly as if he'd been picking dead skin from his toes. It had been a thing that needed doing and he'd done it.

That's what he'd thought at the time.

He wasn't sure if she'd loved Rawang or not, but he was an important person to her, after all, stinkard or no. She should be furious at Numo. She should squish him like a gourd and toss him into the ocean with the dead whales.

But he'd been contaminated. He'd been in a fever at the time. He'd done it for good reason, even if it was perhaps not the best solution. Things had happened so quickly. Perhaps she'd forgiven him.

Or perhaps she didn't know.

Perhaps she hadn't seen it.

But Numo knew.

Suddenly it was very hard to breathe.

"I have to tell you something."

I have to tell you something, too.

Numo's breath hitched. Hammerfist adjusted his pillows as though that might be the problem. He'd graduated from the table to the floor, now, propped up against the side of the wall. Next to Hammerfist's sleeping place. *So I can keep an eye on you*, she'd said. Written.

"Okay." Maybe she already knew. Maybe he didn't have to say it. Maybe she'd say, *I know, Numo. I saw what you did and I forgive you.* "You can go first."

Hammerfist hesitated, as though she would protest, but

she took one of her deep breaths and held up two pieces of paper, side-by-side. Both full of words. She'd already written it out—while he was sleeping, he supposed. It must have been something very important to weigh on her mind like that.

He started reading.

I don't think it's a good idea for you to love me.

He almost stopped there, but he looked up at her and the bits of skin above her eyes furrowed in worry. So he gave a weak smile and kept going.

I have done bad things. And I can't keep myself from doing bad things. I've killed so many people, whether on purpose or not. My brain will keep deteriorating and I won't remember anymore.

I thought I could redeem myself somehow. That's why I wanted the revolution. If I made other peoples' lives better, then mine might mean something. But I've only made things worse and gotten people killed and hurt people like you and my husband. I have done bad things and I am a bad creature who should not be around good creatures like you.

I think it's best if I just—the next few words were scribbled out, replaced with—*go away somewhere and you forget about me.*

Numo's eyes stung when he got to the end and they leaked. He didn't want to, but he couldn't help it; they leaked and leaked and his face was wet and Hammerfist covered her eyes and ducked her head like her eyes hurt too.

"Okay," he said, once his breath stopping bouncing around in his throat. "Now I have to tell you something." He paused. She blinked furiously and rubbed at her face with the back of her wrist and just barely managed to look him in the eye.

"I am a bad creature too."

She shook her head.

"I am. It was my fault. Everything was my fault." Numo snuffled. Snot dripped out of his nose and filled up the inside-tubes in his face. "Remember? I was the one who gave away the revolution. I told my mistress. I didn't know. I was so childish and dungish and ignorant. I got all those people killed. And then I cut off Master Goh's head and got Reddles killed. And then I—" He stopped. She was already in pain. Her face was pinched up like it might explode with pressure. But how could he choose what sort of pain she should be in—self-loathing, or betrayal? Truth had to be better. She had to know. She had to know how awful he was. That in fact, she was the one who was too good for him.

"I killed your husband."

She didn't believe him at first. Then he explained it. Twice. She started to write that he was wrong and made some excuses for him, but he held up his hand to make her stop scratching out that frenzied scribbled writing.

"Why do you make excuses for me, but call yourself a bad creature? You have excuses, too. Either they make you good, or the lack of them make me bad. It can't be both."

She paused. She wrote *I need some time* and went to the far corner of the room.

Numo couldn't hear anything but rumbles. She rumbled vaguely, somewhere behind a mess of tables, somewhere where he couldn't reach her.

It seemed a large fraction of eternity before she came back. In between, Sangja came and went, stumbling in and stumbling out again. He was a busy person, Numo supposed. Had to run all his own errands now. He seemed almost frantic—or he would have been frantic if he weren't somewhat drunk. Something big and heavy and ponderous was about to happen.

When Hammerfist did come back, her eyes had little scabs around them, as if she'd scratched at them. She had more paper with more writing. She slid it on the floor to Numo and sat in front of him, clasping her claws together, waiting.

I forgive you. I wish it hadn't happened, but you were feverish and didn't know what you were doing.

I really wish it hadn't happened.

But the excuses matter.

You are right. Either we are both bad or we are both good. But I feel like I'm awful and you are a victim of my awfulness. It seems you feel the same.

Both of us must be wrong somehow, but I'm not sure where reality is anymore. Maybe we're both good and bad. But I can't stomach it.

Maybe, if we both have good in us, we can redeem ourselves still. Maybe we can still fix this for others like us. Maybe we can still bring down the people who hurt them.

Maybe we can still have our revolution.

Maybe we can fall in love and be awful together.

Numo took deep gulping breaths and a full minute to collect himself.

"I want very much to be awful with you."

404

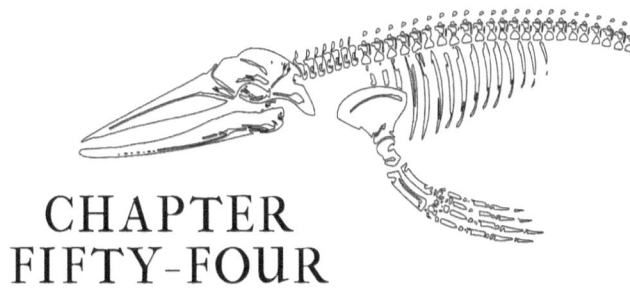

CHAPTER FIFTY-FOUR

Kaizha "Floppacles" Shanyang

Kaizha RAN HALFWAY to Moaki, dragging the body of the veterinarian and some dead infandus she'd found in a field. They were too heavy, so she killed a man with a goat-trap and let his rams pull her the rest of the way.

She wondered if maybe being an infandus had changed her. She should have felt bad about Goat-Trap Man. But she consoled herself by remembering that all people were horrible and he probably deserved it.

Maybe it had changed her a little.

Goat-trap or no, it still took a day and a night to get home. Far too long. There wasn't much time.

She only hoped Turian's transmogrification methods were as fast as he bragged they were.

Kaizha carefully put the vial of the brat's treatment in the inside of her drooping gumline. This made her salivate more than usual, which itched as it coursed down her jaw, but she tried not to scratch; she wasn't sure if, as an infandus, she should notice such a thing.

The guardsmen of Moaki merely looked at her collar and let her in. They didn't search her. They didn't even bother to ask about the dead bodies. Shoddy work ethic, that was. One of the many things she would change.

Her trap bobbled up the mountain and the dead infandus almost slid off the back of the platform. It started to snow. The flakes slapped into her and burned her skin with their cold. The saliva on her chin began to freeze the wisps of hair into filamentous stalactites. She wished she had clothes. She'd grown quite a bit of hair but not enough for this weather. Pants. If only she had pants…

The teat-leech wrapped itself around her legs. A poor imitation of pants, to be sure, but it was touching nevertheless.

Thank you, Bollix.

They arrived at the door. Kaizha was actually nervous. Killing people was a task that no longer worried her as much as it should, but subterfuge was a bit different. Especially when it involved pretending to be the slave of such perfect fools as Turian and Xiongnyao.

She slumped her shoulders and tried to keep her neck exposed in deference. On all fours, she approached the door, dragging her corpses with her tentacles. The infandus guardsmen looked at her collar and nodded. She slunk inside and a drake scurried off to announce her. No one troubled themselves about the dead bodies. Kaizha supposed none of the slaves were familiar with the protocol of someone dragging dead bodies into the foyer.

Excited footsteps hurried through the hallway. Xiongnyao erupted from the archway, clapping her hands.

"Oh, dear Floppacles, well done! I was starting to get worried…" She slowed and looked over the bodies. "Hm. I was under the impression there was supposed to be more of them."

"Yes, mistress," Kaizha murmured. "I'm so sorry, but the drake was lost to wild animals while I slept." She paused. Should she grovel? Talking was difficult with a vial in her gumline, and she was afraid the bouncing of her jaws, together with the overflow of saliva, would dislodge it, and if it fell, or was crushed, or found out—she was lost. But still, she ought to play her part, so she added, "I was stupid. Very very stupid. And I'm so sorry and I deserve punishment."

Xiongnyao gave a pinched smile. She nodded. "Yes, perhaps just a little. But overall, I am satisfied. What did you find out about our outpost?"

"Oh, mistress, it is bad news."

"Don't worry, dear Floppacles. I am expecting bad news."

"Well." Kaizha pretended to fidget with her tentacles. "It turned out the traitors had killed all the Moak soldiers, but the officer was killed by an alchemist. An alchemist of *Trggra*." She didn't know how to make a word that sounded like Trago, but it seemed Xiongnyao understood nevertheless. Her face darkened.

"He said he runs the city."

She bit her lip.

"And he admitted he sent infandi to Moaki to kill the leaders."

Xiongnyao looked like she might slap her. But then she softened. "And why didn't you kill this so-called alchemist and bring him to me?"

"I was ordered to kill the traitors from Moaki, mistress." At least, she hoped. Kaizha didn't remember her exact orders anymore. A dull buzzing coated the voices in all her memories with the desire to smush Xiongnyao's face so hard into the floorboards that the painted whorls in the wood tattooed themselves onto her eyeballs.

It was with difficulty that Kaizha restrained the creature on her arm.

Xiongnyao inhaled and shook her head darkly. She did not look satisfied.

"And I thought you might want to punish the alchemist personally," Kaizha added. Was that too far? It sounded almost too…understanding.

Xiongnyao's brows furrowed. "You thought that, did you?"

Kaizha bared her neck and thought so frantically her eyelid twitched. She came up with nothing. Maybe she should kill her now. Yes, the teat-leech yearned for it. Kill her now and—

And what? Any chance she had at control would be lost. An infandus with a dead master meant execution. An infandus with a puppet who looked like a master, however…

"I asked you a question."

Kaizha stooped even lower. "I'm not sure of myself, mistress! It was wrong of me to presume. To make presumptions! The stupidness!" The vial nearly dislodged from her gums with the exuberance of her disgusting prostrations, and she had to wiggle it back in place with her tongue. "I am infected with it, riddled with it! I am so sorry! I would—"

"Shut up, shut up," Xiongnyao snapped. "I can't understand all your ridiculous snorting noises." She regarded Kaizha for a moment and then waved her off. "Never mind. You're correct. It's best I simply let the army deal with it. No more chances for Trago—they will be obliterated. Moaki is getting overpopulated anyway; we could use a proper colony."

Kaizha bowed.

"You will receive your punishment tomorrow. For now,

Barbara will show you to the servants' quarters, so that you may rest." Xiongnyao tooted on a tiny whistle—four short stops. A plodding drake toddled out of a corridor.

"Yes, mistress?" said the drake with the unpronounceable name.

"Take Floppacles to the servants' quarters and show her where to get her food and the like. Acquaint her with the routine of the household. And get Sawhorse and Hedgestroker to make a public display for these corpses. A nice diorama in the square about the folly of revolutionarism. Understand all that?"

"Yes, indeed, most assuredly!" said Barbara sweatily, and gestured for Kaizha to follow. She left her corpses and lumbered after him. He led her into a side hall and down some badly-worn stairs, babbling all the way.

"Here is the main servants' stair, leading to the main foyer—where indeed much of the prime business is conducted! Receiving things, sending things, scuttling in and out—"

"I'm sorry...what was your name, again?"

"Oh, it's *Barbara*," said the drake, employing some exotic pronunciation. "The alchemist that created me ran out of things to call his drakes and began picking them out of foreign baby-name pamphlets. The mistress liked it so much she had me keep it! Anyway, after the foyer, of course, is the main hearth-room, for dining occasions and the reception of visitors and other grand things involving tables"—Barbara clapped his hands together at the mention of tables—"and after that is blah blah blah..."

Kaizha stopped listening to Barbara, as she lost interest. They came to the bottom of the twisting stair and arrived at a huge windowless room that had a bowels-of-the-house sort of feel to it. The floor was covered in fluffy straw. A smallish infandus turned it over and over and over again with a pitchfork, shuffling back and forth across the floor, performing a mindless and solitary dance.

"This is the servants' quarters. You sleep and rest here when not at work. We go to the kitchens to get food after the masters have eaten in the mornings and evenings and you are to eat that as fast as possible. If a master calls while you are sleeping, you must respond. Your collar will give you a little strangle, there." Barbara pointed at her neck. "But no worries! It is a very gentle strangling, to be sure."

But Kaizha wasn't paying attention to the little meatsack. Instead, she stared at that pitchfork. A heavy thing of sharp, thick metal prongs. Potentially a lethal weapon, and yet Xiongnyao had her servants playing around with it...

Had Kaizha ever been so witless in her own household?

The gardening shears. The fire pokers. The saws. The axes. Even things like access to the food pantry...When she really thought about it, it kind of astounded her that the slaves' little rebellion had failed so completely, given the rampant complacency of their masters. Maybe it wouldn't have, if she hadn't set it off before they expected it to begin.

She might have been murdered in her bed along with the rest of the entire alchemical class. It would have been easy.

But the thought delighted her for some reason.

So easy.

"And around the room you will see all the doors to the various rooms of the household. You are not to go unless you are summoned, mind, and you will be punished if you do so of your own accord. You see there are the main bedrooms, guest bedrooms, kitchen, hearth room, master toilet, hall toilet, the master's lab—"

"The master has his own lab?" Kaizha tried her best to sound incredulous.

"Of course! Every great alchemist has one. And," the portly drake nudged conspiratorially, "since he is now the first seat, Master Turian now has the greatest lab. It is fine and large and full of all manner of accoutrements! The type a lowly drake such as myself wouldn't understand, of course."

"I would very much like to see the master at work."

"Wouldn't we all! But, as I mentioned," said Barbara, wagging a jolly finger, "there is no going into the main house unless you are summoned."

"Of course," Kaizha said vaguely.

"Now, I must be off and see about those messy corpses, mustn't I? Rest here until you are called." Barbara waved her into the room and scurried away.

Kaizha shuffled out to an area of straw in direct view of the entrance to the master's—*Turian's*—lab. Master...it was strange not to call him master. Or maybe it was strange the other way around and she was just rattled from being in this hole with the rest of the slaves.

If she had it her way, she'd spend time learning the ins and outs of the household. Which servants did what, which rooms connected to each other, which servants were oldest and most likely to be in the beginnings of the fall, what hours the ma—Turian—might be in his lab.

But she didn't have it her way. There was no time, thanks to that malicious brat's poisons or medicines or whatever it was she needed to survive.

She'd just have to improvise and hope it didn't blow up in her face.

She slept too long. Kaizha hadn't realized how exhausted she was. When she woke, her body refused to wake with her, remaining flaccid and lifeless for so long that she missed dinner. The teat-leech wilted in hunger and sucked dry what was left.

Kaizha finally managed to sit up. She put the drops in her eyes and waited for the pain to pass and tried to look inconspicuous. And she waited. Waited and waited. In the absence of real adrenaline, her body was sore and sweaty and she very much wanted to fall down and sleep forever.

Finally, an infandus headed towards the door for the alchemy lab. Kaizha got up to follow, gently closing the door behind her. She tried sneaking down the stairs, but she was so much heavier and clunkier than before, and so tired—

The infandus in front of her had stopped. "What are you doing?" she said. Her eyes were odd—one of them was black, but the other was a bright blue with a pupil in the middle—like a real human's.

"I'm…I was summoned."

"He only ever summons me. No others."

How odd. "Perhaps he has an extraordinary project that needs extra hands."

The infandus looked pointedly at Kaizha's teat-leech. "Really."

Kaizha considered strangling the infandus now, but if she made any noise, she might wake the other slaves—them and their pitchforks and fire pokers and who knew what else. She sighed. "I don't know. I only know I was summoned."

The infandus's lip curled, but she said nothing and plodded onward down the stairs. Kaizha followed. At the bottom was a room that would have made her old self come near to climax.

It was the biggest lab she'd ever seen. Even the labs at her old academy couldn't compare. It must have taken up the entire bottom floor of the house. Isolation pods, float tanks, black-caskets, wall-wheels, suspension hooks, and several torture devices she had never seen before cluttered the place like a forest. Some of the float tanks had human subjects in them, or partially-human, treading water and clinging to the grips on the sides. The float tanks were part of the array of experimental theory on isolation—a legitimate science now debased and disgustingly applied to practices like slavery instead of real pursuits like war.

Everyone knew total deprivation of human contact was essential to torture, but the precise methods varied. What if the subject could see other people, but not interact? What if the subject saw nothing—as in the isolation pods? What if the subject saw only a mirror reflection of himself—as in the black-caskets? What if—

"What are you doing here?"

Turian slunk around the corner of one of the pods, his infandus shuffling behind, grumbling "I knew it, I knew you wouldn't summon another, I knew it" in the tenor one would expect of sneery mutterings.

Kaizha blinked. How had she been caught off-guard? How long had she been standing there with her mind wandering like some stupid…slave?

Kaizha took a breath. Her mind wasn't gone. Maybe it

had been affected, but it wasn't gone. She could—and would—reclaim herself.

If she could remember who herself used to be.

Not now. Just do it.

"Oh!" Kaizha said, hunching over, trying to make herself small. "My collar tightened, sir. I thought—I thought you summoned me." Her mind raced. It kept saying *just kill them both right now* but that was not the answer. She'd had the answer planned out—sort of—back before she slept, but now her head hurt and she couldn't remember...

"I didn't." He sighed and pulled at his fat eyelids. "Didn't the mistress teach you how the household works? This kind of thing is supposed to be her responsibility."

"I—er. She did. I suppose I must have been mistaken."

"Well. She must have been the one who called for you. So go find her." Turian waved her away with a limp wrist and his eyes half-open.

Kaizha stood there. There was something she should say. What? What should she say? *Just kill them both...* The teat-leech twitched weakly, excited at her rising temper. But she had plans. She couldn't give in. She still needed Turian...

"Your master gave you a command," the infandus snarled.

The master was walking away. Turian would soon be out of range.

The teat-leech stirred.

It lashed out in two directions, half the tendrils wrapping around the slave's neck and half ensnaring Turian's limbs and smothering his mouth. The tendrils squeezed and squeezed and finally the slave went limp and something in Turian's body snapped. Oops. She hoped it wasn't something important.

The teat-leech was already weakening now. She had to do something with the man, something that wasn't killing him, fast, or the tendrils would slacken and he would scream and the other slaves would come running—

Not if they can't hear him.

She ripped off the lid of an empty float-tank, shut the sliding door that covered the only other opening, and plunked Turian inside. He strained against the lid, yelling, but Kaizha strained right back, clicking all the locks into place. His mouth moved, his neck went taut, and his forehead-veins bulged, but the many-plated panels smothered the noise. Slowly, he stopped struggling, and swam there with his fists clenched around the grips. Glaring hatefully, yes, but quietly.

That worked out better than she could have anticipated.

"Now," she said, and then remembered he couldn't hear her. She stepped away and slid open the tiny partition that allowed air and sound to pass. He hollered and yelled, so she slid it shut again. Kaizha supposed she really didn't need to smirk at him, but she desperately *wanted* to, so she waited and tried again. This time, he kept his voice down.

"Let me out," he said nicely. "I will make it worth your while."

She smirked at him. It felt as satisfying as she thought it would. "I have something else in mind."

"I'll grant you clemency. And freedom. And you can have a thousand—"

"I'm afraid I'm not so selfish as that."

"What do you mean? What could you possibly hope for beyond that?"

"I want some slaves of my very own." She paused. "Oh. I

suppose I'm *more* selfish than that. I got my words mixed up." Kaizha was disappointed in herself. She had imagined this to be a far more sinister and intimidating conversation. But Turian, for his part, looked appropriately horrified.

"You can't, though. It's against the first...law..." He trailed off.

"You realized how ridiculous that was mid-sentence, didn't you?"

"But—but surely you still respect the laws of alchemy, Kaizha? All these years, you yourself fought for the preservation of the laws over all else."

"Something strange has happened to my brain, Turian. It has made me think perhaps certain tenets can be reinterpreted. Tenets like 'only non-humans can be pressed into slavery.' Silly loopholes like 'a condemned human can lawfully be rendered a non-human with thorough disfigurement and erasure of identity.'" She cocked her head at him and wondered if he knew she was smiling. "I'd say as long as there's a slave-lobe, why, you must have a slave, no matter what he looks like."

"But...you..." Turian bit his lip. He glanced at the dead infandus on the floor with an inordinate amount of pain and regret in his eyes. He looked back to her, his face flat and open. Honest, for once. "Is there anything I can do to change your mind?"

"The only thing I want from you, Head Oligarch, is to do exactly as I command. And there's only one guarantee of that."

He shook his head, slow at first, then faster and faster, as though he wanted to spin it off his spinal column. Perhaps he was slowly realizing what she meant. "No one will buy it. They won't believe—"

"I'm not interested in your opinion. I'm interested in where your notes for transmogrification are. Are you going to tell me?"

"Would it change anything if I did?"

Kaizha thought. "If you tell me where they are, I'll leave your genitals intact."

Turian frowned.

"Oh, fine. I'll find them myself. Oh, and let's go see if we can get one of the servants to send your wife down here, shall we?" She slid the door shut before he could start screaming again. *And maybe a hunk of meat or something.* Her body was aching with hunger.

The teat-leech wiggled in glee at the thought. It made the rummaging through Turian's things a little more haphazard than was efficient. But after some time, Kaizha found his pages, weighted under a tureen of scouring fluid.

All she had to do was excise the steps of the process that distorted a body, and she would have two transmogrified slaves wearing oligarchs' flesh.

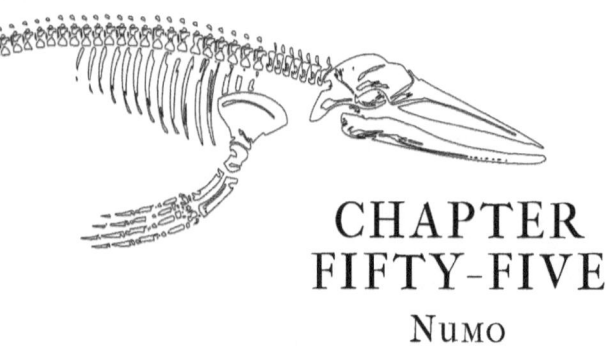

CHAPTER
FIFTY-FIVE
Numo

Sangja POKED NUMO in the shoulder, shaking him awake. Hammerfist growled in her sleep—Numo could feel the vibrations shivering through his skin. He'd fallen asleep in her fist again and Sangja had nearly gotten his head crushed the last time he tried to yank Numo away from her.

He held up a piece of paper. *How far did you get on the whale project?*

"I don't know." Numo hoped that was what he said. The past few days, he had started to forget what his voice sounded like, and how to make it as loud as it was properly supposed to be. Once in a while he'd get a *what?* written in response, so he knew he was making the odd mistake here and there. "It has quite a good deal of various stable fire-bearing materials within it. The things I know and the things you told me—all those fish, anyway—"

Sangja scribbled. *Enough for an explosion?*

Numo hesitated. "You never said anything about an explosion. That would require more unstable materials, sir."

Sangja's face crumpled into angry lines and Numo could tell he wanted to smack him. Sangja had wanted to smack him several times over the past few days, but Hammerfist clung to Numo like a soldier to a casket of gold. She couldn't get too far too fast—the function in her legs hadn't come back—but she was learning to swing on her fists alone, and Sangja couldn't run fast enough in his little lab to risk it.

I said to put anything and everything inside of it.

"You said to put anything and everything I would *put in my ovens* inside of it, sir. I never had cause to make an explosion inside the household. Indeed," said Numo, sitting up, "I would have been a remiss and cuttle-headed fogbrain if I had done so."

Sangja wrote again, and held up the paper, his handwriting turning sideways and falling off the page as it tended to do.

Look, [a word Numo couldn't read but assumed was a Tragan term of non-endearment], *your infandus friend woud be dead without me and so would you. We had a bargain. Do as I say, or I will withdraw my end of it.*

Withdraw his end? His end was to keep the both of them alive. Which Numo should be right well grateful for—why was he being so contrary? He'd never been quite so contrary and ornery and—

Withdraw his end…

Oh.

"You'd kill us for insubordination?"

Sangja grinned broadly, tapping his nose for some reason. *I don't value your lives as much as you do. Understand?*

"Indeed…" Indeed. Gracious, but the boy was a foul creature. But then, so was Numo, now. Perhaps all creatures were foul in some way or another, and their foulness was only natural. The boy was very very natural. He didn't even wear a shirt, after all. "Why don't you tell me exactly how you would like your conflagration, master?"

Sangja wanted an explosion. He wanted fetid whale meat to rain down from the sky and crush the Moak army.

Numo didn't know how to explode a whale.

You used guano, right, like I told you?

The pteropteryx feces that Sangja had him scrape off the sides of some of the buildings. Yes.

"Right, yes. But little, sir. Guano collection does not produce much yield. And besides, sir, I don't know what it does—I included it because you told me to do so, but I had thought it better to concentrate on a more stable fire, agents I was familiar with, and so—"

Sangja slapped an empty bottle off the table and smashed it into the wall. He paced to the other side of the room, rubbing his shaven head and talking to himself. Hammerfist woke up snarling and knocked several of the fish-lamps down in a flurry of panic. Sangja froze. He and Hammerfist murmured to each other. Finally he came back to the table and scribbled furiously, filling a whole page with big clunky letters. Then he held it up in front of both of them, looking pointedly from Hammerfist to Numo and back again.

I've gotten word that the Moak army will be here in two days. We can lure them onto the beach and trap them between the cliff and the ocean. The infandus will serve in a guard that seals off the road from the beach. The drake will explode the whale. I don't care how you do this, but you better do it. If the Moak army is not destroyed, we all die, and I'll make sure you come with me to hell.

Numo spent much of the first day trying to figure out how to make a huge explosion and getting nowhere. His head still hurt and he barely had the strength to move, in any case. He couldn't walk without stumbling—something was wrong with his sense of where the world was in relation to his feet. Everything just slipped over when he wasn't expecting it. How he could make anything blow up was beyond him. Then Hammerfist said *what if you don't make an explosion? What if you just create a massive fire they can't run from?*

That helped.

He couldn't set fire to the place the same way he did the arena, of course. Hunkerwood was hunkerwood, but much more flammable than a stone cliff or a sandy beach, and there wasn't anything like tarpine about Trago.

But there were other things to burn.

Hammerfist helped him gather them: shrubs and dried grass, stolen wood from broken boats, more fungus, more lampfish, a dried-up mummified lizard, and all the packets of alchemical fire the town possessed, which was six. She even helped him sojourn all the way back to the last place there were trees, and punched them over, and they slept amongst the wood for the night before going back to the coast.

Numo, for the most part, sat in her mouth and clung to her teeth. He slipped out a few times—her mouth being a slobbery pool spilling over at certain angles—but the real difficulty of the day was dragging everything down into the whale, where Hammerfist couldn't go. Instead, he sent her off to the clifftops to set up the fungus-line, and for the first time since he'd fallen ill, he was alone.

The sea made no noise. The sounds of birds, wind, wings, moorings tapping against wood—nothing. All gone.

Hammerfist's rumbling was the only thing between himself and the wall of silence.

He swallowed. She'd return soon. For now, he had to crawl inside the face of a decaying whale.

By now, the air inside was heavy as a blanket and toxic as taking a face full of worm-fed smoke, and Numo couldn't see a blasted thing. Even if parts of the whale hadn't been collapsing inward, and even if he weren't as dizzy as a drunkard, his eyes were spilling over with foggy leakage in protest. He crawled on his belly, dragging the firestarters in a carrying-hammock wedged between his tusks. Numo shoved them as far into the belly as he could bear, turned around, threw up, and shimmied out.

He gasped for air in the pupil-withering sunlight. Hammerfist came and made rumbling noises. Numo had no idea what she was saying.

"We're done," he said. Everything was ready; the whale was as full as it could be, and the cliffs were prepared in turn. And yet, the sick feeling didn't go away, even long after Hammerfist had carried him away from the whale's stench.

The truth was, Numo had never attempted anything like this. He didn't know enough about Trago and how to make fire with what was there. He didn't know enough about huge fires, explosive fires, fires meant to kill people instead of warm their houses. It seemed a great perversion of the art.

But then, it wasn't as if Numo hadn't done it before. He

was a low creature now. One that could only redeem himself by paying his debt to Hammerfist. If this didn't work…

He couldn't breathe. It had to work.

It had to.

Maybe he did love Hammerfist after all.

Word came the next day. The Moak army was not far from the cliffs, and already starting to raze the farmland.

Sangja went to the beach, and everyone was gathered there. It was a grand gray day, the sun hiding behind a thick veil of slate. They let him into the center of the crowd. Hammerfist had Numo sitting on the back of her neck. Humans and what few homunculi there were in Trago convened around him in a great circle. Sangja's lips started flapping and Numo didn't hear anything.

There were big arm movements and adze-swings and a low rumble of raucous nothing erupting from the crowd. Something very stirring indeed, Numo assumed, as he sat there and wrung his fingers around his wrists. It was like that first time he'd seen Hammerfist speak. Bollix, inviting him in, perching him on an infandus, trying to get him to understand. Brothers and sisters, that's what she had said, to Numo's utter incomprehension. He'd been disconnected from everyone then, and he was disconnected now, living in an underwater bubble of smothered sound.

But here he was in Hammerfist's mane. Brothers and sisters. How did brothers and sisters love each other? Not like husbands and wives. He hadn't even known what he was thinking before. Romantical attachment? Was that really what had burned into his mind? He didn't know. He didn't understand it at all. It was desperate and thoughtless and berserk and baseless, whatever it was. He'd thought it was perfect at the time. But that was because it hadn't been real.

Nothing was that perfect.

But a brother and sister cared for one another, didn't they? That was what Bollix meant. They grew old together. Fought for each other.

Numo clung tighter to Hammerfist's hair. Her rumbling voice vibrated through his rump-skin like thunder. She was cheering. She was happy. Sangja had said something that made her happy. What?

The crowd suddenly dispersed as though it were the surface of a pond hit by a skipping-stone. They moved away in great ripples: the humans towards the docks and the ships; the slaves towards the main road and the cliffs. Hammerfist sat Numo down at his place—behind a clump of rope, next to the remains of the whale on the beach—and dropped one of Sangja's hoary old swords in his lap. She squeezed his hand. Something tickled his palm. She left to take her own position atop the cliffs, swinging herself up one of the two roads that led out of the rock-hewn city. When she had disappeared from view, Numo opened his hand.

There was a dandelion inside.

Numo's chest felt as unsteady and spilling-over as a tipped cup. She would be okay, wouldn't she? She had to be. Her legs didn't work anymore, but she swung them like secondary fists, using her massive arms as leverage. She was still quite formidable. And she and the other slaves would be in hiding, far out in the watery farmlands and tall grasses, until just the right time.

But against an army…

He thought he felt a distant rumble. There was probably some signal from the drake lookouts he couldn't hear. He hadn't even thought of that.

Another possibly imaginary quiver under his feet. Numo stiffened. He was about to kill the army of the holy city. All of it. Or fail and die.

He supposed it was a bit late to be concerned about the impropriety of it all.

The slaves were all gone from sight. The humans had floated away in the boats to anchor just offshore, "out of range," whatever that meant—except Sangja, who stood on the outermost tip of the longest pier like a tiny smirking half-naked lighthouse with the shiny bits in the wrong places.

Behind him, the men in the boats seemed to be beating drums. Which might account for the rumbling and quivering, which meant that Numo had no idea when the army would come or where—

Oh, there it was.

It was odd, watching a great huge line of people appear on the cliffs above like hairs on a man's chin, raising their spears and slings and swords and axes and meteor hammers, bashing them against shields, all in total innocuous silence. Well, near-silence. Numo could feel the bashing in his own bones, hear a very faint *bum-bum-bum* that competed with the Tragans' *foom-foom-foom*, but gods, the stench of that whale nigh blocked out everything else.

Tiny balls of fire arced out over the cliff from Moak slings. A great rain of embers. Then bigger embers. Fireballs, and contraptions that were much larger than slings—

With much larger payloads....

Oh tiddlefarts.

Rhino-sized wads of fire flumped into the beaches. The docks behind Numo were set ablaze as the smaller wodges of alchemical conflagrations were slung out over the harbor. Sangja opened his mouth in what appeared to be either a maniacal laugh or a wild gobbling scream like that of a rabbit being slaughtered by kittens, then disappeared behind a curtain of growing fire.

Down, down the firestones pelted, for what seemed like hours, until Numo grew weary of the sight of flaming rain. Behind him, the harbors raged for miles down the shoreline, turning shops and mills and moorings and fisherman's shanties into ash. Flakes of it coated the beach and the hapless seawater like dandruff floating upon bathwater. Bits of the whale's tail were starting to burn from the projectiles, but in most places on the carcass, still, fire wouldn't catch on its skin.

Was this Sangja's plan? This was what the Tragans had raucously agreed to? The full destruction of half their city?

Did they know Numo would probably destroy another quarter?

But maybe it wouldn't come to that. The fiery hail stopped. Numo peered out from behind his rock. The men ringing the cliffside had backed away out of sight. The gray sky was gray again, dull and unspectacular in its unmercurial calmness.

The ground, very definitely this time, quivered.

Two halves of the army spilled around the cliffside, tromping down the two roads leading down to the main beaches and the cliff-carved city center. The backs of Numo's knees sweated and his pulses beat everywhere from his eyeballs to his groin to his heels.

This was not meet. This was improper. This was a sin and a blight on the order of things.

Residue from his slave-lobe, perhaps. All the odd things it had filtered into the rest of his brain. Love or not-love. Meet or not-meet. Nothing within his own head was reliable. There was only Hammerfist as his compass. And this time, it felt real.

Numo gripped the sword. Gods, it was heavy—but it had to be heavy. A flimsy needle wouldn't cut through the hide of a sea-beast, and the outside of it wouldn't burn.

He put the sword in between his teeth. He took the watersack from his pouch and left the bag behind—it would be too cumbersome. There was one packet of alchemical fire within the whale, amidst the pile of flammables. The rest were scattered around the tops of the cliffs. Numo had one shot at lighting his own conflagration and hopefully avoid killing himself in the process.

Numo took a deep breath and crawled into the mouth of the beast.

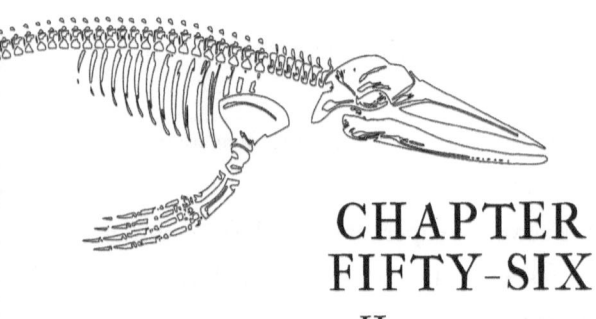

CHAPTER FIFTY-SIX
HAMMERFIST

THE MOAK ARMY took its time descending onto the beach. Hammerfist waited in her hiding spot, her heart pounding thrice the speed of their slogging footsteps. Someone behind her coughed.

"Shut up," she hissed. The drake shrank back. That was all she had in her contingent—well, three drakes and two stringy infandi who might as well have been drakes, most of them armed with sharp utensils and kitchen implements. Hammerfist supposed she was the muscle. It was awfully hard for The Muscle to hide behind such a tiny bush, but the Moaks didn't seem to notice her.

There were two other contingents hidden somewhere with equally small numbers of unimpressive specimens, waiting above the city for their moment. Her group would block one of the roads up the cliffs of Trago. One other immense brute like herself—the most expensive slave in the city, she wagered—would lead a contingent to block the other road.

The third would light the fires.

Finally, the last of the soldiers disappeared down the road. Hammerfist waved her drakes and almost-drakes forward. Her great fists crunched unstealthily on the dry grass, but she tried to go slow and steady. The army couldn't know they were there until Numo set the plan in motion.

Hammerfist stopped just before the edge of the cliff, where the road began its descent, a wide path hammered out of the rock wall. She peered out, craning her neck. There was the army, preparing to fire their slings and little catapults at the ships from the beach. There was the whale. There was Numo's hiding spot—empty.

She waited. The army lit their sling-loads and their catapult fodder. She waited. They arranged themselves into position. She waited. Her slobber cascaded out of her, pushed out by the pounding of her anxiety, and sweat gathered in her furry armpits like lather. She waited. What was taking Numo so long? Had he fainted inside the whale? She knew it. It was too much, too soon. He hadn't recovered. He was still unwell. She nearly started down to go to him, to dash the plan as it was, but then she stopped short. A wisp of smoke curled innocuously out of the whale's mouth. Oh gods, he'd lit the fire. He'd lit the fire and passed out. Her muscles twitched. He'd explode inside a whale. Her Numo, killed by the stench of a dead waterbeast—

A small figure wriggled out of the whale's mouth. Someone at the front of the army formation pointed. Half the soldiers adjusted their aim. *Faster Numo, faster...*

He crawled around the whale's side, to the broadness of its belly—the side facing the beach and the Moak army. A few running paces and they could be upon him. But confusion slowed them. Someone shouted "drake" at him. The air came in slices, chopped to pieces by twirling slings and meteor hammers, prepared to loose on him the moment they decided he was a threat.

Numo took the sword from between his teeth, pushed himself to his feet, dug the sword into the whale, and went sprinting down the side of the creature until he fell face-first in the sand.

Burning rocks piffed into the beach around him, one glancing off his shoulder. But before the attack could become a barrage, it happened.

The gash erupted. Flaming entrails and great black clouds of stench and fire and foulness spurted into the air and came down on the first line of soldiers, coating them in burning black rot. Screams erupted from the beach. The soldiers pushed back towards the cliffs as the guts finished scattering and a thick column of flame shot out of the gash in the whale's side, lighting the fallen bodies like little bits of overdone toast.

Hammerfist turned. The third contingent—all drakes— were sitting in stunned dumbfoundedness in their positions.

"Now! Now now now!" she roared. The drakes jerked into motion and lit the packets, dumping water down the vertical side of the cliff face—a trail for the flames to follow. Little sparks shot out as the fire went along, hitting bits of pteropteryx guano here and there. It wasn't enough, but there wasn't much guano near the top of the rock face. The sparks needed to last until hitting the thickly-encrusted façade of Trago, down near the foot of the cliffs.

Hammerfist took her own group to barricade the road, swinging herself as fast as she could down the rocky trail. The large-ish slave on the opposite road began flinging rocks onto the path to block it. *Damn. I should have thought of that.* But there was no time to go rock-finding now. The Moak soldiers had noticed them.

They tossed fire in Hammerfist's direction and came running back up the roads. The drake behind her brandished a fork and barked. The two stringy infandi growled like angry kittens and waved kitchen knives. Hammerfist knocked the first few soldiers over the side of the road and down onto the shore below, but the second wave was coming, and it was much bigger than her—

And then the cliff exploded.

The little alchemical fires had traced their way down to the guano-soaked façades of Trago. Fire erupted from both sides, trapping the army between the whale and the cliff. Little men on fire, pteropteryxes screeching and crashing and their bellies smoldering, the entire beach lit up in screams and bright white destruction. It was almost pretty. She shouldn't think it was pretty. That was a horrible thing to think. But she was horrible, after all. Monstrous and horrible.

What Samaak would think of her now.

The situation turned ugly. Those not yet on fire streamed up the roadside. The drake charged with his wee little fork and got crushed under the stampede. The other two drakes ran away, leaving her with the stringy infandi. The two of them cut down a few before they were hacked to death. Hammerfist struck out again and again, but the soldiers were overwhelming; they cut her and sliced her and lopped off most of her toes and part of a foot and still she clubbed at them and shoved them over the side and, most of all, hoped that Numo was not already dead.

Finally they knocked her down. Two soldiers raised their swords to skewer her; the others restrained her, sitting on her fists, poking spears through her palms to pin her to the dust.

Rocks slammed into the heads of the skewerers and they

toppled over. Hammerfist looked up. The runaway drakes, positioned at the edge of the cliff just over the road's entrance, were shoving large rocks over the side.

"Move!"

Freed from the spears by the drakes' rockslide, Hammerfist tried to shuffle backwards. Rocks pelted her guts and bruised her thighs and smashed one of her bleeding feet, but they also cracked the skulls of Moaks trying to kill her, and for that she was thankful.

The fires on the beach died out, the whale left smoldering. The pteropteryxes screeched and attacked the wounded soldiers in rightful fury. The boats came sailing in, crunching over the debris and ash to land on the shore, and the Tragans rushed in to finish the job. Stragglers, the wounded, the blackened—those died first, cursorily, as though the militia were merely doing a bit of housekeeping. Then they surged up the roads to cut down the remaining soldiers.

The Moaks swarmed the road like ants. They no longer bothered trying to kill Hammerfist, but she got mowed down anyway under their flailing arms and legs and stompy feet. If nothing else, her body was an effective tripwire—but gods, it hurt. Someone stepped directly on her crooked jaw and there was a snap and holy hellfire demon-runs Samaak's twisted fingernails it hurt as much as being beaten by that tentacle-whip over and over—

And suddenly the stampede was over. She looked up through a haze of pain. Tragans scuttled past her, whooping after whatever Moaks were left alive and running, shoving bodies over the cliffside to get them out of the road. She heard whimpering. It was coming from her chest. She'd never whimpered before. Part of her was ashamed and part of her felt…well, more human. Being crushed was a very human thing to be, she thought. But whether that was good or bad, she could no longer say.

That part of her was dead.

Sangja limped into view, looming over her, casting a very small shadow that hardly deserved the word "looming," but in sooth his face was dark as any demonspawn's. Smeared blood painted the lower half of his face, as though someone had smacked him in nose and it had spilled over his mouth. His leg was blackened from the burns, and his face was wild with pain, but he looked oddly satisfied with himself in spite of it all.

"Is Numo alive?" she tried to say, but all that came out was an incoherent whine.

"Don't whimper like that; you embarrass me," he panted. "Are you dying or not?"

Hammerfist wasn't sure. She tried shoving herself into an upright position against the cliff and her body jerked with an electric current of agony.

Sangja leaned over and peered at her. He called for someone to bring bandages and water. "I'm not sure if you're dying or not. Hell," he smiled, "I'm not even sure if *I'm* dying or not. But I think both of us can make it to Moaki to see if our friend has held up her end of the bargain, wouldn't you agree?"

Hammerfist didn't care where he took her, as long as she knew Numo was okay. Where was he? Did he explode himself? Did he get stampeded? Burned to death? Drowned? She had to get to the beach, but her arms—

"Did you want this as well, sir?" A woman held a drake upside-down by a clubby little foot. Hammerfist peered.

Numo.

Hammerfist's head tightened on itself like her own fist around a melon. He wasn't moving.

"Is it alive?" Sangja poked at him. Numo groaned. Hammerfist's body went rubbery and a noise came out of her like a leaking bellows.

"Seems to be," said the woman. "Keeps throwing up on itself."

"Well," said Sangja, "wipe it off, will you? That's my slave. He has to look presentable for our trip to Moaki. And I'm going to need several of you," he shouted, "to fetch me my shit." He grinned. "After all, we have pressing business to attend to."

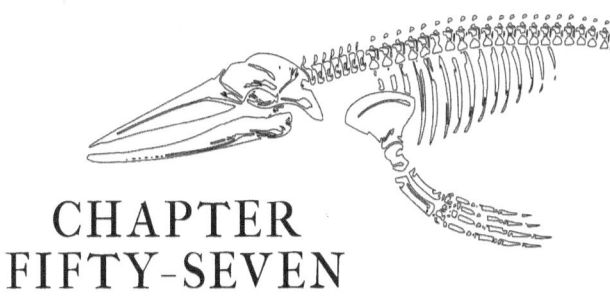

CHAPTER FIFTY-SEVEN
Kaizha "Floppacles" Shanyang

Kaizha STARED DOWN her slaves. They still looked almost the same as before, but the hatred was gone from their eyes, and it had been replaced by a blank look of blissful nothingness. It wasn't that noticeable on Turian, but it looked quite strange on Xiongnyao's face. She wished she had more time to play with them—test them out—but today would be the annual Solstice Convening, and she needed them now.

"Again, what is your objective?"

"To serve you, mistress," Turian droned.

"To make the council think we are very important people," Xiongnyao slobbered.

"Stop that drooling!"

Xiongnyao slurped her tongue back into her mouth and wiped off her chin with her sleeve. Kaizha squeezed the back of her neck. She desperately needed more sleep. The teat-leech purred—sort of, in an internally-vibrating sort of way—demanding more food. It was hungry all the time now. Feed a homunculus his fill and he'll raid the whole larder, as the saying went. She'd forgotten. This whole operation was sloppy and uncomfortable. That damn Tragan brat—if he'd wanted any of

435

this done right, he shouldn't have rushed her so…

"Okay. One more time. You are very important people. You are the head of the council and you are to act like it. Like you are better than all the other human beings and slaves and everyone else on the planet."

"Better than ghosts?" Turian murmured.

"Better than—no. Ghosts? No. It doesn't matter. Can you remember to pretend you are more important than everyone else?"

"Except you, mistress," Xiongnyao said.

"That's the thing. You must treat me as—*goddammit put your tongue back in your mouth*—you must treat me as your slave."

Turian gave a hollow laugh. "A game? We the masters and you the slave, mistress?"

"Yes. A game."

"Great fun," Xiongnyao said.

"Yes. Now, when the people come, you must do exactly what I'm about to tell you. We will go over it several times, but try very hard to remember. Can you try to remember?"

"Of course," Xiongnyao said. "We'd be awful slaves if we didn't." She paused, and then slurped her tongue back into her mouth. "See? Remembering."

That night, the rest of the new council appeared. Half were callow children of murdered oligarchs, and the other half seemed to be newly-appointed young men from the Holy Academy of Moa. Men she didn't know. A council of strangers. As it should be, really—a strong oligarchy demanded some turnover and competition—but without all this "men" business.

Kaizha had her position as waiting-servant, following Xiongnyao and Turian around, bowing and scraping and trying to look innocuous. To her great surprise, they both mostly remembered their lines, although the delivery left much to be desired.

"Welcome, welcome! Welcome to our home! Come to the hearth-room; avail yourself of our vittles!" Xiongnyao burbled, putting her tongue back in her mouth robotically at the end of every phrase.

"Yes. We have many things to discuss," Turian said, theatrically strutting to the head of the dining-table as though he were parading down the aisle in a clown wedding. The oligarchs followed, a few casting hairy eyes and wary eyes besides, but with an altogether satisfying amount of obliviousness.

Slaves served beverages and first courses. Turian and Xiongnyao glanced over at Kaizha. She hadn't told them they were allowed to eat. She nodded. Turian stared at his fork for some time as though he were trying to puzzle out its use. Finally he gave up. Instead he started talking.

"As you all know, we have had quite a disturbing year. Much of the oligarcy slaughtered, the Homomachy lost to the slaves, rebellion from within the city and from those bastards in Trago!" He paused, thinking. Then he thumped his fist on the table. "It has become clear to me, the first seat of the council, that great changes are needed. The universal balance has been put—put off its head." He swallowed. That wasn't exactly what he was supposed to say, but it seemed close enough. She nodded at him to keep going. "The gods are upset with this imbalance. Kiroktera no longer sees us as worthy custardians—custodians of his earth. We must earn back that right and prove ourselves loyal and worthwhile creatures."

"I don't know about that," blurted a bland-looking young man. "I feel there is an imbalance, but possibly only contained to the gods' world itself—"

"Silence," Turian said dramatically, crossing his arms across his chest. "I have many proposals for correcting this imbalance. We shall all discuss them and vote. Keep in mind that we, as the senior members, get to vote twice."

"That is not how we were taught it works," the young man whined.

Turian looked at Kaizha. He didn't have a scripted response to that. "This is how it works because we are the most important people in this room."

"The oligarchy is meant to—"

"Silence," he said again. "Just stop talking." More pleading than ordering. He was sinking. "I'm supposed to tell you about these proposals. I mean, I have to. I have to, because they are important and we thought of them because we are important…"

"These proposals!" Xiongnyao shouted. Kaizha nearly slapped her. But, of course, she *had* told her to step in and save Turian if he forgot his lines. "These proposals are as follows:

"One: we will stop producing homunculi altogether. They are far too dangerous and we have become too soft and reliant on them."

Lili—one of the few survivors of the emergency meeting before her arrest, Kaizha remembered—began to protest, but Xiongnyao only spoke louder. "Two: we will transition back wholly to a tribute economy, with an aim to eliminate slave trading. Our embarrassing defeat at Trago shows just how lacking and unimpressive our armies have become. Other cities will soon rise up against us, thinking us unfavored of the gods. So we will have to once again make our armies glorious and huge and magnificent and…um, scary, in order to crush them all and extract our proper amount of tribute.

"Three: no more men in alchemy. I'm sorry," she said woodenly, "but the gods clearly don't favor you. You do not respect the opposing forces and rely on stability. Chaos is essential to alchemy and you are too weak to uphold its law. You are welcome to act in supporting roles and your wives and daughters may join the oligarchy once their studies have concluded, but—"

The room erupted in soppy shouting. Fists banged on the table, chairs shoved back, at least one dish broke. "But you appointed us yourselves! You hand-picked us! Men have kept this city stable and the region peaceful!"

Kaizha stepped forward and wrapped her tentacles around the nearest young man's neck, lifting him off the floor, turning him a nice shade of bluish purple. As she suspected, the others shut up and sat down instead of trying to fight back. Weak little wealthy children. Sometimes she wished she'd had one just so the city had an alchemist who was raised properly.

Of course, now that she had him, she wasn't sure whether to kill him or not. She waffled about it for a bit, but while she was trying to make up her mind, his neck snapped.

Well. Decision made.

The room was filled with awkwardness. Xiongnyao and Turian stared at Kaizha. She hadn't given them a script for a scenario like this. Xiongnyao's tongue was out again. Kaizha pointed at her own mouth. The woman smartly shoved it back in and wiped off her chin.

"That is our slave," said Xiongnyao. "We are the masters."

Nobody said anything to this. It would have been threatening if she hadn't sounded like a child pointing out which toy was hers.

"Anyway. Proposal number...number next: since we already have quite a lot of infandi, and not much military at the moment, we should commandeer all able-bodied slaves to send to Trago, to do as much damage as possible. Any survivors left with the fall who can't be commanded—tell them that if they destroy Trago, they get a cure. Money. Freedom. Whatever they want. We'll brand them as honorary humans and they can live as a human would.

"If any of them survive, that is." Xiongnyao paused, furrowed her brow, and pushed her tongue into her mouth.

"So," Turian said. "Let's vote, shall we?"

Kaizha, for her part, ensured that the vote went in her favor. If this meant two of the young men ended up donating their masses to the hypocaust-fires, it was a small thing.

Moaki was in crisis. Some would have to be lost to save it.

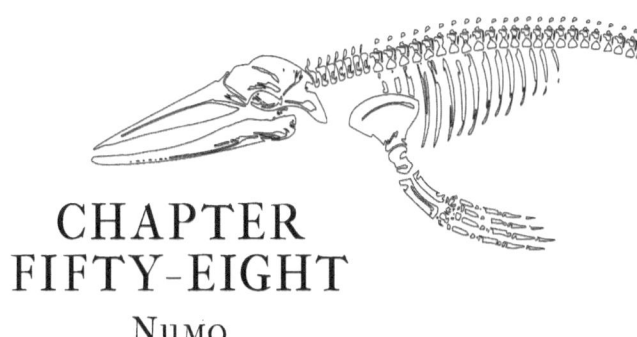

CHAPTER
FIFTY-EIGHT
Numo

NUMO DID NOT care for the bouncing of the goat-trap. Hammerfist sat on the back of the platform, cradling him between her crusty bloody feet as the trap bounced and bobbed and raced under a horridly bright sky. She said things to him—he felt the rumbling in her belly—but nobody seemed to have remembered to bring anything to write on. Staring at the sky made him sick and staring at the lead goat of the trap following behind them made him sicker so mostly he closed his eyes and wished for all the bloody motion to end. He had no idea how much of that whale-belch he'd inhaled, but it still seemed to be inside his belly and lungs and his very skin. It was in the maze-channels of his brain, lodged in the hole he'd made, taking up residence like beetle larvae in a rotting mnoafruit.

They stopped at some sort of inn or waystation. Sangja looked to be in a bad way, all sweaty and glisten-faced, barely able to walk. The men in the goat-trap behind helped him inside and brought bags and things. Hammerfist put Numo in her mouth, which now seemed to be at least half held together by a scaffolding of bandages. She swung her way out of the trap behind Sangja. Numo wondered if she could taste him.

441

Probably so. It was a great credit to her character that she did not throw up herself. Maybe infandi could not throw up. He'd heard that rats couldn't. But she wasn't a rat...

Sangja and the innkeeper had a heated disagreement that involved a lot of pointing at Hammerfist. Sangja ended it by aiming his adze at the innkeeper's badly-shaven throat and waved Hammerfist forward. *Swing thump swing thump swing thump* she went, hastened by the tenseness of the situation, he assumed, but oh how he wished she wouldn't. He tried very hard to have the courtesy not to be sick in someone else's mouth and clutched his mouth tight to pin his lips shut.

Finally they made it to a room with three beds and a heap of straw in the corner. Hammerfist sat him down on the straw, said something, said more things, who knew what, and he couldn't make himself say anything in return but "I'm sorry I taste so bad."

Hammerfist cocked her head and carved something into the floor. *Thank you for surviving.*

"Wouldn't have bothered but for you," Numo said, trying to smile and sound merry. He wondered if he was joking or not.

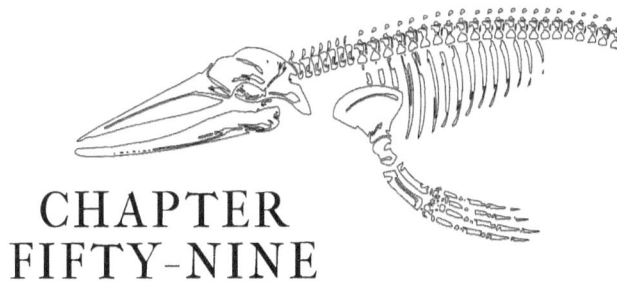

CHAPTER
FIFTY-NINE
HAMMERFIST

THEY PASSED THE night and the next several besides with the two men—some sort of doctors—poking and prodding and cutting and bandaging and splinting and applying ointments and dripping that blue liquid of Sangja's into everyone's eyes. Their days were spent in goat-traps, a discomforting experience in their injured states that got to be an even worse experience once they began traveling up the mountains.

Poor Numo was ill much of the time. The worst of it, aside from the unfaltering pains in her body, was that Hammerfist had no paper or ink, and even if she had, the passage was too rough to write. There was nothing she could say to Numo that he would understand.

She licked him every so often, but she wondered if it was enough.

Moaki's guards were diminished, but there were still at least nine or ten at the gates to brandish various weapons at them, and one to ask for their identities.

"Sangja," Sangja identified himself.

Hammerfist told the guard who she was, but he didn't speak infandus.

"What?" said Numo, and Hammerfist couldn't figure out how to tell him what the guard was asking.

The guard looked at a paper of his and let them in anyway. "The First Seat wants you," he said. "You are to go only to the house of the First Seat, and nowhere else. My men will escort you."

He slapped their goats on the rumps, but the goats did not indulge him with a response.

The altitude strained her breaths as the trap rattled up the main road towards the temple of Moa. Numo clung on to Hammerfist's claw and wheezed. She licked him uselessly.

The trap finally came to a stop at a grand entrance of a large house with a swooping roof, just in the shadow of an enormous temple Hammerfist had never seen before. One of the men in the trap behind approached the infandus footman to announce them. The other helped Sangja limp out of the vehicle. The city guards stood around making sure no one stepped a foot in the wrong direction and making unsavory comments about the smells the party carried.

Thankfully, caring about what she smelled like was a pleasantly bygone feature of Hammerfist's existence.

After a minute or two of waiting, the infandi of the house ushered them inside.

The foyer was a grand thing of intricately-carved wood, grand circular doorways, and a rug of white rhinoceros skin, which Numo seemed fascinated with. He stared at it, stretching his toes and squishing them in the pristine woolly hide before he started to lose his balance. Hammerfist had to prod him back into an upright position. When he started to fall again, she held him steady. He smiled at her and said thank you and all she could do was offer a cock of the head in return.

444

She would have to think of a more steady means of talking to him, when they were alone—

Would they ever be?

Hammerfist wondered heavily about this. If she'd been fantasizing, hoping for something that wouldn't be. If the world was the world she knew, they'd only be separated again, because she was always separated from things that made her happy.

Numo patted her claw. "It'll be all right," he said, as if he could read her face, or the drip-rates in her saliva, or the pensive curl of her tongues.

He was wonderful like that.

A man and a woman pranced into the foyer. It was an odd thing to do, for a man and a woman, and for ones dressed like this. Hammerfist had only ever seen people dressed so finely in parades and on holidays—and when the high oligarchs attended the fights—

"So good to meet you! So good to meet you!" they gushed, shaking Sangja's hand.

"I am Xiongnyao, wife of the first seat," said the woman.

"Turian, first seat himself," said the man.

"We've been told so much about you," said Xiongnyao.

"Did you bring the medicament?" said Turian.

Sangja blinked at them and furrowed his brow. Xiongnyao's tongue was sticking out. If these were oligarchs, something was extremely off. And to Hammerfist, strangely familiar. Their manner, their expressions—they were almost—infandus-like.

"Yes, I brought it. But first I need to speak with Kaizha."

"Oooh! You mean Floppacles. We are only meant to call her Floppacles, you see." Xiongnyao slurped her tongue back in.

"And she says she doesn't need to talk to you. We're

445

supposed to—um. What were we supposed to do?"

"Um." Xiongnyao played with her pectoral necklace. "Oh!" She pulled a piece of paper from Turian's pocket. "This is for you."

"No, that wasn't it. She said something else. She said it was very important…" Turian stared at the rhino hide under his feet. "Have we always had this?"

Sangja unrolled the paper and his eyes scrolled across the page. He raised an eyebrow. "So Trago is independent?" he said.

Xiongnyao cocked her head to the left. Like an infandus. "Is that what the paper says?"

Sangja showed it to her. "You signed it. First seat, yes?"

"Oh, yes. We are very important. We signed it. She told us to. Other people listen to us because we are very important."

Sangja smiled. "I see."

So did Hammerfist. But she had no role here. She stayed silent. She watched Numo. She waited for an opportunity.

Fantasy or not, now or years from now, she would find space and time to run, to carry Numo with her, and for them both to be free.

"What was it?" Turian said dreamily. "There was something else."

"Never mind it." Sangja handed a small satchel to Xiongnyao. "The medicament is in there. Let her know we've upheld our end of the bargain and expect her continued complicity on her end." Sangja banged on his chest once and turned to leave.

"Are you going back to Trago now?" said Xiongnyao.

"Yes," he muttered.

"Oh. Well, maybe you should wait. Until after."

Sangja halted. He lifted his head. "After what?"

"You know. The thing. The attack."

Sangja whirled around as fast as a boy on crutches could whirl. "What attack?"

"Oh! I remember," Turian said. "We're not to say anything."

"Anything at all?" Xiongnyao tittered.

"No. Nothing at all."

"Oh. Drat."

Numo tugged at Hammerfist's claw. "What are they saying? What happened?"

Hammerfist couldn't say; it was too long a thing to scratch into the floor and she wasn't sure the owners of the house would tolerate it. But she began looking about for windows, things she could exit from, and readying a cradle in her mouth with her tongues for Numo.

In case they had to run.

"An attack by whom?" Sangja was growling. "What army is there left?"

In fact—if this went badly enough, and it seemed it would, there might be chaos, and in chaos there were holes of attention where people weren't looking at you, weren't seeing whether you had stayed or left or not, and maybe then—

"Oh, don't worry," Xiongnyao said comfortingly. "Not really an army. But we've got to do something with all the slaves we've got left, see. Infanduses and the like. Floppacles doesn't want them anymore. This way they will have a good use!"

Hammerfist's brain stopped whirring. Her jaw would have come open now, if it were not always open. The constant dripping of her saliva dried. *They'll all die...*

"Very good indeed. And if they die, people won't be as disappointed," Turian said, smiling. "So you see, it all works

447

out fine."

Sangja raised a crutch and swung it into Turian's neck, slamming him to the ground.

A sort of chaos broke out. A lovely sort of chaos that Hammerfist might have been able to run from, if she took Numo now, if she crashed out of that side window by the bookcase and stole a goat-trap and outran the city guards and killed whoever else got in her way until they were long disappeared, and they would both be terrible, so terrible, but—

But the rest of the slaves in Moaki, those who knew their drudgery and those yet to discover it, would be made killers or killed themselves. All of them, the same fate as her, though more likely dead in the end if Sangja was to lead the other side.

The boy did not seem to care what else he lost, or what lives suffered, as long as he won the war.

"What's happening?" Numo said, tapping on her claw. Hammerfist risked a phrase, carved into the floorboards.

They are sending all homunculi to destroy Trago.

Numo stared at it as more guards rushed in from other areas of the house, and Sangja's own men drew daggers, and Xiongnyao and Turian scrabbled to get away from the fracas. Chaos was only growing, but it would be over soon. Hammerfist had to make a decision now—

"Well, we must stop them, mustn't we?" Numo said finally.

Hammerfist swallowed. Her saliva came back to her and dripped on the "destroy Trago" she'd carved into the floor.

She gave a smiling cock of the head at him and put him in her mouth. Then, taking a last look at the window she might have crashed through, Hammerfist entered the fray.

CHAPTER SIXTY

Kaizha "Floppacles" Shanyang

Kaizha HADN'T LEFT the lab since she took over. It was a playground she could have all to herself. She could ditch the slave-making malarkey, at least on its own merits. As an essential ingredient for her new weapon, that would have to continue in some vein—she'd need to go on with her research with new versions of the creature on her arm; distribute it to the military. And restart the alcohol distillation experiments—get the economy going on a strong product before smashing the satellite states with a newly-equipped army.

She'd managed to get her notebook fetched from the little shack in the woods, and was toying with the alcohol, trying to perfect its dose with the distillation. Proceedings were slow, as she was getting more and more ill—weakness set in, and exhaustion slipped over her as easily as a sheet over a corpse. She slipped into sleep during one of the processes, which would have been a small accident under normal circumstances, but Xiongnyao and Turian got into the mixture and became slightly drunk. Or perhaps more than slightly.

But then, of course, the summons from the foyer came.

Kaizha tried to get up and deal with it herself, but she was dizzy and utterly floorbound. All she could do was lie there, sliding around in the film of her own sweat.

At least she knew the brat's threats were real.

Xiongnyao and Turian had gotten through three long council meetings and were improving at mimicking normal human behavior. They had remembered lines and instructions and Xiongnyao's tongue hardly ever stuck out anymore. Intoxicated, they might be a bit different, but they should have been able to handle a simple exchange.

She was in the middle of trying to choke down a sip of water when the Sangja's infandus broke down the door.

A rush of men and slaves and stumpy-footed crutch-children came flying at her. The slaves already in her lab were pummeled into the floor or sliced in their important places before she could get a handle on what was happening. Her brain seemed intolerably slow. Maybe it hadn't made the best decisions after all. But she still had the teat-leech, and it was very good at decisions.

It shot out at Sangja and wrapped around his body. His little posse froze in place. Numo—her sweet fretting Numo—was there with him, looking half-beaten to death, his eyes gone of any sweetness at all.

More of her slaves appeared from behind them and from the stairs to the servants' quarters, aiming rakes and axes and pitchforks at the intruders. She smirked. Then she remembered that the boy probably couldn't read an infandus's smirk and she tried a hoarse chortle instead.

"You lied to me," Sangja hissed.

"What do you mean?"

"You are sending out another attack on Trago."

Kaizha glared at Xiongnyao and Turian. A long string of drool hung out of the woman's mouth and she swayed against her husband. "They told you that? They're intoxicated. They're thinking of the one that already happened."

"No. They said you were sending the slaves. All the slaves."

"As I said, intoxicated."

"Too intoxicated to lie. You, on the other hand—"

"I'm too ill."

Sangja spat at her. The teat-leech constricted its tendrils, making his neck-veins pop out. Kaizha shut her eye and willed the tentacles to loosen just a bit. Much as she wanted this problem to go away, and as much as she hated the kid on a personal level, she couldn't quite bring herself to kill him. He reminded her of herself at that age. Of what real alchemy was. Dirty and dangerous and passionate. She liked that about the child. Maybe there was a way to save them both.

"Tell you what. If you agree not to make any more fuss about this, I'll let you stay here in Moaki. At the Holy Academy. Gratis. No tuition, all free, for the next ten years. And then you can come to the council and rule the city yourself."

Sangja's eyes brimmed with tears. His face reddened. She couldn't puzzle out the reason, exactly. Maybe he was angry. Maybe he was touched by her gesture. Maybe he was still choking to death because the teat-leech—

Dammit. Kaizha reminded it yet again to loosen. Why was it trying to kill him? It had never been at odds with her will before.

Still, after Sangja could breathe freely, he said nothing. He panted. He sweated. He blinked rapidly and his blackened leg oozed with an unhealthy color and viscosity. His pupils moved

451

back and forth across the floor, as though his thoughts were being brought to him by termites marching in a line and he was waiting for them to hurry up and get to his brain.

"There is a condition, though," Kaizha added.

Sangja's eyes flicked up at her. Wet and spilling over and spidery-red with veins. "Beyond the total betrayal of my home, you mean? What more do you want?"

The teat-leech wrapped itself tighter around the base of his skull and squeezed. Insubordinate creature. Kaizha willed it to let Sangja go entirely. After all, she had a small militia of slaves with sharp objects aimed at him. He wasn't going anywhere.

"I'm sorry. It's necessary for all of this to be lawful." Kaizha cocked her head. "Males are no longer allowed into the academy. Which means—"

Sangja's nostrils flared.

"You must sign a statement admitting you were born—and remain—female." She flicked a wrist at his crotch. "And get that leather blasphemery out of your womanhood."

It happened too fast to see. Sangja moved. Metal flashed. The teat-leech lashed out. Kaizha's arm fell away from her side and the creature was ripped out of her, leaving a tiny channel of nothing in her chest, like someone pulling a thread out of the eye of a needle. Blood spurted out of the stump. An avalanche of pain jabbed directly into her bloodstream. The teat-leech thrashed on the floor, wrenching itself around Sangja of its own accord. Her slaves stood there or flapped their arms as the Tragans cut them down with swords.

"Fight back! Fight back! Dammit, why aren't you f—" Her breath fell out from under the words. Her arm; her creature; her blood; *Bollix*—

"Fight back? Kill them, you mean? We're not supposed to kill humans, mistress," murmured a drake standing next to her. "Or are we? It is difficult to consider the propriety of such a—"

Sangja's infandus flattened him like a beetle. More of her slaves dying, her arm bleeding, Xiongnyao and Turian slapping blindly and falling over, the teat-leech still locked in mortal combat with the boy, crushing his body even as it went pale with weakness, blackness fuzzing the edges of her vision, her chest heavy, she was dying—

She ripped one of the leather straps off a torture-wheel and wrapped it around the bleeding stump with her mouth and her free hand but—but oh gods, she couldn't tie it off; she couldn't tighten it enough with one hand and her mouth didn't close properly enough to grip it with her teeth. She called for Xiongnyao but she was on the floor, hiding in a corner, not paying attention; Turian was drinking more of the alcohol…

Numo stared at her. Poor Numo, standing there in the midst of all the carnage. Numo was faithful. Numo had rescued her from slavedom. He would help.

"Numo."

He puttered over to her unsteadily, wobbling to and fro. "Did you say my name?"

"Help me—help me, please. Tie this off. Stop the bleeding. Or I'll die."

He hesitated.

"You remember me, don't you, Numo? You know who—who I am—" Her voice shuddered and threatened to give out. He tapped his ears.

"I can't hear anything, mistress. I've gone deaf." He paused. "I suppose you want me to help you."

"Yes!" She nodded vigorously. "I—I'll—"What could one say to a deaf slave?

"I would, mistress, that I would, if I knew it was right. But I'm not sure what the right thing is anymore."

"Numo! Please!" She pointed at her arm, at the leather strap, the thing that could be a tourniquet if only she had another hand to pull.

"You'll bleed to death. Like the master. I know."

She couldn't breathe. She couldn't speak. He was so different. He seemed almost…sentient…

If he was sentient, then he wanted something. Everyone did. "I'll give you anything, Numo. Anything. I can give…I can…"What had she been saying? Her head was spinning and everything was darkening.

"I've told you, mistress. I can't hear. But I'm thinking. I'm thinking if you are in charge of the people who run this city, there are ways the world would be better with you alive. If, say, you agreed not to send all the slaves to their deaths in Trago, and you decreed that they are to be treated like humans with payment for their services, and if you vowed to research ways to treat the fall and help slaves live happy lives until their natural deaths, and gave them the option of that brain experiment—I suppose I might help you then."

"Fine, yes, I agree." She nodded as much as she could stand, but her neck was all rubbery. It was a lie, of course. Numo didn't understand lies. He never had.

"I'm not sure I can trust your word, Kaizha Shanyang."

Maybe he did now.

That great infandus with the claws—Sangja's infandus— she had a name—Hammerfist? Hammerfist loomed up behind

454

Numo, swinging her bottom half like an upside-down fulcrum. She had something stuck to one of her useless mangled feet. Something white and shimmery.

Kaizha's creature. Her teat-leech.

It wasn't hers anymore.

How? How could it? How could Bollix—

But Bollix had revolted before. That was, after all, where Kaizha had found her. How fitting. And there it was now, on someone else's mangled appendage, while she bled…

Numo looked up at Hammerfist and held her by the claw. "We will stop the bleeding. We will treat your arm. But if you don't keep your promises, we will visit you again and encourage you to remember them. And," he said, holding up a fat leatherbound book—her alchemy journal, *her* fat leatherbound book—"I will be taking this for safekeeping."

Kaizha's heart beat a thousand weak flutters a minute. She struggled for air. Fear—fear was bubbling up in her again—that damn weakness of hers. Poor Numo. She'd turned poor Numo into this. And her creature—her Bollix—was gone. Everything was gone.

"Yes, Numo. Yes. I understand. Please—just help me," she whispered.

Hammerfist nodded at him. He smiled.

"Yes, mistress."

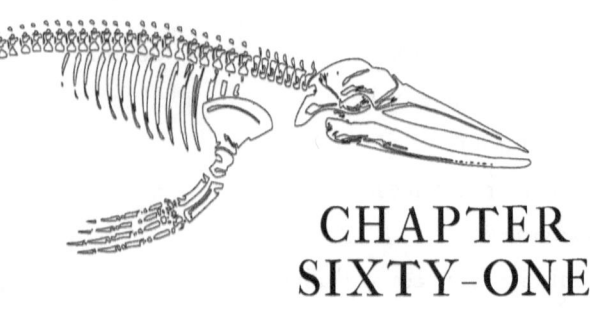

CHAPTER
SIXTY-ONE

IT HAD TAKEN some months for Numo to regain some sense of balance and be able to walk on his own. He'd had to sit there helplessly as Hammerfist trundled him out into the thick of the forest in the interior, built a little place for them to live, constructed a forge of her own to operate her smithery, and produced the finest goat-kit and swords and bolts and hinges and armor-plates he'd ever seen to sell in town. But now he was out and about with her, collecting the wood for her fires. Fire for blacksmithing was rather different from fire for a hypocaust, but Numo fell into it quite naturally, and he loved to stare at the flame as Hammerfist used his little creations to make her own.

Hammerfist held up the mark-board she carried. *What is this wood called?* She pointed at a spindly thing in the distance.

"White gordian." A little sapling, unimpressive in its youth, but soon to turn into a splendorous long-armed twisting miracle of arbory. "We should come back and see it when it's grown up. It'll be ever so pretty."

Hammerfist cocked her head and then froze. Her mouth hung open. She stared at nothing.

Numo sighed and sat beside her. The episodes were more

frequent now. They visited Moaki every now and then to make sure the mistress was keeping her promises, and to give her pages from her own book when Numo felt satisfied. The pages he carefully rationed out, for there were only so many, and he had only her book and her word—and he knew better than to trust her word. But it seemed effective enough. Now there was indeed an entire laboratory in the Academy dedicated to studying and treating the fall, in addition to a clinic for the brain experiments, should slaves decide to take the risk. Most of them, however, didn't. The mistress whined about the expense for something so "useless," but she behaved herself well enough. Usually, she was more preoccupied by plans for hunting down Sangja and his little resistance movement, or taking the rest of the city-states by force, or somelike. Big human things Numo still didn't understand and didn't care to.

Hammerfist had been to the Academy herself for a couple of experiments. But they still hadn't made progress, and she was still crumbling.

But at least they were together now. And everything was all right. Hammerfist was not in pain anymore. She was happy. She sang. He knew she sang because she let him feel her throat when she did it, and a great buzzing went through his whole body.

They were awful creatures, but they were awful creatures together.

Hammerfist slipped back into reality with a cold start, her whole body jerking awake. The world was blank and fierce. The fear of being stalked flowed through her again like blood and she jolted herself onto her knuckles. The creature on her foot shot out and wrapped around the drake sitting beside her.

The drake seemed unperturbed. She held it aloft. How dare it be unperturbed? Was it a psychopath? A monster with no fear? Had it poisoned her? It had. It must have. The creature on her foot shivered in offense and slid across the drake's chest like a boa around its prey.

The drake was singing.

It was a love song.

Her love song.

Numo.

The creature loosened its grip and sat him down on the grass. He kept singing as her brain crawled back into its cubby-hole. He shouted it, off-key, pitch akimbo—he couldn't hear himself anymore, but then, he hadn't been the best singer to begin with. He kept singing until the creature on her foot relaxed and went back to sleep.

"Are you back now?" he said.

She nodded. *I'm glad you're still here*, she wrote.

He smiled. "You say that every time."

ACKNOWLEDGEMENTS

This book is, essentially, me flailing in a sea of people who have been kind enough to help me, and who kept shoving me back up to finish it. More people than I can list, from my closest friends to that person I don't know on an internet forum who supplied the name "Floppacles." Bless you, whoever you are.

Still, I can try.

Lisa, Elaine, Hedgie, Mrs. Fringe, Hippo, Rob, Emma, Bats, Kalli, Donkey, Lusty, Krash: whether you read this book, or pieces of it, or helped me brainstorm, or held my hand while I whined about it – thank you. You made the book what it is, and I hope that's a compliment. Y'all got me through this, seriously; I probably would have given up without you.

To those of you bore the brunt of my insecurity, and I hope you know who you are – you are insufferably amazing, impossibly patient, pants-shittingly marvelous people and I love you.

To the internet community at large – many of you read pieces of the book, or the blurb, or offered me a kind word, or a thoughtful criticism, or encouraged my weirdness – thank you. I needed it.

To everyone, on the internet or otherwise, I've ever met who was nice to me, or told me I should be a writer, or who thought I could do something I thought I couldn't – you enabled me to entertain the idea I could do this in the first place, which is no small thing.

To Tomasz Biernat and the Qambers, who made the cover

art and put the rest of the book design together, respectively: you made this thing look beautiful, and you were all wonderful to work with and accommodating and patient, in spite of my general cluelessness.

And to my family, who I haven't yet told about this book for fear they'll think I'm even weirder than they already think I am...thank you for supporting me, my love of reading, and for loving me. Love you too, guys.